# RED FLAGS

## BOOKS BY JURIS JURJEVICS

*Red Flags*

*The Trudeau Vector*

# RED
# FLAGS

## Juris Jurjevics

*Mariner Books*
*Houghton Mifflin Harcourt*
BOSTON   NEW YORK

First Mariner Books edition 2012

For information about permission to reproduce selections from this book,
write to Permissions, Houghton Mifflin Harcourt Publishing Company,
215 Park Avenue South, New York, New York 10003.

www.hmhbooks.com

*Library of Congress Cataloging-in-Publication Data*
Jurjevics, Juris, date.
Red flags / Juris Jurjevics.
p. cm.
ISBN 978-0-547-56451-7    ISBN 978-0-547-84023-9 (pbk.)
1. United States. Army — Officers — Fiction. 2. Drug traffic — Fiction.
3. Vietnam War, 1961–1975 — Fiction. I. Title.
PS3610.U76R43 2011
813'.63 — dc22
2010050013

*Book design by Brian Moore*

Printed in the United States of America
DOC 10 9 8 7 6 5 4 3 2 1

# RED FLAGS

# PROLOGUE

★ ★ ★

S OMEDAY WAS STANDING on the gravel in front of Bert's store, collar turned up against the cold.

I knew right off. It wasn't like I hadn't been expecting her. Once, when she was an infant, I had imagined her. The grown version demanded a quick revision. She was a stalk. Maybe a twenty-four-inch waist, a bust not much bigger.

"I'm Erik Rider," I said. "How can I help you, Miss . . . ?"

The lips were her father's, the hazel eyes soft, like her touch as we shook hands. The bones felt hollow — a bird's, they were so light. Like his when we recovered the body.

"Celeste Bennett," she said. "Sorry to just barge in on you." She withdrew her hand.

"Pleased to meet you," I said, although *pleased* was the last thing I was.

"You knew my father. I was hoping I could talk to you about him."

"Colonel Bennett . . . ? Dennis Bennett?" I weighed my words, pretending it was taking time for me to recall the man, as though I hadn't thought of him pretty much steadily for nearly forty years. I launched into my fine-man, exceptional-officer patter. *An honor to serve under him.* From her impatient expression, I could tell she'd heard all the customary guff before and wasn't buying.

"Mr. Rider, I'd really like to — "

"How on earth did you find me?" I said, feigning the most genuine curiosity, anything my face might conjure by way of camouflage.

"Your ex-wife." She brushed the hair off her forehead.

"Which one?"

"Hillary?"

"Wife number three."

She looked away, nervous. She had the colonel's angular nose too. His kid all right. Her eyes caught me again.

"She said you were in northern California, around Redding, but she wasn't sure where. You weren't listed . . . or even unlisted. I did a title search online and saw you had property near Creek. I took a chance."

She pulled her gloves on and hunched against the cold.

"Title search, huh? What is it you do in the world?"

"Lawyer. I'm a lawyer."

Shit, I thought. "How old are you?"

"Thirty-eight." She shifted her feet, uncertain. "I was conceived the last time they were together, in Hawaii," she said, by way of corroborating herself, as if that were at issue. "And you?"

"I don't know where I was conceived. Probably the back seat of a Nash Ambassador in Oconomowoc, Wisconsin." She didn't blush and she wasn't laughing. "Sixty-three this year. I'll be sixty-three." I indicated the macadam behind me. "You drive in from Red Bluff?"

"Yes. I'm still swaying. That's some twisty road."

I looked west, toward the higher turns through the pass. Some of it I'd driven yesterday, the S-curves dusted with snow.

"Yeah. There's two more hours of mountain road before you hit the Pacific Coast Highway."

I waved to Bert, visible just behind her in the big window of his grocery store. He had called to summon me down — "There's a gal here looking for you."

She glanced back at him. "Your friend volunteered that he had a weapons permit. His wife also."

I nodded. "Yep. Most everyone here carries. Not many citizens bother with permits."

She squinted against the winter sun. "Why all the weaponry?"

"The nearest law is in Weaver, two hours away. Takes them a day to get here, when they come. Which is why Bert's wife has her pistol out when she takes the night receipts to her car. They make their permits and weapons known to everyone, especially strangers."

"The neighborhood's that dicey?" she said.

"It's isolated."

"Looks so idyllic."

"There are temptations."

She took in the tiny post office and Bert's grocery store and bar, the two connected through a common wall. "I hadn't noticed," she said. "The sign coming into town put the population at twenty-five."

"Sounds about right."

"Not a lot of nightlife in Creek, I take it."

"Bert's bar is it. The temptation's up on the ridges. The hills are full of marijuana farmers, if they're not cooking meth."

She scanned the voluptuous green slopes and pine groves all around us.

"They grow the dope in small patches," I said. "Can't be spotted so easily from the air. Reduces losses if a field gets busted. They've got armed illegals guarding them."

"Should I worry?"

"It gets a little rowdy some nights at Bert's." I pointed to the unlit neon sign in the saloon window behind her. "Otherwise they're respectful neighbors."

"Your wagon full of firearms too?" She looked over at my Bronco, probably scanning for a gun rack.

"No. I haven't kept company with a weapon in a long while. So I have to be especially polite."

A momentary silence fell between us. I was forgetting how to have a conversation.

"How did you come to settle here, Mr. Rider?" she said, her tone light, like we had just met at a cocktail party. She was pretending interest in my life to keep me talking, coaxing the reluctant witness.

"Came for a month years ago," I said. "Never left. A pal from the service asked for help building his house, a few towns over. He had a crop-dusting business, spraying walnut and almond trees from a helicopter."

"The signature sound of your generation," she said.

"What?"

"Those blades beating the air."

"Oh . . . yeah. I suppose."

The day was bright and crisp. A cloud and its shadow passed, and the air turned colder beneath it.

"About my father." She put a gloved hand on her rented car and leaned a hip against the rocker panel. "You're the thirteenth member of the advisory team I've found."

If she was just running through the roster, I could pass her along — fast. "Guess I was next on the list."

"Not exactly. The last couple of men I spoke to wanted to know if I'd seen you yet. So I moved you up."

I was tempted to ask who but suppressed the urge. Instead, I lifted my tattered Dodgers cap, scratched my head, and made homely noises, stalling with hick gestures.

"I didn't know the colonel well. I was just a captain. He was fifteen years my senior, my superior officer. We didn't exactly socialize. You know, you might try his executive officer, Major Gidding."

"General Gidding passed away three years ago. He was the first one I found." She held back wisps of hair fluttering around her face. "Two others are deceased as well. Two begged off. The seven who agreed to meet weren't very forthcoming. Mostly I get lofty sentiments about valor and honor."

"Your mother wasn't . . . ?"

"Told anything? Other than being instructed not to open the coffin, no. Not really. She was so shattered — widowed, pregnant. She just let the protocols and ceremonies carry her along. He was buried at West Point. Afterward it got even tougher for her. A while later I arrived."

"You weren't enough to keep her occupied?"

"Yes. Yes, I fit the bill," she said, sounding impatient, as if being her mother's diversion had been a challenge.

"What did your mom tell you about your father?"

"That he wouldn't have died if he had cared more about us and less about his career."

"Really?" I said, taken aback.

"Mom wanted him to stay an instructor at West Point. She said he had real gifts as a teacher and she didn't see why he felt he had to be an infantry officer. At times I wondered why they had ever been together. He was from a military family. She hated the military, hated all the deference expected of an officer's wife."

"Being an Army widow's no picnic either."

"My whole childhood she was furious with him for going back to Viet Nam when he didn't have to. She couldn't forgive him. I couldn't bear to listen to it. I'd wind up defending him."

"A lot of us volunteered for more tours or extended them. Didn't his awards —"

"'For conspicuous gallantry and intrepidity in action while serving as commanding officer . . .' blah-blah-blah. I could recite the medal citations when I was in grade school, before I even knew what all the words meant. Not much of a substitute for an actual dad."

She was his daughter. Tall, thin as a rail, with that same anxious concentration. The wind rushed through the treetops, swaying the branches.

"Except for those damn citations, I have only my mother's version of who my father was."

"I can see that."

"I wanted to hear about him from people who knew him as a soldier — knew him at the end." She wrapped her arms around her middle, fighting the chill. "A lot of people go to where their loved ones perished to commune with those they've lost: to the site of a plane crash, the spot on the highway where someone they loved was killed. For a long time I thought I'd sense something if I did that — found the place where he died."

I winced. "You're actually thinking about going back there?"

She blinked rapidly. "I did, last year."

Why was I surprised? Young Americans were honeymooning in Ho Chi Minh City these days, frolicking on the beaches at Nha Trang.

"I take it you didn't find what you were after."

She shook her head. "Never got further than Saigon. The aborigines in the mountains were demonstrating against the government. The authorities wouldn't let me into the Highlands."

"Yeah, they're crushing the Montagnards again, poor bastards. So you've come here looking for what you couldn't find there?"

"I'm hoping." She shielded her eyes against the cold sunlight. "I want to know what he was doing when he died . . . if it was true he stupidly put himself in harm's way. I want the facts — unvarnished."

I knew a bit about piggybacking ghosts around and I hesitated, reluctant to disturb hers. She slapped the car, exasperated.

"I've gotten the platitudes and pats on the head. Honestly, I don't want to be spared. It's just impossible when you don't know. It never leaves you." Her eyes cut me. "No matter what the truth is, I need to hear it."

And her gut told her she hadn't yet. I knew the war had burrowed into those of us who had been there, but it was disturbing to see it haunting someone her age. She was stuck with her grief, mourning the father she had never known.

The wind plastered our jackets against our arms and torsos. She trembled, ears crimson. Bert's neon saloon sign went on in the window. The regulars quickly appeared, crunching across the gravel.

"Mr. Rider, I can't keep standing here in the cold. Let me at least buy you a drink."

"Erik. Please call me Erik."

We went in. Bert's wife was filling glasses. The TV played, barely audible, stock quotes and news streaming above and below a talking head. I ushered Celeste to a booth, found out what she drank, and fetched it. She sipped her bourbon. I downed my shot and tipped back a Kirin.

"Haven't much time," I said, checking my wristwatch and feeling the fool for using the transparent dodge of pressing business. She looked exhausted, finding it difficult to keep pleading her case. I needed to do the smart thing and brush her off.

"Whatever you can spare," she said, her voice calming. She took slow, deep breaths, keeping herself contained — patient — even as her heart raced. I could see the pulse in her throat. She was revving for something.

"You look a little peaked," I said.

"Haven't eaten since morning," she admitted, sipping again. "Didn't want to stop."

I signaled Bert's wife and she threw on two bison burgers.

Celeste. Young, alive, and tortured. It was palpable. Even sitting, she moved constantly, darting from side to side just a fraction, as if boxing against somebody in there with her.

"Did you know my dad in Saigon in sixty-four, before Cheo Reo?"

Smart. She was easing me into it. Okay, Saigon was the easy part. I fussed with the chipped Formica and nodded. "I knew who he was."

"How bad was it?"

"There were street demonstrations. Occasional bombs. Otherwise Saigon was pretty much a great duty station early on."

"Oh," she said, surprised.

"Minimal bullshit, quick advancement. Sleepy, tropical. Palms, tamarind trees — like that. Exotic food, exotic women. New Orleans, with bigger and better guns. Perfumed with flowering trees and marsh water and every kind of shit, human and otherwise. I actually miss it. There were only sixteen thousand of us in country then. Most commuted to the war, did their work, and hustled back to town before sundown. We slept in real beds in real linen."

"There was fighting though, right?"

I shrugged. "The guerrilla war wasn't much, just hot enough to qualify us for hazardous-duty pay and put a little zing in life. Shoot-outs stayed in the hinterlands, but most of the fighting was small time — dinky and *dien cai dau:* crazy. The Viet Cong just kept sawing away at the Vietnamese military, a piece at a time. They'd take pot-shots, block roads, hit and run. Drop three mortar rounds on us and be gone before the last one landed."

"But the Viet Cong had such a fierce reputation."

"Yeah, well, in those days the VC didn't even have enough weapons to arm all their fighters. They had to take turns with them — a sad hodgepodge of copies and discards, all different calibers. When they attempted larger attacks, they'd herd villagers into nearby fields to yell and set off firecrackers . . . to sound like there were lots of them."

"Doesn't seem like much of a war," she said.

"It wasn't. More like a bad neighborhood you policed during the day and stayed out of after dark."

Mrs. Bert delivered our bison burgers and the condiment tray. I removed the cap from the mustard. Celeste worked on her burger and waited for me to resume.

"The VC owned the night, we owned the nightlife. The young sergeants partied, the middle-aged noncoms invested in real estate and bars and lived with Asian mistresses they married in Buddhist ceremonies — or not. A lot of servicemen and embassy staff had their dependents with them."

"Wives?"

"Yeah, kids too. Families leased villas in good districts, with pools and tennis courts. Had peacocks wandering the lawns. Cooks, amahs, gardeners . . . a swim before lunch, a round of golf at the Saigon Golf Club in the afternoon."

"Sounds like an American raj," Celeste said. "My mom never mentioned that she could have gone with him. I could have been born there." She sat quietly for a minute, absorbing this possibility.

"Was it exciting?" she said. "Exciting enough to make someone want to go back?"

"Sure. Boring too. Funny every once in a while." I slathered some ketchup on my burger. "Listen, it was never neat or simple. There wasn't just one war, us against them. There were a bunch of wars all going on at once. You had to sort through them. You weren't always sure which side you were on."

I took a pull of beer.

"By the time I served under your dad, two years later, Viet Nam was going through its top bananas like a fruit bat. They were on coup number eight. President Diem ruled for nine years. His successors were lucky to last nine weeks. Every time a regime was taken down, counterinsurgency stopped, the government and army derailed. Then the latest junta generals would replace all the civil and military leaders with their guys and it all started up again."

Action on the tube elicited a small outburst from the sportsmen gathered at the bar. They high-fived and locked on the screen. I took a healthy swig and felt the alcohol bathe my tensed brain. I had to watch it. She was good at getting people to talk. I needed to back away. I waved to Mrs. Bert for the tally.

"Where are you heading from here? Who's next on your list?"

She peered out the window. It was getting late. White flakes threaded the air.

"I'm not sure I should try that road in the dark and the snow." She looked toward the bar. "Mrs. Bert rents rooms, I hope."

I shook my head. "It's not a bed-and-breakfast sort of town."

"Damn." Concern swept over her face. "Might I impose on you, Erik?"

What was there to say? Outflanked. "Where's your stuff?"

"Front seat of the rental."

Mrs. Bert eyed us as we left the bar; the regulars paid no attention. Not minding other people's business was the only town tradition I knew of, other than shooting up Bert's parking lot on New Year's Eve.

"Your place is beautiful." She sounded surprised. And relieved.

I'd driven her up in the Bronco. Her rental never would have made the steep grade.

"Yeah," I agreed. "Hard not to be, with that vista."

The sun set like a boiling rock, turning the Trinity Alps dark green. Faint remnants of gold from below the horizon rounded the rolling hills.

The cabin sat on the edge of a steep drop, giving the back porch an enormous view of our valley, nestled in green twists and slopes. There wasn't another house in sight. The faint whiff of wood smoke was the only sign of other human habitation.

"Do you mind the isolation?"

"I've come to like it."

She put her things in the room next to mine and returned to claim the armchair in front of the hearth. It was growing colder as the light outside died.

I said, "Would you fire up the kindling in the fireplace? It's all set to go. The matches are by the hearth, on the log pile."

She knelt to ignite the wood shavings and splints, baring a band of skin at the small of her back. The room filled with the aroma of apple wood and sage as the scrap caught. Celeste stood up and paused at the framed photos on the mantelpiece. She spotted her father in a group shot.

"I don't have this one. Is this Team Thirty-one? I recognize a couple of faces."

"Yes, some of it."

"You guys ever get together?"

I shook my head but she didn't see; she was still examining the photograph. "No," I said. "We don't."

She looked back, holding my gaze for a moment, weighing something about me. I held up a bottle of fifteen-year-old whiskey. She nodded yes and I got down the cut-crystal glasses, bringing everything over to her. Nothing like kick-ass whiskey in a heavy tumbler. The fragrance alone revived me some. Celeste resettled in the armchair, covering up in a quilt.

"Why do you think he volunteered to go back?" she said.

"To get another crack at a field command, maybe. Career officers needed that on their resumés to advance. That and gongs."

"Gongs?"

"That's what GIs called medals. You needed gongs and a field command or you'd be out of the running for promotion and eventually out of the Army. The higher you went, the harder it got. It was like musical chairs."

"So my mother was right. He was as ambitious as the rest of them."

"General Westmoreland allotted six-month combat commands to as many officers as possible. He rationed them because the fight was going to be over right quick."

"Did you think it would be done that fast?"

"No, but they didn't ask me or other ordinary mortals."

Her cheeks were rosy from the warmth of the fire. I knocked back my drink.

"Whole regiments of North Vietnamese regulars came streaming across, accompanied by Chinese generals advising them. The local Viet Cong armed up too. No more improvised bombs made out of rice husks and sugar. Forty miles north of Saigon, the South Vietnamese lost three hundred men in one ambush, including four U.S. advisers. Just to make sure they got our attention, the Communists decapitated the Americans."

"Good God. Why?"

"Beheading was real popular. The VC decapitated local officials all the time and dumped their heads in the toilet. Burying people alive was big too. Four Americans beheaded, though — the message was clear. We weren't immune. It wasn't going to be a cakewalk if we were truly getting in the fight. The unwritten rules changed as well."

"What rules?"

"They'd never gone after American dependents: no attacks on wives or school buses. One afternoon in Saigon, two VC killed the MPs guarding a movie house and then rushed into the theater with a bucket full of arsenic sulfide and potassium chlorate they'd picked up in a pharmacy. The bomb wounded a lot of our civilians, killed an officer."

I wedged the logs closer together with the poker and stood with my back to the fire. Wrapped in the quilt, she looked tiny.

"They car-bombed our billets, restaurants, the embassy, set off a bomb at a baseball game out at Pershing Field. It was open season on Americans. Dependents were ordered out, the Marines and combat battalions in — two hundred thousand of us. There was no mistaking what was coming. The intelligence on the North Vietnamese elite clinched it."

"What intelligence?"

"That their local officials, their foreign minister, even the mayor of Hanoi — they were all sending their sons and daughters of military age out of the country."

I banked the fire and unfolded the metal screen. The aroma of the fireplace mingled with her scent. I was wound up, mulling the lost crusade.

"Well, Communism didn't win either," I said, sounding regretful. "The old corruption is eating the new Communist state alive." I raised my glass in a toast. "To each according to his greed."

I slumped onto the couch. Even fatigued, she looked pink and delicate, her hazel eyes clear and penetrating, hair luxurious, cheeks perfect. Her teeth were rabbitty though, big, with a gap between the two in front. The imperfection seemed childlike and endearing.

I asked if she wanted coffee; she said she did. I rose to make it, but she waved me back down. "Let me," she said.

Celeste braided her hair while she waited for the water to boil. Been squatting in the woods too long, I thought. Horny at the proximity of a girl twenty-five years my junior. Or maybe apprehension was revving the hormones. Either way, my vision sparkled.

She was efficient. The *café filtre* press was soon on the coffee table. She poured out our cups.

"Your tour," she said, "when you served with my dad." She handed me a cup. "What happened in Cheo Reo?"

I took a sip and didn't say anything.

"If you're worried about sparing my feelings," she said, "don't."

Had the time come for her to hear it?

"I'm aware he was burned. Mom didn't listen to the warning not to open the coffin. My gran said it was two years before my mother slept through the night. What was the slang for it — crispy critter?"

I stared into my coffee. "I'm sorry. Family shouldn't have to — "

"Yes, we do. We do have to . . . even that." She pushed back her hair. "He was a husband, soon to be a father. How could he have been so cavalier?"

"He wasn't," I said. "Your mother married a professional soldier. Your dad went back because that's where the war was. If she couldn't live with that . . ." I took a slug of java. "But honestly, I don't think I'm up to talking about — "

She cut me off. "Out of fifty-eight thousand, two hundred and sixty-three casualties, do you know how many full colonels, like my father, died in Viet Nam?"

I shook my head.

"Eight. Pretty damn rare, wouldn't you say?"

"Very."

"Did you hurt a lot of people in the war, Erik?"

"More than I wanted. Why?"

"Do they haunt?"

Something had shifted in her tone and my comfort level. Suddenly I felt like a hostile witness.

"I'm not sure where you're going."

"Some of your former comrades intimated my father didn't die as officially reported."

"You mean — not in combat?"

She froze, realizing what I might have let slip. "Are you suggesting he *wasn't* killed in action?"

"Who did this intimating?" I said, evading the question.

"It's not important. What's germane is they implied you were involved."

I closed my eyes for a moment, tilting my head back.

"Were you?" she said.

"Was I what?"

"Did you have any part in it?"

"Not the way you seem to be thinking." I opened my eyes.

"One person referred to you as Captain Sidney. Said you weren't who you appeared to be."

"Maybe because I wasn't. Listen — " I held up a hand, stopping her as she was about to press me again. "If I tell you . . . you have to put it away and move on."

"I'm not sure I can promise that."

I went to my jacket hanging on the wall rack and slipped my wallet from the inside pocket. I took out the military scrip I'd carried since the sixties and unfolded the mauve and green "funny money" on the coffee table.

"What's this?" she said, peering at the woman's profile printed in place of George Washington's on the military money.

"You're a lawyer. It's a retainer."

She let the peculiar-looking dollar sit on the low table between us.

"You feel you need a lawyer?"

"I need attorney-client privilege."

"Why?"

"There's no statute of limitations on what you want to know."

Her face hardened; she was no longer anyone's child. *Someday* reached out and picked up the bill.

# 1

* * *

**M**ISER GOT US rooms at the Five Oceans in Cholon and we went out to get reacquainted with the city. Saigon was still sordid and fabulous. Neither of us had eaten actual food since departing San Francisco so we indulged ourselves, feasting on lobster and salted crab at classy La Miral and then savoring small dishes of unimaginable flavors cooked in modest family restaurants with just a few tables in the yard, sampling morsels of eel grilled on stove carts in the street and unidentifiable meat smoldering on braziers yoked across the cooks' shoulders on *chogie* poles and lowered to the curb. We strolled on, flirting with all the other food on offer: shrimp from the Saigon River, sparrows roasted in oil and butter, frogs' legs, skewered snake, buffalo-penis soup, steamed mudfish, baked butterfish, shark. We finished at the open-air place near the Old Market that had cobra on the menu and bananas flambé for dessert. Both of us settled for espresso.

We walked again under the brilliant crimson blossoms of the flamboyante trees, moved through the flower market and avoided clusters of Vietnamese draft dodgers who idled on shady street corners hustling hot watches. At the PX, GIs and the odd American deserter scored reel-to-reel tape recorders and electric fans for locals to resell at inflated prices. Chinese drug dealers scooped coke off sidewalk tables with elongated pinkie nails, and Macanese hoodlums carted bricks of cash to their moneychangers. Outside the British embassy, turbaned

Gurkhas guarded the gates while, close by, street urchins hawked one-liter bottles of gasoline. Whatever lit your fire, Saigon had it all.

Astrologers trading in futures, mama-sans extolling taxidermied civet cats and live bear cubs. Stick-thin men selling U.S. Army–issue rations and assault rifles, flak vests, toilet paper, jackets made from GI ponchos lined with speckled parachute silk. Whether it inflicted pleasure or pain, whatever you desired was yours. Hell, armored personnel carriers and helicopters if you had the cash, a howitzer for four hundred bucks, an M-16 rifle for forty, a woman for ten. Or a tooth yanked out curbside for a dime.

We ambled past clubs with live bands imitating famous rock groups, and Cholon gangsters taking their leisure in open-sided billiard halls. Near the Central Market, refugees squatted in giant sections of stock-piled sewer pipe. We stepped around night soil and lean-tos on the pavement. Lights burned in MACV SOG and in General Westmoreland's old office on 137, rue Pasteur. The brass was working overtime.

In the morning we put on our work clothes — civvies — and reported to the Headquarters Support Activity, Saigon (HSAS), office. A dozen of us worked out of the rickety place, not much more than a bunch of desks. We were special agents loaned out to HSAS by our various investigative and counterintelligence agencies — ONI, OSI, CIC, CID. U.S. Navy, U.S. Air Force, and us — U.S. Army, "El Cid." GI slang for Criminal Investigation Division; "Sidney" behind our backs. The work didn't make us popular with our fellows, who considered us barely better than snitches.

No investigators were commissioned officers, although we frequently went undercover with officers' ranks. Our mandate was mainly to investigate crimes against U.S. personnel and property. Miser and I had been teamed up for a couple of tours, him an E-7 noncom, me a warrant officer, a rank halfway between the lowliest lieutenant and the highest-ranking sergeant. Early on we investigated the occasional homicide, but mostly we looked into the pilfering of supplies, scams like selling the U.S. military thousands of inedible eggs for thousands of American breakfasts, and the unexplained deaths of dozens of sentry dogs. As terrorist acts began to target U.S. personnel and dependents, the American head count rose steadily, along with our caseloads. We didn't get much support. Our little outfit had to improvise even as we found ourselves investigating suicides, rapes, security violations, even espionage and treason.

Our boss, Major Jessup, gave us a perfunctory welcome-back and instructed us to trade our civvies for jungle fatigues and fly up to Pleiku to investigate a threat against a company commander who had called in artillery on his own position, earning him a medal for valor and a bounty on his head of eight hundred and seventy dollars. Not from the VC; from his own men, for shelling some of their buddies into hamburger. The brass hats loved their heroic young West Point star. Eighty-seven recent high-school graduates had pledged ten bucks apiece to see him dead.

"Local talent in Saigon would've done it for fifty," Miser growled. "The kids could've saved their fucking pennies."

"Never mind that, Sergeant," Jessup snapped.

The U.S. Army wasn't about to charge nineteen-year-old survivors of horrific combat with mutiny and solicitation of murder. The solution was obvious; Major Jessup strongly suggested we put it into effect the moment we got to Pleiku: "Get his ass out of there!"

"Yes, sir," we answered.

The second case Jessup assigned us was out in the boonies and wasn't going to be anywhere near as simple or quick.

A chunk of our work involved GIs' attempts to smuggle dope home: cannabis and heroin, both extremely high grade and insanely cheap. The purest scag went for a dollar or two a dose, commonly sold roadside by kids. A buck would buy you the quintessential experience of the exotic East: a dozen pipes in an opium den. Fifty dollars got you six pounds of marijuana, though most everyone bought rolled joints, ten for fifty cents, or special cartons of Salems — ten bucks instead of the two you'd pay at the PX. The Salems were perfectly repacked by hand with opiated grass, and the carton artfully resealed so you couldn't tell it had ever been opened.

All you had to do was step up to the perimeter wire anywhere holding a sprig of anything, and you'd be set upon by vendors of marijuana and heroin. Business indicators were all good. Mainlining GIs were on track to outnumber stateside addicts. Normally the South Vietnamese drug trade was off-limits, untouchable, none of our concern. Saigon was a smuggler's wet dream, as Miser often pointed out. We couldn't even arrest Vietnamese nationals who were stealing from American supply ships and American supply depots, much less the ones smuggling narcotics in and out of their own country. Besides, transporting and refining them was practically a South Vietnamese government enterprise. Which is why the second assignment came as a surprise.

The major said, "We need you to bust up a drug operation in one of the Highland provinces." Miser and I exchanged glances, wondering if the major was serious. "*Half* the proceeds turn up like clockwork in the Hong Kong bank account of a Viet Cong front organization. Their cut's way too big to be just a tax or a toll. Which means the VC are in partnership up there — in business with somebody."

He paused to see if he'd gotten our attention. He had.

"Since the forties, the Communists have sold captured Lao opium to traffickers in Hanoi to help finance their arms purchases, and even bought quantities to sell. But actually growing dope . . . that's new. They denounce the imperialist French for their government-sponsored drug dealing, but evidently the North Vietnamese need an infusion of U.S. dollars to buy supplies, so they've parked their ideology while they stock up on arms and ammo. You with me so far?"

"Yes, sir."

"Good. The money the VC are banking is major. Ten times their usual five- or ten-grand rake-off. An informant puts this cash crop of theirs somewhere in Phu Bon Province."

"Sir, do we know what kind of dope they're growing?" I said.

"No, and I don't particularly care." Jessup assumed his best hands-on-hips command posture and looked us each in the eye. "No way we're going to wipe out their drug trade, that's for sure. The Vietnamese and their neighbors have been at it for five hundred years. Screw the dope. I don't care if they're growing pistachios. The higher highers don't want our guys getting the bang from those bucks. Slow the cash. They don't like their having so much capital. The buying power needs to be contained — at least for a while. Sabotage as much of the money as you can for as long as you can. And then bail."

"What are our specific orders, Major?" I said.

"You heard 'em: fuck up their revenue stream."

"But how, sir? I doubt the money ever touches down in that province, just shifts from one Hong Kong account to another. So what do we do? Kill their pack mules? Kidnap their women?"

"Do it any way you can. Just don't tell me about it. Especially if it's hinky." He tapped the unit shield hand-painted on the piece of plywood mounted on the wall behind him bearing the CID motto: DO WHAT HAS TO BE DONE.

What he meant was, since we didn't have any jurisdiction over Vietnamese nationals — couldn't arrest them, couldn't so much as detain them — he didn't want to know about us getting over on any South Vietnamese who might be involved. No such strictures applied to Communists who got in the way. Their only right was to sacrifice themselves for their cause. So we had to make a case for any casualties being VC if it came to that, and stick to our story.

Miser assumed his *Oh, great* look as we stood at ease in front of Jessup's desk while the major finished speechifying. He gave us nothing to go on — neither where to start looking for the operation nor what to do once we found it. Zilch. The absence of direct instructions kept him conveniently free of blame for whatever we wound up doing. Never mind that it left us in the dark about how to carry out the assignment. That was our problem.

As usual, we were to do our work unnoticed: fall back on our early occupational specialties as signalmen, put on field uniforms, and pass as regular soldiers. Or as the major put it, "Do your thing and get out of there as quietly as you came."

"Will the commanding officer know what we're about?" Miser asked.

"No. Nobody. And keep it that way."

A month earlier, an American general had been court-martialed for dealing American arms to God knows who. The shock was still reverberating around Saigon and the Pentagon. If Major Jessup had hung his personal motto on the wall, it would have read TRUST NO ONE. Beginning with him.

"The less they know, the better," Jessup said.

Which was perfectly okay with Miser and me. The rank and file didn't exactly love us, and this little chore wasn't going to be quick or easy. Still, law-and-order work for the Army was way more interesting than coaching the South Vietnamese on how to wage war. Miser and I had both done our time as advisers before signing up for the Army's agent training course; he a former Pittsburgh cop, me the brat of a widowed Wisconsin county sheriff with my own cell to sleep in on the nights he pulled the graveyard shift.

Jessup tossed me some captain's bars. "Congratulations. You're a captain — for the duration."

"Yes, sir," I said.

"I want 'em back when you're done."

"What about me, sir?" Miser said.

"You're perfect the way you are, Sergeant."

I said, "Can we talk to the informant who linked the Hong Kong account to this Phu Bon Province?"

"Try holding a séance."

We left. Outside, I said to Miser, "Have you ever heard of the Communists growing dope?"

"Fucking never. The Viet Cong tax the smuggling and retailing and will traffic the shit to finance their war effort, but they don't produce it."

I turned to Miser. "Sending us is odd, don't you think? Viets with police power and fluency in the language would make more sense. Unless our masters don't trust the Vietnamese to get to the bottom of it."

"Now, Mr. Rider, why ever the fuck would you say such a thing?"

# 2

★ ★ ★

**U**P IN PLEIKU, we extricated the company commander with the bull's-eye on his back and saw him safely off to Nha Trang. After which the two of us rostered to fly out on the only regular flight that made a stop in the province capital of Cheo Reo. The six-seat, single-engine de Havilland Otter was an oversize Canadian bush plane, totally reliable, totally slow. The nose housed its one enormous motor and the shaft on which spun the single propeller in a blur in front of the windshield. The landing gear didn't even retract. Crossing Pleiku at two thousand feet, we passed over the city's fifty thousand souls napping through the worst of the midday heat. Below us, across the red laterite prairie, stretched the long runways of the air base, Titty Mountain, the evacuation hospital, Camp Holloway, the MACV compound, and the billboard antennas on Tropo Hill, big as apartment houses.

The plane droned across the cloudless Asian sky on a long circuit of stops, carrying the two of us passengers and a large heap of courier pouches containing classified paper. The one saving grace was the instant relief altitude brought as the air turned dry and cold. It was better than sex.

The pilots, in gray jump suits, lounged at the controls, unfazed. They sported shoulder holsters and yellow-lensed, aviator-style shooting glasses, like they were spoiling for a dogfight over goddamn Darmstadt. This in a courier plane with no armament and one lousy engine.

The pair of them sat in the elevated cockpit, with us in the well of the fuselage behind them. It was too dark to read by the light of the dirty porthole window, so I rubbed the pane with my elbow and gazed out at the vast green growth that ran to teal toward the mountains. Behind me, Sergeant Miser snored.

Why had I come back?

On my leave a year before, I'd eloped with the girl I'd loved since high school. Months later, that tour finished, I headed stateside, my Army hitch done. Twelve hours after landing in Tacoma I mustered out, a newlywed, although technically we'd been married half a year. She was in graduate school in New York. I was barely in the door, she said I smelled different and that we were history. I stopped. I was standing on a land mine. She'd withdrawn to a safe distance, entered the future alone. I was still thirteen time zones away, my night her tomorrow.

"How could you do this if you love me?" I said.

She gave me a tender look. "I couldn't."

Not sure what to do, I walked along Broadway, diagonally down the island, carrying my life in a valise like a refugee, one foot following the next along miles of insect-free concrete. People stared at my uniform but no one came near me. Increasingly I felt unlike my contemporaries — a stranger in my own life. I had a month-long going-away party by myself in a series of bars and then re-upped. Volunteered for another go-round in Southeast Asia. I went back on the levy and ran into Staff Sergeant Miser at Fort Dix.

As he often did when inebriated, Miser started crooning a pop song in a rich baritone: "'Cross the ocean in a silver plane, see the jungle when it's wet with rain . . .'" He was coming off leave and nursing a pint. Miser hummed a couple more verses, then abruptly stopped to complain.

"I haven't a fucking prayer of living on fucking Army pay stateside," he said. "Every leave, I bunk in cheap-ass bachelors' quarters on base, shop only at the dippy PX, eat shitty mess-hall grub on the government, drink cheap at the NCO club, even fucking bowl on the freakin' base, and I still come up short at the end of the motherfucking month."

He shook his head. "Overseas is the only place for assholes like us. No taxes. Extra pay for hazardous duty. Food allotments . . ."

Miser liked intimidating officers with his foul mouth and swagger. The only thing he liked better was boasting about his contacts and overseas investments. He owned shares of massage parlors in Qui Nhon, a truck wash in Long Binh, two laundries in Saigon, a bar in Kontum, and a piece of a saloon and a film-production shop in Bangkok. I didn't want to know what kind of films.

Nam, he argued boozily, was wide open and free in ways only a besieged society could be. Regulations were lax. Hell, everything was available, removable, salable. Nobody sweated the small stuff, he said, and launched into a pitch on how he could get noncoms going on Riot and Recreation to smuggle gemstones back for him. He said it was nuts to risk our butts for the kick alone and the simple thanks of a grateful nation. We were entitled to bennies from all the sweat and risk.

"Back in loosey-goosey Nam," Miser said, "the whole fucking thing is to make it work for you."

The Otter whined across the sky. I yawned and said, "Can you find out where the hell this windmill is going next? We're cranking east. Cheo Reo's south."

Miser talked to the crew chief, the two shouting over the engine, then came back to me. "We're going to the freakin' coast," he said. "Qui Nhon. Gotta pick up some priority stud."

The VIP passenger was a full-bull colonel, a beet-red newbie just arrived. He loaded on and we climbed over the azure ocean before turning back inland high above the several hundred thousand citizens of Qui Nhon City toiling in the heat. A hundred supply ships stretched across the horizon, waiting their turns to unload. Some would wait months. I knew how they felt. The Otter wasn't taking us anywhere soon either.

The crew chief beckoned us over. Cheo Reo, he promised, was next. For sure. Half an hour. Miser gave me a cynical glance. I occupied myself lightening my load of new issue. I jettisoned my shelter half, abandoned the tent stakes, tent cord, collapsed air mattress, and carrier, my gas mask and its pouch, the poncho, and six pairs of olive-drab underpants. Cutting the plates out of my flak jacket, I reduced it from nearly seven pounds to three, thought on it, and threw the flak vest away too, dumping everything into a wooden trash box in the back.

Columns of red dust rose behind long convoys of trucks and armor; the pilots spotted a wide dirt road off the major route and followed it south. No plumes. Aside from a lone bus or rickety truck, nothing. Everything bound for Cheo Reo arrived — like us — on a military air transport or helicopter, whether it was cases of Coke, grenades, or help in the event of an attack. Volcanic plains floated by, green jungles, and dry scrub. We followed the road and the lazy coils of a river looping across the flat land toward its junction with the larger Ea Pa and the province capital.

Cheo Reo. Finally. We landed and deplaned. The crew chief threw a bag of mail out after us. A spec-4 idled in a small truck. Farther on, a Vietnamese sentry box stood empty, its barrier pole vertical and unattended. No air-control tower, no other planes, no buildings, not so much as a forklift. Only a lone walk-in cargo container.

"You think that's the f-ing arrivals terminal?" Miser said, jutting his little knob of a chin at the CONEX. "What do you think we did in a former life that Buddha sent us to this shit hole?"

The light was a stiletto after the plane's dark innards. I made my way across the perforated steel planks that were latched together to make the runway. The sixty-five-pound planking was patched and worn, some of it blasted and jagged, the target of heavy bombardment.

"Well," Miser said, "at least somebody thought enough of the place to shell the shit out of it."

"Pilots must hate this strip," I said, grateful we hadn't blown a tire. A new asphalt runway was under construction, and dirt fill was being trucked in. A grader and backhoe belched diesel smoke as they worked.

A jeep sped toward us, churning dust, its windshield lying flat on the hood. The driver, red-haired and hatless, jumped out and greeted us with a genial smile without saluting. He had on threadbare stateside fatigues, no nametag or rank insignia. Freckles and golden-red stubble speckled his cheeks.

"Sir," he said, gesturing for me to get in while he signed for a courier pouch and handed the clipboard back up to the crew chief.

Miser said, "Good day . . . Private, is it?"

"Yes, Sergeant. PFC Checkman. I clerk for the CO, Colonel Bennett."

He hefted the mailbag and our duffels, threw them into the jeep, and slid behind the wheel as the Otter taxied away. Miser stepped up into the back, I took the front passenger seat, and we drove off at a leisurely pace.

"Which way should I look for the skyline?" Miser said.

Checkman's forehead furrowed. "I can make a quick loop and show you."

We passed by the Vietnamese guard post and rolled down a straight dirt strip, flat and wide. Across the airfield were the outskirts of the town: a scattering of tin-roofed shacks and two-story stucco buildings.

Miser scanned the horizon.

"Jesus H. Christ," he said. "Who the fucking hell lives out here?"

"Montagnards," Checkman replied. "Thousands of 'em. Jarai especially. Cheo Reo is the Jarai heartland."

"It's strange," Miser said. "I never even heard of Phu Bon Province."

Checkman beeped a goat out of the way. "It didn't exist until recently. It was just Montagnard territory. Saigon decided it wanted a stronger government presence and made Cheo Reo a provincial capital."

We turned left, past the MACV compound, and entered the metropolis.

"Cheo Reo's a Montagnard clan name," Checkman explained as we slowed. "The government forced them to rename it Hau Bon. Changed all the Yard names of villages and rivers to Vietnamese. But everyone still calls it Cheo Reo."

The so-called capital was a shantytown. "The whole place is maybe six thousand Vietnamese," Checkman said, stopping the vehicle. He slipped out from behind the wheel, courier pouch in hand. Kids immediately made a playground of the jeep as we walked away. Each child was immaculate, wearing clean if worn clothes. Unlike urban waifs, not one propositioned us for candy or cigarettes or tried to rent us his sister.

Nothing was paved. A hard-dirt street led to the market square, an open area circled with canvas-roofed stalls, goods spread on the shaded platforms beneath them. One dais held produce; another, stacks of dried fish. An old woman squatted beside a pyramid of rice. A butcher displayed the heads of monkeys and a small black deer the size of a Labrador. Two slaughtered ducks and a chicken hung upside down beside a goat and a couple of bats. A man bicycled past, holding an umbrella against the sun, and called out a melodic greeting to Checkman. Checkman answered in Vietnamese.

Nearby, a few barefoot women in sarongs and black shirts sat on their haunches beside carrier baskets in which they'd brought modest piles of tomatoes, onions, and peppers.

"Yards," Checkman said. "Jarai. Don't often see them in town. The Viets won't let them hang around long."

A small truck lumbered into the market area, a gorgeous dead tiger draped across its hood. A crowd gathered.

"Catch this," Miser said. "Commercial opportunities in Cheo Reo."

"You picturing clients on safari?" I said.

We went to touch the beast's fur and huge teeth. A GI, passing on the other side of the road, shouted to Checkman: "Hey, Private Muff Diver! Careful that slope pussy don't eat you." He ducked away fast when he saw my captain's bars.

Checkman interviewed the hunters and turned back to us. "They're saying it walked into an ambush last night. I don't know. Militias haven't gone out patrolling at night in months, and it's not all shot up. The pelt's near perfect." He ran a hand over the rich coat. "Must be worth a lot."

Miser said, "Its choppers and guts are worth even more."

"Right, right," Checkman said, "local healers. I'll show you the neighborhood pharmacy," and he took us to a stall where a bear's full hide, including the head, lay draped over one wooden barrel. A large preserved iguana was curled up on another. Glass jars on a plank held potent-looking elixirs with bees and less identifiable things floating in them. Checkman pointed out the bat's-blood-and-rice-wine cocktail for tuberculosis beside jars of land leeches beckoning like miniature fingers.

A few stalls offered modest black-market booty, mostly stacks of green c-ration cans and field gear. Nothing like Saigon's extravagant contraband. Along one end of the hard-packed square stood shops filled with cheap wares, a café, a photographer displaying large framed samples of hand-tinted portraits, the town barbershop, and an open-sided billiard hall. Pigpens and slop troughs immediately behind it gave off an acrid stench.

"Shit," Miser croaked. "Who could play pool next to that?"

Checkman grinned. He shooed the kids out of the jeep and we got back in. We drove by some thatch huts roofed with metal sheets imprinted with beer-can logos and halted at the empty back side of town, a plain of dry, baked earth and scrub. We hadn't passed a pagoda, a church, not so much as a gas station or streetlamp.

Checkman nodded toward the landscape. "End of city."

Miser frowned. "Ass end of nowhere."

Turning back, we passed some two-story stucco houses with second-floor balconies edged with Chinese filigrees. Checkman showed us a shop front screened in at ground level, sparsely furnished with a few low stools and tables on a concrete floor. It was a bar in front and a brothel in back.

"Homey as a garage," Miser said. "What a place to get laid."

Checkman pointed out a stucco building that looked Mediterranean. "The Korean medical team's quarters and clinic. They treat Vietnamese. Two docs, three nurses. Dr. Towns's dispensary is on the other side, down that alley." He indicated a wide passage lined with shops.

"He European?" I said.

"She's American."

Miser's head swiveled around. "An American woman, here?"

"Yep. She does the health-care thing for the Yards. There's also a Christian Alliance missionary who runs a Yard leper colony a few klicks upriver. The Jarai never used to isolate their lepers but he talked them into it to reduce contagion. And there are two missionary couples: one here, the other in a Yard village way south."

I said, "What's the American headcount in the province?"

"Thirty Green Berets at the two Special Forces camps. Big one's north of here, the other's southeast. Also half a Special Forces team — that's seven Berets — and two MACV officers at a district headquarters. An A-team may soon go in on a mountaintop at Buon Blech too."

I said, "Thirty-nine. Is that it for our side?"

"Yeah, and the personnel here, and a dozen Army engineers bunking with us while they build the new airstrip."

"What've we got locally?"

Checkman downshifted to first as we bounced along a water-eroded stretch of road. "You gentlemen just brought the compound's total strength back to forty, sir."

"What?" Miser exclaimed. "Did you say *forty?*"

"Fifty-two, counting the engineers on temporary duty."

"How close is the nearest support?" I said. "You know. Firebases? Reinforcements?"

"Pleiku." Checkman braked for a goat. "Like, fifty miles."

Miser sighed. "Eighty klicks. So a plane with Gatling guns is the best we can expect if it hits the fucking fan."

Checkman said, "The First Cav is straight north at An Khe, about forty miles. I don't think we're a top priority for them either."

"South?"

"Empty for a couple of hundred miles until you get down around Saigon."

"Crap," Miser mumbled. "So eighty-nine Americans in a province the size of . . .?"

"Like, Delaware," Checkman said, grinning. "We do have an ARVN battalion right across the road, and lots of strikers at the camps. Village militias too; most are Montagnard, a few are Vietnamese."

"And that's it for round-eyes?"

"Oh, the pinko French priest nobody ever sees. Likes to badmouth Americans and is supposed to be chummy with the VC. The Special Forces guys are always threatening to off him."

"You think they're kidding?" Miser teased.

"You never know with them, Sarge." He downshifted. "There are two American USAID reps in the little compound next to ours. They just built a reinforced bunker for the province chief — under his quarters — and a tennis court on the edge of town. The prov chief's playing with the AID guys. Sometimes with Major Gidding."

"Aren't USAID people supposed to do useful shit like dig wells and put in public-address systems?" Miser said.

"The province chief wanted a pool table," Checkman said, "he got a pool table. He wants a tennis court, he gets a tennis court. Everyone works at keeping the man happy. I'll show you." He veered left.

Miser's chin rose in indignation. "No sewage pipes or running water, no streetlights. Wish I'd brought my fucking racket. I'd love to bust some USAID balls."

We rolled up to the tennis court. A short, imperious Vietnamese in regulation whites was volleying with a lanky preppy in cutoffs and a T-shirt, his horn-rimmed glasses low on his beak.

"USAID taking on province chief Colonel Chinh," said Checkman.

The court wasn't much more than a concrete slab with no fencing. There was no net, just a clothesline strung across. A half-dozen Vietnamese troops acted as ball boys, and a dozen more formed a human backboard, though a horde of kids did most of the chasing of errant shots and passed balls. A plastic jug and water tumblers waited on a small table between two chairs draped with towels. A bowl of ice sat next to the tumblers.

A badly hit ball skipped past us, chased by a dozen boys. Miser took the opportunity to cadge a cube of ice to suck on.

"Would you mind keeping your hands out of the ice?" the USAID guy whined at him and pushed his eyeglasses higher on his aquiline nose. "That's very unsanitary, what you're doing."

Miser gave him the fisheye and slowly spat the cube onto the court. The guy's colleague glared at us from the sidelines. The USAID pair were familiar types. I'd have bet a week's pay the onlooker with the short hair was ex-military and the one on the court a pedigreed preppy who was getting a leg up on a foreign-service career while keeping out of the draft. The young man returned to his serving position at the base line. A local came up and engaged Checkman in animated conversation.

"He says something's going on down by the river that we should see."

It was only a few hundred yards to the river's edge and we covered it quickly in the jeep. Using scrub for handholds, we descended the steep bank. At the wide sweeping curve where the two rivers met, a huge waterlogged corpse lay beached on the sandy bank, face-up and nude, bloated arms outstretched like a sleepwalker's, its sausage lips exaggerated and swollen like its erect penis. The tongue protruded from the giant round mouth. The eyes bulged. The scrotum was the size of a grapefruit. Judging from his short stature and sparse body hair, I guessed he wasn't Caucasian.

Vietnamese circled the reeking body, awed and curious, as if some exotic form of sea life had washed up. They tried to move him with bamboo poles but the saturated cadaver was impossibly heavy, his features so distorted we couldn't tell whether he was Vietnamese or an aborigine, or even how he had died. "What do you make of this, Sergeant Miser?"

"Something fucking nasty going on upriver."

Checkman called out. They'd found another one, a long loincloth unwinding behind him. Definitely Montagnard, definitely dead — horribly so. The head, nearly severed from the body, bobbed alongside like an appendage, the neck crudely sawn, rending the flesh and leaving a jagged flap.

"I hope to hell he was dead when they did that," Miser said. He shook his head. "We're back in the shit for sure."

Little kids coming to see the odd floating thing called out to Checkman as we scrambled up the bank to the jeep on the road. Driving again, Checkman slowed for a Vietnamese girl hauling river water in two square cans hanging from opposite ends of a yoke pole balanced across her shoulders. A file of Montagnard women marched past her in the other direction, their woven back baskets laden with manioc.

We rolled up to the compound gate, guarded by a lone American in a big, open-sided sentry box with a wood roof. He lounged on a three-foot-high wall of sandbags behind a concrete barrier painted with the MACV shield bearing red ramparts, an upturned yellow sword, and

TEAM 31 below it in black. The sentry rose to his feet, his hands occupied with a baby civet cat the size of a mouse. He motioned us by with his chin. No barrier pole, no salute, no mirror under the chassis to check for bombs. Just the guard bottle-feeding the civet from a pricked condom.

# 3

★ ★ ★

WE CROSSED THE quad and stepped up onto the walkway, following Checkman to the sign that said OFFICE
and into a cramped bullpen shared by the colonel's immediate staff and a local interpreter. Lieutenant Colonel Bennett came out
of his tiny office to greet us. Bennett was tall and slender with the long-
muscled build of a distance runner. His translucent-frame Army-issue
glasses and wispy blond hair gave him a bookish air. A West Point class
ring was prominent on his hand, like an extra knuckle. More than half
a dozen Montagnard bracelets jangled on his wrist. We went into his
office. A Vietnamese kitchen worker brought us lemonade from the
mess hall.

Bennett said, "I was pleased to hear you're willing to lend us a hand.
We don't often get volunteers here."

"Happy to help out, sir," I said. Miser eyed me suspiciously.

"You've both advised before. I have no doubt you will handle the
duties. Between bouts of tedium, we'll try to provide some diversion, I
promise."

"We look forward, sir."

"Okay," he said, smiling. "Your duties. You and Sergeant Miser will
be running the six-man signal detachment that keeps us linked to
the outside by multichannel radio and encrypted teletype. You need
to keep the landlines open to the province chief at the sector headquarters, USAID, and so forth. What else? Maintain your vehicles and

weapons, help harden the fortifications, and man part of the perimeter during alerts."

"Yes, sir," I said.

"Your people may also be called on from time to time to stand watch on the shortwave radios in the commo bunker. And to support patrol missions and assaults."

By which the colonel meant humping through the woods with a backpack radio and a whip antenna sticking up out of it like a SHOOT ME sign. Miser looked glum.

"Yes, sir," he said. "We know the drill."

"Captain Rider, besides your signal oversight, I've got you down for intelligence. Are you all right with that?"

"Absolutely, sir."

Jessup had outdone himself engineering that one. It was perfect, giving me access to information and the freedom to snoop around the province. Running the detachment was going to be the exact opposite for Miser — a ball and chain.

Bennett looked pleased. "You'll review the intel coming in, liaise with our three Special Forces camps and with the ARVN battalion across the way, gather up the local intelligence from them as well, and distill it all for me. Every evening you'll transmit *our* intel to the head shop at Pleiku and the Green Beret camps, and pass on to your Vietnamese counterpart across the street whatever's permissible to share."

"Yes, sir."

"Take extra care with security. It seems we've been compromised."

"Sir?"

"The harassing artillery fire put out from next door hits nothing. The VC seem to know our radio frequencies — even come up on them to gab. They monitor communications between our units so closely, I'm hesitant to put men in the field. Maintain radio discipline and be extra careful with your codebooks and shackle code sheets, and burn your work product, of course."

"Yes, sir."

Bennett leaned against his desk. "My door's open if you have problems. If I'm not here, my XO is Major Gidding, one door down. He's the civil affairs officer — coordinates building schools, repairing bridges, funding agricultural projects, and the like. Naturally, he's our go-between with USAID in the little compound next door." He pointed vaguely over his shoulder. "Most civil affairs projects stop halfway through, though all the financing invariably gets used up," he said, smiling ruefully. "It's a mysterious process. Education is our one big civic accomplishment. We've got three thousand kids in school in the province and so far the teachers haven't all been run off or murdered by the VC."

"Probably are VC in that case," Miser volunteered, "or they're cooperating with them."

I shot him a look — like, *What the fuck? We just got here.*

"You may well be right," Bennett said, "but they do a decent job of teaching arithmetic and reading." He sat down behind his desk and tossed his glasses onto the desktop. "The principal has a good head on his shoulders — and has managed to keep it there, so far."

"Sir," I chimed in, to deflect Miser, "has there been recent enemy activity?"

"Last monsoon season twenty-one battalions of North Vietnamese regulars infiltrated four Highland provinces, ours included." Bennett shifted uneasily in his seat, which squeaked as if in pain. "They surrounded and isolated us. Blew bridges, blocked roads, stopped all traffic coming into Cheo Reo. Then cut off our two district capitals the same way, pinned the ARVN there, encircled them, and took over the undefended countryside piecemeal. We couldn't go to anyone's aid and no one could come to ours. They jammed us up good. Did the same in the three other provinces."

"How did you defeat them?"

"We didn't. The Air Force flew South Vietnamese reinforcements into Cheo Reo continuously in Caribous. Our little airstrip can't handle any bigger aircraft. ARVN got bloodied. Third day of June they took three hundred casualties."

"In one day?"

"Yes, one day. They fell back on Cheo Reo and haven't really ventured out since. Which is why we still hold so little of the outlying rural areas and why going overland anywhere around here remains so risky."

"What's your main concern at the moment, Colonel?" I asked, worried that Miser might open his mouth again and get us on the colonel's shitlist before we'd even unpacked.

"Normally the North Vietnamese troops pass through, heading to objectives near the population centers on the coast. Lately they've stopped and are just hanging around. We don't know why. Last fall they tried to cut the country in half across the Highlands until the First Cav arrived to block them. If they'd succeeded it would've been checkmate — they win. They're cranking up for something like that again."

"Sir," Miser said, "if there are that many hardhats and VC in these hills and mountains, what's to keep the Communists from just shutting down Team Thirty-one?"

"Not much, Sergeant. If we annoy them enough, they might. It wouldn't require much. Getting their forces off this plateau we're on . . . that would be the hard part. They'd get punished from the air."

Provided the weather allowed our warplanes to fly, I thought, but I didn't bring up the obvious.

"Hopefully we're not worth the price," the colonel went on. "We try not to tempt them. Which is why we don't keep so much as a helicopter on the airstrip overnight. A single-engine Cessna is all."

"We hope our addition to the team won't tip the scales, sir," I said.

Bennett smiled. I appreciated his candor and didn't envy him his vulnerable compound. I wanted to do a good job for him handling the intel, despite our sub-rosa work for Major Jessup, and get out.

Bennett said, "Private Checkman will show you around. He's a foreign-service brat, smart as a whip. Speaks and reads Vietnamese." The colonel rose. "Good to have you with us."

Checkman took us across a gravel truck park. A Dodge pickup, now Army green, had obviously been Navy gray before being liberated from our sister service. Just beyond a two-seater latrine hut stood a sandbagged shed housing a pair of backup generators under its corrugated metal roof. Overhead rose a thirty-foot mast with a two-panel antenna grille pointed toward Signal Hill at Pleiku, fifty miles away, ten miles farther than by rights it should have reached. The antenna was stretched past its limits, like all our signal equipment in Viet Nam.

We glanced into a pair of metal shelters, heavily layered with sandbags and steel plate, connected by a corridor of more sandbags to a wooden shed between them. The Mickey-6 in the first van transmitted and received encrypted messages in high-speed bursts that punched themselves into paper tape from which they were printed out by a teletype machine. The facing rig was paneled floor to ceiling with racks of electronics carrying the teletype transmissions and six radio-voice channels up into the rectangular antenna.

We proceeded down the short corridor and stepped inside the signal shack. Half a dozen signalmen stood to attention. The shack was crowded with replacement parts and GIs. Two M-14 rifles and ammo pouches hung from pegs. A library of Signal Corps manuals filled a wooden ammo box mounted above an obsolete switchboard, and a large pot of chickenless Army chicken soup simmered on a small hot plate. A helmet parked on top was inscribed *Make Fuck, No Kill.*

I put the men at ease and Miser took the report from Sergeant Rowdy, a buck E-5. He couldn't have been more than twenty and was a three-striper already. He had high clearances and ran the crypto rig, encoding and transmitting the classified traffic.

The other experienced man was a spec-4 called Geronimo, though he wasn't an Indian or even American. His name was Macquorcadale and he was Canadian, evidently a point of pride with him, as he boasted that there were "more f-ing Canucks in Viet Nam than candy-ass draft dodgers in Canada." Miser liked the tall, brash kid right off, I could tell. The rest were privates: two regular Army and two draftees.

Miser, Sergeant Rowdy, and I went out back to a sandbagged firing position surprisingly close to the chest-high steel-plank wall that circled the compound. Beyond it lay the broad, curving Ayun River, where we'd seen the bodies.

Rowdy gave us the rundown on equipment and warned us against inspecting the backup generators.

"They out of commission?" Miser said, hackles rising.

"No, Sergeant." Rowdy was all business. "Cobras."

"As in hooded?" Miser growled. "As in snake charmers?"

"Yes, Sergeant. Two, we think. We ran the generators several nights this week and they must've liked the warmth."

"Great," Miser said. "Cobra fuck buddies."

"Well," I said, "at least we don't have to worry about rats."

Miser and I excused ourselves to walk the compound.

"Sarge, what do you need from me? What signal work do you want me to do?"

"As little as possible, *Captain*. Sign the paperwork and stay out of the way. Stick to the intel charts-and-darts. We're spread thin. We got three jobs now. Your cover job, my cover, and our fucking chore for Jessup. Looks like that's going to be on you. I have my damn hands full."

"You remember enough to run the commo crew?"

"In my sleep. So long as we don't get attacked and bum-fucked."

"Not liking the odds here, Sarge?"

He shook his head. "This is fucking Fort Apache without the defenses. No mines, no flares, no claymores, not a single mortar."

We walked toward the perimeter. There wasn't much to the compound: a water tower, a couple of scraggly trees, hootches for the enlisted, the main generator shed, several sandbagged bunkers shored up by ten-foot-long perforated steel planks driven vertically into the hard earth, some laid across like beams for roofing. Villas in Saigon boasted more grounds and security.

"Yeah." I had to agree. "If Charlie's willing to face the morning after, he can absolutely have his way with us."

"Once the dumb-ass monsoon grounds our air support, they could screw with us easy."

He was right. Small units in the hinterland were expendable. No big deal if we got overrun. It was just a fact of life in the military. We were a tiny piece of the machinery. Somebody somewhere up the food chain was betting that our value as a target was offset by the possible cost of taking us down. But it was a safer bet that that officer was never going to spend a single night in Cheo Reo.

Miser bared his jagged teeth. "Anyone with a decent arm could throw a grenade halfway into this fucking compound, drop satchel charges on us, no problem, and knock out communications. The bungalows and hootches aren't even sandbagged. Mess hall either. Talk about lightly defended."

"What's the good news?"

"Gooks can't throw for shit." Miser exhaled loudly. "Still . . . we'd be dead meat in minutes if they decided to have themselves the propaganda victory of taking a province capital."

"Even with our valiant allies bivouacked across the road?"

"Yeah, right," Miser growled, indignant. "Uncle Ho's birthday is coming around again. I'm not interested in being a goddamn party favor."

"We better hope we're done here soon. I don't want to spend the monsoon mildewing in Cheo Reo, waiting for Charlie to drop by some stormy night when nothing's flying."

"How exactly are we supposed to do this little job for Jessup? Maybe we should hop over to Hong Kong and stick up that bank. Probably easier than fucking up their wholesale business from here."

"If we knew who was growing the stuff and where, or how they're moving it, we could mess with the fields or the growers — or the pipeline."

Miser shook his head ruefully. "You haven't a goddamn clue how to do this, do you, Captain, sir?"

"Not yet."

I left Miser to get acquainted with his men. Checkman, who had stood off at a discreet distance, fell in step as I passed and directed me back along the covered walkway to my new quarters, the third bungalow from the end. He didn't bother knocking, just showed me in.

"Your roommate is a civilian. He leases a place in town, which is where he mostly stays. He's only in the compound when there's trouble or meetings run late."

"Agency?"

"It would be presumptuous of me to say, Captain."

He had to be the spook-in-residence.

The room was small. Two metal bunks up against opposite walls. Between them, a desk with two gooseneck lamps and a green Army field phone was pushed against the windowless back wall. A flag with a yellow star in the center of a red field hung above my roommate's bed. A Vietnamese farmer's hat and a forty-two-shot Zephyr automatic rifle with scope sights hung beside it on a peg.

"What's his name?"

"Ruchevsky. John Ruchevsky. Big John."

Checkman left. I emptied my dopp kit of everything but shaving gear and soap, unpacked one set of civvies and shoes, additional fatigues, and an extra pair of jungle boots. At the foot of each bed was an actual bureau. I clamped some socks and underwear to my chest with my chin and opened the top drawer of mine. Inside was a perfect cone of fine wood shavings topped by the metal stem and trimmings of a handmade Montagnard pipe. Somebody's souvenir. Invisible bugs had devoured the wooden bowl, leaving only the aluminum stem and brass ring fittings cut from different calibers of spent bullets.

I emptied the sawdust out the door onto the grass, tossed my stuff into the top drawer, and slid it back in place. The next drawer down held a large card. The English text addressed *Advisers*.

> *There is a Reward for your capture and death!*
> *Surrender Now and Live! We will pay for your*
> *information on your training.*

As an afterthought it said *This Girl and $10,000.* Dead center was the girl, a sedate brunette in a coy pose.

"Come on, Charlie," I muttered to myself, "give it a rest."

I tacked the card over my bed — home sweet home — and went about draping the mosquito netting over the T-frames attached to either end. I shoved my agent's paper ID deep in my left thigh pocket and buttoned it shut. Outside, a spent artillery shell clanged like a gong, announcing chow. Struck repeatedly it would have meant an alert, all hands to the wire. Some things were the same all over Viet Nam.

The mess hall was modest and served all ranks. Oilcloth covered a dozen tables. French-era Sten guns hung around the pastel walls, below the screens and shutters of the window openings.

"Decoration?" I asked Checkman.

Checkman shook his head. "More like fire extinguishers, sir. They're oiled and loaded."

Dinner in the mess hall was thoroughly cooked and tasteless. The meat was white, the mashed potatoes white, the French beans albino. Miser and I declined the cream sauce. The potatoes, like the milk, were dehydrated and then reconstituted from powder and water. Forensics couldn't have identified the meat.

Miser eyed his portion suspiciously. "This looks like it's been done with an acetylene torch."

"No germs, that's for sure."

"Tastes just like chicken," he said.

Whatever unimaginable creature or organ we were eating, Miser always made the same observation. This time it actually was chicken. You could tell by the drumsticks. We went through the motions of eating and looked for the bar.

A side door opened onto a modest concrete slab roofed and sided with thatch, not much more than a screened-in patio with half a dozen stools and a small bar that served all ranks. Team 31 was far too small to have separate drinking establishments for enlisted, noncoms, and officers. Over the bar hung Christmas-tree lights and a hand-forged VC submachine gun, its trigger housing and magazine holder welded to a gun barrel made from a lead pipe. Crude but lethal. The ashtrays were empty c-ration cans, with linked rounds of spent machine-gun ammo snapped shut in a ring around each one.

Miser eyed the handcrafted receptacles skeptically. "Glad to see the campers are keeping busy."

The bartender was a huge black guy named Westy whose chief jobs were keeping the main generator running and the water tower filled and treated.

"What can I do you gents?"

"Larue," I said. Everyone concurred and he served up bottles of cold Tiger beer all around.

We were joined by the intel sergeant, Joe Parks, who was celebrating twenty-four years in the Army and his third war in Asia. Parks declared himself a homesteader who rarely left the compound. A major once, he'd been caught in the downsizing after Korea and given the option of leaving the Army or accepting a severe reduction in rank. Parks stayed, as a sergeant E-7.

He unfolded a sheet of paper and slipped it in front of me. "No doubt you've seen these before," Parks said. Prominent in the middle, my rank and name — *Di Uy Erik A. Rider* — and the bounty on my head: sixty thousand piasters. Something like three hundred bucks, a small fortune in Indochina.

He passed Miser one too. "Your reputation precedes you, Sergeant."

Miser beamed when he saw the price on him. "I'm at a hundred thou!"

I leaned over Miser's sheet. "*Ellsworth* Miser?" I said. He snatched it back.

We carried on like it was funny, but here we were in the back of nowhere, and the VC knew us by name.

"Makes you feel kinda important," Miser said. "Gives me the fucking creeps."

Back in country less than forty-eight hours and the sarge and I were already on the local hit list. A cheap propaganda psych-out, but it worked. We needed to watch our asses if we didn't want to finance some VC farmer's next planting season. I slid off the barstool, took our sheets over to the one solid wall shared with the mess, and added our bounty chits to the two dozen others pinned around a red battle flag with a large yellow star in its center.

As the light faded, several Montagnard aborigines drifted past, dark-complexioned and black-haired, their skin like bark. Three Montagnards, barefoot, dressed in black long-sleeved native shirts and matching loincloths trimmed in red. The fourth wore a French military shirt and shorts. An old soldier. All four shouldered or cradled vintage bolt-action rifles and smoked homemade pipes as they strolled.

"Our night guards," Parks said as they ambled by. "Jarai tribesmen. There aren't enough of us to man the perimeter at night, so we've hired them. They're all veterans of the French colonial forces."

Made sense. Vietnamese hated the Montagnards, looked down on them as repugnant inferiors. The Montagnards returned the sentiment and quietly despised the Vietnamese. When Americans took casualties, the Yards expressed regret. *Chia buon.* I share your sorrow. When the casualties were South Vietnamese, all you got were blank looks. Whatever courtesies might be observed during the day, no Vietnamese was allowed in the compound at night. The simple truth was, we all liked the Yards better and trusted them a whole lot more.

In addition to the Jarai, an American stood guard on the gate and an American manned the shortwave radios all night in the MACV commo bunker, monitoring the three Special Forces camps in the province and periodically warning aircraft about impending artillery fire from the guns across the road so they didn't unwittingly fly into the trajectory. The signal detachment also maintained a separate radio link to Pleiku around the clock.

One of the Jarai bent down, picked up a large beetle, admired it, stripped off the hard shell, and crunched down. Protein on the hoof. A delicacy. I'd seen hootch maids in Saigon do likewise with cockroaches.

I turned back to Parks, a little embarrassed to outrank a man who had served longer than any of the rest of us and might have qualified for a general's star. "What's the lowdown on our ARVN friends across the road?"

"It's the usual: awful morale and lethargy. We equip them with obsolete World War Two weaponry and boss them around. Their brass doesn't so much as house or even feed them properly, skims their pay, and lets them gamble and piss away what's left. After which they go grabbing up chickens and appropriating rice from the civilians. Endears them to everyone. Soldiers sell their military items and then nag us to replace them."

"Meanwhile, their officers avoid anything that looks like a decision."

"Yeah. Bugs the hell out of the colonel. Bennett is career military. He respects the idea of service. Here, government and military appointments go to whoever has the connections and the wallet. How many exceptional officers have you seen stuck at lower ranks because they couldn't afford the rank they deserved, while untrained incompetents parade around with generals' stars? You ever see anyone above the rank of captain out in the field?"

"In their system," I said, "field-grade officers don't have to go."

"If Bennett had gotten the combat command he'd wanted, he'd be leading troops like he did in Korea. Instead, he's stuck as senior adviser to this ingrate bunch. He's diplomatic, he does a good job, but any time we plot an operation, the ARVN go into slow motion. Every preparation takes forever. By the time the troops get done getting ready, the VC are long gone. Lately they aren't even bothering to go through the motions."

"And why do we? I wonder."

Joe Parks puffed on his pipe. "They're embarrassed to have us land on them with all our strategizing and machines as if they couldn't do it themselves. And they're embarrassed and resentful that they can't. They don't trust their lousy excuse for a government, and their government doesn't trust us. They see us pouring in men and equipment, erecting huge aerodromes and monster camps, and it makes them suspicious that we have permanent designs on the place, like the French."

"Meanwhile, the Montagnards worry that we'll abandon them to the Vietnamese, who will grab up their land and evict them the minute we're not here to protect them."

"The Yards in Pleiku call the Vietnamese land eaters," he said. "They're not wrong. The generals and cabinet ministers are busy snapping up the best land for their summer homes and business ventures. Our Two Corps commander, General Vinh Loc, and a bunch of his subordinates are building an amusement center up in Pleiku on Hodrung Mountain, next to where the Fourth Division builds its base camp this fall."

Miser perked up. "Amusement center?"

"Brothels and bars." Parks sucked on his pipe. "They're expecting to make a fortune. Plei Poontang, the enlisted call it." He relit the bowl with a wooden match. "The Jarai think that's the volcano they came out of at the beginning. Bellybutton, they call it. Holy ground."

"Is that Titty Mountain?" Miser said, contemplating investments.

Parks nodded and puffed. "Yup."

Other members of Team 31 drifted into the bar, including Hump, the guard who'd been on the gate when we drove in, also his sidekick Lucky, and a pale newbie wearing fresh jungle fatigues and boots — no nametag, no patches, only his second lieutenant's bars. He nearly dove to the ground when an artillery shell shrieked by overhead, outbound. Hump offered him a Camel and Lucky offered a Lucky Strike to try and calm him down.

Westy poured the guy a whiskey and said, "Just Harassment and Interdiction, sir. Vietnamese gun bunnies across the street blasting their cannons to rattle infiltrators and maybe waste some if the H and I lands lucky."

Miser lifted his beer. "Your tax dollars at work, a hundred and ten bucks a shell. To attrition," he toasted, and sucked on his bottle.

"Attrition!" we repeated and hoisted ours.

"Infiltration traffic's growing all the time," Parks said to the lieutenant. "The guns go off a lot. You'll get used to them."

Another artillery shell launched. The lieutenant flinched again as it screeched and rocketed across the sky.

The lieutenant rubbed his palms on his uniform. "How far out are they firing?"

"Seven miles max," Parks said. "The ground they can reach is nominally the government's. The rest is the Viet Cong's." He winked at us as he slid the lieutenant's bounty sheet over to him. "I think this is yours, Lieutenant Lovell."

"Holy shit," the young man said, staring at his name on the poster. He knocked back his shot and offered the glass for a refill, blinking rapidly, eyes tearing up from the booze.

Westy switched on the tape deck in back of the bar and blasted out some rock. Something stirred in the thatch overhead. The dinks' artillery hurled another shell. Westy replenished the lieutenant's liquor and poured himself a shot.

"Yeah," he said, "*nam lu*," and downed the whiskey. "Attrit the funky bastards."

My roommate took up most of the doorway. Ruchevsky was big. Six three or four. Over two hundred pounds. Thinning hair and a somber expression. He wore the requisite short-sleeved shirt, baggy khaki pants, and Hush Puppies, and looked like someone who sold sporting goods for a living. Anything but a spook. He dropped his backpack by his bunk.

"Captain Rider?" he said. "John Ruchevsky."

"Pleasure." I shook his hand.

"I run the agents in the province," he said, "and spy on everybody."

"I'm honchoing the signal detachment."

"And freelancing intelligence for MACV. I just put in dibs on you myself."

"For what?"

"Mutual benefit. You can watch my back and tell me everything you get from MACV that's super secret. And I'll selectively brief you on the local doings."

"Why doesn't that sound equitable?" I said.

"Hey, somebody's gotta be the top bunny. And we *are* on the same side, no? If I don't help you sort through the avalanche of intelligence bullshit, you won't know what's important in the daily shitstorm of classified crap coming your way out of Saigon and Pleiku and clogging your encrypted channels. Besides, your colonel is okay with it. We're all a little thin on the ground in this place."

I buttoned my jungle fatigue shirt. "You want me to go undercover downtown in Cheo Reo City?" I teased. "Blend in with the locals?"

Ruchevsky snorted. "You may be smaller than me but you'd stick out a mile too. No, I need you for company when I go out in the woods. You could hold my hand, operate my fancy radio for me. Hey, you don't like country and western, do you? I *hate* C and W."

"Rock. I like rock."

Ruchevsky grinned. "We're golden. You absolutely get to play with my guns. Your jacket says you're good with them."

Shit, had he really seen my file? "I didn't think your outfit liked to share," I said.

"True, but I'm more generous than most. Besides, you're gonna get bored pushing classified paper. You'll want to get out from behind that desk, get a little fresh air. I can offer you some fun and frolic, nature hikes, introductions to interesting people."

"We'll see," I hedged, not eager to take on more duties.

His eyebrows rose. "Come on," he coaxed. "I'll keep your secrets if you'll help me with mine."

I didn't respond. He sighed, disappointed. "Don't make me resort to blackmail."

"Like what?"

"Like who you really are and what you're really after. You and your pal from El Cid," he stage-whispered, using the slang for Criminal Investigation Division.

So much for working anonymously. I gave him a cold eye and walked to the door, closed it softly.

"You're smarter than you look," I said.

"Hey, I've seen your shop in Saigon. You've got no backing. We've got two floors in the embassy, our own air service, Special Forces at our beck and call, the ear of the ambassador and his lips on the buttock of our commander in chief. You got Ellsworth Miser and a stapler."

"You know anything about major dope fields in the province? Poppies? Marijuana?"

"That your assignment?" he said with disdain. "You seriously looking to wage war on drugs *here?* Save the world from snorting, shooting, smoking that shit? How many fingers you got, Dutch boy?"

"No. I just need to screw with this one operation."

"Just the one? Why?"

"At harvest time there's this Viet Cong bank account in the crown colony that grows fistfuls of American dollars with every load they run from here. Dope is giving them a lot of purchasing power in the arms market."

Ruchevsky blew a smoke ring. "Hmm. Maybe our interests do overlap. Did you know Hanoi is negotiating with Moscow for field-fired rockets?"

"Jesus," I said.

"Katyushas. Two meters long, black steel. Thick as your leg. A hundred pounds, forty of them high explosives. They'll fly maybe fourteen, eighteen kilometers. We're supposed to keep watch for one. Capture a sample, if possible. Can't you just see me hauling ass through the jungle with a hundred-pound rocket under my arm?"

"Eighteen klicks. Damn. That would give them artillery, if they're accurate and they buy enough of them."

"VC in the dope business," Ruchevsky said, musing. "Whaddya know. There's been nothing in my informants' reports so far. But it's an eye for an eye. We got a deal or what?"

"Okay," I said, reluctantly.

"Good. That's settled. You up for a walk in the woods?"

"How long? How many of us?"

"Just you and me, overnight. We'll stage out of my villa. My main man, Little John, will drive us. We'll hike in, hike out. It's not far."

"Where are we going? What are we after?"

"Little John gave me a lead on odd doings in the bush: a market servicing the NVA in the jungle. I want to see the scope of this thing, count customers, maybe get a handle on what kind of force is massing in the province."

"Sounds promising."

"Are you good to go without reporting your whereabouts?"

"I have to tell someone I'll be away."

"The colonel."

"And my sergeant."

"Okay, but that's all. It's our ass if the wrong people hear. We won't have backup."

"The colonel says you think our security's compromised and there's a leak. Any ideas where we're sprung?"

"Well, anything that goes across the street to ARVN is practically broadcast the next night by Radio Hanoi. We identify a target for the Air Force and it promptly vanishes. If there's a mole in the camp, I don't know where. We've looked at the usual suspects: Bennett's interpreter, old Mr. Cho. The hootch maids, food servers, cooks, the Montagnard guards — even our servicemen with security clearances."

"You checked *my* people — the signal detachment?"

"The two handling really classified stuff, yeah. And Miser. You too." He smiled. "That's when I found you out." A self-satisfied grin spread across his face.

"You come up with anything on the signal detachment?"

"Sergeant Rowdy's got a girlfriend downtown and likes to party. And your pal Miser habitually seeks out ridiculous investment opportunities wherever he goes. Thinks he's gonna be the next Howard Hughes from running bingo parlors in Asia. But that's about all. Given how leaky it is on the other side of the road, how would we even notice a trickle here?"

"Not very reassuring. When are we going on this little picnic?"

He consulted his watch. "Tomorrow afternoon. Right after I see Major 'Civic Action' Gidding. Why don't you tag along? Could be an eye opener."

"You and the major work closely, do you?"

"Not if he can help it. He hates my guts. Says I'm an arrogant, self-centered anachronism."

"Now, why ever would he say such a thing?"

# 4

★ ★ ★

I LAY ON MY bunk midmorning reviewing intel reports, hoping like hell I'd find something to point me toward the source of the drug coffers in the province. There was a knock on the screen door and Checkman said, "Excuse me, Captain Rider. The colonel wants you."

I picked up my boonie hat, strapped on my .45 pistol. The MACV compound was abuzz. The girlfriend of the gate guard on duty — Lucky — had strolled out from town to visit with her American paramour at his post. But the Vietnamese sentry across the road didn't like the idea of her fraternizing, so he'd stopped and hassled her. She gave him some lip and he struck her with his rifle barrel, splitting open her scalp and knocking her to the ground. Lucky ran to her aid and got into it with the South Vietnamese. The province chief was notified and intervened officially to eject our security guard from the province.

Apparently the young man was serious about the girl, but the province chief's authority was total, his word law. It was his province to command, his country. We were his guests, his advisers. There was no appeal. Lucky was to be on the first available aircraft out of Cheo Reo, no matter where it was headed.

We passed a small group of enlisted men in the quad commiserating with the kid as he stuffed sundries into his rucksack while waiting for a ride. The snatches of conversation were of the tough-break, motherfuckin'-slope variety. Hump and his bunkmates promised to send the girl to him on the next plane. They'd talk the pilots into it and slip them a bottle of Jack.

Checkman led me into the office bullpen, where the colonel stood holding a mug of coffee.

"You expecting trouble?" he said, indicating the pistol on my hip.

"Force of habit, sir."

"A good habit. Remind me to get you and Sergeant Miser issued carbines. It's what the ARVN carry. Most of the rest of us too, when we go out with them or with the territorial militias. Meanwhile, I sent for you because Mr. Cho here says the province chief is expecting a courtesy visit from you. We'd best get that out of the way before I hear back that I've been disrespectful. I've already sent over a note of apology for our gate guard's misbehavior."

"No chance he'd cut the kid some slack?"

"Not a prayer. The colonel delights in any American screwup. He isn't a guy to bargain with. I set a precedent like that with him and I'm done."

"How did he get the job?" I said.

"Chinh?" Bennett looked straight at me. "The usual way. Bought it. Five months ago. For about sixteen thousand dollars, U.S."

A high price for a post in the sticks.

Colonel Bennett elected to drive the short distance. We were immediately delayed by a column of ARVN troops ambling in the direction of the airfield. The soldiers flopped by in shower clogs, carrying their rifles on their shoulders or holding them by the barrels or slung muzzle-down, some cradling them like infants. A few wore their metal helmets; most hung them off their packs. A live duck dangled upside down from one soldier's belt. Pots and canteens clanked as they herded past. A number of them held hands, the custom among friends and comrades.

"What's their actual head count," I said, "when you subtract the no-shows and the phantoms and deserters?"

"Chinh's battalion? He claims seven hundred on the payroll, but it's four hundred, tops."

"Is it hard to get through to this outfit, sir?"

"Like tying knots in spaghetti." He glanced over at me. "What's your experience been with our Vietnamese allies?"

"The ranger battalion I advised my first tour was good. The regular army units left a lot to be desired. One time several of us went out with a platoon that tripped a firefight. The next thing we knew, it was just us and our radio. They slipped away and left us to face a company of NVA by our lonesome."

"You almost can't blame them," Bennett said, "given how they're treated. And they're drafted to serve until they're fifty-five. It's like a life sentence. How can morale be anything but miserable?"

"Do any of your advisers get along with them, sir?"

"Divivo. They love Sergeant Divivo."

"Why is that?"

"He's easygoing. Seems genuinely interested in their welfare. Got a second Silver Star from Westmoreland for risking his ass saving some of their wounded."

"Sounds like a good man."

"The best."

"So they listen to him."

"No. But they like him. He was a mason in civilian life. Divivo risked his life making an overland run to the coast for bricks and cement for them to build their families better quarters. He scrounged the materials and made it back in one piece. Took some fire coming back. The ARVNs thanked him profusely but never fixed their quarters. Sold every last blessed brick and bag of cement."

"How did he take it?"

"The sergeant is a saint. He's nonjudgmental, no matter what they do."

The column finally cleared the road, and we rolled past the ARVN gate sentry unacknowledged.

The provincial seat was also the sector headquarters, located in a barn of a place in the Viet garrison, surrounded by a bare parade ground, deserted and quiet. In front of the building, a barbed-wire cage the size of a doghouse was staked to the ground. A Vietnamese man lay inside, naked to the waist, arm bent over his eyes to block the sun. There wasn't enough headroom in the cage for him to sit up, hardly enough to turn over. Sweat dripped off my chin and temples; the captive had stopped sweating.

We climbed the tall set of steps. The building was closed up and dank. Bennett led the way. The floor creaked, and our footfalls echoed. We encountered a lone, unarmed soldier seated at an old-fashioned switchboard, mouth open, asleep. No clerk or typewriter visible anywhere. No papers, no files. No calls. A weak light bulb burned high up by the ceiling. The vast space and the dim light gave the illusion that the still air was vaguely cool. But there was no breeze.

Bennett said, "Chinh's English is much better than he claims, by the way. So be careful what you say around him. He understands far more than he lets on."

The province chief's office was in the rear, dark and huge. A pool table stood lost in one corner; facing it, a couch and the kind of straight-back armchairs you might expect in a law office. Behind a table flanked by two shuttered windows sat the province chief, smoking and looking minuscule in the gloom. A covered birdcage hung nearby. The floor complained as we crossed, stood before him, and saluted.

Colonel Chinh returned our salutes. He wore the insignia of a full ARVN colonel pinned to his shirt front: three flower buds above a gold bar engraved with a flowering branch. In addition to being the highest-ranking officer in the province, he was also its civilian head.

"Colonel Chinh," Bennett said, "I'd like you to meet Captain Rider. He's come to look after our communications and act as your battalion's intelligence adviser."

We took our seats on the other side of the table that served as his desk. Its surface was naked: no paper, not so much as a pen.

Chinh Doa Cao was thin and delicate, his khaki shirt and trousers immaculate, like his manicured nails. His only unattractive feature was a wart on his chin with two long hairs dangling from it. Letting them grow was an Asian thing: it warded off bad luck. At least he wasn't sucking on them or twirling them, like some Vietnamese I'd done business with. Still, it was hard not to stare.

The ARVN interpreter slipped into the room, looking nervous, and quietly took up his station, standing beside the seated Chinh. Bennett reiterated his apologies about the gate guard's effrontery, brought the colonel up to speed on the latest intelligence reports, recounted some information passed along by Saigon about larger actions around the country, and reminded him of the upcoming elections. A complaint had been lodged that the government's candidates were all on red ballots, the color of luck, and the opponents' on unlucky green.

The colonel grunted and said he would look into it. Not that elections mattered. Every important post, his included, were bought appointments. Province chief, district chief, village chief — all appointed, all military officers. That left the voters only village councils to elect. And even so, police often went right into the voting booths with people to facilitate the proper outcome.

Lieutenant Colonel Bennett asked about the deployment of the three companies that were currently in the field. The province chief gave only a vague description of their whereabouts and mission.

"But why you inquire? Your Sergeant Divivo is with Second Company," the interpreter translated. "I am sure he inform you."

"Of course," Bennett said. "Colonel Chinh, forgive me for bringing it up, but I am wondering why yesterday the battalion's companies marched south when we advised your officers of NVA activity to the north."

Chinh cut him off.

"My commanders, they reluctant to follow suggestion of adviser when they disagree. But they polite. No say . . . at this time."

"Colonel, it makes your units seem unwilling to seek out and engage their enemy, unwilling to fight the invaders."

"They not want fight, at this time." Chinh seemed amused. "These soldier from seacoast — low country. Buddhist. No loyal this place we ask they defend, no loyal to Catholic people of our Phu Bon Province. Soldier heart ill. Miss home. No like food in mountain, want creature from sea."

"They no like Montagnard," the interpreter translated, though Chinh had used the Vietnamese word for savages — *moi*. Wild men.

Chinh went on through the translator: "My soldier not want Highlands very much and not wish fight. Casualties no can. Wounded officer have ration payment cut" — he made a slicing motion. "Forty cent a day. Wounded soldier man get eighteen cent. Not much paid. Many less piaster than mercenary savages of you. Vietnamese soldier family here, with soldier. Soldier know wife and childs in danger if they don't protect. VC come. Kill son, daughter, wife."

Chinh leaned to one side. "What can do?" he said in English, arms open in a magnanimous Western gesture.

Chinh reverted to his own language. The nervous interpreter wet his lips, listening. He turned back to us.

"The army men no care what fall down upon Saigon or foreigner who tell government do this and that. They want aborigine to patrol mountain place."

"The Montagnards would like nothing better," Bennett said, but stopped when he saw how perplexed the interpreter looked.

The man blinked rapidly. "Say, please."

"The Montagnards want to defend their Highlands but need better weapons — mortars, machine guns, grenade launchers. Saigon will not stand for that. But your government opposes giving them heavier arms."

"Army of savage? No, no. Cannot."

"Didn't think so," Bennett said under his breath. "Sir, we are also concerned that your men keep setting up their ambushes in the same locations time and time again. It's . . ." Bennett groped for an inoffensive word.

"Silly," Chinh suggested in English, and resumed speaking to the interpreter in Vietnamese.

"Yes — ridiculous if you wish pounce on enemy," the translator said. "They no wish. They happy make understanding with VC."

Chinh spoke to us directly: "Alive and permit to alive, yes?"

"It's your conflict to win or lose, sir," Bennett said. "You are at war."

"Correct," said Chinh. "But we battle for very much time. It not excite my mens or call them to fight like tiger. They think you, Colonel, and other American, you alien government. Give too many advise. Make them *n guy*." He looked to the interpreter, who was stymied and pantomimed the word, lifting his hand with an invisible wire.

"Puppets," I said.

The interpreter beamed, relieved. "Puppet! Yes, yes."

Speaking quickly, Chinh continued. The interpreter nodded as he translated.

"They feel to be on Washington string. They bored of it. Many desert. We so need, we welcome runaway mens if they return and give them all old pay. You fly to home in less than year. My men and myself, we go no place. Last eleven month in Highland, six thousand seven hundred Vietnamese soldier *fini*. Deads. Yes? Much war left. Too few us."

Chinh rose. "Thank you for views . . . at this time."

Bennett and I stood. Bennett congratulated the province chief on his latest medal and invited him to a celebratory dinner. The province chief declined: duties called him away. Or maybe he didn't like all-white food.

"Perhaps another time," Bennett said.

"Perhaps. Yes, yes." Chinh came from around his desk.

We took our leave and went back through the echoing hall. The colonel's door shut behind us.

The prisoner was still in the cage outside, the sun steadily baking his brains. He didn't look too good. Lips cracked, tongue dark and starting to protrude. It would take days to restore him, if he didn't dehydrate and die today. The man mopped his face slowly and tried to lick the sweat from his fingertips. There was none. A last sign before heatstroke.

"You think they worry about the Geneva Convention, sir?" I said, wishing I had carried a canteen.

Bennett got into our jeep on the passenger side. "Doesn't actually apply."

"I should have guessed. He's not a prisoner of war, is he?"

"No," Bennett said, "he's one of their own."

"What will happen to him?"

"They'll broil him for two days, allow him one cup of water every eight hours, one bowl of rice every twenty-four." The colonel pulled on his cap. "If only they were as hard on the enemy."

"You met the Chinny Chin Chinh." Ruchevsky chortled. "Whaddya think?"

"A charm boat. He has an answer for everything . . . at this time."

"You definitely get to play with my guns," he said, pulling a wooden ammo crate from under his bunk. I noticed a heavy strongbox shoved in the back. Out of the crate came rifles: a Schmeisser, a Swedish K, an AK-47 in three pieces, and two banana clips.

"My arsenal," he said. "Part of it, anyway."

I inspected his weapons. Each was perfectly serviced: clean, oiled, ready to do its work. Though nothing in his physique or his bearing was ex-military, the man knew his guns. They weren't just well-maintained tools. They'd been looked after, cared for, and were uncomfortably reassuring to hold, their power alive in the inert metal. The feeling was enhanced by the devotion he'd shown to their well-being. They were appreciated. I worked the mechanisms and dry-fired the Kalashnikov at a gecko stalking an insect on the wall.

"C'mon," Ruchevsky said. "Time to chat up Major Gidding."

We went to his room. The major came to the screen door in his undershirt and fatigue pants, dog tags taped together. He held the screen door open for us.

"What can I do for you, Mr. Ruchevsky?"

"I'm here to complain about the gas siphoning."

"Again?"

"It's getting more serious."

"How so?" Gidding said, walking back to half-sit on his desk. Ruchevsky leaned against the wall, arms folded across his chest.

"The missing quantities are escalating. The daily tally of gas your depot sergeant dispenses legitimately and the supply the next morning used to jibe at least some of the time. Not anymore. Not even close."

"That's classified information, Ruchevsky. How the hell — ?"

"Gas goes missing in the night every night. How does your depot sergeant account for the difference?"

Gidding shrugged. "Leaks?"

"You're telling me that's the official explanation? That's what you put in your reports?"

"Seepage, actually."

"*Thousands* of gallons of seepage?"

"Yeah," Gidding said. "Slow but steady." He pointed his clasped hands toward Ruchevsky. "Look. The POL sergeant is just covering his ass. He's got no way of securing the bladders. You and who else is going to spend the night outside the perimeter guarding a bunch of fuel and oil and aviation gas? The ARVN guards on duty see nothing and say nothing about what goes on there after sundown. If I underscore the discrepancy, the sergeant gets burned. What would you have me do?" he said, exasperated. "Close down the supply point entirely to stop the siphoning? Not fuel our vehicles or the aircraft that land here? If you haven't noticed, half of all our supplies coming into Viet Nam go missing. A lot goes missing before it even reaches a dock. More disappears *from* the docks and supply depots onshore and the trucks hauling them away."

"More seepage, I suppose?"

"That's our story."

"You and I know where that gas is really going, Major. The difference is you think it's perfectly okay."

"I don't condone it. I just think it's . . . realistic to expect it."

"The price of operating here."

Gidding exhaled a great sigh. "I really think you're exaggerating the problem, John. Okay, we pour him a concrete slab and call it a tennis court. If that's what it takes to keep him happy, why not? General Westmoreland presented Premier Ky with two prototype helicopters after the premier signed over land for Westy's new headquarters complex. How's our concrete a big deal?"

Ruchevsky frowned. "It's not just the gas. The Chinhs are really pushing it. You want the latest? His wife just cut a deal with some Chinese moneymen in Cholon for them to log hardwoods here in Phu Bon."

The major looked bemused. "The roads aren't exactly secure," he said. "How do the loggers expect to get this lumber out of the province?"

"They've gotten a pass from the local VC provisional government."

"You mean they paid a tariff."

"I mean they bribed the Communists with cash money — dollars we probably supplied."

"Look, John," said Gidding. "I'm not happy to hear it, but it's not any different than what our local merchants do to bring in luxury goods on trucks. They pay Charlie's road tolls and we get to drink Cholon cognac downtown. How do you think barges loaded with Coke machines get shipped around the damn delta intact? Or the huge petroleum depot south of Saigon avoids even a single tracer round from setting it off?"

"Besides the safe-conduct fee, the VC are also getting heavy timbers out of the deal to build sturdier fortifications and bunkers."

Gidding assumed a bored expression and looked at his wristwatch. "I think you're absolutely exaggerating Chinh's situation."

"He's a crook."

"He's a realist. The country runs on graft, if you haven't noticed. Whatever you make, however you make it, you keep forty percent, gift the rest to your superior, and the next guy does the same. We're not here to critique their damn society. We're here to win the war. What's the big difference between us giving them rice and arms and their *taking* some gasoline? We're the sugar daddy."

"Supplies get diverted and sold on the black market," Ruchevsky said. "Not nice but — okay. What's not so okay is that Chinh's biggest customer is the opposition. If you're arguing he's no worse than any of the others in his position, we're in trouble. Good day, Major."

I walked Ruchevsky to his vehicle.

"Meet me back here in an hour. You didn't shower this morning, did you?"

"No, boss. I know the drill."

The less aftershave and deodorant, the better. Then again, no way was I getting close enough for the VC to smell me. John got in his Bronco and drove out of the compound. Checkman came along the walkway heading toward the perimeter.

"You gotta see it, sir. Come quick."

"See what?"

"The house trailer, sir. It's got a real bathroom, air conditioning, kitchen, fridge."

"We're getting a deluxe stateside trailer here?"

"No, sir. The USAID compound next door is."

Every off-duty enlisted was headed over to the big event, as were several officers. An unkempt airman named Lewis came up behind us, trailed by his pet pig.

"Rut, sit," he commanded, and the pig did, sort of. More like flopped. "Good pig," Lewis said, and scaled the wall of perforated steel planks and sandbags. Settling on top, he gave Westy a hand up. More men stood atop a tall bunker.

Westy said, "Not too exposed for you out here, Airman Lewis? I know you're short. You maybe oughtn't ta risk yourself."

Lewis shrugged. "I felt a moral obligation." He tossed his pet a piece of bread. "I'd hate myself if I didn't. I'll be back in the world soon enough."

Westy hooted. "Son, this is the world. Back there, that's Disneyland."

On the USAID side the tennis-playing preppy, now in chino pants and short-sleeved checked shirt, paced in front of their little residence, looking at his watch and peering at the sky through his horn-rims. Mr. Ex-Military, similarly attired, leaned against a post, hand raised to his forehead, shading his eyes. Soon we heard the thump of heavy rotors.

Westy pointed heavenward. "The Shit Hook!"

The Chinook was less than half a mile out, a large rectangle slung beneath it.

The enlisted men stood as the copter hovered and descended, easing the sling earthward. The rotor wash whipped us, raising a growing storm of grit. We all squinted.

"It doesn't take much to draw a crowd in Cheo Reo," I observed.

"No, sir," Westy said. "You gotta take your entertainment as it comes."

At a height of maybe fifty feet, the cables unlatched and the trailer plunged. The onlookers roared and whistled their delight as it came down.

The preppy danced around in agitation but that didn't keep the luxurious quarters from crashing hard into the dry earth with a great noise and a cloud of dirt. Wall panels flew off as the trailer crumpled. Coolant and propane sprayed the air before fizzling out. He flailed his arms and yelled something we couldn't hear over the rotors. The USAID tough guy surveyed the proceedings impassively. He didn't look like someone you'd want to dig you a well.

"Did you see that?" Westy exclaimed. "Did you see?" He smacked palms with another soldier. "That was some shit."

Airman Lewis looked impressed. "Definitely persons in need of guidance up in that chopper."

"I thought that USAID motherfucker what's in charge was gonna stroke out," Westy said.

We all got down and walked back into the center of the compound, the pig following Lewis. Checkman and I trailed after them toward the bungalows.

"What was that about?" I said to Checkman.

"Oh . . . ah, that was the latest attempt at delivery. The same . . . ah . . . accident keeps happening. Third time in a row."

"Almost as good as a drive-in," Westy said over his shoulder. "Sheeet, somebody somewhere's got a serious case of the ass for USAID."

"Can't understand why," Lewis replied. "Maybe we should bring them a meat-loaf casserole to console 'em. You know, welcome them to the neighb."

"Now, that's cruel," said Westy. "Really uncalled-for, Airman Lewis. That meat loaf is lethal. You know the survival rules we learned in Basic — don't drink untreated water, don't eat the mess sergeant's meat loaf."

The pig trotted on past them.

Our gear lay on Ruchevsky's bunk. Blood expander, dressings, morphine Syrettes, eight pounds of water in four canteens, grenades, smoke — the usual. VC ammo vests that fit high on the chest. Hammocks much lighter and better than our regular issue. Counterfeit NVA boots made on Okinawa for the Forces. My size too. The man planned ahead.

Not so usual: a silenced pistol for each of us and two extra magazines; a very fancy, very sharp knife and sheath; AK-47s (the enemy's assault rifle); and three twenty-round magazines apiece, a fourth already inserted. A heavy weapon and heavy ammo, but it would make the right sound going off in a hostile neighborhood, and ammunition would be everywhere for the taking. That was the only way we could resupply. Officially no one knew we were going or where. Nobody was going to be standing by to rescue us. Under the circumstances it was safer not to announce our intent, or so I kept telling myself.

Ruchevsky packed black pajamas for himself and an NVA pith helmet. It would make the right silhouette at a distance, even though he was too tall and the outfit huge. He offered me several styles of camouflage fatigues. I opted for the tigers. A little baggy, but baggy was okay. We stuffed everything in our packs, including cotton bandoleers containing the long rolls of cooked rice that would be the extent of our food supply. Breakfast, lunch, and dinner — a chunk of coagulated rice pinched off from the roll, VC style. We would even smell native. The radio was one I'd never seen before, a cigarette-carton shape with a weird metal tube for an antenna.

Ruchevsky said, "If we get completely compromised and we're done for, push the red button on the radio."

"That'll put us out of our misery?"

"No such luck. Fries the circuitry. It won't keep us from wishing we were dead."

I tested the radio by calling into the MACV commo bunker and tossed it into my NVA rucksack.

"Party time," he said.

We got in the back seat of Ruchevsky's Ford Bronco.

"Boss," said the driver, a black-haired Montagnard in sports shirt and black trousers.

"Little John," Ruchevsky said by way of introduction, and turned to me. "Little John's a Westernized Montagnard. Hangs out in town. My number one man. Runs my agents and informants. His Jarai name is something crazy, like Pig or Asshole — one of those nasty names Yards use to keep spirits from eating their kids." Leaning closer to me, he whispered with genuine glee, "He's a little shady."

Clever, I thought. If anyone could be trusted to dish the dirt on the Vietnamese, it was an alienated Montagnard.

"Little John, this is Captain Rider."

Little John wore an odd two-fingered glove on his right hand and shook my hand with his left as I leaned over the seat. He held his forearm with his free hand as we clasped, and I reciprocated the custom.

"Don't worry," Ruchevsky murmured, glancing at the glove. "Just a touch of leprosy." His eyes crinkled with amusement, watching it sink in that I had just shaken Little John's ungloved hand.

We slowed at the gate and turned left, going west along Road 2. We didn't pass a single conveyance. Ruchevsky and I rapidly changed into our outfits and blacked our faces. About seven klicks along, Little John pulled up and eased into the brush far enough for the vehicle not to be seen from the road. Ruchevsky bloused his black pajamas in his boots; I taped my pant legs shut to keep out land leeches and biting critters, took up my gear, and stepped into the undergrowth after Ruchevsky. He looked like the world's largest Vietnamese peasant. Little John quickly drove off.

All around us lay steep hills and tight valleys filled with ten-foot-tall reeds and grass. We slithered through and around them, trying not to let them cut or bruise our faces. I followed Ruchevsky, covering the signs of our passage as best I could. He put us on an actual trail.

After going west for an hour along the worn path, we switched to an animal track that took us up a long slope onto the ridge of a high foothill. We followed the ridge and descended to a little outcropping. John signaled a halt. We took up firing positions — him forward, me facing back — and waited.

No sounds. No one following or passing by. The partial canopy dimmed the afternoon light. Ruchevsky brought out binoculars and directed me to look northwest. I peered at a trail below us, clearly visible in a small valley. The tall grass lay parted like someone's hair. Normally the NVA came down out of the mountainous Highlands and plodded east toward the densely populated coastal provinces. But this trail wasn't the normal route of infiltration. It ran north.

I spotted a thatched shelter. A box stuffed with paper stood on a short post outside it. In the shadows, men prepared for the night's march. I couldn't count them. All I caught were glimpses of arms and elbows in the doorway. Two stood outside.

Ruchevsky signaled us closer. We descended toward the trail and approached to within sixty yards of the shelter before going to ground again. Keeping low, we crawled slowly another ten yards and lay still for fifteen minutes, making sure we hadn't been detected. A stream flowed nearby.

Ruchevsky handed me the binocs again. The box on the post held newspapers and magazines. After a while, men in green khaki came out and stood in the failing light, noisily talking and coughing. A dozen North Vietnamese *bo doi,* foot soldiers, ragged and tired. They'd been living rough on the trail for months, trekking south nocturnally through Laos in large groups, then breaking into smaller groups like this one. At some point, they'd crossed into South Viet Nam, Montagnards guiding them through the mountain forests.

After they rested all day at a way station, a new Montagnard guide escorted them halfway to the next overnight hut and handed them off to another guide for the rest of that leg of the trail. As a security precaution, the guides knew the locations of their own stations only. That's all they needed to know—one stretch of trail and its one rest hut.

Finally, the group set out on the night's march. The Montagnard at the front and the last man in the file each carried his assault rifle in both hands. The rest had their weapons slung on their shoulders or across their chests.

They crossed a bridge made of four young bamboo trees laid across the narrow stream, and slipped away into the mass of black foliage. Their upcoming shelter might be seven miles from here; nine if the route of march was easy. They'd arrive well before dawn, rest all day, and repeat the cycle again until they reached their final destination.

We listened for a quarter of an hour to the jungle around us and watched the light fade. When it was nearly gone, we snuck across the trail and retreated up the next gradual slope for a hundred yards, quickly plunging into double-canopy jungle that completely dwarfed us. In an overgrown grove of teak trees, we slung a pair of hammocks close to each other among the vines and moss and bedded down. I buttoned my cuffs and my top collar button and raised my lapels to keep out the mosquitoes and gnats. With my floppy hat pulled low, my ears presented the most tempting targets, but I'd hear them coming, even in my sleep. I propped the AK-47 across my chest and tucked my hands in my armpits to hide them from the mosquitoes.

A torrential downpour began shortly after nightfall. We huddled under the weatherproof cloth of the NVA ponchos, easily protected beneath the umbrella of double-canopy foliage. I signaled that I'd take the first watch. John waved me off. With only two of us camped out, accidental discovery was unlikely. Or, bedded down like VC, we might get a pass. If they did find us, it wouldn't be much of a contest. Ruchevsky opted for audacity: we would take our chances and get some real sleep.

I awoke once, around midnight, and ate some rice balls. Drops still pelted the large vulgar leaves overhead but the rain had stopped coming through. The deadfall on the floor of the jungle glowed, the rot luminous. The jungle was growing like a cancer, dripping and klacking, forcing and appropriating, choking everything within reach. Given the slightest opening, it wedged in. I draped my head in an olive-drab towel and slept.

# 5

* * *

I T WAS BARELY light. Ruchevsky took the lead along a faint animal track that wove over a ridge and into another valley. The track dipped behind a small hillock near the bottom, then went over it. As we neared the top of the smaller rise, we left the path and eased to the ground, crawling slowly forward through thick grasses into tangled foliage. I crawled after John on hands and knees, wishing that whatever the hell animal's trail we were using, the beast had been taller. It took forever. Eventually we crawled into a double-canopy forest of tropical hardwood trees speckled with orange flowers growing on their trunks.

The growth merged with a dense stand of elephant grass basking in a rare slash of light. The stalks loomed ten or twelve feet over us. Our continuing through would leave a visible trail. Not that we could. The individual blades were treacherously sharp.

Ruchevsky slid off to the left. I lost him momentarily and followed blindly, stepping onto another small animal trail on a hillside covered in creepers, praying that none was the thorny variety that latched onto you and didn't let go. A gang of yellow flies descended and bit our scalps. We slithered across the wet jungle floor, soft and quiet with dead vegetation, beneath broadleaf plants and nipa palms that looked like giant green shark skeletons. We were on a downward slope.

At the bottom of the hillside, the vines and thick undergrowth gave way to a crude road twenty feet wide, flanked by lush plants and sheltered on both sides by enormous trees that rose like redwoods, well over a hundred feet high, dwarfing us beneath their interlocked limbs and leaves.

At Ruchevsky's signal, we went to ground in a slight depression beneath a fallen log colonized by ferns. We camouflaged our position with fetid, damp rot and beards of moss, then waited, lying parallel to the road and facing in opposite directions, our feet touching. Sweat dripped from my chin and nose and ran freely down my face. I was exhausted and began to fade out as I lay still, hoping nothing too painful or deadly had decided to camp in my pants or under my shirt. A slight touch of John's foot had me instantly alert.

Small engines putt-putted through the stillness as scooters and motorized carts arrived, impossibly laden with goods. They parked and unloaded. Tradespeople began setting up shop by the roadside, piling their goods on tarps and erecting stalls for their produce, rice and dried fish, purple mangosteens, green jackfruit, yellowish papaya, even live fish in plastic bags filled with water. A rickety truck, a three-wheeled Lambretta, and a row of motorbikes soon lined the roadbed. Two women set out beer bottles and sundries, another piled cigarette packs on a tarp. The town market had come to the jungle.

Guards appeared — local Viet Cong. The guy in charge was stocky, his jowls shaded with several days' growth of beard. Unusual for an Asian. Judging from the rustling and talk behind us, we were within the circle of their security. Holy Jesus. What the hell had Ruchevsky gotten me into?

He was playing the odds that we'd be safe because the likelihood of anybody knowing that we would be out here was nil. Nor would anyone anticipate our presence, since no one in his right mind would do what we were doing. Me included, if he had warned me ahead of time. I desperately wanted to scratch the fly bites and dislodge whatever was feasting on my calf.

Guards trudged past, talking loudly. I held my breath. Vietnamese, thank God. Montagnards were great trackers and might have picked up signs of our presence. One of the sentries climbed high into a tree and perched in its branches to look for approaching threats, concentrating on the opposite ends of the road. A second guard posted himself with his ear to the trunk, listening for any signals the lookout tapped out.

Customers appeared, peaked and worn, their clothes threadbare. Up and down the road, passing the Viet Cong in their conical hats, armed North Vietnamese Army regulars strolled in shorts and black pajamas or pale green uniforms prudishly buttoned to the throat, confident they couldn't be spotted from overhead through the canopy. They all looked emaciated from living in the wild. None had more than a single magazine in his Kalashnikov, so their waiting comrades couldn't be far away. Their wants were modest — candy, cigarettes, beer, fruit — treats. Some small personal essentials: needles, thread, aspirin, that sort of thing. Each man bought just a few items and moved back into the forest, permitting other soldiers to funnel out of the jungle and take in the wares on offer. The entrepreneurs haggled loudly. Negotiations were short but intense, accompanied by loud banter. Everyone was enjoying the day. The surrounding foliage both muted and magnified the sounds, hollowing the air as it held it still.

The larger bulk purchases looked official: rice, cooking oil, live fish, mosquito netting, pharmaceuticals. Every soldier hefted a bag of supplies for the unit onto his shoulder as he departed, counted off by cadre. They exited in the same northerly direction they had come from.

A stick smacked the fronds behind us: a sentry wading through the ferns and leafy plants on the other side of the fallen tree trunk, beating the foliage as he went. I thumbed the safety off and breathed shallow, through my mouth. A bead of sweat inched down my spine. Another hung from my nose and dropped. An insect staggered past my eyes, dragging a vanquished enemy twice its size. Its cousins had taken up residence in the soft flesh at the back of my right knee. *Bo cho* ticks, judging from the pain of the bites.

Shouts erupted. A sentry hacked at the growth, bringing several others. They were chasing a snake, excited by the contest, yelping like children. The footfalls and shouts receded. I breathed again.

The shoppers thinned out, and the vendors hurriedly struck their stands and packed their wares. The sentry in the crow's-nest tapped out a signal, alerting those on the ground that somebody was approaching.

A two-stroke motor scooter came down the track, operated by a Vietnamese in green ARVN fatigues and aviator sunglasses. Behind him sat a Westerner in khaki pants, poplin shirt, and leather sandals: the USAID tough guy, wearing a shoulder holster. Their machine pulled up as a priest in shirtsleeves and clerical collar arrived on an ancient bicycle, its gears and chain clacking. A new white pickup truck brought a third Caucasian. What in the hell? I was dumbfounded.

The ARVN and each of the Westerners silently waited his turn and met briefly with the stocky Vietnamese leader. He exchanged a few words with each man and gave him a packet. When he'd met all of them he promptly left, walking into the jungle with his entourage of VC. The priest remounted his bicycle and pedaled off. Mr. USAID and the South Vietnamese soldier got back on their motor scooter, and the white guy climbed into his pickup. They all departed the way they'd come. The guards withdrew, and the last sellers straggled off, putt-putting away on their motorbikes and pedaling their bicycle carts.

We lay still. When we were utterly alone, Ruchevsky tapped me with his foot and we painstakingly crawled out through the tangle, our limbs stiff and numb. Back on the ridge, Ruchevsky drained his canteen and spoke for the first time since Little John had left us in the brush.

"Need more water," he whispered, sprinkling his face with the final drops, his cheeks bright red. "Let's pinch some from that stream near the rest station."

I raised my thumb in agreement. The new bunch of pilgrims would be snoozing by now and wouldn't be up again until they set out at nightfall. He led us up the hill near the rest station, where our faint animal track crossed their well-worn trail. The hut was to the right, the sound of running water to the left. We staked out the spot, listening and watching. The invaders slept. He handed me his two canteens and signaled *go*. Rifle slung, pistol out, I stepped onto the trail and padded toward the bubbling of the stream. It flowed rapidly with the previous night's rain. I filled all four canteens and hurried back, the fingers of my left hand hooked in the caps' plastic ties.

The discharge was faint but unmistakable. I ran to John. When I reached him, an NVA soldier in green shorts lay on the trail flat on his back, clearly terrified. Ruchevsky knelt on his arm, holding the silenced pistol an inch from the boy's forehead, a hand over his mouth.

He was no more than sixteen. Scrawny, gaunt, his hair overgrown, out for a walk in the beautiful woods to savor a minute's privacy, or maybe to fetch water to wash his clothes, boil his bamboo shoots. He must have been heading my way when Ruchevsky took him down. Shit. If only the boy had slept. A diagonal rice sleeve crossed his body.

The youngster whimpered. Blood streaked his arm. Ruchevsky made faint soothing noises to put him at ease and popped a shot into his temple. It didn't exit. Just banged around the brainpan for the instant it took to send him into eternity. He lifted the weapon away. The silencer had burned a red circle around the small black hole.

We each took a leg and dragged him off the trail and along our track, into heavier foliage. I went back and brushed away all marks of a disturbance while Ruchevsky stripped him of his rucksack and AK-47. He examined the weapon for a proof mark but it had none: a Chinese knockoff. He removed a bullet from the magazine, peered at it, and held it out to me. The base was stamped 1964: two-year-old ammo. I nodded in acknowledgment and signaled to hurry. If we were lucky, the soldier wouldn't be missed until tonight's march or might not be found at all.

"Take his rice," he whispered. "My people can identify where the grains came from."

I slipped the bandoleer sleeve off the body and draped it over myself.

Ruchevsky lifted the rucksack and rifle and what looked like a shiny penknife but turned out to be a harmonica. We covered the body with broad leaves and were off, back over the ridge toward our rendezvous with Little John.

We reached it two hours later. No Little John.

"He's supposed to be here ahead of us," John hissed and gulped water.

We stayed in the tree line back from the road and waited, trying not to talk, not knowing who might be nearby. After a while, curiosity got me.

"What do you think that little powwow in the jungle was about?" I said in a whisper.

Ruchevsky shook his head slowly. "God and Lenin striking a truce? Fuck, I don't know. Nothing good for us."

"What the hell's the story on Mr. USAID?" I said very softly. "I wasn't exactly expecting to see him confabbing with the Viet Cong."

"No kidding. His name is Whalen Lund. I keep wondering if he might be working for my employer."

"You don't know if Lund is one of yours?"

"Field people with different gigs aren't identified to one another. We don't coordinate — or cooperate. I'm here trawling the civilian population for Reds. I got a directive to make lists of VC and their sympathizers and order up air strikes. Lund? My station chief says he knew the guy a few years back, says he was a Marine looking to do dark deeds for God and country. Like running a Truong Son death squad. Offered himself to all the intelligence shops while he was still in the Corps. No takers — allegedly. Winds up a construction contractor for a short time. Well, a contractor, anyway. Then he joins USAID to push fertilizer and new rice strains, if you buy that."

"And the priest? There to bless the provisions, you think?"

"That was Father Calogaras, is my guess. I've only seen one old photo of him."

"The lefty French priest they say has gone native? The one the Berets talk about offing?"

"From a Greek family near Marseilles. Worker-priest in a factory there. Been in Indochina forever. Reportedly knows everything that goes on in the province. Has the locals' loyalty."

"Which locals?"

"Vietnamese — Communists, Catholics, Buddhists. It's kept him alive, so far. He's been in these mountains for two decades and everyone wants what he knows. But he stays completely off our radar, even while he's rumored to be running social services for the *other* provincial government."

"For the Communists, you mean? Like schools?"

"Schools, village wells, irrigation. Medical stations. Food for those on hard times. Some of our schools are his schools after sunset."

"God, what was he doing there in the jungle with Lund?"

"Beats me. Comparing notes on well digging?"

"And the Westerner in the Ford?"

"A local missionary, Judd Slavin. He and his wife are from St. Louis. Liked by everyone."

"Including the Viet Cong, apparently."

"He's the least worrisome. The humanitarian workers over here stay as neutral as possible . . . for their own safety. Even so, the Viet Cong aren't very consistent in their official positions on Western do-gooders. Makes socializing iffy. They have a committee called Friends of Workers in Christ that's supposed to liaise with the missionaries. Slavin makes contact with them from time to time."

"The ARVN dandy looked nervous."

"Can you blame him?" Ruchevsky said.

"Think he's a turncoat?"

"He'd never be that obvious. No, he's there probably to negotiate new prices at the gas pumps or some other commodity his boss is dealing in. Must be a hell of a feeling, going in alone to bicker with armed VC."

"Who was the odd-looking dude with the jowls and five o'clock shadow?"

"He's the top comrade in the province. Chinh's counterpart. The VC boss, most senior official in the area. Outranks even their military leadership. Joe Parks calls him Wolf Man."

"Amazing he would meet so publicly with Westerners and an ARVN."

"Probably wants word to get around that they recognize his authority. Acknowledge his position."

"What bio have you got on him?"

"Former Viet Minh commander. Led a Montagnard battalion against the French. He remained in the Highlands after they kicked out the French. When President Diem launched his campaign to eliminate all ex-Viet Minh fighters in the south, he fled into the bush. Hid among the tribespeople."

"What was with his teeth? They looked odd."

"Wolf Man had himself tied to a tree and had his front teeth filed down like theirs. Trained for a year at the Gia Lam school for ethnic minorities, in Hanoi. Speaks several Montagnard languages, knows their customs, how to use a crossbow. Ingratiated himself with a chief. Took a daughter as his wife, put on a loincloth, lived the Montagnard life, and patiently swung everyone in the vil to the Commie cause, mostly by telling them Ho Chi Minh will give the Yards the Highlands and autonomy after the war. They were reluctant to believe it — until they heard it on Radio Hanoi. The Reds broadcast it in the major Montagnard languages."

"And the teeth are why he's called Wolf Man?"

"His pointy teeth, yeah, I suppose. And the heavy beard. His facial hair is unusual as well. Like Vietnamese, Yards haven't much body hair to speak of. A beard is the sign of someone with the qualities to lead. Like Ho Chi Minh. Like the Yard holy man they call the King of Fire. Also, Wolf Man bellows. Gets loud when he harangues villagers. He's got an agitprop team that roams the province proselytizing, and intimidating when needed. You miss your twice-monthly tax of two hundred grams of rice or your annual tax payment of five thousand piasters if you're a shopkeeper, and you're likely to get a visit from Wolf Man."

"Do we know where he is now?"

"He gets around, never beds down in the same place two nights running. Sleeps five hours — if at all." Ruchevsky darkened. "He's executed half a dozen village chiefs, lots of minor officials, teachers, wives, even kids, for collaborating with the Saigon government. Like those two who floated into Cheo Reo."

"How large an NVA force was being supplied by that jungle market?"

"Their buddy system is built on units of three," he said. "Everyone we saw made purchases for the other two."

"The cadre allowed sixty soldiers at a time into the market for no more than fifteen minutes. Two hundred and fifty total."

"Right," he whispered. "Multiply that by three and that's their unit, bivouacked up there in the mountains someplace."

"Seven, seven fifty."

"Seven hundred sounds right. And there are signs of lots more hardhats out there in the hills — more than two or three times today's group. More customers for Madame Chinh's next country market."

"Our province chief's wife?"

"It's her show, according to Little John's sources. She's behind the black market operating in town too, but that's small potatoes compared to this."

"Then Madame Chinh's running a fucking supermarket for the NVA. Forget the snacks and smokes; they were selling enough staples to keep a large group fed for a week or more."

Ruchevsky sipped his water, sweat pooling in the corners of his eyes.

"Whatever you do," said Ruchevsky sternly, "don't put a word of who we saw at this shindig in your report."

"You don't think the colonel should hear about this?"

Ruchevsky stared me down. "Not a word until we figure out what we're dealing with. A priest, a missionary, a USAID rep, and an unarmed ARVN meet with a VC commander in the jungle. It's like the setup for a joke. But what's the punch line?"

"You know," I said, "you could have warned me the two of us were going to get so up close and personal with hundreds of VC."

"Well," Ruchevsky said, "if I had, you might not have come."

Little John finally showed. We mopped off the face blacking and changed into our regular clothes. When we got back to MACV, Ruchevsky went straight to our room, and I went to report to the colonel, but he wasn't in his office. So I sat down at Checkman's big Underwood and, using two carbons, typed up an intel summary describing the scope of the market and our encounter with the infiltrator we'd killed. As instructed, I made no mention of the meeting between Wolf Man and the odd quartet, and I gave the reporting agents a high reliability rating of B. Colonel Bennett would know they were John and me, but we went unnamed. In case the information leaked, we didn't want our methods known.

I left a copy on Bennett's desk in a sealed envelope and marked it *commanding officer — eyes only.* He wasn't going to be happy about the market, and even less so about the growing NVA force out there in his province.

The original went in the courier bag Checkman would swap tomorrow morning at the airstrip for one coming in. I took the carbon papers and the second carbon copy to Sergeant Rowdy in the signal shack to teletype immediately to MACV in Pleiku and Saigon and warned him not to discuss it, even with the other enlisted man who had clearance for the crypto van. He gave me a surprised look. I hesitated, said, "Never mind," and ducked into the crypto rig and typed it myself. Afterward I got Miser to follow me out to the barrel in which the detachment burned its classified paper and handed him the sheet. He shook his head in dismay as he read.

"How are we supposed to look for Mary Jane and opium production with NVA and VC crawling all over the province, stocking up like fucking squirrels for winter?"

He reached in his leg pocket and pulled out a map that he snapped open. "The province is five thousand square kilometers — five thousand itsy-bitsy one-kilometer grids on this map. You could hide a whole division in a corner of a single grid, much less a bunch of VC dope. Who knows how many NVA are out there. What do we go looking for and where do we look?"

"Not me, not tonight," I said, feeling the waves of fatigue.

I set the sheet aflame with my lighter, holding it by an edge until I was satisfied, and burned the two carbons. Before I left, I filled him in on what wasn't in my report.

"And Ruchevsky didn't want you to write up the meeting in the woods?"

"No."

"He doesn't trust it won't leak," Miser said, guessing correctly. "Fucking hell." He sighed. "What have we stepped in?"

I walked to my quarters. Ruchevsky, naked to the waist, fresh from his shower, was bent over the rucksack we'd brought back. He tossed aside two NVA uniforms and a pair of boots and laid out currency, scraps of writing paper, a notebook, some photos, and two crudely dried cannabis leaves rolled up in a shirt.

He examined each item with a flashlight and a magnifying glass.

"I'm sorry I had to do that kid," he said, not looking up.

"You didn't have much choice."

"I hate it when they're kids."

I peered at the materials spread on the bed. Vietnamese loved photographs; the boy had secreted his in the journal. He wasn't supposed to be carrying either. A girl, maybe fifteen, smiled in one photo. Sister, girlfriend? A snap of him, a family gathering . . . His people would not have the solace of a grave, much less his remains. Perhaps they'd get them back after the war, more likely never. Whether his comrades discovered the body or not, the youth's death wouldn't be reported to his family. The NVA didn't notify soldiers' families about casualties. Hanoi had declared funerals detrimental to morale. Even if his kin learned privately that he'd been killed, they were forbidden to conduct a funeral. Most probably his family wouldn't know he wasn't coming home until the war was long over.

I picked up a photo of the kid and two North Vietnamese Army buddies. Written on the back: *Nam do a di da phat.* May God protect us.

"You think they'll find his body?" I said.

"I hope not. I don't think his fellow travelers will stop to look for him. On average they lose four or five men from a company on the march south. His mates will leave the rest hut in the morning and trek on. If we're lucky, they'll assume he deserted or hurt himself in the jungle, or ran into a tiger."

Wanting to get my head off the subject of the dead boy, I pointed to the articles on the bed. "What are you seeing?"

"They're supposed to surrender all personal letters and papers at the border before stepping onto the trail in Laos. But they're inveterate journal keepers." Ruchevsky flipped open a notebook filled with handwriting. "Checkman did a quick read-through for me."

He held up a sheet of paper. Checkman's summary fell from his fingers, and Ruchevsky picked it up off the blanket and gave me the highlights.

"They started out seventy-one days ago, it says. Each got issued twenty kilos of rice for half the journey. They subsisted on two small meals a day, pepped up occasionally with wild game, since they're expected to provision themselves. They boiled ants for condiments, picked wild bananas, gathered bamboo shoots."

Ruchevsky held the notes closer to his gooseneck lamp.

"He's lost a lot of weight, so have his buddies. They're jaundiced, fevered. A couple can barely carry their weapons. One of his comrades was hurt during an air raid. They packed the wound with cow dung and dirt to stop it bleeding. They buried him at station fifty-seven." He looked up. "The stops aren't numbered sequentially so we don't know where that was." He referred again to the synopsis. "Another comrade came down with dysentery so bad he couldn't get out of his hammock. They cut a hole in it so he could relieve himself. Made him smoke weed. He succumbed during the night."

"Can you tell where they were," I said, "where they got the marijuana?"

"Not really. You know the problem. The trail is a twelve-mile-wide corridor of paths."

Ruchevsky opened the journal to a place marked with a strip of paper.

"They pass a shed with Montagnards bundling cannabis plants. This is the third entry from the end, just before their comrade checks out from dysentery and before they turn north. They're in the province at that point. Somewhere vaguely west of here."

Rubbing his eyes, Ruchevsky said, "They trek down in small groups and get assigned where needed when they arrive at their destination. This soldier was a replacement. Most are joining NVA divisions. Some are getting assigned to the local VC battalions, which are filling out their ranks with northerners as they lose men. Here's his trail ID." Ruchevsky laid a small rectangle of paper alongside the notebook: D-384. "The *D* stands for *doan* — group."

"What does this trail ID tell you?"

"Nothing much. The first and last digits always add up to seven. That's all I know."

His name and rank followed: Nguyin Thanh Sin, private in the People's Army of Viet Nam.

"His group was hiking north," I said, "not toward the coast?"

"Their comrades are camped up in the mountains, getting supplied and refitted. It's like a rear area for the NVA."

Ruchevsky took a cigar from the ledge. "Did you notice the items bought in bulk? Either they're stocking up so they can avoid contact with civilians to keep their location unknown, or they're camped somewhere where there are no locals to provision them or eavesdrop." He lit the cigar. "Gathering their strength."

"Maybe rehearsing their upcoming campaign for the monsoon season," I said.

"That's what I need to find out." Ruchevsky puffed until the end glowed.

He stared at the picture of the three Red soldiers going off to the defining adventure of their young, uncertain lives, a small flag stretched between them, their faces smiling above it. TOAN THANG printed across the bottom. Complete Victory. Odds were none would see home again.

"How many NVA are out there in the province, do you think?" I said.

He gave me a wary look and dropped his voice. "You really want to know?" Ruchevsky buttoned his shirt. "Something like five thousand."

"Holy shit. What's five thousand to fifty-two of us? A hundred to one?"

"Fifty-three if you count me." He tucked in his shirttails. "They're not about to risk manpower like that to take down this little compound."

They wouldn't have to. They didn't need anything approaching such numbers to overrun us. Two hundred and a dark and stormy night would do it. "Right," I said.

The gong signaled supper, but neither of us could face food. We decided to drink our dinners instead. Westy set 'em up on the bar and we knocked them back without speaking. I threw mine down quickly so no one would notice my shaking hands. Ruchevsky was quaking slightly too.

"We look like two alkies," I said, downing another shot. "You ready for AA?"

"Assassins Anonymous? Hell, yeah."

After the third round, I excused myself and went to the signal shack to check on the encrypted transmission of my report. If I had another drink, I knew I wouldn't stop.

The sky was darkening again, a blanket of black clouds fighting the remaining light. The rainy season would soon be upon us. A huge swarm of winged termites had found an open door in a new hootch lit with fluorescent lights. The residents stood outside, staring through the screened upper walls at the creatures shedding their wings in some kind of frenzy. The bugs covered the screens inside and out, as well as most of the concrete floor. Every surface in the hootch rippled under a mass of tiny frantic bodies. Two of the Montagnard night guards appeared with broad sticky leaves and started rolling up the bugs to cook them.

I left the guys to their show and continued toward the signal shack to pick up the perfunctory confirmation of receipt. At the four-foot-high wall of sandbags across the front, Sergeant Rowdy, Geronimo, and some other enlisted stood peering into an empty cookie tin from home. Inside, in slow motion, two fierce-looking beetles clutched and slid across the bright metal, pincers at the ready.

"They're not fightin' yet," whined one of the privates. Deros, the compound's hound, barked with excitement.

"Fuck," said Geronimo and doused the pair with lighter fluid. Sergeant Rowdy set it off. The beetles hissed in anger or maybe agony as their bodies roasted. I stepped behind the backup-generator shed and leaned on the sandbags, my stomach churning. After more than three years in country, I was hardly the innocent. But today I felt like a murderer. I'd been in Asia long enough to believe the universe wasn't going to give me a pass. There'd be redress.

As I walked back toward my quarters, the sky opened. Rain dropped like a curtain. In an instant I was soaked. A couple of young men came out hooting and hollering, soaping down as they showered in the downpour. On the walkway outside my room, I sat on the elevated edge and let the cataract cascade down on me from the overhang. I lay back. The bottom of me disappeared, cut in half by water.

Since I was a kid in Wisconsin I'd been killing creatures: slaughtering chickens, cows, pigs; shooting deer from the family deer blind out on the back acres. But I couldn't if the animal was looking at me. Didn't like it when I could see a buck's eyes either.

Admittedly, it was exhilarating to drop a creature at a hundred yards. Three hundred even better. Anything becomes an *it* at that distance, brought down by metal punching through at nine hundred miles an hour. From far off, it was like being in the Air Force. Hey, look what I can do! Killing a person up close was different. The sounds, the smells — they didn't leave you. The eyes.

A serious soldier in combat arms gave no more thought to capping somebody than he did to operating a lawnmower. He could waste his quarry without breaking a sweat. He'd grown used to it. I'd seen these soldiers inventory their own wounds with the same professional distance, weighing how long they could keep functioning before their ruptured hydraulics gave out. Not me.

The actual moment was exciting, almost joyful. But when the killing was intimate, the deed steadily turned back on you. Demons and *yang* took to coursing through the vulnerable channels of your body, the vessels that carried blood to the tissues and fragile bones just beneath the skin. For days, the tiniest nick would upset me. It sent fear rushing into my own flesh, and tremors into my fingers that showed up unexpectedly long afterward.

I'd passed some test with Ruchevsky. The next morning he was all over me.

"You gotta come see my digs downtown," he said, "and the rest of my war toys."

I'd been invited for tea with the CIA. John sported a holster on his ankle and I had a personal sidearm stuck in the waistband under my jungle fatigue shirt, a weapon I cursed — a .22 Beretta automatic loaded with two whole rounds. It was impossible to find ammunition for.

Other than the American on guard on the MACV gate and a sleepy ARVN sentry at the entrance of their garrison, we only passed two saffron-robed monks walking briskly by the side of the road. Faces peered out from holes in the walls of hovels along the way. I'd seen some dilapidated ARVN housing, but this was the worst. Just ruins.

Breakfast was under way. Soup pots, limbs, and the bums of naked kids appeared in large breaks in the walls. The South Vietnamese Army did not feed its soldiers, so groups of half a dozen military families pooled their meager allotments and prepared communal meals. Likewise the bachelors.

"You can bet Chinh's dining better than that," Ruchevsky said. "Funds we supply for constructing military housing are regularly diverted. And there's the government tit. Chinh's battalion does jack shit but it's collecting from us for the cost of combat operations and training as if all equipment and supplies were getting depleted. Used or not, it all vanishes. A little turns up locally. Most of it is sold in the markets at Kontum and Pleiku. Guess who buys most of the loot? And of course, his battalion is way under strength. He's carrying two hundred and sixty nonexistent infantrymen. Emperor Chinh pockets their pay every month — around a million piasters, fourteen thousand dollars. He also banks some serious bucks arranging government jobs."

"He sells them?"

"Never personally. From the presidential palace on down, the women are the fixers. They cut the deals, receive the gifts of esteem, subtract their shares, and pass the rest up the ladder. Colonel Chinh's lady is a real operator. Lays off the military promotions and civil-serpent posts to the wives of the interested parties. Chinh flies down to Saigon regularly to see her. At least once a month she comes to him and receives visitors. She negotiated all his promotions."

Ruchevsky fanned himself with a manila envelope.

"Chinh grants all the licenses needed to operate anything anywhere in the province — stores, market stalls, brothels, opium dens, restaurants, you name it — and he issues trading permits for the few goods that come in or get shipped out. Of course, his wife takes the pick of the best ones for herself. Anyone shorts her on a gratuity, he yanks the license and shuts them down. Sell or rent anything, he gets a cut. If you're in business, you're in business with Chinh."

We stopped in front of a two-story stucco house with a balcony. An armed Montagnard — pistol holstered and automatic rifle in hand — met us at the door.

"Home sweet home," Ruchevsky said and ushered me in.

His villa was spacious but crude. Everything in Cheo Reo was basic, dirty, and worn. Even new structures looked played out. A frontier town without the boom, old before its time.

The tall, thin windows were draped with heavy cloth so you couldn't see in. A second Montagnard peered out through a crack, watching the exterior. Golf-ball grenades lay scattered through the room and at each window. Also sidearms and Soviet-bloc assault rifles and Type 56 Chinese knockoffs. And one Australian L1A1 self-loading rifle. All had seated magazines; all were loaded.

The house was built Chinese style: two stories high and deep. Ruchevsky occupied the front. He announced he had to pee and led me to a sort of courtyard between his building and a more modest one-story structure used by his housekeeper and the guards. Behind a curtain was the toilet, Asian style — a squat hole set in a concrete slab — where he relieved himself. Alongside it sat a Western commode with no plumbing, shifted over the hole as needed, with a cistern of water to flush. Next to the commode sat a stack of outdated magazines and yet another handgun.

"My in-house," Ruchevsky said as he peed in the floor hole. "I hope the VC never bust in here while I'm on the throne. I'd hate to check out sitting there with my pants down."

"My sergeant says he knew he was a real soldier when he could shit under fire, lying on his side like a baby."

The shower nearby was a bucket of water and a scoop. A squat table with some bowls and a brazier on the floor served as the kitchen. By the back doorway a small Japanese refrigerator ran on propane. Ruchevsky greeted his housekeeper and showed me upstairs to his spartan bedroom. A large wooden platform supported an Air Force mattress half its size, a luxury, since most Vietnamese beds were just bare planks. A stool served as a night table. In a shallow box on the bed was a snub-nosed .38 Special with an aluminum frame, the CIA's standard issue.

A trunk decorated with carved fruit sat at the foot. Weapons were everywhere. In a corner Ruchevsky had a sideband radio and an Army field phone connected to the compound by landline.

"I think it might be cooler on the deck," he said, and we stepped outside.

Ruchevsky offered me the solitary plastic chair and perched on the waist-high wall decorated with Chinese filigree. The sun baked the empty expanse of the Cheo Reo airfield and the droopy palm trees at its near end. Two huge black rubber bladders, like giant hot-water bottles, added their rubbery-oily aroma. Small figures in green fatigues were using hand pumps to siphon gas into metal drums.

"That the famous seepage?" I said.

"Gasoline in the bladder on the left. Aviation gas in the other. Comes in by air in those five-hundred-gallon tires. Heavy as hell."

The collapsed blivets, recently emptied, lay deflated alongside the runway.

Ruchevsky pointed. "After the elephant nuts get delivered, our guys transfer the gasoline from them into those bladders. Our gas, our bladders, but like Gidding said, no American comes near them after dark. Emperor Chinh's got his snorkel in there daily. One night they sucked out aviation fuel by mistake and the next day mopeds were exploding all over town. The VC pay Chinh double for petroleum."

"Still a bargain," I said, "if it saves them having to truck gas a thousand miles down from North Viet Nam."

"Yeah." Ruchevsky flipped open a box of cigars. I declined. "There's a couple of reports they're actually laying a pipeline along the trail."

"Gasoline seepage, the jungle market — what are you going to do about Chinh?"

"What are my options? Complain to Major Gidding? Or the general in Pleiku who's Chinh's patron? Or his patron's patron in the palace in Saigon? Can't. Loc is Premier Ky's boy. Chinh is General Loc's. I'd love to turn in Chinh's name to the counterterror groups and depopulate his ass, but he's too well connected.

"Every few weeks I complain about the gasoline situation. You saw how well that goes. What can I realistically turn him in for, his capitalist tendencies?" He exhaled. "I'm supposed to be rooting out Communists, not chasing corrupt officials. Gidding and Bennett don't have the stomach to take Chinh down."

I slapped a mosquito on my arm, leaving a bloody skid mark. "But selling gasoline to the Viet Cong? Provisioning them with government rice? Doesn't that cross the line?"

"The gas scam. Yeah, well." Ruchevsky puffed up a blue cloud of smoke. "Gidding and the USAID reps argue that it's sold to all comers, that locals run their motorbikes and trucks and generators on it. Some of it just happens to be bought by VC agents. Looked at that way, Chinh is an entrepreneurial patriot who sells to all without discriminating and keeps the provincial economy rolling."

"So we should just be pragmatic since there's no way for us to secure the gas depot anyway."

"You heard Gidding," he said, taking out a note from his shirt pocket.

"What? We just write off Chinh as another government official trading with all sides?"

Ruchevsky blew out a cloud of pungent smoke. "You know the Vietnamese. They're pessimists. And paranoid. Hedge all their bets. They've stopped trusting each other, won't even have other Vietnamese for servants. They know all the contenders will extract the maximum from them, so they're as self-protective and as noncommittal as they can get away with being. They pledge allegiance when they have to and bury their loot . . . disperse it to relatives, or convert it into those paper-thin one-ounce gold strips they like to smuggle."

"The big dippers don't bother with the gold toilet paper. They go straight for ingots."

Ruchevsky tilted his head back and groaned with joy.

"What's so funny?"

"Intel gossip from Saigon. You gotta love it. Somebody's buzzing in Westmoreland's ear that we should permanently sabotage the de-militarized zone with radioactive waste. Drop some dirty A-bombs along it. You sneak across, you glow in the dark and die."

"Are they serious?"

"Perfectly." He dropped the note in an ash tray and set fire to it with the cigar. "They're working up a similar plan to block the mountain passes between China and North Viet Nam in case the Chinese decide to join in. But neither will happen, I don't think."

"Thanks be."

Ruchevsky looked at me closely. "Secretary McNamara wants an electronic wall instead. A Flash Gordon thing with sensors and crap. God, I wish he'd go back to Ford and build some more Edsels." He slid off his perch. "It was so much simpler when it was just us and them in the alleys. It's a damned shame we're marching all these young GIs into this demented fucker. I mean, what are they doing turning this civil war–revolution combo into a children's crusade?" Ruchevsky blew on the embers of his cigar. The tip glowed orange. "They should have left it to us and kept the kids out of it."

"How long have you been at this?" I said.

"All my life, it feels like. Born in the Ukraine. My family fled toward the end of the war. Wound up in a DP camp in Germany after it was over. I came down with mumps and got put out of the place with my father — quarantined. Just then the Allies announced the immediate repatriation of nationals from the Iron Curtain countries — forced repatriation. We never saw my mother or sister again."

"You hate the Communists."

"Yeah. You notice how many Green Berets are Eastern Europeans? Same story. They don't care if being in Special Forces is a bad career move. They're here for maximum payback."

Muted flashes registered in the rain clouds over the mountains to the northwest. Ruchevsky checked his watch and counted silently, as if timing the arrival of thunder instead of bombs raining down from thirty thousand feet, churning the mountain jungle like a tornado. You couldn't see the planes. No booms. The bombs crackled, like cloth ripping.

"Eight kilometers maybe," he said, puffing on his cigar and looking pleased. An empty Coke can fell off the balcony railing.

"Think they hit something?"

"There's always a first time, Captain Rider."

# 6

**B**ENNETT ORDERED ME to report behind the mess hall for an overnight trip to Mai Linh, the biggest of the three Special Forces camps in the province. He had to meet and greet some general. It was an opportunity to do some snooping for Jessup, but I was less than thrilled about the mode of transport. Convoys fifty trucks long escorted by armor and aircraft got attacked. Ours was three small vehicles.

Lack of advance notice offered some protection en route, but any road trip was a gamble. Either you'd get there or you wouldn't. Each of us had a weapon at the ready but, done right, a road ambush was close to impossible to counter.

I was assigned to drive the American doctor, Roberta Towns, in her tan English Land Rover. Colonel Bennett, with Private Checkman at the wheel, rode in the open jeep behind us. A sergeant and a private manned the third. Everyone was unusually clean. Even slovenly Checkman had on his best fatigues with proper camouflage insignia.

The doc was a looker, about ten years older than me — somewhere in her late thirties — and dressed in a linen blouse and slacks that showed off her figure. She'd been summoned from her dispensary in town to help with a complicated pregnancy in a village near the Special Forces camp. The doctor asked me to switch to a civilian shirt and the light blue baseball cap on the dash. She explained she couldn't afford to be seen consorting so openly with the U.S. military. I borrowed a flowery Hawaiian shirt from Miser and donned the cap. It wasn't much of a disguise but at a distance I'd pass for a Western do-gooder with questionable sartorial taste.

When I got back, two enlisted men were loading her Rover with ten-pound bags of rice and wheat.

"Black-market rice for the Jarai villagers," she said. "They're hurting. They haven't much stored, and the VC have been exacting an extra rice tax from the hamlets, or buying it with chits. The colonel bought this load out of his own pocket."

Each vehicle carried a PRC-10 radio, just in case. I ran a quick check on ours and reported our imminent departure, then placed my rifle and web harness on the floor and took the driver's seat on the right side. The doc slid into the passenger seat to my left. We pulled out of the MACV compound a little after eight and turned right, toward town. Over the radio, Colonel Bennett ordered me to maintain a wide interval with his jeep: fifty yards. They would eat our dust the entire way. We passed through Cheo Reo quickly and picked up Road 2 heading north toward An Khe.

The VC mined roadbeds with pressure-sensitive devices and electrically detonated explosives. In the irrational belief that increased speed would allow us to outrun a blast, I pushed the speedometer to thirty miles an hour, so we bounced uncomfortably over the pocked roadbed until finally my jarred innards and the Rover's shocks demanded I slow down. The road was abysmal. I stayed in second gear and checked on the vehicles well behind us. Colonel Bennett wore his steel helmet. The others had opted for cotton boonie hats, flattened against their foreheads by the onrushing air. They fondled their weapons and scanned the sides of the road.

We eased by Montagnard villages but soon even the rice fields thinned out and we were surrounded by the vast emptiness of the Highlands. After a few kilometers of scrub and savanna, the adrenaline backed off and I distracted myself by examining my passenger.

Dr. Roberta was large boned, with a strong-featured face and thick curls cascading to well below her shoulders. Not the kind of hair you wanted in a tropical climate, but she obviously thought it her best feature and put up with its challenges rather than cut it off to accommodate the humidity and grit. She'd tried to tie it down with a kerchief but it streamed out behind her, buffeted by the blast of hot air as we bounced down the bumpy road.

I said, "I'm surprised the Special Forces medics couldn't handle this delivery."

"Probably could. Berets have a rule, though: one medic in camp at all times, and they've only got one at the moment. The mom's nearly due and the child is presenting feet-first. It hasn't inverted. Could get tricky."

"A breech birth."

"Right. I've seen an awful lot of them here. Medical care in this country is beyond inadequate. Not many Montagnards make it to adulthood." She turned to me, hair fluttering across her face. "They're old by forty and plain lucky if they live much beyond that."

"What brought you to Viet Nam?"

"The Quakers. I worked for an Aussie missionary doc for a bit. After that, at Patricia Smith's Montagnard hospital in Kontum. Worked a couple of seasons with Dr. Pat and decided to start my own clinic. The shortage is desperate. All of South Viet Nam has seven hundred doctors."

"The whole country?"

"Afraid so. And half of them are military. It's even worse for the Highland tribes. The hospitals the French built for them are in utter disrepair, and Vietnamese facilities don't really accept Yard patients."

"How did you land in Cheo Reo?"

"I was holding a day clinic in a village halfway between Kontum and Pleiku City. Colonel Bennett had brought them rice. Just bought it with his own money when he saw they were half starved. Anyway, he pitched in. Took patient histories for me and kept talking about the lack of health services for the tribes around Cheo Reo. The staff at Kontum gave me their blessings and all the medicines they could spare. I packed up and came down."

"And the local Vietnamese were okay with you setting up a Montagnard clinic?"

"Nah. They were outraged. Mind you, I never said the clinic was only for Yards. I just brought along a couple of nurses who happened to be Montagnards and, what do you know, the Vietnamese wouldn't come near the place. I wasn't surprised but, hey, they've got the Korean medical team all to themselves. Not that they like Koreans either. Me, I've got maybe a hundred thousand Montagnards to service and only the one of me to look after them all."

"They walk in from the province districts?"

"Sure. Me going to them would be impractical, never mind dangerous."

If Montagnards from everywhere came to her clinic, she had eyes and ears in places I had no way to get to. She could be invaluable, but I couldn't risk asking her anything specific, not yet.

A barefoot Montagnard in a loincloth stepped out of the scrub into the road. Instinctively, I put a hand on my rifle. The old man bowed deeply, bush ax resting on his bare shoulder as we rolled by.

"What was that about?" I said.

"The bowing? Colonial etiquette. The French insisted on deference. They used to shanghai the tribesmen to clear the land and work for them as laborers. The Montagnards couldn't read, so the French made them put thumbprints on contracts that practically enslaved them. They were like press gangs: cutting roads into the wilderness, chopping down forests, harvesting crops. Most plantations employed many thousands — thirty-five, forty thousand."

"Are we talking actual slavery?"

"Practically. They'd get paid five piasters a day. Three or four cents, when the plantations were making fortunes for their owners. The Communists collect eighty grand a year in tribute from them. Despite the merciless exploitation, the French encouraged the tribes to believe they'd be autonomous someday. The Communists, they flat-out promise it once the American war is won. I practice my Jarai and Rhade listening to their propaganda broadcasts."

"Do the Yards buy it?"

"Many have. The North generally deals better with the mountain people. When the French returned to claim their colonies after World War Two, the Communists retreated into the mountains, and Highlanders' aid was vital. The top Red general learned some of their languages and won their loyalty against the French. He made a tribesman his second in command. The old warriors I treat brag about their units all the time: the One Twenty-sixth Rhade, the One Hundred Eighth Jarai, the Eight Hundred and Third Bahnar . . ."

I scratched a bug bite. "So why aren't *all* the Montagnards around here supporting the North?"

"They just don't trust Vietnamese." She held her hair to keep it from whipping into her eyes. "The tribes have no great loyalty to either side. Or to one another, unfortunately. They're insular. And there must be sixty different tribes. The whole country was theirs once, before the Vietnamese forced them into the Highlands and kept the coast and the lowlands for themselves. When the French colonized Indochina they barred Vietnamese from the mountains. Ran the Highlands like their private preserve."

"The Vietnamese didn't protest?"

"Not really. They were happy to stay away. They're convinced the rivers here give you malaria. That the mountains are haunted, full of primitives practicing sorcery and cannibalism and performing cruel sacrifices. At the turn of the century, the Vietnamese told their French masters that living here in the forests like wild beasts were feral men with footlong tails who fed on children. An expedition was sent in to capture some for the Paris zoo. That attitude persists."

"So why are they here at all if they can't stand the Yards?"

"The government coerces Vietnamese to relocate, especially Catholic refugees and Buddhist villagers. It offers Montagnard land to entice them. Mind you, the government doesn't buy — just grabs what it wants. They'll even bulldoze Montagnard graveyards to get tracts they want."

"No wonder the Yards are pissed."

She struggled with her hair again and recaptured some of it, wedging tufts under her kerchief and braiding the rest into a manageable tail.

The scrub thickened. We rolled past tall bamboo and trees towering more than a hundred feet high.

I said, "You mind if I raise the rifle up?"

"Be my guest."

I drove one-handed and put the M-16 across my lap.

She tipped her head to the side. "And what's your story?"

"Wisconsin farm kid. My old man's a World War Two vet. County cop. I grew up with manure and sideband radios. Wanted to be a lawman too. He wouldn't have it. I went to agricultural college. Aside from great ice cream at the college dairy, there wasn't much else to recommend it. Didn't want to take up farming, so I joined the War Corps to see the world."

"Why the multiple tours?"

"Didn't think it was safe to stay home."

"You didn't feel safe back in the States?"

"Didn't think it was safe to have me there."

I maneuvered around a gaping hole.

"It's too tame back in the U.S." I said. "I'm comfortable in Viet Nam. It never seems hard to leave but it's hard to stay away."

She recaptured a wisp of hair. "*Le mal jaune,* the French call it. The yellow fever."

"Viet Nam keeps adrenaline levels up even when things are dull."

"Men," she said, shaking her head. "You're adversarial-violence junkies."

"What can I say? Guys like it. It's practically erotic."

"Not something most people would admit to." She glanced over. "Say more."

"This one night my first tour, I slept on top of a ruined bunker in the jungle. The ARVN platoon I was out with, they pitched a lean-to next to it. Their sergeant worried that I was so exposed. Tried to talk me into coming down off the roof. I was stubborn and stayed out under the stars. Two in the morning we got mortared. The very first round lands right on them. Me, I didn't get a scratch."

"You felt lucky."

"I felt awful. My breath wouldn't stop quaking, I kept shivering. But the morning was indescribable and everything was completely clear. I was scared, elated . . . starving. Devoured breakfast."

She leaned closer, the better to examine me. "You actually like this war."

"Well, it sure wipes away the mundane. Nobody worries about smoking or the condition of their liver. Everything's now. There's no later."

"You're a prisoner of your hormones." She smiled. I couldn't tell if she thought I was amusing or hopeless.

"The male is a destroyer," I said. "We kill for peace. It's our idea of a good time. We like to knock other people down, whether it's in a game or like this — for keeps."

I downshifted on a long slope to make it less jarring as we bounced over ruts and in and out of holes. "You must get an equivalent charge in your line of work, like when you've got five minutes to save a limb or a life."

"Sure, but it doesn't come from mayhem. I couldn't cope if it did."

"You would, and you'd like it."

She gave me a skeptical look.

"It's true," I insisted. "You do now."

"I don't think so."

"Remember your first incision? First cadaver?"

"Yes."

"How did you react?"

She hesitated. "Almost threw up."

"Because it seemed unimaginable — violent — cutting into flesh. Even a corpse's. And now?"

She didn't answer.

"See? You got used to it. Our work isn't so different. You can do something other people get nauseous even thinking about." I looked at her. "Everything's war and violence in this place. Without it I'd be just a security guard with a radio and you'd be another do-gooder ministering to the needy in a backwater nobody ever heard of. The war raises our work to a high calling."

"Is that right?"

"Yeah. I bet you've done more doctoring in the last three years than you'd do in a whole career back home. Bet you treat diseases and wounds your colleagues only read about."

"True," she conceded. "Plague, beriberi, every kind of tuberculosis imaginable — bone, brain, lung, skin . . ."

"Illnesses they only know from history books." I looked her in the eye. "You ever fire a weapon?"

"No."

"You should. It's a kick, putting the sights on a tiny figure. Dropping it."

"Godlike?" she said, pointedly.

"Like making an incision."

She shook her head.

I said, "I wouldn't know what to do without Viet Nam anymore. I've given in to the fever. You too, I bet." I turned back to the road.

"You are such a boy, Captain Rider. Boys want to hog all the fun and danger."

"Life's too fucking short not to." I knit my brow. "You're not exactly a homebody yourself."

"You know what the Vietnamese call us?" she said.

"*Khi dot*? Big monkeys?"

"That too, but I was thinking *khong goe.*"

"I don't know that one," I said.

"It means, loosely, 'people who don't know who they are.'"

"You think I'm in Southeast Asia chasing myself?"

"Something like that."

I said, "Isn't this as straight as life gets? Doesn't this mess let you face yourself and make you grateful for morning?"

"So you like what you see in your shaving mirror?"

"Not completely, but here I accept me — who I've always been — without apology."

She made a face. "Have you been reading Kierkegaard or something? Give me a fucking break. Where was this cow college you went to — Amherst?"

I laughed. She snatched the baseball hat off my head and smacked me with it.

"Ow!" I squirmed. "Hey, Doc."

She smacked me again. "Hold still. I'm trying to beat some sense into you."

"Ow!"

"You're *right* about violence," she said, "I *do* like it," and she swatted me one more time.

The Special Forces camp looked ancient and primitive, a fortress more suited to catapults and boiling oil than modern assault rifles and mortars. The dry moat encircling it was filled with sharpened bamboo spikes and three concertina coils of barbed wire. One roll rested on the other and ran up the side of the earthen parapet. Within the wire, claymore mines were fixed in concrete posts so they couldn't be pinched or swiveled around by sappers at night and redirected against the camp. Home-brewed fougasse in plastic jugs — jellied-napalm cocktails — lay half buried in the sides of the earthen wall. Lethal speed bumps. The VC version used blood and sugar to jell the gasoline. The Berets detonated fougasse and the embedded claymores electrically.

Dr. Roberta pointed out low shrubs growing amid the coiled barbed wire. "*Kpung*," she said, "poisonous as snakes. One scratch from those nettles will inflict a week of excruciating pain."

The camp was a five-sided star, each side one hundred meters long. At each point a machine-gun barrel protruded from a bunker. Over the gate, a sign in several languages posed the Green Berets' standing challenge to their enemies: ANYTIME, ANYPLACE. A human skull wearing a green beret sat atop a post. A ring of machine-gun bunkers and earthworks in the center formed a second line of defense, a fort within the fort. Mortar tubes at facing sides of the camp tilted toward each other so they could each defend the other's side of the wire in an attack.

Jarai kids were everywhere. Barefoot and bare-breasted women, the dependents of the Montagnard militiamen, poured out of two fortified barracks. Dr. Roberta pointed out the Bahnar tribesmen mixed in among them, easily identified by their long, mangy hair. Half clad, wrapped in gray Navy blankets, they looked squalid, like forlorn street people.

Outside a smaller building, Vietnamese Special Forces soldiers in speckled tiger fatigues and silk scarves lounged on fortifications in studied postures of boredom, red berets tilted low on their brows.

Even motionless, they managed to convey disdain and contempt and elicit wariness, like teenage gangsters. All they needed was a street corner and a victim.

I parked at the inner ring of defenses by the Green Berets' team house and got out. The colonel's jeep and the truck pulled up behind us. My gaudy shirt and hat drew stares.

"*Di uy,* you are down, man," a black Special Forces sergeant teased. "Thems some fly rags." He offered a fist and we dapped as he introduced himself. "Grady. Demolitions. Welcome to Fort Sucky-Sucky."

The doctor needed no introduction. The team members lined up to greet her and salute the colonel. They all looked gaunt and underfed. Several Montagnards rushed forward to welcome Bennett warmly. I changed back to my jungle fatigue shirt and boonie hat while they all caught up.

The Special Forces captain, George Cox, popped out of the team house flanked by two intimidating Nungs in black Aussie bush hats and black uniforms. He welcomed Colonel Bennett with a salute and shook hands with the doctor. "Ed," he called out and a sergeant emerged from an open-sided tent, stethoscope looped over his neck and kids bunched all around him. Brass bracelets chinged faintly on his wrists.

"Ed Sprague," Roberta exclaimed with real verve. Arm in arm, they walked off to speak privately above a growing sea of children, curious to see the pig-colored woman. Other youngsters cornered Checkman, fascinated by his head of red hair, which he obligingly lowered for them to touch. He smiled, passed around candy, and tried out his linguistic skills, but they didn't understand Vietnamese.

"Colonel," said Cox, "Captain Rider — this way," and he led us into the inner, second defensive perimeter to the command post at the camp's center. "During the day, only Americans and Nungs are allowed beyond this point," Cox said over his shoulder. "Once they accept your money, Nungs will watch over you, waking and sleeping. They're great fighters — loyal, ruthless — and handsomely compensated to cover our backsides. Sixty bucks a month, more than a Vietnamese captain. Pisses off the Vietnamese no end." He grinned. "Even so, after sundown it's Americans only inside the Alamo."

Checkman and I trailed behind Colonel Bennett and the Special Forces captain as they stepped up into the elevated bunker. Mahogany logs formed the roof, their ends exposed. Firing ports and weapons circled its walls. The whole structure was encased in sandbags many layers thick and topped with antennas.

Cox turned and said, "I'm sorry you missed our intel sergeant. He just took out our nightly five-man patrol."

Cox ushered us down some stairs into a short corridor that led to an underground room, spartan except for the torrid photographic studies plastered on one side. In front of the facing wall were radios stacked on a sawhorse table, and the captain's tiny work area decorated with tactical maps and gear. Behind a crude partition a dozen cots occupied improvised cubicles. Field equipment hung from pegs and lay draped over stools and locally made tin lockers. A long narrow table flanked by benches occupied the wide middle aisle.

"When's the general expected?" Colonel Bennett said.

The captain consulted his watch. "About eleven hundred, sir."

Despite the heat, we retrieved ceramic mugs from a side shelf and accepted the boiled coffee the captain offered. You could have stood a spoon in it. Army diesel.

"This is all their fault," a sergeant on radio watch grumbled, pointing above the sideband rigs to a framed color photograph of two Green Berets seated alongside commanding general Westmoreland, who was holding the working end of a very long straw arcing up from a ceramic jar of Montagnard moonshine. A shaman was putting a brass bracelet on Westmoreland's wrist to symbolize his initiation into the tribe.

The two Green Berets in the snapshot, Cox explained, had come up with this public relations ploy to put Mai Linh on the map of somebody who could actually do something for the Yards.

"And it worked, big-time. That photo of Westmoreland in Mai Linh appeared in the press worldwide."

"Westy has a distinct bias toward Airborne anyway," Bennett observed, "and Green Berets are all paratroopers, like him."

"The bracelet just helped seal the deal," Cox said. "Mai Linh has but to ask and supplies, equipment, air support, and helicopter assets arrive."

The downside was the camp also received an endless string of ranking officers hoping to get tribal bracelets like their leader's. They'd become coveted status symbols. A two-star was due within the hour. Technically, as Captain Cox's superior officer in the sector, Colonel Bennett should receive whatever general officer came through, but duties often occupied him elsewhere and he couldn't always show up.

Captain Cox jingled when he moved. He wore the serious carved bracelets on his right wrist, the more casually bestowed plain ones on his left.

Sergeant Grady climbed down the steps into the room carrying a box under his arm.

"Our camp's chief scrounger and purveyor," said Cox, by way of introduction.

"What exactly do you purvey, Sarge?" I asked.

"I got it all goin' on," Grady said, taking a mug. "Mostly war souvenirs. Real quality goods."

Cox stirred his coffee. "Grady takes them to big bases to barter and sell, or lays them off on our visitors and chopper crews."

Grady ticked them off on his fingers. "VC flags, Montagnard crossbows and pipes, pith helmets. AK-Forty-sevens when we've got 'em. NVA rucksacks too."

"Captured?" Bennett said.

"The weapons and rucks, yes, sir. The crossbows and pipes the Yards make. The ladies do the flags." He held up a yellow-blue Hanoi flag, soiled and bloody, with a yellow star in the middle.

"Very convincing."

"We're trying to lay in a money supply and build up an armory for the Yards for when we're not around and they done need hard currency and guns. Whenever we capture weapons, they cache some."

"You have reason to think we won't stick it out?" said the colonel.

"Not me, sir. It's them. They don't believe it anymore."

Bennett stroked his cheek. He turned to Captain Cox. "What's the current head count of Yard militia in the camp?"

"CIDG? Just under eight hundred Montagnard irregulars: mostly Jarai, some Rhade. A few Sedang and a fair number of Bahnar refugees. All together — with dependents — maybe three thousand souls. And ten of us Big Noses."

"Did I see Vietnamese Special Forces as we came in — LLDB?"

"Yes, sir," Cox said. "But just for today. I know their reputation and it's well deserved."

"They'll be out of here by tomorrow," Grady added.

Cox said, "They're posturing, showing they're not afraid. Not many Vietnamese have been in the compound since the uprising."

"Uprising?" I said.

"There've been a bunch."

Bennett motioned me closer. "Captain Rider's our new intel officer. It might help to make him aware of our skeletons."

"Yes, sir," Cox said, and turned to me. "We got brought in five years ago to organize the Montagnards into defensive militias. Found the Yards completely disarmed. Anything that looked like a weapon, the government had confiscated. Crossbows, guns, spears, bush axes. Montagnard province chiefs and leaders had been forced out. Vietnamese Catholics were running everything."

"Real honky shit," Grady muttered.

Cox ignored him. "We got along great with the Yards. Although the South Vietnamese forbade us to train them to lead troops, we armed 'em up with surplus carbines and taught them to defend their turf. They proved themselves real warriors, scrupulously honest."

"I swear, they'll banish a thief for life," Grady interjected. "In their eyes, stealin' rice or even water is worse than murder."

Cox silenced him with a raised hand. "The South Vietnamese freaked out. Carried on that we'd created an army of mercenaries poised at their backs. Two years ago they demanded we transfer command of the Yard militias and the strikers in the A camps to them. Their country, their call. The South Vietnamese Red Berets took command and we went from being independent operators for CIA to being advisers reporting to MACV — officially anyway."

"More like allegedly," Sergeant Grady added.

"Yeah, well. Real authority didn't shift so easily. The Yards and Vietnamese despise each other — have for centuries."

Grady banged down his cup. "The dumb slopes even tried to confiscate some of the arms we'd given the Yards. That didn't work out so good neither."

"No," Cox said. "The Viets started in with their usual crap. Their special forces jerked the Yards around on their pay, which the Red Berets took over issuing — and pocketed. Pushed them to go on the offensive too and take on the heavily armed NVA regulars streaming in, guided by their Montagnard allies. Our strikers were deployed to distant camps straddling infiltration routes, far from their own villages. They couldn't fathom fighting for some other tribe's turf and they sure weren't into fighting other Yards."

"The dinks were completely okay with usin' them for cannon fodder," Grady mumbled. "Fine with laying air strikes on their villages too. A little depopulating of the real estate for after the war, it seemed like."

Cox said, "Our Yards didn't trust their new Vietnamese masters."

"Or us either after that," Grady said.

"We'd promised them autonomy, title to their tribal lands. Trained them to defend their villages, then handed them over to the South Vietnamese, who were forcibly relocating tribespeople into government settlements — dumps — and ordering the men to fight main force North Vietnamese battalions coming across the borders. We had no say in the matter, but try telling them that."

"So what happened?" I said to Cox.

"Spontaneous firefights between the Yards and ARVN. Mass desertions to the VC. Sabotage. Finally, mutiny — armed revolt."

"Two years ago," Grady said, "Rhade militia in the province next door seized the Vietnamese Special Forces commanders and soldiers and the administrators in five camps. They just detained our guys, but absolutely mutilated the Vietnamese. Slit their throats. Shot 'em. Seventy of them. Did 'em up bad."

"Declared their own independence movement," Cox interjected.

Grady shook his head in resignation. "The Yards wanted their mountains. They thought we'd stand with 'em. Kick the North *and* South Vietnamese the fuck out of their Highlands."

Cox looked a little pissed. "You still got a hairball about this?"

The sergeant stood with his hands in his pockets. "We strung them along and sold 'em out."

"The Yards go bat shit and you figure we're responsible?"

"We let them think they were our troops — American legionnaires — doin' for us like their daddies did for the French. The young bloods even got uniforms made like ours — patches, flashes, berets, the works." Grady pointed at the Latin on his shoulder patch and translated. "'To Liberate from Oppression.'"

Cox sighed. "Sarge, stow it. What's done is done."

Grady stared back. "They have went through hell cause we made 'em think it was gonna happen."

"What happened to the rebels?" I said.

Cox poured out another cup. "Three thousand marched just across the border into Cambodia and set up FULRO — their own liberation front."

"The ones who surrendered mostly got amnesty," Grady said. "But for months guns went off whenever our Montagnards bumped into ARVN or Vietnamese militia. 'Accidental meetings,' according to Saigon. Full-out fights is what they were."

Cox nodded. "Meanwhile the Viets put General Vinh Loc in charge of Two Corps, an aristocrat with a pathological hatred of the Yards and no great love for us."

"Where were the Berets in all this?"

Grady looked downcast. "Transferred, reassigned, scattered all over. After the uprising, the U.S. Army treated us like we was Hell's Angels. They didn't trust us *not* to side with the Yards."

"And the Red Berets," I said, "they're still scared to come around two years later?"

Cox glanced at Grady. "It didn't end back then."

Bennett rubbed road grit from his face with a handkerchief. "Four, five months ago, the week before Christmas — this is fifteen klicks west of here — Jarai militiamen were standing guard on the perimeter at the Phu Thien District headquarters. They turned their guns around — then sounded the alarm. As the South Vietnamese soldiers poured out of their barracks, the Yards cut 'em down. Forty-three Vietnamese and an ARVN captain who'd been installed as the district chief."

"Jesus," I said.

Cox grimaced at his coffee and put it aside. "Their leader marched his column of rebels here. The plan called for simultaneous mutinies, but our Yards hadn't taken us down, thank God. When the dissidents saw it wasn't gonna happen, they surrendered."

"General Loc convened a military tribunal in Pleiku," Bennett said.

"Evil shit." Grady sat down on the edge of the table, one foot up on a chair.

"Sentenced four men to death," Bennett went on. "The first two in Pleiku. They tied them to poles on the soccer field, with a thousand Vietnamese looking on, cheering and munching pineapple-on-a-stick like it was a football match. The firing squad killed one straight off, succeeding in wounding him a second time. Propped him up, bleeding, and shot him again. Wounded him a second time. He looked like Saint Sebastian, just pierced everywhere. The crowd jeered. A French priest pleaded with the soldiers. The third volley finally killed him."

Bennett put away his handkerchief and stood for a moment with arms folded. "Two of the condemned were from here and were brought back to Cheo Reo for a hurried execution. Bob Reed, our local missionary, got called to the airstrip and was told they were going to die that day. At the barracks, the Montagnards got a last meal. They didn't eat. They prayed with Bob, then were taken to the edge of town and tied to posts in front of a crowd of onlookers and a nine-man firing squad. The two prisoners searched the faces, looking for friends. The one Yard called out to someone, 'Oh, Uncle. Come and take my hand before I die.' Nobody stepped forward. So Bob asked the Vietnamese captain to wait. He walked out to the posts, placed his hands on their shoulders, and said a last prayer."

"The execution was quick," Grady said. "No cheers, no applause."

Cox lit a menthol cigarette. "Since the mutiny at Phu Thien, the Vietnamese Special Forces keep their distance. They're petrified of the Yards."

"Can't blame them," Bennett said.

Captain Cox leaned against a wooden post. "The only bright note was that one of the few Montagnard army officers got appointed our new camp commander."

Grady smirked. "No slope officer would take the slot."

"You have any FULRO rebels among your strikers in the camp?" I said.

Cox laughed, expelling smoke. "Here? Only a couple hundred."

"You're okay with that?" I said.

Grady shrugged with indifference. "They're not a problem to us."

Cox looked at his sergeant suspiciously. "Especially since certain Green Beret noncoms have been known to drive them around, helping them recruit young Yards from the different villages."

Grady sat silent, avoiding looking at the captain.

"It does get a little old," Cox went on, "having Yards on our payroll who the ARVN field police are looking to lock up. Luckily they haven't the balls to make arrests out here."

Grady snorted in derision. "Yeah, good luck with that."

"What's trickier," Cox said, "is the hundred or more Montagnards we bed down with each night who are VC."

Checkman started. "*Here?* Inside the camp? Viet Cong?"

The captain smiled, amused. "In every Special Forces camp. There are VC all through the ranks of the Montagnard and Vietnamese militias. It's a great deal. They get to keep an eye on our every move, and we train and feed and pay them. Three squares, a bunk, and free military training, all courtesy of Uncle Sam."

Grady harrumphed. "No way to know which ones are VC until they're cuttin' your throat or the wire and swingin' open the front gate for their comrades."

"Could that happen?" Checkman said, incredulous.

"Already has," Grady said. "Thirty VC agents in among the Yard strikers at Plei Mrong sabotaged the mortars and cut the perimeter wire, then turned their guns on the defenders. They let their friends in and took down the Special Forces camp. Same thing at Hiep Hoa and four other camps."

Cox said, "We're always finding soil dumped in the feed tray of the fifty cal, or rags stuffed in the mortar tubes."

"God Almighty." Checkman grew pale, his freckles darkening.

Cox slapped him on the shoulder. "So watch your back tonight, young man."

Checkman swallowed hard. "I need my own Nung."

We all laughed. The radio squawked: "One Six. This is Dog Six, we're twenty klicks out."

Cox took the mike and acknowledged. "The general's inbound," he said.

# 7

★ ★ ★

**T**HE GENERAL HAD half as many stars as Westmoreland but arrived with nearly as many birds. The first two helicopters bore down on the camp from the west and shot across it breaking left and right, looking like homicidal sperm, guns trained on us.

"Gunships," Cox said, shielding his eyes, "carrying nails and gun pods."

Meaning, armed with seven fléchette rockets strapped on either side and electronically operated Gatling guns tethered to both flanks. They circled low and close, the visored door gunners bug-eyed. Grady waved with his whole arm, like a little kid, as the general's Command-and-Control ship swooped close overhead, trailed by his chaser.

"A slick shadowin' the boss," Grady said, "in case the old man's Charlie-Charlie bird goes down and he needs *immediate*" — he drew out the syllables — "rescue."

I cupped my hands above my eyes and looked up. The customary altitude for a general was twenty-five hundred feet over his troops, well out of range of ground fire. Commanders formed a kind of airborne chain of command: the general on top in his plush C-and-C chopper, brigade commander in the middle, battalion commander below him, all of them laid back in their flying armchairs, demanding answers and issuing instructions while the shit flew on the ground.

The general's helicopter banked and flared, hovered level, and descended. Twenty feet above the ground, Major General Donal stood on the skid, flanked by two troopers in flak vests, their assault weapons pointed skyward. As the chopper touched down, they stepped off as if from an escalator. An aide jumped to the ground behind them. They all looked like they'd just come from the dry cleaner's. Two stars shone on each of the general's lapels and on the front of his cap.

Camp commander Siu Broai snapped off a salute and welcomed Donal to Camp A-226. The pilot kept his rotors cranking, reducing the rotations but keeping them spinning, just in case. The three other choppers circled, zooming in and out over the fortifications, adding their pulse to the anticipation. The Montagnards stayed under cover, staring out from doorways and windows at the commotion.

Colonel Bennett and Captain Cox saluted the general and invited him to inspect the honor guard. Smiling broadly, he strode by the Yards standing at rigid attention in a variety of mismatched partial uniforms, most of them barefoot, one in a loincloth and olive-drab shirt bearing French medals. Next to him, a twelve-year-old in fatigues wearing ammo pouches and bearing a carbine. The general didn't pause. Quickly done with the military courtesies, he clapped Colonel Bennett on the shoulder and made straight for the open-sided hut just inside the wire where the shaman waited, holding a live chicken upside down by the legs.

The rest of us drew closer to witness the general sealed to the tribe forever. Donal assumed a profound expression appropriate to the honor. He had waived the all-day, all-night blood sacrifice, and—by placing his unshod foot on a bronze ax head—he skipped directly to the moment the shaman places the brass band around his right wrist. The general tried to fake the required sip of rice wine from the giant jar but actually sucked some in when a large roach skittered out the top, startling him.

Bending, Cox whispered, "An acquired taste, sir." Donal gave a brave grin, eyes a little wide.

Back at the helipad, Sergeant Grady was finishing negotiations with the general's helicopter crew, war souvenirs and currency discreetly changing hands. An aide signaled the pilot to crank it up. The prop increased rotations. After the briefest discussion, the colonel and Captain Cox escorted the general right to his command ship, its rotor slicing the air at full power. The din was deafening. To my surprise, Colonel Bennett accompanied the general aboard. The bird pulled pitch and rose aloft to speed away, rejoined by the gunships.

"Captain," Cox called to me as he returned, beret clamped in place against the rotor wash of the chase ship lifting off.

I leaned toward him to hear over the rising noise.

"The general invited the colonel to lunch at his mess. Wanted Dr. Roberta too, but she had to decline. Sorry I couldn't get us on the guest list. I hear he serves real coffee. With real cream from the Navy."

"I didn't bring my mess jacket or calling cards anyway," I yelled in his ear, my eyes slits. "And I'm not wearing any skivvies."

"Me either," Cox shouted.

Dr. Roberta watched the chase ship rise, her clothes plastered to her body by the wash.

"Well," Cox yelled, "she's wearing hers."

Dr. Roberta and I loaded her Land Rover with more rice, a bottle of Lysol, and four large plastic jugs of treated well water. I ran a quick radio check and we set off.

"Anything I should know about how to behave when we get there?" I said.

"Yeah. Spirits control everything. Some are good, most bad. The Montagnards spend their lives trying to keep them placated. You can easily violate a taboo. For starters, stand still if you sneeze. No kidding. It's hellishly bad if you don't."

"Got it," I said. "Okay. What else?"

"Don't relieve yourself in the village. That's a total no-no for outsiders. If you have to go, go beyond the fences."

"Right."

"Only use your right hand to shake with."

"What?"

"Why are you smiling?" she said.

"I — never mind. Go on."

"When you shake hands, hold your right elbow with your left hand.

That way whatever evil spirits are in you will be blocked from entering the other person."

"I've always done that but I never knew why."

It was only three kilometers to the village of the expectant mom, but we didn't see a soul on the way. The first sign of a community was a group of Jarai grave houses on a hillside. Dr. Roberta directed me onto a rough track that led us past the cemetery. I slowed the Rover to a crawl. Each tomb had four main posts and a peaked thatch roof over a raised platform, underneath which a dirt mound covered a very shallow grave. The overhead supports were elaborately carved, and the crossbeams bore mystical designs, bursts and sun symbols. Tall jars of wine and personal effects rested on the newer platforms.

"Comforts for the dead," Roberta said.

Near the graves stood lone posts with carved tops. A wooden monkey crouched on one, a plane balanced on its nose, its propeller still in the hot air. A French legionnaire braced at attention atop another, facing a bare-breasted Montagnard woman. High overhead, on a mast rising over a tall grave-house roof, two wooden birds perched on opposite ends of a horizontal stick. I pulled to a stop.

"What do you make of the carvings?" I said.

"Haven't a clue. They're so strange. Like cargo-cult art, some of it."

"Cox says they consider stealing water a heinous crime. Have you heard that?"

"The gods of water and rice are especially powerful. Stealing either is considered a high crime. Pissing off either god means major trouble for the whole village. The offender has to make amends. Not to the victim. To the god."

"Make amends how?"

"Sacrifice. Pigs, chickens . . . for a really bad offense, a buffalo. Sometimes several. They ring gongs to summon the gods, beat drums, consume whole jars of rice wine. They think gods live in the jars."

"But they don't sacrifice the offender?"

"No. No capital punishment. That would be an unnatural death. The worst."

"Right."

She took in the cemetery. "Not Western, is it?"

"You'd be surprised," I said. "About thirty miles north of here, off Road Nineteen, there's a graveyard in the Mang Yang Pass where a Red Montagnard regiment decimated a French column a dozen years ago. The legionnaires who survived buried their dead standing — hundreds of them, facing toward Paris, *Mort pour la France* on every headstone. We spent part of a morning there."

"You stopped to pay your respects?"

"No. For coffee and doughnuts. God, I still dream about those doughnuts. The French-trained cooks made them for the MACV mess at Kontum. Four of us liberated a couple dozen and headed out on a small jeep patrol to try and triangulate an enemy radio transmitter. We stopped at the graveyard, ate all the doughnuts with a thermos of Army coffee, then shot it out with two Charlies we bumped into a few kilometers down the road."

"Have you been in a lot of firefights?"

"Some. Usually by accident. Small actions."

"So where have you served?"

"Mostly around Saigon these days. My first tour I was sent everywhere."

"Why? What were you doing?"

"Our radios were never intended for this climate. They're susceptible to moisture, and the jungle absorbs transmissions. Whenever somebody had problems with them, I'd get sent to fix things."

"Couldn't the Army come up with new equipment meant for the tropics?"

"Sure, but by the time the military gets it right, we'll be fighting in deserts or on ice floes."

I shifted into first gear and got us rolling again.

"You married?" she said.

"Briefly."

"That's unfortunate."

"We eloped. Didn't have much time together. The day I came home she announced it was over."

Roberta nodded. "So you came back."

We were within sight of the village, passing by fruit trees and a garden. In among the tobacco and vegetables stood waist-high stems topped with darkly ripe knobs. The notched pods oozed white lines of resin that scented the air with a sweet aroma. Roberta saw my interest.

"The sap turns brown in the air. This goes on for five or six nights running." She pointed at a dark, resin-streaked pod. "In the morning they'll collect the tar in little bamboo pots they hang around their necks."

"Smells inviting."

"The village pharmacy," she said.

"Do the Yards around here ever grow opium to sell? I mean, in large quantities?"

"Not that I've seen. They're not business-minded. This is for their own use. Drinking is a bigger thing in their culture. But they don't sell their moonshine either."

Thirty longhouses came into view, built on stilts six feet off the ground, the longest over forty feet. Entries at both ends fronted on raised porches, with notched logs for ladders.

"They've got fifty people sleeping in those big ones," Roberta said. "They pull the ladders up at night to keep out animals and marauders."

I wasn't completely unfamiliar with the layout of Yard villages but didn't tell her that. I liked listening to her talk.

"The elevation helps keep out rodents," she continued, "and the smoky interiors discourage mosquitoes."

A man sat on his raised veranda, singing something in Jarai.

"You understand that?" I said.

"Some." She listened a moment. "It's a courting song. 'Your skin is soft like a dove's. Your nails like a falcon's. Your breasts are full and beautiful.' Something something."

She listened a moment.

"'You are close in my heart . . . but far from my eyes.'"

In the center of the village we passed a post smeared with blood.

"This is where they tether the animals when they're sacrificed." Stuck on another post was the bleached skull of a buffalo.

Though Roberta was eager to get to her patient, protocol demanded we sit with the village chief for a respectable amount of time and receive a formal greeting. Several men offered us tobacco leaves, bowls of cooked rice, and eggs. Roberta instructed me to take a leaf from each man and to touch an egg.

"You're symbolically accepting the food," she said. "If you're offered rice wine later on, drink. To them, drunkenness is a spiritual state. Makes the gods happy."

"If I gotta, I gotta."

"No, it's really important. More than half their rice harvest goes to make rice wine even in the leanest times. It's a huge part of their lives."

The chief sent two young men to the Rover to fetch Colonel Bennett's gift of rice and wheat, and a bag of candy for the kids. Finally the chief led the way toward the patient's home.

A small, dark woman drew near. "The shaman," Roberta said, and translated for me as the two of them launched into a discussion of a patient they shared. Roberta listened intently to the description of the steps the shaman had taken and described to me the sequence of sacrifices, culminating in the draping of trees with the intestines of a buffalo.

"Big medicine," she said to me, and returned to the conversation. The shaman was clearly pleased by the consultation with her Western colleague and bade us farewell.

"I'm impressed you've got time for her," I said.

"A little collegiality goes a long way, Captain. I can help her patients a lot more if she feels we're working together than if she thinks I have no respect for her treatments. She's much more likely to send for me if someone's in real trouble."

"Like calling in a specialist."

"Exactly."

"Smart, Doc."

Spurred cocks slashed at one another, wings spread. A young woman in front of a longhouse pounded a wooden post into a mortar, mashing grain. Beside her a young child played with a furry toy: a dead rat. The mom-to-be reclined on the ground nearby. She looked exhausted. Squatting around the supine woman, a circle of wizened old women smoked their pipes and waited.

"Not good," Roberta said. "These Montagnard women urinate standing and deliver their babies upright. They used to birth their babies alone, outside the village. These days they hold on to a longhouse post and squat. This mom, the way she's lying on the ground — definitely not good. And there are a lot more ladies in attendance than usual."

Four beautiful, bare-breasted women smiled at us, displaying their gums, black from the mildly narcotic betel-nut cud they chewed all day. All were missing their front teeth. I smiled back.

Roberta said, "You might want to stop smiling."

"Smiling's taboo? They smile so much."

"They file their front teeth down to the gums because they think those teeth make them look hideous, you see. As in feral, beastly, repugnant."

My smile collapsed.

At the back of the longhouse a man chopped at the innards of a tree trunk, scooping them out. A dark knot of tissue under his collarbone marked the track of a through-and-through bullet wound.

"The dad," she said.

"Making a trough?"

Roberta frowned. "No. A casket. If she or the child dies, they won't be interred in the village graveyard. He'll have to bury them, probably alone, and abandon their home. His neighbors will dismantle it."

"Why?"

Roberta pushed strands of hair out of her eyes. "Being killed by wild animals, suicide, murder, dying in childbirth — they're all considered unnatural deaths that make for unhappy ghosts who bring bad fortune on the community."

Roberta asked the chief to tell the pregnant woman I was assisting her. The expectant mother didn't seem embarrassed in the slightest about being examined in front of me, though the midwife and the encircling women deftly preserved her privacy, holding open a sarong like a curtain just as Montagnard women did so elegantly when bathing in the rivers toward evening.

Roberta spoke to the chief, and the chief to the woman. The chief gave his blessings, and Roberta and the midwife began manipulating the mound that was the child, trying to turn it around manually so the head would lead the way through the birth canal. The woman didn't utter a sound, though she was drenched in sweat from the pain.

It didn't work. Roberta briefly tried a second time and gave up. She said something else to the chief, who conveyed it to the woman.

Roberta came back to me. "No go."

"You going to try again?"

"We don't dare. It's exhausting her, and the placenta could detach. It's going to be a breech birth."

The circle of women squatted, waiting. Roberta sent me to retrieve some packing paper from her Rover.

"This whole country is a petri dish," she said, "I swear." She sat down next to me on a log. The husband kept chopping; the blows carried across the village.

"All you can do is your best," I said.

"In one sense they're tough as nails. Have to be to have survived into adulthood. Yet their bodies have been heavily taxed. They haven't much endurance."

"They look sturdy enough to me."

She shook her head and indicated the pregnant woman. "She's got leprosy, like so many of them. Suffers from vitamin and iodine deficiencies, and I can hear the effects of TB in her lungs. I don't know if it's active. I treated her earlier with isoniazid, streptomycin, and para-aminosalicylic acid, in case. Probably has malaria too, hopefully not cerebral. And maybe dengue. Worms and parasites . . . God, their parasites have parasites. I've never seen a specimen from a Montagnard that didn't have parasites."

I looked at the woman's husband. "You think she could check out?"

"She's not in great shape." She stood with hands on her hips. "Fuck."

"What can you do?"

"I had her on dapsone last year for the leprosy. She's chronically anemic, like they all are . . . luckily, because that actually keeps her malaria suppressed. I can't give her anything for the worms until she delivers. The medicines are too toxic."

"What doesn't she have?"

"No tetanus or yaws." Roberta gazed ahead. "Plague either. I haven't detected plague. But if you look over there, you'll see the carriers in those little corrals."

Caged rats.

"They raise them," she said.

"Pets?"

"Food. Roasted rat. It's not bad."

"I've had some, caught in the wild. I didn't realize they actually raised them for food."

"What you're seeing" — she indicated our surroundings — "this is four thousand years old. They've been like this forever. They farm rice without plows or water or tools other than sticks so as not to make the gods mad. Only the men make the holes for seeds, only the women plant them in the holes. Every grain of rice gets harvested by hand to keep their pissy gods happy." Worry lined her face. "In some villages, if the mother dies in childbirth, the baby gets buried with her whether it's alive or dead."

"Is this one of those villages?"

"I don't know."

"What are you going to do if she doesn't make it?"

"What I did the last time — try to buy the baby. See the sorcerer sitting under the longhouse?"

A distinguished-looking man sat by himself next to a tethered dog and a pig, enjoying a huge joint.

"If she dies, he'll sacrifice those two immediately and purify the village with their blood. Sprinkle the ground everywhere and stamp on it."

"You got any good news, Doc?"

She leaned back against a support post, staring at the sky. "Yeah, at least it's not twins on board," she said, her hair a mass of curls from the humidity. She looked back at me, amused. "It gets better."

"What?"

"The dad. He's VC."

Half a dozen kids drilled with bamboo sticks on their shoulders, imitating their elders in the militia at Mai Linh. More women and kids gathered, talking and cavorting. This birth was attracting a lot of attention, perhaps because we were involved.

"Got anything you can give them as a present?" Roberta asked. I patted my pockets, hoping for some candy or gum. All I had was a pack of cigarettes. Roberta nodded. "Two each."

I distributed the cigarettes. The old women flashed their black, toothless grins. They stripped off the paper, stuffed the tobacco into their pipes, and puffed away. A swarm of small boys cleaned me out of the rest. They strutted around puffing, obviously experienced smokers though they couldn't have been more than five or six.

"You're sure about the father?" I said, quietly.

"Yes."

The women held up the sarong again so Roberta could check on the labor. The mother was dilated ten centimeters. We sat on the packed earth and waited. The old women waited with us. Roberta put her hair up and tied it in place with her scarf. She produced a cigarette and lit up.

"Those older ladies are the movers and shakers of the village," she said and exhaled. "Jarai women do most of the work, run everything and own everything, including the men. Mothers get together and buy and sell sons for marriage."

"What's a guy go for these days?"

"About two dollars' worth of piasters and a pair of water buffalo. Maybe a brass gong thrown in. The groom marries into the wife's clan and moves into her family's longhouse, takes her name. So will their kids. The guy has no power; the clan makes all decisions. He's there to service her relatives. He can't buy or sell anything without the wife's approval. If they divorce, she keeps everything."

"How modern," I said.

"You see the old one?" Roberta nodded toward the circle of skeletal women.

"Which one? They all look old."

"The oldest — really shriveled."

"Yeah," I said, still not knowing which.

"She's the guardian of the land. She says who farms it and when, and how much of a harvest goes into the common emergency reserve."

"Why isn't she the chief?" I said.

Roberta looked at me with condescension. "This is Asia, Captain. The men only think they're chief."

"I take it you wouldn't mind being a Montagnard?"

"I . . . no. I wouldn't want to."

"Why not?"

She took a long drag. "Can't say." She blew out a stream of smoke. "It's sort of a secret."

I lit the lamps we'd brought and turned on the one big flashlight. The pregnant woman rose to her feet, slightly hunched, and took hold of one of the posts supporting the longhouse overhead. The women in the circle slid her covering away and she stood naked, flesh glistening with sweat. She looked fevered. Roberta and I rushed forward.

Roberta spoke to the woman, examined her, and made a quick movement. Water gushed.

"It's clear," Roberta said, relieved, clicking off her flashlight.

"Is she going to lie down again?" I said, kneeling behind Roberta.

Roberta didn't take her eyes off her patient. "Whatever her body tells her to do, we follow her lead. She wants to stand, she stands. But get the packing paper in position on the mats behind her just in case. If I have to do surgery, God forbid, it'll be on the paper. The odds of infection will skyrocket if I have to operate, damn it."

The woman began grunting. The circle of old women stopped puffing their pipes. I lit two more Coleman lanterns and suspended them from the bottom of the longhouse while Roberta laid out covered metal trays of her obstetric and surgical tools on a low bench. The younger women rose to their feet to peer at them. This wasn't going to be good if Roberta had to cut her open. How would the villagers react? Worse still, what if the mother didn't make it?

On the porch of the longhouse, the baby's father unrolled a mat and placed a jar and a bowl on it. I turned to Roberta.

"He's got a cooked rooster in the bowl and alcohol in the jar. And a sharpened piece of bamboo to cut the umbilical cord."

The husband chanted something.

Roberta listened. "He's asking for it to be a girl."

"Girl? Don't the men want sons?"

She shook her head. "Why? Girls do the heavy labor and own the property. Boys don't have any power. When Dad's done, he'll pour a cup of alcohol for his wife to sip, and fetch fresh water to bathe the baby. He's already dug a hole under the house to bury the placenta."

"Good. He's staying positive. We like that."

"Well, he's also notched that little pole."

"Stuck in the ground next to the log casket?"

"Yeah. It'll go at the head of the coffin. Kind of a ladder to the underworld."

The woman went down on all fours. Roberta examined her again by flashlight, turned it off, and settled on the ground alongside her, me at her back.

"The kid's coming," she said. The woman went to her knees.

I squatted and snapped on the flashlight. I was gazing at the birth canal, which was filled with flesh, not feet. "Is it crowning?"

Roberta stepped around and shook her head. "The baby's coming butt-first. Its ankles must be up by its ears."

"Can she possibly pass it through her — you know?"

"She has to. We're not pushing that kid back in and cutting her open. Please, God. Shine the light again, Captain."

I trained the flashlight and saw the cleft in its ass. "I see it! I see it!"

Roberta turned toward me, amused. "You see it," she said.

"Yeah." I was breathless. More wound up than the dad.

"Good thing you see it." She turned her attention back to the pregnant woman and applied the stethoscope to her chest. "You're catching this kid."

Its bottom slipped out, its little back, legs and finally feet, arms, and tiny fists . . . Mom was facing away. Most of the baby was in my hands and its head still inside the mother.

"Jesus," I said, terrified.

"One advantage of malnutrition. The baby's little. Probably made the trip easier."

"Can it last like this?"

"Not long," she said, voice hoarse. "Minutes. Five. Maybe ten."

The baby hung headless in my hands, its little chest motionless. Roberta spoke words of encouragement to the woman. The umbilical pulsed less and less. The shaman stepped close and streaked us with ash.

"Doc—"

"Wait."

The mother growled, brow touching the ground. On the next contraction the head emerged with a sucking pop.

"I got it!"

Roberta took it from me instantly and rose. She inverted the infant, holding it by the ankles, umbilical trailing. Fluids dripped from the newborn. I saw its penis, smaller than my pinkie.

"It's a boy!" I said. He had arrived ass-backwards but alive.

Roberta cleared his mouth and the newborn cried out.

I stood bent at the waist and rested my hands on my knees. "I know how you feel, kid."

I was warm and cool at the same time. My knees were shaking. Roberta made me hold the kid anyway. The father approached and purposefully blew in his ear.

"What's he doing?" I said, surprised.

"Blowing the child's soul into its body."

Roberta washed the baby with the treated water and I passed him to the dad. He stood grinning, overjoyed, holding his son.

# 8

★ ★ ★

IT WAS ALMOST ten at night by the time we were ready to return to Mai Linh. The colonel came on the radio, impatient with us, like a dad whose children were deliberately flouting their curfew. We had been drinking, but in subdued celebration. The Montagnards feared making the *yang* spirits jealous of the newborn, though the father couldn't tamp down his joy. He could barely contain himself. Neither could I.

We'd been invited to the parents' hearth in the family's longhouse for a meal, where the chief unsealed a jar of rice wine. I accepted the long straw and imbibed. A wooden marker made sure we each drank a proper portion. I was buzzed and still high as a kite from the birth, so I didn't realize what they were doing until the brass bracelets were already on our wrists, our bare feet resting on an ax blade, anointed with blood dribbled out of a headless chicken. Dad shook our hands and took his leave, disappearing into the dark. Mom and child were nowhere to be seen. The chief looked self-satisfied and content.

Coconut shells went on the fire for kindling, and we were served roasted chicken and fish on banana leaves. Roberta hugged me. She couldn't stop grinning as she dismembered the fleshy chicken, her fingers glistening with fat.

"Maybe they'll name him after you," she teased. "More likely they'll wait and name him something like Harelip or Mole, or worse." She threw back her hair. "But they won't even do that until he's around five. They'll want to see if the *yang* let him live before they give him a name."

We wobbled down the notched log ladder and barely made it to her Rover. The Yards had carefully repacked it with her medical supplies. On the passenger seat was tree bark with a moon-white orchid growing from it.

"What's that?" she said.

"The doctor's fee, I'd say."

Two bamboo containers lay next to the flower. She switched on her flashlight and opened the first. "Raw opium," she said. She opened the second: "*Broial* root, which they use to treat sties. They're replenishing my medicines."

I tossed my gear in back and radioed Mai Linh.

"Wait one," the operator said. "Six wants you," and the colonel came on.

"Red Fox, what the hell's your situation?"

He sounded less worried when he heard our report.

"Well," he said. "What was it, boy or girl? Over."

"Boy. Maybe five pounds."

"What's he called?"

I looked at Roberta, stuck for a reply. She took the mike and keyed it. "Old family name. Victor Charlie."

There was silence for a second at the other end. "Seriously? Over."

"Yes."

"Do you require assistance? Over."

"No, we're fine," she said, exuberant. "How's the area? Would you advise we stay the night?"

"Negative, negative. Come back. Be quick." He sounded worried again.

Roberta turned the ignition. "Rider," she said, thrilled. She leaned over the shift stick, clutching her bracelet, and kissed me on the cheek. "We did it, we did it."

In the dark I couldn't tell if it was sweat around her eyes or tears.

We rolled toward Mai Linh, Roberta driving, me riding shotgun, rifle stock at my shoulder, radio handset resting on the other. The headlights were nearly blacked out with tape and we were creeping along.

"You ever prescribe heroin for your patients?"

"No. Raw opium's easier to obtain in Cheo Reo. We buy French barbiturates like Binoctal at a pharmacy when we can, and cadge dextroamphetamines our military men are issued going into combat."

"Can you do me a favor?"

"You looking to score?"

"No, I draw the line at weed. Never been fond of needles. But could you ask your Montagnards if they know of any big new fields of poppies or marijuana plants in the province? It's an intel thing."

"They all grow a little weed in their gardens, right alongside tobacco. How big is big?"

"Big enough that people take notice and talk."

"What was that?" she said.

"What?"

"That light."

I grasped her shoulder sharply and she braked. "Switch off the headlights."

"What are we doing?" she whispered.

"Did you really see a light?"

"I thought so, but I don't see it now. Maybe the headlights reflected off something. Why?"

The dad had been grateful, sure, but did our protection end once we were out of the village? The VC could easily know by now that a pair of tipsy, barely armed Americans were heading back toward Mai Linh in the dead of night.

"What was that click?" she whispered.

"My rifle. I switched off the safety."

"What should we do?"

"We're too far along. Keep going. Try for Mai Linh."

"Now?"

"Just a second. If you even think you see a light at the side of the road, tell me immediately."

"You mean like a flashlight?"

"More like a candle in a can."

"Held up, like a lantern?"

"No, no! On the ground. A number-ten can — the kind coffee comes in — with a little window cut out."

"You lost me."

"They cut a square opening in two number-ten cans, put a lit candle in each one, place them on the side of the road, maybe twenty feet apart, with the windows toward the road. Then they take up a position a safe distance away, where they can see both lights, and they wait."

"Shit."

"Even if it's dark as death — like now — they can see their target block the first light as it rolls past. When the target crosses the light of the second can, they detonate whatever explosive they've set up."

"Okay, okay," she said, "now I'm scared." She strained to see in the inky dark. "What do I do if we see a light . . .? Rider?"

"Spin us around and haul ass."

"Shouldn't we wait for some moonlight or something?"

"No. The less time we think about it, the better. Okay," I said. *"Fast."*

"Hang on."

She put the Rover in gear, let out the clutch, and we were off. In the pitch-black, with little slits for headlights and bouncing madly, ten miles an hour felt like we were doing a hundred. Something clanged loudly against the undercarriage and Roberta slammed on the brakes, skidding us to a stop on the sandy road.

"What was that?" she said.

"Don't know."

"Did we drop the transmission?"

"No. No. We're okay."

"Are you sure? What was that awful bang?"

"I have no idea. A rock, maybe. Drive straight forward twenty yards. Don't turn the wheel. Not even a little bit."

She nodded and obeyed, edging us forward.

"Now what?"

"Just drive on normally."

She hit the gas. We covered the three kilometers in record time and came screeching up to the Mai Linh gate. It flew open instantly and we rolled in. The colonel, Cox, and Grady were sitting in an idling jeep, all wearing harnesses and bearing arms: a rescue party.

Sergeant Grady took Roberta's bag to the "guesthouse," an abandoned bunker in the inner defensive tier. The colonel took charge of her and the orchid. Grady came back to the Rover, and he and Cox took me in hand.

Cox said, "Congratulations on the bambino. First delivery's the hardest, I hear."

"Drink?" Grady said. "Man, you look like you could use one."

We walked past a white screen onto which a film was being projected, turning part of the camp into an open-air movie theater. Two hundred Montagnards sat on the ground, enthralled.

Grady said, "We got a mixed film batch tonight. One *Batman* episode, one *Combat*. Oh, and the third reel of some western. You don't want to be around when the western comes on. The Yards get carried away."

"They root for the Indians, right?"

"Used to. Recently they've decided the Indians are Vietnamese and they root for the cavalry—us." Grady took a swig of brandy from his canteen and passed it. "Then again, they root for the Germans in World War Two flicks. We had one feature with a forest fire—that really got them agitated. They just about stampeded. And *King Kong*, that was a wow. But they've gotten used to movies, mostly."

We circled the audience. The Vietnamese Special Forces in their red berets stood at the back.

I noted the obvious: "They're still here."

"The LLDB? Yeah, till tomorrow." Grady sniggered. "They're struttin'. We gotta watch out for feuds among the Yards too. The Jarai and Rhade get along okay. But the Bahnar and Jarai have been fighting each other forever."

A poker game was in progress in the team house. The pot was formidable: the table was littered with chips and military scrip and piasters and personal weapons of every variety, put up as collateral by Green Berets strapped for funds. Sprague, the medic, was trying to bet his Rolex but no one would accept it. No one wanted to risk winning a medic's watch.

"You wanna sit in, Captain?"

"No, thanks, my hands are shaking too badly. I wouldn't wanna embarrass myself."

In the corner, an E-7 strummed a ukulele as he sang to a caged monkey with a powder blue snout and pale orange circles around its eyes. The monkey was dipping its fingers in a cup of beer and licking away. I pointed to the triple locks securing its chicken-wire cage.

"Does it jailbreak a lot, or is it prone to attack?"

"That's Bobo the Third," Grady said. "Belongs to our commo sergeant. A mean drunk. Bobo, that is. Just like Bobo the First, and lots worse than Bobo the Second. It'll bite you for no reason, drunk or sober. But nah. The locks are to keep it safe. The guys death-squadded the last one and let the Yards eat it. They're plotting against this one too."

Grady retrieved two cold beers from a large shiny refrigerator the size of a station wagon and offered me one. We clinked bottles and each took a pull.

"You liberate the fridge from the Navy?"

"Nope," Grady said. "Graves registration in Qui Nhon."

Two Montagnard kids appeared out of nowhere and stood stiffly in front of the icebox. Grady said something to them in Rhade and pulled open the door. He removed an ice tray and cracked out a couple of cubes, handing one to each. They bravely accepted the ice he put in their palms and stared at the cubes. Grady shooed them out.

"Yard kids ain't never seen ice, much less touched it."

A beet-faced sergeant scowled at Grady. "Will you keep those f-in' kids out of here? They are gonna hand you a grenade one day."

"Cool it, you dumb fuck. They're just bein' curious."

"You're stupid as a sack of rocks, Grady."

Sergeant Grady and I stepped outside, past two stone-faced Nung, to get out of range of the other sergeant's anger. A cloying odor drifted over us. Montagnards watching the movie were smoking fat cigars rolled with homegrown dope.

"Man," Grady said, "best we keep upwind. They marinate them bliffs in opium. Just bein' near that shit will knock you on your ass."

A Bahnar with bushy hair rose from the crowd and walked unsteadily by us. One of the Vietnamese Red Berets said something as he passed. The Montagnard stopped.

"*Lu mat*," he said to the soldier and bared his filed piranha teeth, lacquered black.

The Vietnamese recoiled. "*Du mi ami*," he snarled. Motherfucker.

"What did the Yard say?" I asked. Something as fierce as his rictus grin, I presumed.

"Nothing bad. He don't speak Vietnamese. He's a sweet guy. Said he's drunk, is all."

Grady chuckled as the man passed us and tottered off into the dark.

The Bahnar was barely able to stand, so we tagged after him to the men's longhouse to make sure he made it in one piece. Grady climbed up the pole ladder to the thatched porch and together, him pulling and me pushing, we hoisted the guy up. The Bahnar grinned again.

"*Kahan*," he said with dignity, touching his chest.

"What now?"

Grady looked proud. "Said he's a soldier. A rifleman."

The man staggered inside, the two of us close behind. Fires smoked in several hearths, seasoning the air in the long hall and stinging our eyes. Our host curled up on a long wooden slab and immediately went to sleep.

"They all look kind of shaggy."

"It's the hair," Grady said. "They don't like to cut it." Grady squatted next to the guy and covered him with a handwoven blanket. "Their souls leave their heads and go wandering when they sleep. You know, like in their dreams. Then come back in the morning."

The Bahnar snorted and turned over.

Grady stood up. "If they cut their hair they worry some enemy will, like, voodoo them — take a lock of hair and bury it to make their soul think their body's died and been buried, and the soul will never come back."

Something on the exposed rafters caught my eye and I gasped. Human skulls.

"Damn," I said, stepping back, "that's some home décor."

"Yeah, well," Grady said, "Bahnar are into some wild shit."

"I'd hate to see their souvenir shop," I said. We left and climbed down the notched log leaning against the front porch to the ground.

Grady laughed to himself. "We gotta watch 'em in the field. If a Yard gets hit, it's like they're all insulted. They're liable to take big vengeance—just chop a dead VC's head right off. Scares the crap out of helicopter crews when the Bahnar hold up the thing like a trophy as the bird's comin' in." He scratched the stubble on his face. "You'd think Bahnar would be easy pickings for the Commies."

"Why?"

"They're practically Communists already. Divide up every bit of food among everyone in the vil. Everybody gets an equal share. I've seen 'em divvy up a scrawny-ass chicken among a whole damn village. Not more than a pinch of food for each person, but that's what they do. Reminds me of my grandma. Every kid got somethin', even if it was nothin'."

Grady walked me back to the innermost part of the camp where only Americans and the camp commander were allowed at night.

"Di Uy, radios are your bag, right? You ever see one of our Sneaky Pete specials?"

He took me into a shallow bunker and lit a lantern to show me a wall of portable radios on a long shelf. I took one down. A Japanese transistor model.

"Those Melvins at psy ops stuck us with a whole batch of these, rigged so they lock on this one Saigon propaganda station. You know, Viet happenin' tunes and silky talk to jones the VC into turning themselves in to the Chieu Hoi 'Open Arms' centers for some R and R. The VC are all hungry as hell, they figure, and hurtin', so they broadcast this sweet deal: come shoot the shit, turn in your piece, get some serious bucks, a couple months' rack time, home cookin', a little volleyball. The psy ops jerks want we should drop them radios where Charlie is gonna pick one up, turn it on, and be rockin' out." He snapped his fingers in rhythm.

"Does the come-on work?"

"Sorta. But whaddya know, a lot of 'em just treat rehab like a paid vacation. They kick back, fatten up, buy new weapons downtown with their bonus money, and go right back out to Jungle World. The psy ops ladies don't wise up. Them fools keep sendin' us these heavy-ass radios, give us orders to scatter 'em along the infiltration routes. They want we should haul all this extra weight and risk our necks playin' Santa Claus so's Charlie can catch some gook soul tunes and the Sacred Sword of Patriotism bullshit broadcasts outta Saigon."

"I can see where you might be annoyed."

"Definitely. So we do a little rewiring. Reconfigure the receivers and deliver them trailside, as ordered. Includin' the flier."

He held one up and translated. "'This radio will bring you knowledge and relaxing entertainment.'" Grady laughed to himself. "You know what those psy ops goops call their program? Winning Hearts and Minds. WHAM for short."

I hefted a set. Grady grabbed my wrist. "I wouldn't."

He opened the back. Two wires ran out of the C-4 packed in the battery space and around the speaker to the on/off switch.

"The gook finds it, puts it to his ear, and turns it on — it's good night, Chuck."

"Sweet Jesus."

"We call our thing WHAMO! Winning Hearts and Minds of—" Sergeant Grady beamed. "Whaddya think?"

"I think you have a very black sense of humor."

"Very black!" Grady giggled. "Yo."

"You blow my mind," I said, and he actually hooted.

"What a blast!" he said and shrieked with laughter, his eyes tearing.

It wasn't that funny but I couldn't help joining in. It was infectious. I was nearly howling when I realized I was staring at one-kilo packets wrapped in paper and plastic wound with tape.

"What's this?"

"That?" The timbre of his voice slowly changed. "Shit. You shouldn't be seein' that."

"Sarge, this looks like heroin."

"Don't it just."

"Refined?"

"Yup. Nearly pure, man. Twenty kilos of Laos Gold."

I admired the logo on the wrapper. "Where the hell did you get a load of refined heroin out here?"

Grady grinned. "From the sky. Swear to God. The shit floated down on top of us. Nearly bagged one of our strikers."

"Where?"

"Northwest. We and some of our Yards chased an NVA patrol way out of our normal tac area. We were in an open stretch. A transport plane appeared overhead — Vietnamese air force — and down came this bundle. Manna from heaven. Must have mistaken us for whoever was waiting for the delivery."

"What are you going to do with it?"

"Donate it to the Yards to cache with their guns and money. Sort of a nest egg." He picked up a brick and hefted it. "Wish I knew what it was worth."

"In Saigon a kilo like this goes for two grand. Maybe two and a half."

"Jeez. Twenty kilos . . . forty thousand dollars."

"In San Francisco it's ten times that."

Grady looked at me oddly. "How is it you know?"

"I'd move it now, if I were you. They won't be able to do it without you. Besides, you don't want to keep it in the ground. It won't age like wine."

"I hear ya," Grady said. "If you could forget you saw this, Di Uy, I'd owe you large."

"Saw what?" I said.

Grady smiled. He showed me to a spare bunk in the team house and I collapsed for a couple of hours. When I came to, the camp was quiet under a quarter moon. I stripped off my shirt and boots, got fatigues and floppies, slung my weapon on, took my towel and soap, and made my way toward the water tower. Suspended beneath it, a tank fed by a well served up shower water. A wooden grating made from cargo pallets is what you stood on. A skimpy bamboo half wall passed for the bathhouse.

The shower worked beautifully. I let the water deluge me as I stared up at the stars. I hadn't felt as clean or peaceful since I'd arrived. I felt lighter than I had in years. When I'd used up more than a generous amount, I put on fatigue pants and floppies, slung my rifle over my shoulder, and climbed up to the highest point in camp. It was a beautiful night. Half a joint lay abandoned on a sandbag, crimped by a matchbook. I ducked down to shield the light, struck a match, and lit up. Dope cured in opium. I cupped the burning end and inhaled deeply. World class.

Checkman appeared next to me as I stood up.

"You're keeping late hours," I said. He leaned against the sandbags, facing me, his back to the camp, his eyes not yet adjusted to the dark.

"The guys on radio watch woke me. First they were listening to their favorite disc jockey playing rock on Pathet Lao Radio. Then they got into making their own music."

Down below, someone strummed a ukulele and softly sang a barracks ballad: "'My mother's a Montagnard princess. My father's an LLDB / And every night around midnight / They turn into hard-core VC.'"

Checkman massaged his neck. "But what really woke me was I dreamed VC were breeching the perimeter wire and swinging open the gate."

"Here." I handed Checkman the smoldering joint.

"Really?"

"It's an order."

Two tokes and his eyes pinwheeled. "Wow."

Two figures in black VC pajamas made their way down to the shower point and disrobed. The Special Forces guys liked to sleep in peasants' black garb so they'd already be dressed in the event of an attack. They also didn't want to have on uniforms that would identify them in the dark as Americans.

Checkman slumped against the sandbags and slid to the floor. Down at the showers the two doused themselves and lathered their heads. Then each other. I exhaled the dope slowly, staring. It was a man and a woman. The woman had long spiraling curls. She turned her back to the guy and reached behind her. The mutual washing turned sexual. His hands came around and fondled her, everywhere. She turned to face him and leaned back against the bamboo barrier. He pressed close and took her. Halfway through, she turned again and bent forward, holding the half wall.

A trip flare popped into the sky over the western perimeter. The bunker sentry on that side ratcheted a .50-caliber machine gun, seating the first six-inch shell.

"What's up?" Checkman slurred, smiling.

"Nothing. A prowling animal, is all. Just keep the lit joint down there. Don't get up."

"I'm not sure I can," he said and chortled.

The flare descended slowly. Nothing in the kill zone. A brief ghostly light swayed over the spent lovers. Roberta and the colonel.

# 9

★  ★  ★

I WAS PAIRED UP with Colonel Bennett for the drive back. He obviously wanted to speak with me privately, but not about what I'd thought.

"I understand John Ruchevsky had a set-to with Major Gidding," he said.

"Yes, sir. Big John is pretty frustrated about the, ah, seepage situation."

"As are we all, Captain."

"Sir, isn't there anything we can do about Colonel Chinh's profiteering? The gasoline? The rice?"

"You know the score. He writes my report card. As senior adviser, I'm judged by how happy I keep my counterpart."

"And is he happy?"

"So long as I get him what he wants by way of materiel and air assets and don't demand too much from him or his troops."

"So we give him what he wants."

"Don't always want to, but yes. I manage to get him the supplies, the copters, the toys. Hard to deny him since Chinh holds all the cards. He's the Man. My job is to bolster, persuade, cajole, get him to act. And I won't be able to do it if Big John starts seriously rattling Chinh's cage and challenging his perks."

A line of Jarai boys stood along the roadside, waving. Bennett waved back. I was still jumpy from the trip back to Mai Linh after dark. Hav-

ing investigated incidents of Vietnamese kids delivering lethal greet-
ings to unwary Americans, I switched off the safety.

"You have children, Captain?"

"No, sir," I said, eyes fixed on the boys. "Any waiting for you at
home?"

"Afraid not. I'd like to snatch a couple of these little guys to bring
back, give them a chance at a real future. Have you had much contact
with Montagnards?"

"Nothing like this, sir." We were past the line of boys, and I relaxed.
I glanced at the colonel. "You like the Yards."

"They're innately honest, don't have a calendar, don't read or count,
rely almost entirely on barter to get by, and insist that everyone get
looped at their ceremonies. You gotta love 'em."

Big John was waiting for me, enjoying one of his stogies and writing
something longhand. My head was killing me.

"I hear you're godfather to a little Victor Charlie," he said, not looking up.

"Yeah, the doc said the dad's VC. Not sure how she knew."

"She treated him for a gunshot last year. He's full-time local cadre.
Nearly the top dog's right hand. Remember Mr. Wolf Man?" Ruchevsky
fussed with his cigar ash. "You think Roberta might be willing to persuade our grateful new dad to help us, ah . . . interview his boss?"

"C'mon. She takes sides and she and her clinic are history."

"Yeah. Thought you'd say that." Ruchevsky held up his hands defen-
sively. "Won't push it."

"Yeah, and the colonel wants you to put a lid on the seepage com-
plaints. You're making his job harder."

"Sorry to hear that," he said sarcastically. "Excuse me for trying to
do my job."

"Odd thing at the Mai Linh Special Forces camp," I said.

"Yeah, what?"

"A Yard patrol got twenty kilos of pure Laotian heroin dropped on it
by a South Vietnamese aircraft."

"That's the weather in Southeast Asia for you," Ruchevsky said, "hot
and humid with a chance of falling heroin. It's raining dope bundles in

Pleiku Province too. The traffickers are moving so much product they can't land it all in Saigon. So they drop it in the sea where it gets fished out by colleagues, and they drop it in the jungle at collection points to have it trucked to Saigon. The province chief in Pleiku collects five grand for every shipment. Talk about falling in your lap. Five large for doing fuck-all."

"Why can't we get work like that?" I said.

"Here," Ruchevsky said, producing a manila file folder. "Take a peek at this."

I read it with one eye closed, fighting the ache in my head. The current set of ruling generals, the report said, were providing safe passage for Cholon's Chinese and Corsican syndicates smuggling raw opium and processed heroin into and out of South Viet Nam. Two refineries in Saigon's Chinese district, run by survivors of Chiang Kai-shek's Eighty-fourth Regiment, were operating around the clock. Refined and unrefined dope came in on regular commercial carriers like Lao Air and on South Vietnamese military transports once commanded by Vice Air Marshal Ky. Now Premier Ky. Dumping his politically incorrect French wife and mother of his brood, he'd taken up with an Air Vietnam stewardess and built a modest mansion for them right on Ton Son Nhut Air Base, overlooking the runways bringing in the stuff.

Ky had consolidated his control of law enforcement and intelligence by making an old classmate the director of the Military Security Service and head of their Central Intelligence Organization, and director-general of the National Police. The classmate, in turn, appointed his own brother-in-law the mayor of Saigon.

Hundreds of kilos were being carried into Saigon by military attachés, diplomats, stewardesses, civilian travelers, and intelligence agents, in unaccompanied luggage and diplomatic pouches. More arrived on Vietnamese naval ships and river patrol vessels and fishing boats that picked up drug shipments dropped into the Gulf of Siam. Shipments sailed for Europe, for Hong Kong, for America. Coming in or going out, the contraband was protected. Police, the military, and customs looked the other way: *courtesy of the port.* A footnote identified the port director as Ky's brother-in-law.

Closing the folder, I said, "The South Vietnamese can't be happy with the competition of VC trafficking. Or having hard currency diverted to the People's Army when it could be filling pockets in Saigon."

"I don't know," Ruchevsky said, standing up. "If the VC get the dope raised around here and smuggle it all the way to Saigon, the syndicates wouldn't care whose goods they were moving. Likewise the customs and port officials. The admirals and generals either. War or no war, business is business."

Big John stooped, his hands resting on his knees, and stared at me closely. "Rider," he said.

"Yeah?"

"You don't look right."

I didn't feel right. My head swam and an awful pain blossomed behind my left eye, clouding my vision. The next second I was on my ass, every joint in my body blazing with pain.

Dengue. The recurrence of the fever took me by surprise. One second I was feeling tiptop, the next my body seized up and my joints hurt so bad that my mind went fuzzy and objects turned liquid. Not for nothing was it called breakbone fever. The MACV medic, Doc Wright, popped me full of pills and put cold cloths on my forehead.

A day later I felt light and empty and a little weak in the knees. I was upright, though, and insisted I was functional. Wright didn't buy it. He ordered bed rest and put Mama-san Duc on the case. The old woman was a staunch Viet Minh nationalist who did our laundry and cleaned our quarters. Years earlier she'd portaged supplies into the mountains for the guerrillas fighting the French. The men in the compound had grown fond of her and of the way she'd berate anyone who crossed her, regardless of his status or whether or not he understood her. Mama-san Duc popped in regularly to check on me and dressed me down in rapid Vietnamese if I made any move to get up. I knew when I was beaten and slept the day away.

When Bac-si Wright stopped by early in the evening to take my temperature, I was alert enough to be alarmed.

"Doc!"

"What?"

"You look like hell."

"Yeah? I feel punk."

"Your eyes are yellow, Doc."

"Fuck," he said and glanced in the small shaving mirror on the back of the door. He muttered, "I gotta go," and bolted.

I passed out again. The doc came back a few hours later, or so I thought. But it wasn't Doc Wright or Mama-san. It was Roberta bringing me cold water.

"Sergeant Wright's not doing so well," she said. "I'm making house calls for him."

I thanked her and quaffed a whole glass. It was painfully cold going down. My knees and elbows burned, and a white pain blurred my vision.

"How are you feeling?"

"Broken."

"Here's another blanket," she said, and covered me with it. "I'll check on you later. Oh, a Sergeant Miser came by earlier. He said you should stop malingering."

No matter how hard I tried to keep from slipping away, sleep took me again.

I was woken in the night by a commotion and shuffled outside. First Sergeant Mote, in green skivvies and flip-flops, came out of the medic's room four doors down. To the east a distant flare floated earthward in complete silence, haloed by humidity.

"What's up, Top?"

The first sergeant stopped. "Bac-si's yellow as a gook."

"Hepatitis. Shit."

"Yeah," Top commiserated. "I hate those shots. How are you holding up?"

"Better." I returned to my bunk and slept normally the rest of the night.

The first sergeant and the perimeter guards coming off duty medevaced Doc Wright in the morning, swapping him for a load of gamma globulin. The whole team needed inoculation. Westy climbed the water tower and doused our water supply with an extra load of purifier. I went to the mess hall and mixed salt and sugar into a glass of powdered milk and gulped it down. Outside, enlisted men stood around the top steps of the commo bunker, speculating about the leper colony upriver and what might have gone into the current there. But hell, lots of Montagnard villages were upstream, and bathers and washerwomen from town. No telling where the hepatitis originated: food or drinking water.

In the absence of an Army medic, Roberta stepped in to administer the large doses of gamma globulin. Team members convoyed to her clinic all day, a few at a time. The commo bunker advised all approaching aircraft that, by order of senior adviser Lieutenant Colonel Bennett, anyone who landed at the airstrip and set foot on the ground had to be inoculated as well. American pilots didn't even cut off their engines. They'd land and drop open their back ramps as they taxied, sending aviation-gas blivets bounding along the perforated steel planks toward the petrol dump. After they'd dumped them all out, they gunned their engines and took right off again. I was at the strip enforcing Bennett's order when a twin-propeller Caribou with kangaroo insignia landed with supply pallets. The Aussie pilots taxied over to us at the CONEX to inquire about the day's luncheon menu. I radioed in to the commo bunker to check. Hearing it was meat loaf, the four of them deplaned. We warned them our cooks weren't exactly Paris trained. They didn't care.

The Montagnards they had on board to handle the heavy lifting were less eager to be dartboarded by our female shaman and elected to remain behind, squatting on the lowered ramp.

"We'll send the little bleeders back some lunch," the aircraft commander said. I radioed the commo bunker and had them summon the doc.

Roberta drove out to the airstrip and injected the big dosages into the Aussies' keisters. The Australians enjoyed themselves thoroughly, taking snapshots of the lady doctor jabbing their bare bums, cigarette dangling from the corner of her mouth. Afterward they posed for a group picture mooning Viet Nam and then hitched a ride into the compound on the bed of the engineers' truck. They invited me to join their upright luncheon party. They'd brought Worcestershire sauce, a jar of something revolting called Vegemite, and their own Australian beer, chilled at altitude.

"You blokes take this whole dustup too seriously," the copilot said.

"You oughta sample the output from those beautiful fields due south of here."

"What do you mean?"

"Gorgeous poppy fields up on a mountain, about twelve miles south. Ruddy fantastic at the moment. Flowers everywhere. Looks like Flanders."

After they finished eating, I made the copilot point out the peak on my map and thanked him. This was my first real lead. The Aussie crew left a gift bottle of Bundaberg rum for the bar and rode back to their plane standing on the engineers' truck, singing four-part harmony:

> A short-time girl wore thirty-eight Ds.
> Rather much for a Vietnamese.
> So they searched her with pleasure. And discovered this treasure.
> One grenade, one plastique, two punjis. Oh . . .

My name was on the clinic list for the afternoon. I walked into town, not expecting to sit again that day. The clinic's six beds were occupied by sick and injured Montagnards surrounded by their families. Relatives prepared meals in the aisle and slept under the beds, on the floor, even in beds with the patients. I had to step over several napping Jarai to reach the dispensary. Roberta, harried with cases, whipped through the prep for my shot, then stopped, amused that I still had my pants on.

I was sweating profusely. Besides the embarrassment of baring my butt, I hated hypodermics and grew queasy at just the thought of sharp metal driven into my body. Even a dentist's syringe made me anxious. The end of my second tour, my buddy Stolz and I had sat outside the Air Force snack shack in Pleiku forging the mandatory vaccinations on each other's shot cards to process out. The shots for Viet Nam were a bitch: black plague, typhoid, yellow fever . . . but the absolute worst was gamma globulin for hepatitis.

"Which is it," she said, "me or the spike?"

"Usually it's the needle. This time I'm sure it's both."

She couldn't resist teasing. "Valiant captain enfeebled by a syringe. Tell you what," she said, lighting up a Salem. "You're going to be sore afterward. It's intramuscular. But I'm very good at this. I can do it with my eyes shut — and I will — if you'll just bring your backside in range."

She took a step closer and shut her eyes, cigarette burning. I bit the bullet, tipped myself over her exam table, and slid my pants down.

"You there?" she said, blowing smoke past me.

"You're not doing this with your eyes closed."

"You want them open?"

"I'd prefer you see your target, yeah."

"Your call." She stubbed out the cigarette.

I tried to block thoughts of the steel sliding into flesh but failed. My body temperature rose with a rush of adrenaline and turned my hands clammy. She impaled my buttock as expertly as promised, but the pain began to spread almost immediately.

"Hey," she said, slowly pushing the plunger on the huge dose. "It's a fair turnaround. It's not like you haven't seen me . . . compromised. It *was* you on the parapet that night, wasn't it?"

"Is this some new interrogation technique?"

"You might have turned away."

"You might have stopped."

"That was unlikely at that particular moment," she said. "Besides, I kind of liked being watched. I'm afraid I'm long past being shy."

"Ahhh."

"First one done." She withdrew the hypodermic. "You okay?"

"No. What do you mean *first?*" I exclaimed. "Two?"

"Double-header. You had close exposure. You get two."

"Hey, it wasn't like Doc Wright and I were dating," I argued. "Haven't even shared a meal with the guy."

The second shot jabbed my other cheek unannounced and I groaned.

"You jungle warriors are such wimps." The plunger took forever and the serum was growing larger in my backside. "Done." She swabbed the site. "Cute ass, Captain. Aha, what's this? Nice stitching job. Not much scarring."

"Doc!"

"Okay, okay. I was just admiring the handiwork. Glad they missed your . . . vitals."

She paused, and then said, "I did want to thank you."

"For what?"

"For not saying anything. For being discreet. I worry for the colonel if it gets around. He's married. Loves his wife. Loves his Army. I'm just . . . here."

"Thanks." I pulled up my fatigue pants and wobbled away, aware for the first time that an audience of curious Montagnard patients and their visitors crowded in the doorway, probably discussing the strangeness of my body hair and whatever else they'd seen.

I didn't care. Roberta had installed doorknobs in my hindquarters and had eyes only for the colonel.

She reminded her Bahnar nurses to make up some permanganate solution and have the staff wash their hands with it immediately. The young patient they'd been handling was suffering from bacillary dysentery. Her attention swung back to me.

"Rider," she said, filling in my shot card. "Can you spare half an hour? There's a problem at a village and I need some backup."

She handed me a hemorrhoid cushion and pointed me toward her Land Rover. I got in gingerly and tried to find a comfortable position on the doughnut, but it only felt like somebody was twisting the new doorknobs in my ass. Roberta came over and got in, flashed me a sympathetic glance, and pulled away, trying to keep the vehicle from bouncing.

"Tell me about the wound," she said.

"Professional curiosity?"

"I wouldn't have said anything if it was just a dimple."

"Got wounded two months into my second tour."

"They ship you home to recover?"

"No such luck. I rehabbed at the field hospital in Pleiku. There were a bunch of us shot — ah — similarly injured and recovering on our stomachs. A friend of mine brought me my Purple Heart. Read out the citation and pinned it to the seat of my pajamas."

"Did it scare you, getting wounded?"

"Yeah. But afterward it was like being initiated. I'd made the fraternity."

"How long were you laid up?"

"About four weeks. Never felt more like a soldier."

"You make it sound almost enjoyable."

"Getting hit wasn't, but the hospital stay was a lark."

"What do you mean?"

"On either side of me were a private and a sergeant. One steamy evening the Sarge and I stole half a gallon of ice cream from the hospital mess. A nurse let us hide it in a refrigerated medicine cabinet for a share and got us spoons. We waited for lights-out. Instead, sirens went off and they blacked out the hospital. The staff rushed everyone to the bunkers. Except the Sarge and me. I retrieved the container and we slipped under his bed. While a mortar barrage rained down somewhere close, we were in hysterics, joking. Then, in the dark, I felt this odd wet warmth creeping along my body."

"Snake?"

"No. We were feasting on this beautiful cold ice cream, lying in a warm puddle of his blood."

"He had popped his stitches."

"Yeah. I thought, Wow. We're really here."

The Rover hit a pothole and bounced.

"Christ," I moaned.

"Sorry."

"We shouldn't go anywhere too remote," I said. "I'm in no shape to run."

"It's about a kilometer and a half. Right off Road Two."

Yeah, right. She had no idea how far out we were. She was just making it up, little realizing the odds were excellent that I would have gone to hell and back if she had asked me to.

"Okay," I said. "So what's happening there?"

"Fuck, it's just so discouraging. ARVN keep uprooting Montagnards from their villages in the mountains and shoving them into government hamlets close to the main roads and the district seats. 'For their protection,' Chinh says. The Vietnamese are screwing the Yards out of their land, forcibly relocating them and pretending it's for their own good. The tribespeople hate it and sneak away first chance they get."

"You think they'll go off the reservation again and revolt?" I said.

"I wouldn't blame them if they did, but I don't think they'll ever overcome their tribal feuds and wars. The clans hate each other as much as they hate Vietnamese." She looked over. "The Jarai really botched the uprising last December." Roberta braced against the dash. "We're here."

The old Jarai village was flanked by fruit trees and surrounded by small steep hills covered with brush and grasses twice the height of a man. Outside the village fence, the whole community — men, women, grandparents, and little kids — were stacking long, freshly cut bamboo logs. Tough as they were, the Montagnards looked worn and badly bruised by the hard labor.

Half a dozen Vietnamese soldiers lounged in the shade of the fruit trees, helping themselves to bananas they'd cut down and drinking from coconuts they'd appropriated and gouged open. Fifty yards off lay a water buffalo, hobbled by bullet wounds. They'd been amusing themselves taking target practice on the animal, shooting out one leg at a time. Embracing the suffering creature, its six-year-old herdsman wailed over his beloved beast. Roberta was seething. She got out and confronted their sergeant, went off on him in Vietnamese, the vessels in her neck and forehead pulsing as she waved her arms at the injured animal and the large cache of wood: six stacks of long bamboo logs piled chest high in alternating, perpendicular layers. The sergeant smiled benignly, as if everything were swell.

"Shit," she exclaimed, turning away from the impassive clutch of Vietnamese to talk to the old chief and his deputies standing nearby.

"What's going on?" I said.

"The whole village is being disciplined. They have to harvest bamboo."

"What are they being punished for?" I said.

"Their old chief had the temerity to complain to Chinh about their measly rice rations." She stood with hands on hips.

"Where's all this bamboo going?"

"The province warehouse. It'll get sold in a few days or weeks, and the money — lots of it — will go into the province chief's pockets. The village will never see a dime. The bastard's taking a page from the French planters' book. Forced labor. Corvée."

The Vietnamese soldiers continued to peel bananas and chat languidly. Roberta stomped over to the pile of their stuff and pulled a live trussed chicken from an empty sandbag. She untied the bindings and freed the flapping bird the troops had obviously confiscated. The soldiers looked resentful but did nothing to stop her. Roberta continued her rampage through their rucks, yanking out tobacco leaves, yams, marijuana plants, spilling coffee beans all over the ground.

The Montagnards watched their doctor storm. I was glad I had my rifle, in case the ARVN stopped grinning like fools and decided to give us the water-buffalo treatment.

She returned to my side, cheeks pink, breathing hard.

"I know their military doesn't do right by them, but they've got to stop pillaging the Yards at every opportunity."

"I think you've made your point. Are the Yards done with their — their punishment?"

She called out to the dozen Jarai standing silently by the cut bamboo. A toothless old woman answered.

"She says the villagers can do no more today. They're exhausted."

"Right. All done," I said to the sergeant and made a point of waving the soldiers away with my left hand — a huge insult. "*Di di.* Go. Go." The gesture wasn't lost on the Yards. Or the sergeant, whose face went slack. They slowly gathered up their rucksacks and sauntered off toward town.

The chief borrowed my pistol and went over to the wounded water buffalo to console the boy and dispatch the stricken animal. Roberta got out her medical bag and set up a quick sick call, treating the deep cuts and welts inflicted by their harsh labors, while I carted two sacks of rice from her Rover and presented it to the village chief. More patients appeared as word of her presence spread. She had me record their names and illnesses on cards and note the medications she handed out and the dosages. Malaria, dengue fever, vitamin and iodine deficiencies, intestinal parasites, toothache, skin infection . . .

"Most of them suffer from the same half a dozen illnesses," she said.

"A reasonably adequate nurse could handle most of this. I've got to get more of them trained."

After an hour of her impromptu clinic, the line had barely decreased. Montagnards kept appearing to replenish it.

"Appreciate your help, Captain Rider. You'll tell your colonel about this crap of punishing the village, won't you? See if he'll raise some hell with the province chief."

I said I would, though I didn't think for an instant it would do much good. Neither did she.

"You got somebody back in the world?" she said.

"Not since my ex dumped me."

She flashed me her best smile. "You should put some work into that situation."

"Don't smile like that," I said.

"Why not?"

"Makes my head swim."

She looked pleased.

"Everything in the army is hard and coarse," I said. "After a while, what you miss most is a woman's softness. It's like an ache."

"And you don't think women find this place hard-edged or have longings?"

I brushed back sweat and handed her the tube of ointment she pointed to. "You should drop by the compound some evening when we've gotten in all the reels of the same movie. I'll drive you back afterward."

"Thanks. I could use some American company. But if you're asking me on a date, that might be inadvisable."

An old man stepped forward to present an elbow with a festering sore.

"So it's not just a wartime fling?"

"I was hoping it was." She winced. "I outsmarted myself."

"How so?"

"I fell in love."

Roberta drained the sore and wiped it with antiseptic, and swabbed again with a dark salve before applying a dressing.

"Not exactly the guy I expected to fall for," she said. "I mean, he's a professional soldier in the business of inflicting harm. Here I am, repairing the sick and damaged." She laughed. "We're kind of a ridiculous pair."

"How do you explain it then?"

"He's just the kindest, smartest, most sincere man I've ever known. The Montagnards think he's favored by the gods."

"Does he know how you feel? How much you care for him?"

"Not from my lips, but maybe. Probably." She thought a moment. "It would be hard to miss."

"What are you going to do?"

"Suffer. Eventually I'll suffer more. For now, I cherish every minute we can steal from this damn war."

"You don't mince words," I said.

A mischievous grin crept onto her face. "Life's too fucking short, an insolent young officer informed me recently."

I grimaced. "Yeah. Captain Badass."

She finished wrapping the wound and tied off the white bandage. "You remember when you asked if I'd like to be a Montagnard?"

"You said no but wouldn't say why."

"Because I'd have to stand in the river with my lover and eat shit off a stick, that's why. That's their punishment for adultery. It's sort of smart, if you think about it."

"There are worse things than guilt, Doc."

"Yeah? What beats it?"

"Regret."

She took me in with a sidelong glance. "I'm not sure I want to know how you came by that piece of insight." She turned to the next patient. "I appreciate your not judging me."

A bullet buzzed by, the report echoing through the hills a fraction of a second later.

"What the hell?" she blurted out, her head swiveling as the line of patients scattered. I pulled her behind the Land Rover. "What was that?" She started to stick her nose up over the door.

"Keep down. Listen to me. He's a ways off. He'll need time to sight between shots. We have to move after the next one."

"Oh my God. We're being shot at."

"Yes, and we need to move."

"Can't we stay here, behind the Rover, where we're safe?"

"Only works in the movies, Doc. He's using an assault rifle, a Kalashnikov. It'll bang right through."

I pulled her behind the engine. She cried out as a round punched straight through both front-seat doors, leaving a gaping hole. Trying to be clever, I peered into it, lining up both punctures to see where the shot might have come from. All I could make out was a tangle of scrub. No landmarks. Still, it gave me the hillside he was on. Roberta shrieked again as I popped up to spray a burst at the slope: eighteen rounds in a blink.

Nobody hearing intermittent gunshots would pay attention. Maybe more sustained fire might be noticed, an alarm raised. I was about to do it again when a third shot struck the ground near my feet.

I fired off another magazine fast and said, "Move!" Grabbed her by the elbow and hauled her across open space into the banana leaves. When all lines of sight were blocked, we moved laterally. I pushed her into a crouch. We inched forward.

"VC?" she said, gasping, as she wrestled with the idea of an indifferent stranger intending her harm. A shot hit the fronds where we'd entered the foliage. I pulled her farther back.

"Yeah, VC or our southern allies expressing their feelings about being humiliated earlier." Sweat dripped from my chin. "Vietnamese either way. Though probably not NVA."

"What makes you say that?"

"They're better shots."

"God, Rider. Anything can happen to anybody in this place and who would know."

I pulled her deeper into the leaves and had her squat next to me again. We waited. The afternoon was hot and peaceful. Everything normal, except somebody was out there looking to kill us. My inoculated backside felt like it'd been shot again. Luckily the locals weren't great riflemen. Ammunition was scarce. The VC didn't expend much of it practicing. Neither did the South Vietnamese, who got plenty of ammo from us but were lackadaisical about training.

I peered through the large leaves, praying there weren't enough gunmen out there to maneuver around our side. Nothing. Minutes passed. No more shots. The guy was gone, or very patient.

"A lone sniper, most likely."

"You sure?" she said.

"I'd bet my life on it," I quipped.

"Don't kid."

"They would have tried to flank us by now if there were more of them. It's just the one guy."

A hot and empty day in the tropics: a hundred and twenty in the shade. We shared my canteen. I was dying for a cigarette but thought better of risking the smoke giving us away. A large spider ambled down the trunk of the banana tree behind her.

"You ever married?" I said.

"No. Never had the time to think about it when I was studying and one day it was too late."

She tried to peer out around the broad leaves but I shook my head no.

She said, "You know the colonel well?"

"Not very. Company-grade officers aren't exactly chummy with field-grade officers."

"So you wouldn't know why he's disappointed with his career?"

"I don't know that he is." Did she really think captains did career counseling for colonels?

"Trust me," she said. "He doubts he's going to make full colonel. He says two MACV assignments and no troop command means his career is permanently stalled."

"That could be. But so what?"

"He says he never got the combat command he'd been promised. The one he's been dreaming of since he was a cadet. He captained a company in Korea, but he doesn't think he'll ever get a battalion here."

"I'm sure he'd do okay commanding troops again, but there are a couple of thousand amped-up lieutenant colonels hot to strut their stuff, desperate for a battalion command. Personally, I don't know why anybody would want responsibility for a bunch of heavily armed teenagers, having to harass them to produce higher counts of enemy dead and worry about them crapping themselves to death from dysentery in jungles buzzing with flies and bullets. I mean, he could switch to intelligence or logistics and do great. You wouldn't really want to see him go off to a combat unit, would you?"

Her head tipped back against an elephant-ear frond. "He says he won't shovel paper in the Pentagon. Says if he can't have the infantry, he's going back to teaching at West Point or the War College. If he accepts a permanent teaching position, he says he'll never make higher rank but at least won't lose his commission when this conflict winds down and the government cuts back. He just won't ever make general."

"That's true," I said, "he won't see another promotion if he commits to teaching. So what? You ready to be a faculty wife at West Point?"

"I told you. He's already got a wife. He just saw her not a month ago. All I can do is hope this war never ends."

"I know people who'll give you odds it might not."

"I must sound crazy," she said.

"Not really. A lot of old hands don't want to think about it ever being over. Or how it might end."

"Badly," she said. "How else?"

"Don't you think we're going to pull it off?"

She pinned me with a look. "Do you? From what you've seen so far? This could be the Hundred Years' War if we play our cards right."

"Look at the bright side. Eighty years to go."

She wasn't amused.

"Listen up, Doc. I'm going to jump in your Land Rover, crank it, screech over here, collect you as I roll by, and hightail it. I'm not going to stop. You'll have to hop in as I go. You with me?"

"Roger, dodger."

"If I don't get there — "

"Don't say that."

"We gotta be real. If I don't make it, don't think. Go." I pointed my rifle barrel. "Head for the thickest growth and go to ground. Hide. Wait for someone to come find you. Don't show yourself. Stay put."

I didn't give her time to object. I crept back to the British Rover, opened the passenger's door on the left side, and crawled in. I hit the ignition. Half in the cab, I used my hands to depress the clutch and shift into first, and let out the clutch. The high idle rolled the vehicle forward. I sat up in the driver's seat and called her. She rushed out of the fronds and into the passenger seat. In seconds we were on the road, the hemorrhoid cushion around my neck, Roberta whooping as we drove like hell for Cheo Reo, light as angels.

# 10

★ ★ ★

WHAT A ROACH coach," Miser said as we sat down on the long wooden bench at the counter of an open-air food stand just off the marketplace in town. Miser passed me a curt teletype message from our boss: *Another Hong Kong deposit 100K.*

"Any ideas?" Miser said.

"I need to get a look at that poppy field the Aussie flier pointed out."

"Your hard work makes me hungry," he said, raising his chin toward the cook.

The stand was skanky wood with a corrugated roof, sided with metal sheeting covered with row after row of identical beer logos. We ordered *pho* for ourselves and for Checkman and Rowdy, who had tagged along and were cruising a small pile of black-market items. A man lay back in an empty handcart, hat held to his face, while a friend picked lice from his hair. Miser remembered something and giggled.

"What's funny?" I said.

"The first sergeant just heard this from Pleiku. General Vinh Loc, head of Two Corps, is gonna hold a fucking Heroes' Day up there to honor an outstanding American officer and an enlisted man for their courage in battle."

"You sending out your uniform to be starched?"

"The officer they're gonna honor is that prince who called in artillery on his own damn position." Miser sniggered. "Think he'll show for the do?"

The proprietor produced a loaf of hot French bread. Miser tore off the end and passed the baguette to me. Checkman and Rowdy stared at Miser flicking worms from his piece and declined the great-smelling bread.

"Thanks for comin' out," Miser said. "I couldn't face another mess-hall meal."

"Yeah." Rowdy nodded. "Another morning of fuckin' shit-on-a-shingle and foreskins-on-toast."

The proprietor put out our bowls. The *pho* had cooked for hours: a boiling soup of oxtails and beef bones, anise, onion, cilantro, hot chili pepper, lime, black pepper, cinnamon, and scallions that he ladled over flat noodles.

"Lay it on me," Rowdy exclaimed, rubbing his chopsticks together.

"Fuck," said Miser. "We could be in Saigon, drinking artichoke tea, chowing down on geckos pan-fried in batter cooked to perfection." He sampled his soup. "Armadillo, duck eggs, watermelon with guava, durian . . . Instead we're ordering boiled-bone soup and noodles out in the sticks."

I held the tin spoon at my lips, enjoying the aroma.

Even more pungent, twenty feet away a barrel stood open, waiting to be sealed. In it symmetrical layers of silvery fish alternated with layers of salt. After the fish rotted and liquefied, it would be nuoc mam. A bottle of it stood on the table. The flavor wasn't bad once you got past the idea of it.

"Nuoc mam." Miser curled his nose at the dark liquid as he dumped it in. "God, the stuff smells like my ancient aunt."

"Essence of armpit," Rowdy said, making a face and waving off the offer of it.

"At least it's not durian fruit," I said.

"Thank God," Rowdy exclaimed. "Durian smells like my *dead* aunt Mae."

Miser scowled. "It's a fuckin' acquired taste, you peasants."

The same way he'd grudgingly come to appreciate durian, I realized,

Miser had developed a thing for Viet Nam, loath though he was to admit it. He was tight with lots of Asian old boys from Kontum down to Cholon. It occurred to me he wouldn't ever leave Indochina of his own volition.

Rowdy and Checkman started arguing about which meat tasted more rubbery, elephant or dog. In all probability neither of them had ever tasted elephant, but that didn't mean they couldn't argue. In the middle of it, Checkman spotted his favorite whore carrying her shopping basket and ran over to flirt, which clearly made her nervous. The public attention was bad for business. There weren't enough of us in Cheo Reo to keep her solvent without Vietnamese clients, who were easily bent out of shape by Americans bedding their women. Fraternizing with American soldiers was frowned upon; sleeping with them, even worse. Word would get around fast and it could be a while before any local fancied her.

"*An com*," she said, pushing back her big head of hair and hurrying on.

Rowdy took her in from the back. "What a choice mama. What'd she say?"

"She said to eat my rice."

Checkman's ability to speak the language certainly gave the boy an advantage with the ladies, though he seemed oblivious to the Vietnamese resentment of us American mongrels consorting with their women, or his woman's concern about associating openly with him.

Miser grunted and bent to his work, wolfing down his food.

I reached for my wallet to pay.

"Don't bother, Captain."

"What?"

"I'm part owner of this emporium."

"No kidding?"

"I'm workin' on a steam-and-cream also," he said, drinking the last of his bowl. "But my partners are getting a lot of pressure for me to kick back to the civil authorities — in appreciation for their letting me operate in this thriving metropolis."

"What are you gonna do?"

"Me? I told 'em I'm not paying sixty bucks a year to any grafting slope fucks."

"So you're finding the area more attractive than you thought."

"Yeah. It's virgin territory. A frontier, really. Wide open. It's gonna grow like crazy when the shooting stops."

"If this fighting ever ends, maybe the Yards can figure out a way to benefit too."

"Never happen," Miser said. "They'll get screwed no matter who wins. The lowlands are overpopulated as hell. The Central Highlands, they're practically empty. The Vietnamese will go home after the war's over and start makin' babies. They've already got their backs to the sea. They got no choice but to push into the mountains. They'll log the timber, burn jungle, grab up land. It's beautiful country. Their only problem is the Yards, and they're afraid of 'em. Whatever they do with the tribes, it ain't gonna be pretty."

"Why don't you drive the boys back?" I said. "I'll walk."

"You sure?" Miser bit into the plastic tip of a Hav-a-Tampa and lit up.

"I'm sure." I nodded.

Miser scowled and headed for the jeep. Checkman and Rowdy finished their bowls and bounded after him. They vaulted into the back, and Miser rolled out.

"Captain."

I looked up to find Dr. Roberta standing over me. She was wearing slacks and a wrinkled khaki shirt, looking disheveled and disarming.

"Doc."

Nearby, on a raised platform overhung with canvas, an old woman squatted beside a perfect cone of rice she was selling. Her young granddaughter stared openly at Roberta's exotic Western features.

"Would you like some breakfast?" I motioned to the place on the bench next to me.

"Thanks, no. But I wouldn't turn down some coffee."

I ordered *deux café sua,* two filtered coffees sweetened with condensed milk. She slid down beside me and took out a mentholated cigarette.

"How are you?" she said, lighting up, enjoying the luxury of the day's first drag. "You still look a little feverish," she said, exhaling.

"Just tired. Could use some caffeine."

The coffee arrived, smelling of chicory.

I said, "Any word on the new mom at Mai Linh?"

Roberta perked up. "Ed Sprague says she's doing well. The baby too. Eating like a little water buffalo."

We finished our coffees and she accompanied me back toward the MACV compound. Roberta walked with arms crossed. As we passed through the small market square, I noticed Colonel Chinh having a morning coffee with Whalen Lund in the corner café.

"No doubt they're discussing some new strain of rice that will grow like gangbusters in the hills," she said.

"Or the net for their tennis court."

Roberta looked at me, amused. "You are an iconoclast."

Near the South Vietnamese garrison, she pointed to a large metal shed with galvanized siding and a corrugated roof.

"That's Colonel Chinh's magic warehouse. The rice harvest of the entire province is hauled into town twice a year and stockpiled under that roof, allegedly to deny the enemy food supplies."

"What's magic about it?" I said.

"The way the rice disappears. Goes right out the back, onto the local market. Meanwhile, very little comes out the front door, and the Montagnard villages in the province go hungry. Makes me livid."

"What about donated rice?" I said. "The stuff Lund and his pals bring in?"

"All sold too. The flag and handclasp symbol right on the bags."

A group of young Vietnamese men and women in conical hats had just finished clearing brush and ground wood from the bare field adjacent to the MACV compound. They started drifting back toward town along the worn path that ran diagonally across the field. They came toward us at an angle as we walked up the road, away from them and toward the gate. Roberta looked hard at them.

"Something wrong?" I said.

"Who are they?"

I shaded my eyes. "Just kids the first sergeant hired for some day labor, cleaning up that empty area so the guards' sightlines aren't impeded. Why?"

She studied the retreating figures. "Have you seen any of the older ones before?"

"No. They look like local youths."

"The girls, they're northerners."

"How do you know?" I said.

"Young Vietnamese women all wear their hair long. North Vietnamese cut theirs straight across. See? All their hair, right across."

"Catholic refugees probably," I said. They were nearing the edge of town, strolling casually. I stared too, trying to catch the outline of a weapon.

"What's the matter?"

I said, "Vietnamese men don't collect ground wood unless they're charcoal makers. They think it's beneath them."

"You might mention this to someone," she said.

Back at the compound, I went to the office to tell the colonel.

"Northern visitors?" he said. "Casing us?"

"Seemed that way."

He leaned to the side and called past me: "Private Checkman."

Checkman's flaming hair and face appeared in the doorway. "Sir?"

"Have Sergeant Durando put an extra American guard on the perimeter during daylight and . . . four on at night. One on each wall. Ask First Sergeant Mote to have the fifty-caliber on the northwest corner checked."

"Will do, sir." The redhead vanished.

"Anything for us in the EEIs and intel from Saigon?"

"Nothing good, sir."

"You should know," Bennett said, "the Army engineers working on the airstrip reported a dozen VC at the far end of the runway this morning. They hung around for half an hour, just observing, turned away, and left."

"I don't suppose our southern allies challenged this squad in any way."

Bennett shook his head. "Acted as if they weren't there."

· · ·

The humidity rivaled the temperature. I sent Jessup a brief encrypted message that I might have a lead to pursue and proceeded to plow through a stack of intel paperwork until Joe Parks interrupted.

"Got a hot intel item for you, Captain. Some Yards are saying the VC have Montagnard villagers trapping gophers for them."

"For food?" I said, making a face.

"Excavation. The NVA set them loose in their tunnels to dig air shafts to the surface."

He tapped out his pipe bowl into a shiny can of sand. "Let's you and me go over to the ARVN compound and see if we can shake any useful intel loose from your esteemed counterpart."

I readily agreed, not having met the man yet, and we drove over.

Captain Nhu grinned when he was happy and grinned when he was embarrassed, and he was one or the other most of the time. Nhu was hoping to run his family's pharmacy business after the war and already had his degree. His father was a civil servant. His mother ran the family enterprises: two pharmacies in Saigon, a rice-trading company in Hue. A younger brother was an ophthalmologist in Paris. Everyone in the family spoke French and English and some Chinese.

Joe Parks and I looked over the intelligence Captain Nhu handed us. Calling it *thin* would have been too kind. *Negligible* was more like it. However the captain was occupying his time, it wasn't in the pursuit of information on the enemy. No surprise. Intelligence was hard to come by if you never left your barracks, never put out a real patrol. Without the Green Berets leading patrols out of their camps daily and our own infrequent forays, we'd be completely in the dark about the thousands of NVA infiltrators backed up in the province.

We excused ourselves at the first opportunity and regrouped on the wooden steps of the sector headquarters building.

"God," I said, "we're not getting much from him, are we?"

Joe propped his Army-issue baseball hat on his bald pate and simply said, "Nope," and repacked his pipe with fresh tobacco.

"And you're not giving him much either."

"Nope."

"So he couldn't be compromising us by sharing with third parties?"

"Is Captain Nhu feeding our intel to the enemy? No. Don't see how he could. The really sensitive items go to Chinh marked 'eyes only.'"

Good to know, I thought, since Captain Nhu was the South Vietnamese in tailored fatigues I'd seen in the jungle-market meeting. I found Ruchevsky in our room and broke the news to him.

"You're sure?"

"I'm sure."

"Shit. Is he freelancing, or is he just Chinh's bagman?"

"If he was that enterprising, I think his mama would've bought him a higher rank. I'd say he's an underling carrying the can for Chinh. Maybe fetching Wolf Man's shopping list for Mrs. Chinh."

"No wonder we get no useful intel from across the street about the NVA gathering in the mountains. Why rat out your best customers?" Ruchevsky rubbed his brow and sighed. "Well, you've certainly given me something to obsess about. Let me return the favor. I've set you up to fly the backseat on a recon with our best Bird Dog pilot. See if you can get some better intel on your assignment from the air. If anyone can find your pastures of plenty, it's Major Hopp. And count NVA noses for me while you're up there."

I went by the signal shack to check in with Miser and let him know I was headed out on an aerial reconnaissance, following up on the Aussie's lead.

"Glad to hear it," he said. "Looking at your reports going out and the intel coming in, it don't look promising for long-term investment in Cheo Reo. The sooner we can get our asses out of here, the better. The scuttlebutt ain't good."

I noticed the fresh sandbags outside. And the tear-gas canisters and masks everywhere. Ammunition boxes, grenades . . .

"Sergeant Miser, you starting an armory?"

"No, sir. New procedures."

"Really?"

"There's a bad vibe. Trouble coming. We're getting ready."

He was completely serious, I realized, and it sobered me. He held up a gas mask like a stewardess demonstrating an oxygen mask.

"If we get fucking overrun, we pull our rubber cunts over our snouts, smoke the place with all these CS grenades, just saturate the area with tear gas, grab a Prick-Twenty-five for communication, and haul ass."

"Where to?"

"Some fucking rendezvous point we're supposed to find in the pitch-black night and wait there to get extracted by helicopter. There's an escape-and-evasion plan up in the colonel's office. I got it from Checkman. The usual circle jerk. You know, step one: sneak through the goddamn human-wave attack and un-ass the area. Step two: wade through the motherfucking gooks and jog out. Like that's gonna happen."

I noticed a wooden box in a corner with half a dozen Mason jars. Each held a grenade floating in a pinkish liquid.

"What 'n the hell?" I exclaimed. "Av gas?"

"Three parts aviation gas, one part motor oil, a dash of badass battery fluid."

"This your grandma's recipe for Molotov cocktails?" I picked up a jar and examined the metal egg seated in it.

"Fits perfect. They work good," Miser insisted.

"The pin's missing on this grenade."

"Right. All of 'em are set to go. You throw the jar. The glass breaks, splashes the juice, and pops the arming spoon. *Ka-boom* and *whoosh*. Should scare the gooks good if we fry a few. Pretty good, huh?"

I replaced the glass jar very carefully. "Just don't — "

"Break 'em? *No, sir,*" snapped Miser.

"Fucking-A, Sarge. Carry on."

An Army major buttonholed me in the mess hall half an hour later as I was trying to jump-start my overheated brain with boiled coffee. He sported a gray crewcut, aviator sunglasses, a chaw of bubblegum, and a small pistol buried in a shoulder holster that might have been his granddaddy's in the Great War.

"Cap'n?" he drawled, inflecting up into a question. "Name's Hopp? Big John asked me to take you up for an overview? Says you want to see our visitors from the north, and something about fields?"

Major Hopp of Gloversville, Oklahoma, was neatly groomed and compact in his comfortably baggy flight suit. He came by his flyboy look honestly. This was his second shooting war. He was all business and experience, with a generous dash of country yahoo. And blew the biggest pink chewing-gum bubble I'd ever seen.

"Pleasure, sir," I said. "You're a Bird Dog pilot, I take it."

"One of two." He popped his gum — it sounded like a gunshot — and parked it on his spoon to sip his java. "Yep. I fly the friendly skies for Colonel Bennett."

"When is this sky cruise of ours scheduled for?"

"We could go right now, if y'all are of a mind and done with your joe?"

I took a last gulp and was good to go. Hopp pulled out photo reconnaissance black-and-whites.

"An RF-One-oh-one Voodoo took these. And these" — more came out of his bag — "OV-One Mohawk overflight shots."

He spread them in front of me and pointed out the movement detected at night using SLAR — side-looking airborne radar. And heat-sensitive photographs of emissions from cooking fires, bodies, and generators. I whistled, taking it all in. Miser had reason to be jumpy.

"Lots going on up in that neck of the woods." He tapped the last photo and traced the blobs of heat detected in the mountains. "That's where we're headed first."

"How about here second?" I said, and opened my map with the Aussie's red X.

Hopp squinted at my grid map and nodded. "Can do. Let's roll."

We stopped by my quarters to pick up my web gear and rifle, along with my compass and .45 pistol. Major Hopp's mechanic drove us out to the airfield at speed, raising an impressive plume of ocher dust. At the end of the long, straight stretch of open road, we passed the raised barrier pole and the Vietnamese guard shack, complete with comatose guard. Hopp popped a huge bubble at him but he never stirred. We were the only people at the strip.

Hopp's plane was the standard civilian-variety two-seater O-1 Cessna, with rigid landing gear and a lone propeller on its snout. The pilot's seat was in front, mine directly behind. There was a clear canopy over us and a windshield in front, but you could toss grenades or beer bottles out the open sides without impediment. It was sort of airy.

This Bird Dog had seen better days. Oil streaked the engine cowling, and the cockpit was skuzzy — worn and stained. Swatches of duct tape adorned the fuselage. I peeled one back and instantly regretted it. A bullet hole.

"Great."

"Say again?"

"Nothing."

The mechanic appeared. "Put on the helmet, Cap'n. It's miked."

I tucked my boonie hat in a pocket, donned sunglasses, and put on the helmet the mechanic handed me. It was as heavy as a biker's.

"Grinch Niner," I heard Hopp say over the intercom, "this is Ptero-dactyl Five Zulu."

The commo bunker acknowledged and he sped through his pre-flight checks as the engine revved. Wasn't much to check off. His air-ship was pretty much a kite with a propeller.

"You ready?" Hopp said.

"Just trying to find the ejection-seat button."

Hopp chuckled. "You can't punch out of this buggy. No armor and no emergency flashers either."

"Amen."

"You know how to use this?" he said, holding up a 35-millimeter camera. When I said yes, he handed it back. "Excellent. You'll earn your keep then, Cap."

Hopp taxied off the concrete apron onto the metal planks of the airfield, turned, and gunned the engine. Everything around me shook and clacked as we bucketed down the metal planking and lifted into the air.

We climbed to two thousand feet and churned slowly north over meandering streams and fields of crops. Almost nothing with wheels moved along the tracks and roads, only a forlorn bus with half a vil-lage tied to its roof, trailed by a single flatbed truck hauling freshly cut logs. Montagnard villages nestled in the valleys. Trails threaded up onto the slopes and along the ridges. Leaving the Cheo Reo basin, we sailed above the mountains. The peaks grew steadily taller. Soon we were in among them. Hopp took us down to treetop level and we sped at full throttle through interconnecting valleys, over dense foli-age, most of it triple canopy with no real breaks except over wider rivers and several breathtaking waterfalls. The occasional interruption in the mass of green revealed colossal trees over a hundred and fifty feet tall.

"Regulations say I'm to stay out of range of ground fire, fly no lower than fifteen hundred feet. Same as the lowest altitude for an infantry commander's chopper. They zoom around at ninety-five miles an hour at least two thousand feet up. Too fast and too high to see good. Bird Dog pilots prefer stayin' on the deck, flyin' low. Safer that way. Gives 'em less time to put their sights on you. And you see what's on the ground better."

And they you, I thought.

"We'll fly nap of the earth," he said, "and ease back to forty miles an hour."

"I take it you've got a good supply of duct tape."

"Not to worry," Hopp said, and popped his bubblegum. "Ain't a problem usually."

"You're not going to turn me upside down or anything?"

"Not unless you insist. And it'll cost you extra."

As we got farther into the mountains, the growth thinned out, except around the many streams.

Hopp passed back his overlay map. He had marked out the north quadrants where Phu Bon came together with two neighboring provinces.

"That's the area Big John wants us to check."

"What did you fly in Korea?"

"Jets. Fighters. Now I drive this crate around Nam six hours a day searchin' for the little people."

"Any luck?"

"They stay spread and hidden. But I've got a rough idea where they're hangin' out."

We roller-coastered along for another five minutes through tight valleys, some not much more than ravines, and dipped into a wide gorge. Our destination. Hopp pulled up and banked us into a big circle. I saw nothing but green. In the thinner scrub on the ridges and where there were openings in a tree line, I spotted a few huts. A woven bamboo platform sat at the end of a crude field, with tall grass parted along paths running through it.

"I'm taking us lower. Don't get nervous. Odds are they're not gonna shoot."

With that, Major Hopp descended and slowed our speed to a crawl.

We banked and orbited in a tight circle. Below us, men in olive shorts were out in the open, playing volleyball. NVA, without a doubt. They paused, hands sheltering their eyes, showing no sign of being wary. A couple of them waved.

"You see? They're being gentlemen." Hopp dipped his wings in salute.

"Incredible."

"Yep, friendly Charlies. They'll even come up on my frequency for an exchange of views."

"They know your freqs?"

"They know my freqs, they know my call signs. We're practically on a first-name basis. Never mind I tried to kill 'em the other day. They don't seem to be holding it against me."

"Major, how is it that they have your freqs?"

"Wish I knew. They're always listening in, intercepting. A chopper or a Bird Dog instructs a ground unit to mark its position with purple smoke, and purple smoke grenades go off in four different places."

"Major, you've been all over Phu Bon Province."

"Yep."

"Ever come across any huge fields of opium poppies? Or marijuana? I mean, a *big* cultivated field."

I hoped he could confirm the Aussie's story and that we weren't on a wild-goose chase.

"You're not talkin' about the tiny-ass patches of weed the Yards grow along with their tobacco."

"No. Really large fields."

"Large fields, well . . ." He seemed to confer with himself. "No poppy fields — but weed? Sure, yeah. About half a dozen in different spots around the province."

"Big ones?"

"Yeah, big. Hectares."

"Did you ever report them?"

"God, no. Marijuana fields are as common as volcano cones over here. My mission is to find enemy to kill, not chase dopers."

"Where's the biggest one you've seen? I mean, in the province?"

Hopp pulled a map out, unfolded it to the section he wanted, and handed it back.

"I'd say the one in Phu Thien District. They burned off the north slope of a whole mountain there last year."

"A cultivated farm?"

"Farm? Hell. More like a plantation. First time I flew over it I thought it must be tea. One day they were burnin' some and I flew through the smoke. Marijuana, take my word. More grass than you've ever seen. That soil and climate gotta be ideal. Some ol' boy is growin' himself one huge crop of weed."

"Would it be convenient to fly over that area today?"

"Sure thing. It ain't far. Afterward we'll go look at that mountaintop that's got you all excited."

A tiny rectangle appeared and disappeared back into the foliage. "Whoa," I said. "That structure in the trees, on the left side? What's that?"

"A stage. For coed entertainment troupes. They come in to bolster morale. Mostly musicals. Skits. Dancing tractors. You know, patriotic shit?"

I could make out trench lines and bunkers at the edge of the trees, and shelters. Faint smoke rose through the canopy.

"Their cooking fires are belowground," Hopp said. "It's their invention: horizontal chimney shafts in the ground that dissipate most of the smoke. If we're seeing this much, there must be a *lotta* cookin' goin' on down there."

Hopp straightened the Bird Dog for a minute and tipped us into another shallow turn. A break in the green revealed a waterfall with a pool filled with swimmers. I glimpsed a bunker on a knoll, radio antennas barely camouflaged.

"Three antennas," I announced. I tried to mark my map but got too lightheaded.

"We're eyeballing only a fraction of what's down there. This is as crowded as I've ever seen it in this sector. They're usually better hidden than this."

We corkscrewed still lower. "You'll see more at less altitude," Hopp said. The plane banked steeply. Hopp itemized what he somehow made out in the green mass: "Kitchen, sleeping platforms, storage maybe, trench lines . . ."

Observation from a low-flying, single-engine plane tipped on its wing must have been an acquired skill. I caught Hopp in profile, casually gazing out, inflating a pink bubble. All I saw when I looked down was broccoli rotating overhead. I had the sensation of falling *up* into a vortex. My eyes wouldn't alight on any one spot; they flitted ahead, fighting vertigo as we turned.

"Where exactly are we?"

"Circling Charlie's R-and-R center. Their rear area. A quarter of a mile beyond the border with Phu Bon Province. We tilt the other way and we're in Pleiku Province. The three provinces come together right here."

"You going to call in an air strike?"

Hopp chuckled and clicked his gum. "Nah. The Air Force keeps tryin' but they're wastin' their time. The Cong are too smart. Let me show you."

He leveled us out and we flew horizontally. On the port side, a huge naked swath appeared, torn out of the double-canopy jungle. The gash was about the width of Central Park, and twice as long. Godzilla had plowed through, vaporizing the jungle and tossing enormous trees aside like kindling.

I said, "Looks like the wrath of God down there. What kind of air-power did it take to do that?"

"Two B-Fifty-two cells, three bombers each." Hopp recited the deadly math. "Six aircraft, one hundred bombs apiece: seven-fifties and five-hundred-pounders. Carry 'em stacked in the bomb bay, on racks outside the fuselage."

"How many enemy casualties, d'you think?"

"None."

"None?"

"Zero. The NVA was encamped on our side of the province border. Big John Ruchevsky snuck close enough to see classrooms, a rifle range, bunkers, comrades copulating. Got all excited. Set up a strike. But — surprise — when the Air Force drops by, nobody's home. Helluva waste of ordnance."

"Ruchevsky scouted them by himself?"

"He did. Prefers it, he says. Says alone is safer."

"They've gotta be afraid of you calling in an air strike," I said, "after seeing damage like that."

"It's scary, sure, but they know the odds are in their favor. It's not precise, just massive. Six B-Fifty-twos will pulverize three square kilometers — three kilometer grids — in one raid. Which is why the NVA spreads way out, so as not to get the crap pounded out of too many of 'em if the bombers get lucky. Wait one."

Hopp raised his hand, listening to Cheo Reo issue an artillery warning. Then he resumed.

"B-Fifty-twos bomb by radar. If the super bombers connect, the target gets vaporized. But often as not they're blowing up empty jungle — killing lotsa ferns. Most of the time the Cong moves out of the way beforehand. They know when we've got an Arc Light laid on."

"Their intel's that good?"

"Better than ours. They get tipped off way in advance. On the day of the raid, they get a heads-up from Soviet trawlers offshore that clock the azimuth and air speed of our bombers coming in from the Philippines and Okinawa. VC eavesdrop on our broadcasts that warn friendly aircraft of an impending air bombardment and pass the warning along. On the ground, their observers clock my Air Force colleagues overfly a target in advance of the bombers, and they sound the alarm. But by that time more than likely everyone's already long gone from the target area."

"Why didn't we take any ground fire earlier?"

"They know from the markings that I'm Army recon, not an Air Force forward air controller. They know I don't direct air assets and I can't call on artillery bases that can reach here. But if they fire on us, we'd technically be engaged and might just qualify for immediate support without having to go through the usual million steps and channels. Which is why they treat me tenderly, except of course when they try to snare me out of the damn sky with vines strung across the tighter valleys. I'm starin' down, not lookin' where I'm flyin', and they try to net me like quail. They'll only take the odd potshot to discourage my snooping when there's something on the ground they don't want seen."

Hopp adjusted course. We flew south for some minutes and descended.

"Here it comes," he said. "That badass field I was telling you about."

Hopp pointed to long geometric shadows — structures — projected out from a tree line by the sun. At altitude, the field looked like green savanna, but Hopp brought us ever lower until we shot across it with our wheels brushing the tops. It went on forever. Acres and acres, circled by a narrow track. The whole side of the mountain. Montagnards worked among the plants, their upturned faces visible in the six-foot-tall growth looming over them. We'd found part of the VC's revenue source.

A few green tracers sped by without our hearing them, drowned out by the drone of our engine and the slipstream.

"I'll be damned," Hopp exclaimed. "Some fool's poppin' off at us."

Metal crinched, like a beer tab pulled open. We'd been hit. He dinked the ship, and my elbow banged against the fuselage.

"Gonna need more duct tape," he said. "That was close. Must be important for them to drive us off like that."

"I think it's what I've been looking for."

We dinked the other way and climbed, right up through a thousand feet. At two thousand, we leveled off.

Hopp half turned toward me, chewing laconically. "Looks like we're not gonna make it to your Big Rock Candy Mountain today. I think that lone gunman put a knock in my engine. You mind flyin' to the coast? It'll take about forty-five minutes. We haven't got much by way of parts back at the Cheo Reo aerodrome."

"No problem." I shoved my face into the air stream outside. I was drenched in sweat and adrenaline.

We flew east, out over the peaks, winging across foothills and another mountainous region that gave way to a narrow band of rice paddies, heavily dotted with hamlets full of huts and livestock and farmers in turtle-shell hats stooped over their work. We crossed that skinny stretch in no time and were out over the pale green sea. A heavily populated strip flowed along the coast toward a formidable military base and airfield. A stubby peninsula drooped around a piece of the South China Sea, forming an azure bay. Despite the enormous air traffic, we were down in minutes.

I was happy to deplane and leave my combat harness behind. Hopp explained his problem to a mechanic as they inspected the bullet hole and the engine. A spec-4 drove us in to the base. We passed mess halls, the Post Exchange, and a beach dotted with GIs in bathing suits lounging on pristine white sand.

The jeep climbed up to a flattened peak with a hospital on top, an Air Force building, and hootches professionally constructed by contractors. Hopp led the way into the officers' club. The air conditioning nailed me at the door. The perfectly appointed bar was like a meat locker. I shuddered. Armed Forces Radio was reporting that young American anarchists waving Viet Cong flags had charged a phalanx of police in San Francisco.

A sign said NO GUNS, so we checked ours with an Air Force sergeant and pushed on past a row of slot machines onto a wide terrace. A Hawaiian-style bar covered with bamboo and thatch stood at the far end, elephants' tusks holding up the corners. A pair of jet jockeys, perched on the tiger-skin stools, leaned across, flirting up the Vietnamese woman tending bar. A medallion above the bottles read BEVERLY HILLS HOME SECURITY — ARMED RESPONSE. We took an umbrella-shaded table and slumped into our patio chairs. The air was soft.

A stunning Vietnamese woman in a white blouse and pedal pushers appeared and took our order, then came back almost instantly to pour our beer, angling it into chilled glasses to form perfect heads.

"This was worth helpin' the Charlies out with their target practice," Hopp said, "don't ya think?"

"Didn't at the time." I took a long swig. "Do now."

The waitress returned with our hamburgers, slathered with onions and cheese. Hopp parked his gum under the table, anointed his burger with ketchup and relish, and took a giant bite. I slipped most of the onions off mine.

I said, "What does Big John think about nobody being home for his air raids?"

"Well, every planned strike has to be run past MACV in Saigon and the whiz boys in Washington, and by our allies in our province, and their headquarters at Two Corps in Pleiku. Pleiku runs it by the South Vietnamese tactical headquarters in Saigon too. Four or five clearances. All this mostly to make sure friendlies aren't in the area we want to bomb. Takes weeks. The enemy knows within the first eight hours what we're planning. Just when we finally get all the okays to lay on the strike, the NVA ups and moves a coupla hundred yards next door."

"Into the neighboring province?"

"You got it. And the whole clearance thing has to start all over again, this time going through channels in *that* province. Eventually the raid gets the green light, but the Charlies up and move out again the night before."

"They're playing our bureaucracy."

"And winning."

"Saigon leaks," I said. "Pleiku must too, and Cheo Reo. The VC have agents everywhere."

"Yup," Hopp said. "The South Vietnamese military government is more penetrated than the whores in Saigon. But Big John Ruchevsky thinks there's a particular leak sprung in Cheo Reo."

"How can he tell?"

Hopp licked ketchup from his thumb. "We simulated a priority air strike a while back. Put in for clearance only at the sector headquarters level in Cheo Reo. Kept it entirely local. Just before the bombs were supposed to drop, the NVA carouselled out of its bivouac."

"That still leaves a bunch of possible suspects," I said.

"Yeah," Hopp said. "I guess. Though all of 'em in Cheo Reo."

I pointed to Hopp's Yard bracelet. "You've been initiated."

"Oh, yeah, yeah. Whenever I can, I tag along with Bennett on his visits to the Jarai villages to help with the kids. Have one from the Sedang tribe too. Had the ceremony and the moonshine. Got rightly drunk."

The terrace was several hundred feet above the beach, with no guardrail or barrier between us and the vista of the water below and the air base launching warplanes every few seconds round the clock, afterburners trailing fumes. The South China Sea spread to the horizon, so beautiful it nearly hurt. I turned my face to the sun, closed my eyes. It blazed behind my lids. The clear air smelled of blossoms and burned jet fuel.

"Where are we?"

"The land of flush toilets and hot water." Hopp groaned, basking in the sunlight. "Shangri-la, son. Shangri-la."

# 11

★ ★ ★

HOW BIG?" RUCHEVSKY said, munching his cigar while he tried to align two shaving mirrors to catch sight of the bald spot developing on the back of his head.

"Humongous." I plopped the exposed roll onto our shared desk, atop the open map where I'd marked their locations. "The field looks ready for harvest. Plants taller than the field hands." I told him about the warning shots we'd taken. "We didn't even make it to the Aussie's flower field, but Hopp on the way back from the body shop flew us over three other huge tracts of dope. They're all a few weeks from harvest, I'm guessing."

Big John gave up the beauty exam and put the mirrors back on his dresser.

"They're smuggling it south out of the province how?"

"Only two passable roads in and out of the whole province. Neither is paved. They couldn't move it overland with any confidence."

"Assume they're flying the dope out," Ruchevsky said. "Whose aircraft?"

"Vietnamese air force flies most of it for the various parties. Big shipments for the syndicates. The air corridors from Burma and Laos are choked with their flights."

Ruchevsky fussed with his hairbrushes. "We'd be aware of South Vietnamese military flights into the province, though."

"Sure. Our air controllers would log the activity."

"Civilian aircraft on the other hand —" He stopped and fixed me with his glare. "Shit."

"What?" I said.

"Air America — the Agency's private delivery and taxi service."

"You think they might be flying the dope out?"

"Those aren't Boy Scouts at the controls. Hell, we airlift opium harvests all the time for our favorite warlord in Laos to help him finance his huge anti-Communist army. Air America flies in four hundred loads of material every day to keep his forty thousand troops and their families supplied. No problem flying a few loads out."

I exhaled hard. "Doesn't sound like their aircrews would give a cargo of grass a second thought. What do they fly, DC-Threes?"

"Mostly. STOLs and helicopters too." Ruchevsky bit his lip. "You got any idea about load capacity and dollar value?"

I grabbed a pencil and did some quick calculations. "Bundled in forty-pound bales, a DC-Three load of marijuana would be around two tons. Each load would command — what — a quarter of a million U.S?"

Ruchevsky said, "To grow the weed and move it they need all sides cooperating. The Viet Cong for security. Somebody cultivating. Americans for the airlift. And Colonel Chinh's South Vietnamese military authorities to be struck blind at appropriate times."

"If you take off fifty thousand for pilots, bribes, and incidentals, that leaves a two-hundred-thousand-dollar profit. Could we interdict the air route? Can you do anything about Air America?"

"The pilots are contract players and hard to control. Did you see an airstrip near that first marijuana field?"

I shook my head. "Nothing flat or wide enough to land a plane."

"The closest is the strip by the Phu Thien District headquarters," Ruchevsky said, looking at the map. "Though I doubt they could steadily airlift quantities of anything from there without the Green Berets noticing. There's a split A-team at Phu Thien and two MACV advisers."

"So how would they manage it?"

"Road Seven is dirt but plenty wide in places," he said. "Only low scrub. No vehicular traffic to speak of. Seal off an open stretch and you can put down a DC-Three on it, no problem. Those boys can land on an eyelid. Haul your weed to a road like that, guide the plane down, toss it aboard, and go."

I scratched my sunburned arm, which was beginning to peel. "You think the Air America pilots cut their own private deals?"

Ruchevsky thought for a moment. "The odd trip? Sure. Five a month? Less likely. That many blacked-out flights would need someone like me to make them happen — or at the very least, somebody affiliated with our beloved State Department."

"Like a USAID rep?" I said. "Lund?"

"Or the geek sidekick of his."

"You said Lund might even be from your shop."

"Possibly."

"But you wouldn't know."

"No. We're not identified to one another." Ruchevsky drew himself up. "What size deposits are the VC making?"

"A hundred thousand U.S." I sat down on my bunk.

"So who's getting the other hundred thou?"

"Their partners."

"What do you want to do about that marijuana field you spotted?"

"Fuck it up."

"How do you propose to do that?" he said.

"A bombing raid." I peered at the map.

"If we go the official route, the South Vietnamese in charge of looking the other way will make sure we're denied permission. We'll just hear there are friendlies in the target area and we can't bomb."

"Not if we don't submit a request."

"How do we get B-Fifty-two sorties then?" said Ruchevsky.

"We don't. We don't order up heavy bombers from outside the country. We use lighter aircraft from bases in country, already airborne and carrying unexpended ordnance. Fighters carrying napalm."

"Go on."

"I'll get Major Hopp to do a little theater production: we'll fly up there and incur heavy ground fire. If we're engaged by the enemy, it might be enough to eliminate the requirement for prior clearance and allow Hopp to call in air support immediately."

"I've underestimated your less-than-sterling qualities, young captain."

"The fighters will unload their nape onto the crops, set the field ablaze. Burn it to an unsmokable cinder."

"You won't get more than a pair of fighters. We'll never get all the fields in one go."

"We Zippo the rest when we can these next few days, before the Vietnamese and MACV wake up to what we're doing."

"Yeah." Ruchevsky laughed. "Before they handcuff us."

"Hope you don't mean that literally."

Ruchevsky chewed his cigar with glee. "It's sort of perfect. Their troops always manage to scoot out of the way of our air strikes, but their money supply is rooted in the ground this time. No way to vanish." Ruchevsky sobered. "Know this: The folks we're messing with are not the type to amortize their losses. There's immediate blowback from this when they figure out who to be pissed at."

"I know. We've got to watch our butts," I said.

He puffed his cigar, sending out a cloud of pungent blue smoke. "Okay, Captain, go put it to Major Hopp."

I found Hopp socializing outside his quarters. We walked toward the perimeter where we wouldn't be overheard. When I finished laying out our plans for the VC grass crop, I said, "You think it's doable?"

"Hell, yeah." He grinned, eyes dancing, and slapped me on the shoulder. "Finally a little sizzle. How soon do we perpetrate this arson?"

"Soon as possible."

"Okay, we'll hand-roast the product for them. Could be a marketing breakthrough."

Miser emptied out the signal shack and set Hopp up with a secure voice channel to talk to his Air Force pals in Tuy Hoa. An hour later, it was a done deal.

"Hallelujah," Miser exulted, practically dancing for joy at the possibility of trashing the dope crop and getting back to Saigon.

We flew out at first light, Hopp in front, me in back again. Airman Lewis went on duty in the commo bunker. We reached the field and circled. Major Hopp reported our hot contact: massive ground fire, figures on the ground maneuvering, and all hell generally breaking loose. Lewis acknowledged and requested a forward air controller and any available flight. A pair of Skyraiders armed with napalm zipped over from a neighboring province to lend assistance and assumed a slightly higher orbit than ours. The FAC arrived and joined the circle. Union rules: only Air Force personnel could direct Air Force pilots. The FAC confirmed enemy structures and movement on the ground.

Hopp rolled in to mark the field with white-phosphorus rockets and resumed his position in the aerial wheel. The FAC added several more. The lead fighter peeled off over the target and dropped its pods along one sloped edge. The fire would spread up the incline if we were lucky. The second plane rolled in, and the lower margin of the field burst into an orange fireball. The Skyraiders made two more passes with rockets and really got it cooking, then turned toward the coast to return to base. It was the most we could risk at one go. We didn't really dare report any more ground fire to get additional fighter-bombers diverted.

Airman Lewis and the forward air controller observed the usual etiquette, thanking the fighter jocks and each other, after which Major Hopp thanked his counterpart, the fighter pilots, and Airman Lewis. Tomorrow we'd hit another field. While they were stroking one another in the customary manner, I got ready to empty an AK-47 into the thin fuselage of our light plane.

"Hold your ears," I said on the intercom.

"Whoa!" Hopp exclaimed.

"What?"

"Aim at the sides, not the floor. Don't hit any wires. I don't wanna lose the tail controls or we'll have to fly circles all the way home."

"Right." I contorted myself and pulled the trigger, putting rounds into the skin. The report wasn't too terrible given all the noise in the cockpit. Hopp turned for home. Shell casings needed gathering up and the bullet holes required doctoring so they wouldn't reveal anything. I broke down the Kalashnikov and stuffed the pieces in a kit bag. We were given a heroes' welcome by Hopp's mechanic, who set to work on the fuselage. Airman Lewis and Major Hopp filed their reports and made ready for a repeat performance the following morning over the next field, twelve kilometers farther west.

Ruchevsky and I procured two large cans of Australian beer from Sergeant Miser's small stash in the mess-hall fridge and retired to the northwest-corner bunker, on the roof of which resided the .50-caliber machine gun, its long shells glistening in the linked ammo belt. We ducked inside, checking first for tripwires. We made ourselves comfortable and congratulated each other on our campaign against the profit motive in Asia.

Our private drinking establishment provided an unexpected benefit. The firing ports overlooked the road to the airstrip and the modest USAID compound next door. Before long, Captain Nhu drove past the dozing guard into the barren USAID compound and hurried inside the residence. He came back out with Whalen Lund, and the two of them went off in the captain's vehicle. I called our gate guard on the field phone to find out where the pair were headed.

"They're just turning into the ARVN garrison," I announced to Ruchevsky.

"Hmmm. Off to see the wizard?" He burped. "Command performance by USAID man? Looks like Lund's in this business all right. Probably using USAID fertilizer to boost the yield per acre, and the newest herbicides. You know he's getting his." He took a pull of beer. "There's no way Chinh wouldn't have his snout in the trough too. Lund and his VC partners are undoubtedly keeping the colonel happy. So that's at least two entrepreneurs we've pissed off today. We should do some probing while they're agitated and vulnerable. See what we can dig up."

"I doubt Captain Nhu or Whalen Lund are in any mood for a heart-to-heart," I said. "Chinh either — at this time."

Ruchevsky actually giggled.

"How about their friend from the jungle market," he said, "Father Calogaras? I'm pretty curious to meet the invisible frog priest, find out what he knows about this all. How do we find him?" He looked at me. "Well? You're the gumshoe."

Actually, I'd given it some thought. I took out a map of the province and located the place where we had spied on the jungle market.

"He arrived on an old bicycle, without a rucksack or even a water container."

"Right." Ruchevsky nodded.

"With the poor condition of the road and in this heat, it's unlikely he'd pedal more than an hour."

"How far could he ride in an hour along that track?"

"Five or six kilometers," I said.

I spread out my map on the sandbag ledge. Measuring six kilometers with a tie-off string, I drew a crude circle around the meeting spot.

"The only Catholic Montagnards I know of," I said, "are Bahnar. None around here. The converts in this province are all Protestant. If Calogaras has parishioners, they're likely Vietnamese Catholics."

There was only one Vietnamese village between Cheo Reo and the jungle road where we had spied on the NVA market. It was less than two kilometers from where we stood.

"Cao Tin," I said. "A mile away."

Ruchevsky looked embarrassed. "You think he could be living that close and stay out of sight this long?" He paused for my answer.

"Only one way to find out."

VC roadblocks tended to come down at around four in the afternoon, the day's toll-taking and blockading done. We let the commo bunker know our destination and estimated return time, gathered our gear and a radio, and set out by jeep five after the hour. Road 2 ran west–southwest through scrub and tall grasses twice the height of a man, past a Montagnard village on the outskirts, past groves of trees and stands of bamboo flanking streambeds. I radioed in our progress.

Just before the hamlet, we passed a checkpoint manned by South Vietnamese militia in conical hats and peasants' black pajamas, barefoot and armed with carbines. They made no move to stop us and we rolled past unacknowledged.

Locals in heavy black cotton padded about the town's market square, even more modest than Cheo Reo's. Muslins and tarps interlaced and formed a shaded alley for platforms and stalls. Vendors and shoppers looked up as we drove by. The sun beat down and there wasn't a whisper of wind, not so much as a breeze. We squinted against the sharp tropical light. The flag atop a pole hung limp and barely visible. The colors were wrong: yellow and blue. A yellow star undoubtedly hidden in the folds. What had we driven into?

I nudged Big John and nodded toward the Communist flag. Ruchevsky casually slid his weapon off his shoulder. We pulled up outside the only structure in the town that was roofed and sided with wood, with a slightly elevated wooden floor. We sauntered in, as if the circumstances called for bravado. A gray-haired Caucasian male wearing shorts and a blue work shirt with the sleeves ripped off was bent over the floor in back, hammering. When he stood up, he looked haggard and hollow-eyed, his complexion like leather. He didn't seem happy to see us.

"Father Calogaras?" Ruchevsky said.

"Yes. I am he," he answered in English and tossed the hammer aside with a loud bang.

"We have been searching for you for quite some time."

He wiped his face with a plaid cloth. "*Voilà*. I am here, you are here, we are here. And soon *they* will join us, damn it."

Ruchevsky attempted an ingratiating smile. "We wanted to talk to you about the political situation in the province, and we wonder if you might help us."

Father Calogaras was already shaking his head no before Ruchevsky finished. "I have no side in your conflict," he insisted. "I'm a Franciscan. My purpose, my mission, is people."

"Might we persuade you to help us?"

"Please." He held up a wrinkled palm. "Don't bother."

I said, "Are you a Communist sympathizer?"

"Though my politics are left, I am not a Communist, no. What I *am* is unsupported by my church and the Saigon government. The provincial commissar and I, we have an understanding that permits me to continue my work for the time being."

"How is that possible?" Ruchevsky said.

"We are similar, he and I. He is also a believer."

"In a faith that denies yours. Is it true you administer social services for the Communists?"

"It is. *Action civique.*"

"Why?"

"Because I have the skills, and persons here are poor and need services, because the provincial commissar funds them as opposed to making off with the allocations."

"Do you know his name?" Ruchevsky asked.

"*Comrade,*" he said facetiously, batting away the question. "What does it matter? They don't use their actual names anyway."

"Are you aware how he finances their insurgency and your work?"

"Extortion, I assume. The sale of whatever contraband comes to hand. Taxes? The VC demand a bottle of rice from each of the families once a week and maybe a couple of hundred piasters more from the few shopkeepers at year's end. I am uninterested in how the National Liberation Front finances the programs. I am indifferent."

I said, "Even if it includes harvesting and selling opiates? A practice Hanoi condemns?"

His fingers pinched together in front of his face. "To finance their colonial empire, the French sold opium to the Vietnamese through state-sponsored dens and shops. They rendered the drug commonplace." The hand flew open. "I wouldn't condemn the Front for exploiting this. Perhaps it is part of their strategy to return the favor and cloud the minds of the West. In any event, the brown genie is long gone from its lamp. I can only try to do some good in my immediate environs. As long as I do not proselytize, the commissar lets me do my work."

"Father Calogaras," I said, "do you meet regularly with the Viet Cong?"

"Of course. From time to time I go to the Southern Liberation Army to plead for more funds, more school supplies, medicines, for help digging channels for irrigation or sewage. Occasionally they will lend me their troops for these labors since there are so few young men left in the villages. In return, they tolerate my presence." The barest smile crossed his deeply creased face.

"How long do you think they will let you operate here?"

"As long as I am useful to them" — he shrugged — "and they to me. I pose no threat. They want their country. I would be happy for them to have it."

The town had gone quiet. Not a person on the street.

"Is that what you were doing at the market in the jungle," I said, "agitating for more resources?"

Mild surprise registered on his face. "Yes." He eyed the open front doorway. "I really can't say more. They will not be pleased that we've spoken. It will take many hours to persuade them I am not collaborating. The longer you stay, the more difficult they'll be to convince, and the more unpleasant. You need to leave. It would be unfortunate for us both if you were found here when they come."

I stood fast. "Why were the others at your rendezvous in the jungle? The ARVN and the two American civilians?"

"Monsieur, you two really must go," he said.

"Is that what he handed you out in the jungle in that package? An allocation for your programs?"

"I need you to leave."

"I need an answer."

"*Yes*," he said, exasperated. "Money for the hamlets."

I said, "Why is there a Communist flag on the mast outside?"

He glared at me as if the question were absurd. "Because . . . they claim the village as theirs."

"Aren't those South Vietnamese militiamen at the road checkpoint?"

"Regional militia, yes. What of it? They wisely never enter the village. You would do well to emulate them."

"Are the people all VC sympathizers here?"

"Not all, no. You know the Vietnamese. Their sympathies are complicated. If one son goes north to the People's Army, they send the other south to the Army of the Republic. Family is all the southerners are really loyal to."

"Why doesn't someone take the flag down then?"

"If someone does, the VC will kill his children in front of him, slay his wife, their relatives, pets, livestock, and bury him alive. But if you are tempted, by all means." He extended his arm toward the doorway, daring us. "If you like, you can wait some moments and discuss it with them personally."

A Vietnamese youngster burst in through the back, shivering from fear. He muttered something to Calogaras.

"People's Army irregulars," the priest announced, "less than ten minutes' walk."

"We're going," I said.

We bade the priest goodbye and left with as much decorum as we could manage, but we didn't breathe easy until well after we had passed the regional militia checkpoint and not gotten shot in the back.

"If Calogaras got a packet of money from Wolf Man, it stands to reason they all did," I said. "So Nhu's packet could have been Chinh's tribute money for his part in ensuring the shipments' safe passage. And Lund gets his cut for arranging the transport flight."

"Do you think the French priest is as innocent as he says?" John asked. "Or that missionary Slavin?"

"You seem to have it in for the clergy."

"Hey, spooks do the same as you Army agents — use whatever cover is available."

My jaw dropped. "You've infiltrated the missionaries?"

"The opposition doesn't hesitate; why would we? They infiltrate Vietnamese seminaries, Buddhist monasteries, Polish pulpits — "

"Communist priests?"

Ruchevsky shrugged. "Just picture them in the confessional. The rectory. No coercion. No torture. Secrets spilled voluntarily. Makes my pulse race thinking about it."

I said, "They'd actually submit to years of religious training to establish a false identity?"

"Sure," Ruchevsky said. "Anything to do in the bad guys — us. Look at Wolf Man learning to speak Rhade, filing his teeth down, marrying into the chief's clan. They're damn committed. We're the ones playing the field over here and calling it monogamy."

He pointed accusingly. "You have to look at everyone. You can't assume. What's Sergeant Grady willing to do for his beloved Yards?

Where are his loyalties really? Why does your pal Dr. Roberta listen to Communist broadcasts in Rhade all the time? What's Checkman confide to the Vietnamese girl he's so smitten with?"

"I can't believe —"

"You don't *know* what any of them would do for a cause or people important to them."

# 12

★ ★ ★

**B**ACK IN THE compound, the shit had hit the fan. Sector headquarters in Cheo Reo had already lodged Colonel Chinh's formal protest with ARVN II Corps headquarters in Pleiku, which passed it along to MACV next door, charging that an unauthorized bombing mission in Phu Thien District of Phu Bon Province had mortally endangered friendly troops on the ground, wounded civilians, and destroyed needed crops. Bennett received copies delivered by hand from across the road, along with a curt note.

Major Hopp was summoned to the senior adviser's office to speak by radiophone to his superiors in Tuy Hoa. Ruchevsky and I tagged along. Hopp feigned innocence with real panache, claiming he had sighted North Vietnamese regulars in the open. He insisted something big was going down in the province and he had stumbled into a piece of it. Bennett got on the line and backed him up, which was easy to do with all the recent NVA activity.

General Loc's staff had made such a stink that Hopp was temporarily grounded anyway, pending further inquiry, so he retired to a beach chair outside his hootch with a pitcher of whiskey sours and played fetch with the compound dog. Our other Cessna pilot made an assessment flight in the afternoon and confirmed the field was a charcoal briquette. We had undoubtedly put a crimp in a certain bank account. One for our side.

Colonel Bennett appeared in the bullpen just as Major Gidding came in, his face grave, followed closely by the first sergeant.

"Evening, sir," the XO said to Bennett.

"Good evening, Tom. What's up?"

"I have a priority message for you," Gidding said, "from MACV headquarters, Saigon."

"Crap. Break it to me gently."

"Your promotion's come through." A huge grin spread across his face. "You did it, Dennis. You did it. Full colonel."

"Well," Bennett said, looking shocked and rubbing his sunburned scalp. "Talk about surprises."

Seems somebody in the higher echelons thought he was doing a worthy job advising Colonel Chinh, and no doubt Chinh's reports were favorable. Why not? He got Chinh what he wanted and looked away when the province chief appropriated U.S. supplies. Gidding shook the colonel's hand with a heartfelt exuberance. I had more mixed feelings.

First Sergeant Mote beamed like he had done it himself. "Congratulations, sir."

The artillery-shell gong announced the evening meal. The first sergeant went out, Checkman close on his heels.

"Sir," I said. "Can we buy you a celebratory drink?"

"Thank you, no, Captain. How about some supper and iced tea instead, gentlemen?"

"We'd be honored," Gidding said.

The three of us retired to the mess hall. As we crossed to the chow line, the diners hooted and applauded, a few rising to their feet. Deros, sensing the excitement, barked loudly and got kicked out.

"So much for classified messages," Bennett joked.

"Not many secrets in Cheo Reo, sir," Gidding said.

*He should only know,* I thought. We filled our trays and retired to the corner table nearest the door.

"I'll have to buy the bar," Bennett said.

"Captain Rider," Gidding said. "What are the Special Forces patrols reporting?"

"A lot of signs the NVA are prepping to inflict damage."

"Let's hope we're not part of their plans." Gidding poked at a meat patty with a knife. "I'd hate for this to be our last meal."

Bennett smiled. "Don't say that. If I want to keep the promotion, I have to survive at least twenty-four hours after receiving it."

First Sergeant Mote appeared at our table. A staff officer who served with Bennett's father had snuck a set of silver eagles into the daily courier pouch, and the sergeant presented them to the colonel. Bennett asked Gidding to pin one on and the first sergeant the other, which they did proudly to more applause and whistles.

As we dispersed, Checkman brought the colonel a message. Bennett read it and sighed.

"From Chinh," he said, leaning in close to me. "His men did a sweep through Cao Tin. No flag, no priest. No VC." He crumpled the paper. "Faulty intel, he says."

The following morning, Judd Slavin and his wife sent an invitation to the colonel for a cookout on their lawn celebrating his promotion. Bennett was surprised.

"They're inviting the whole team," he said to First Sergeant Mote. "A bad idea for missionaries to associate so openly with combatants, wouldn't you say?"

Mote sighed. "You've done an awful lot for them, Colonel."

"They're good people." Bennett read the invitation again. "I don't want them to risk retribution from the VC, but I don't want to slight them either."

"Sir," Mote said, "they've been here longer than any of us and are completely aware of what risks they choose to take. This is obviously important to them."

"You're right as usual, First Sergeant."

Bennett accepted the Slavins' invitation, and asked Sergeant Durando and me to take added precautions. The gathering could be an easy target, with so many of our people and our Vietnamese counterparts together in an undefended private residence.

I returned to my desk and scanned the classified communiqué from Major Jessup in Saigon, looking for congratulations on the drastic dip in VC fortunes and revenues. Nothing. Not even a downtick. The latest deposit was over a quarter of a million American dollars. We blast a nice-size hole in the side of their operation and their take goes up. What the hell?

Ruchevsky had his guards take up posts outside, ten feet from his house, so he and I and Little John could speak freely. I told him what I'd gotten from my boss in Saigon.

"At this rate," Ruchevsky said, "their monthly total will come to over a million bucks. Shit. That's got to be opium, with those numbers."

"Opium poppies like altitude." I spread my map across the chest Ruchevsky used as a coffee table and we examined contour lines. "Thirty-two hundred feet to maybe a mile high. The Aussie pilot's peak is four thousand feet above sea level — there." I traced a route to the mountain. "Hard, vertical jungle, with poppies growing on steep ridges and in ravines. Irregularly shaped patches, he told me — not really fields. Hard to spot except for the short time the plants are in flower."

Little John turned pensive, staring at the grids.

"What's the matter?" I said.

"Katu."

"Katu?"

Ruchevsky nodded. "Another Montagnard tribe. Their chief territory is up north, in Eye Corps. Last year the South Vietnamese government relocated a thousand Katu down to the southwest corner of Phu Bon Province, where you've marked that mountain."

"Katu scare," Little John said, making a face.

"That's the general word on the Katu from all the Yards," Ruchevsky said. "They're not exactly sociable."

"You know the Katu area?" I said to Little John.

"No."

"Anyone know it?"

"No. But Reverend Slavin know Katu."

"The padre at the jungle market?" I turned to Ruchevsky. "Does he mean the reverend's familiar with the Katu or that he speaks their language?"

Little John held up two fingers.

Ruchevsky glanced at Little John and back at me. "Both."

I drove Checkman and some of the enlisted over to the celebration at the Slavins'. The party hadn't been announced until the last possible moment for the sake of security. Sergeant Durando deployed a discreet cordon: six guards for the corners of the quarter-acre property, six more who'd attend the party and switch off with the others every half an hour until it was over. Concealed personal weapons were welcome. Colonel Chinh surprised us with a second security ring: a hundred of his men in five armored personnel carriers. Everybody who was not on duty showed up.

The invitation was for a back-home barbecue on what passed for the front lawn of the Slavins' home, next to a Yard village not far from town. The Montagnards we passed driving onto the grounds seemed more Westernized than the ones living farther out. The women were all demurely draped, the kids neatly dressed in uniform shorts and shirts and red kerchiefs. A couple of thatched longhouses had bicycles on their elevated patios. The Slavins' residence was modest, though made entirely of local teak and mahogany. The lawn consisted of a few tufts of weeds.

A pig had roasted all night in a covered pit. Tribesmen carved it into hefty chunks presented on two platters, with yams and asparagus, potato salad and French bread. Coolers of beer were strategically placed around the yard. A choir of barefoot Montagnard boys in shorts, white shirts, and red neckerchiefs sang something that sounded oddly like "She'll Be Coming Round the Mountain."

Everyone wore mufti in deference to our hosts' civilian status except the guest of honor and Captain Cox, who drove in from Mai Linh and appeared at the gathering covered with orange road grit. He looked like an owl when he removed his goggles. Old Mr. Cho, in his tropical suit, stepped away as Cox dusted himself off.

Colonel Chinh arrived fashionably late in an armored personnel carrier, dressed in white linen. He stepped lightly, as if from a carriage, and took his wife's hand to help her down. She was tiny and wore a black *ao dais*. Perfect emeralds set in heavy green gold sparkled at her ears. Captain Nhu came down the little ramp behind the Chinhs. In addition to MACV personnel, all five of the Korean medical staff came by, and Dr. Roberta Towns in a sunshine-yellow sundress.

John Ruchevsky wore his customary scowl and tropical attire: Hush Puppies, cigar, short-sleeved shirt, and khaki slacks held up by the saddest-looking leather belt.

Spying Chinh's dainty wife, Ruchevsky muttered, "It's Madame Antoinette herself, come to eat cake."

Colonel Chinh stepped up to Bennett and snapped his fingers at an aide, who immediately brought over his gifts for the new bird colonel.

"Felicity," he said to Bennett and presented him with a long-playing record of a traditional Vietnamese concert. Also a mahogany box the size of a humidor containing a captured Chinese K-54 pistol. The underside of the lid was inlaid with a large round replica of Bennett's new eagle insignia in burnished silver. Chinh handed the colonel a third gift wrapped in coarse brown paper. Bennett undid the wrapping and unveiled a leather-bound volume and a small book of poetry.

"*'Essential Summary of Military Arts,'*" Bennett read, "'Marshal Tran Hung Dao.'"

Chinh said, "Our marshal fight Mongol invader. He retreat to mountain. Mongols far from home. Dao make guerrilla fight." He turned to Judd Slavin and Bennett and spoke in Vietnamese.

Checkman translated: "Marshal Dao wore down the Mongols of Kublai Khan and destroyed them with a trick. In 1287."

"Many best advise. For you," Chinh said in English, patting the book. "America next birthday, one hundred ninety. Viet Nam, three thousan'. My country old, like this war. We fight French, Japan, Chinese all time, Burma, Khmer Krom, Cham, and Montagnard, Mongols three time, and many time other Vietnamese. Now America teach to us how make war."

"Colonel Chinh," Bennett said, "we are here as partners. My country has vowed to stand with yours. As have the Australians, South Koreans, Thai—"

"Yes, yes," Chinh said, impatient. "Free World Force. You come fight war for us. Like Lafayette in American Revolution. George Washington same me. He have not many soldier — eight thousand? Lafayette bring forty-four thousand French to fight. Many warship. Defeat English emperor. French make you free." He giggled gleefully, hand to his mouth.

"You are well informed about our history," Bennett said. Chinh appeared pleased and accepted the compliment with a slight bow.

The second book was from Madame Chinh, he explained: a famous poem in Vietnamese written in the 1700s and translated into French. Chinh apologized for the lack of an English translation.

Checkman, interpreting, said, "She doubts it could be done because the language of the original is so remarkable."

"Please thank her for me," Bennett said. "Ask her what it's called."

Checkman spoke to Madame Chinh and turned back to him. *The Lament of the Waiting Warrior's Wife.*

"Thank you so much," the colonel managed, looking uncomfortable.

"Duty," Chinh said, half bowing. "I go."

Chinh spoke to Judd Slavin in Vietnamese and turned on his heel. He tromped down the porch steps and into the open back of his armored personnel carrier. Captain Nhu and Mr. Cho helped his wife board, and the hatch closed. The machine pulled away, raising dust from the hard-packed earth. A battery of howitzers fired, their booms familiar as thunder at a lawn party. No one flinched, not the children long used to it, not even the newbie, Lieutenant Lovell, talking to his Vietnamese counterpart.

Everyone savored the food and the rare opportunity to socialize. John excused himself to talk to the hostess. Roberta took it as her cue to come over. Her A-line sundress was plain and hid her shapely figure but there was nothing restrained about her. Roberta, who hadn't paid attention to Madame Chinh's gift, was visibly happy. A barefoot Jarai choirboy held out a tray of hors d'oeuvres for us to sample.

"God," she said, "the children are the single bit of relief from this war. Especially those who are too young to grasp what this all is. Or maybe they're just unfazed because they were born into it and don't know anything else. I sometimes wish I had one," she said, eyeing the disarming boy.

"I had the posterity urge too," I said, "not long ago. I thought a kid would be really cool."

"Had?" She shaded her eyes. "Where did the urge go?"

"Lost it when my wife annulled my ass."

"Well, you're what—in your midtwenties? You've got time." She brushed crumbs from her fingers. "I need a favor. Two, actually."

"Sure. Just say."

"When this breaks up, I need you to give your boss a lift to my place. And pick him up in the morning, early. First thing. Can you do that?"

A pang of something passed through me and kept going. "Sure," I said.

Roberta touched my forearm and slipped away to talk shop with the Korean medical team. Judd Slavin stepped forward, looking like a Kansan at a barbecue: short blond hair, short-sleeved blue plaid shirt, chinos, white socks, silver Timex on his wrist. Slavin clinked the side of a bottle and made a short, earnest speech thanking the colonel for his many kindnesses:

"The rice he brings our Montagnards, the medical supplies and building materials that just appear, along with seeds and donated clothing from his hometown parish. I won't go on. I don't want to embarrass Colonel Bennett. He doesn't react terribly well to praise, as some here will attest."

Applause interrupted. Judd turned toward Bennett. "Audrey and Ted Baxter have come a long way to be here. Not a journey lightly undertaken. We wish they hadn't run the risk but I'm delighted they're here. They want to say a brief word."

The couple stepped out of the group, straight as sticks, both in their forties, graying and modestly dressed: she in a madras wraparound skirt and a blouse, he in black slacks and white shirt. Audrey Baxter presented the colonel with a black tribal sarong and shirt for his wife, and addressed him.

"We're pretty isolated where we are. You folks can imagine our surprise seeing an American officer amble into our remote village and ask what was for lunch. He just appeared one afternoon and he's never forgotten the way. He never came empty-handed. Dennis, I just want you to know there are tribal kids who are clothed because of you, fed because of you, alive today because of drugs you supplied. We are so immensely appreciative for all your help and compassion . . . and proud to congratulate you on those most appropriate eagles."

Audrey Baxter hugged him and everyone clapped and whistled. Bennett actually blushed. Her husband took the colonel's hand in both of his. Both Baxters looked anxious and frail, as though they didn't eat much more than the Montagnards they ministered to. The colonel admired the sarong and thanked them, bussing Audrey on the cheek. He thanked everyone for coming, singling out the Slavins for their hospitality. More applause.

Ruchevsky came back around as the crowd began to disperse. "The gall of that smug son of a bitch Chinh," he muttered. "Three-thousand-year-old civilization and they're still shitting in holes." He filled a plate with food.

Roberta waved goodbye from afar.

Ruchevsky said, "You playing Cupid now, Rider?" Big John missed nothing.

"Feel more like the rat driving Cinderella's pumpkin."

"And here I thought you might have a thing for her yourself." He took a bite of potato salad.

"She's crazy for him. It's bigtime stuff."

"Tragic thing, unrequited love," he said, sighing, and dug into the food on his plate. He nodded in the direction the Chinhs' armored carrier had gone. "You catch the emeralds on that corrupt bastard's corrupt wife? You could buy all of Cheo Reo with one stone. How much black-market rice you think they cost? I'd like to rip them off her teeny-tiny ears."

"Tell me, John," I said as Roberta pulled away in the buttery light. "How is it you got into the stealth business?"

Ruchevsky massaged the slight paunch developing above his belt. "I dunno. Just liked working with people, I guess." He handed me a small box. "You get a gifty too. I wouldn't be without just now." He clasped my shoulder.

Inside were the impossible-to-find .22-caliber bullets for my pistol.

Ruchevsky arched his eyebrows. "What do you say we have a little chat with our host?"

Judd Slavin appeared surprised by our request for a private talk but showed us to some Adirondack chairs in a shady corner of the broad porch. I could see their vegetable garden over his shoulder.

"I understand your parents were missionaries in Viet Nam," Ruchevsky said.

"For over a decade, yes. I boarded at the Dalat Missionary Children's School back then and spent my summers and school holidays with my folks wherever they were. Had a whole year with them one time at their mission station."

"And you learned Montagnard languages?"

"From my playmates and classmates at the time, yes. I speak at about the level of a ten-year-old."

"Rhade, Jarai . . . Katu?"

"Yes. Some Bahnar and Sedang too."

"What is it like," I said, "ministering to the Montagnards?"

"Challenging. For all the powerful deities they live with, they don't easily grasp the idea of a single God. They're happy to add Him to theirs, but most tribespeople don't readily understand the concept of exclusivity."

"One God is a hard sell?"

"No." Slavin smiled warmly. "They mostly like the idea of a God who can protect them from their troublesome spirits and lesser gods. To be fair, the Triune God is what's difficult to explain. Naturally, they see Him as three. We insist He's one. They mouth the words but don't really get it."

"Have you had any success with the Jarai?"

"Reasonable success, I would say, yes. Five years ago we had five hundred Jarai converts here. Double that today." He gave a resigned shrug. "It's slow work. Fraught with problems. They're very communal. When they convert, we require them to burn their magic amulets and idols and forbid them to participate in any more pagan feasts and ceremonies."

"Sacrilege to the rest of the tribe," Ruchevsky said.

"Exactly. Upsetting to the *yang* spirits. Whose displeasure threatens the whole village. So the shamans and neighbors harass families not to accept Christ. Sometimes we try to win over the whole village at one go."

"All or nothing?"

"Exactly. Convert some critical number all at once. If that doesn't work, we might build a church on a facing rise and invite the believers to slowly migrate over to it, hoping this makes the division less traumatic for everyone. But there are dilemmas no matter what we do."

I said, "Was it difficult for your parents to proselytize the Katu?"

Slavin tensed. "The Katu believe in lots of spirits but a single god, the King of the Sky. They're nearly monotheistic."

"Did that make them easier to reach than other tribes?"

Slavin shook his head. "When my parents preached the Gospel, the Katu were keen to adapt Christian belief. They were transfixed by the Eucharist, fascinated by Jesus on the Cross. Even competed at putting up crucifixes in their longhouses. My parents were surprised and encouraged at first. Until one day they realized it wasn't Christ that called to the Katu. The Lord's Body and Blood wasn't a transcendent religious experience for them. What fascinated them was the technique of crucifixion."

"What do you mean?" Ruchevsky said.

"They wanted to understand how we performed sacrifices, how we consumed the Body and Blood during communion. They were offended at being turned away from participating unless they converted. Their old chief explained they wanted to hear everything about *percée de sang*—bloodletting. 'There Is a Fountain Filled with Blood.' They'd beg my mother to sing that hymn in their language. My dad nearly tore down their crucifixes one day but thought better of it."

"How long did he and your mother work with the Katu?"

"They only lasted a couple of years. My mother and father felt they'd failed them. They baptized hundreds in the rivers all over Viet Nam. Not Katu. Not a one."

"They sound seriously primitive," Ruchevsky said.

"They're dark souls, the only mountain clan that metes out capital punishment. If a Katu accuses another of using sorcery or witchcraft to murder and doesn't prove it, the accused has the right to kill his accuser. They deliberately isolate themselves in inaccessible places so they can maintain their customs and primitive ways unbothered. They encircle their village with a stockade and a confusing maze of approaches, most of them lethally booby-trapped. They're always braced for attack. It's a mystical, wary society."

"An inhospitable tribe," Ruchevsky suggested.

"Not really a tribe; more like a cult of intermarried first cousins. They wear their hair long, decorated with cone-shaped bones or the tusks of wild boar. The skulls of the creatures they sacrifice are kept in the highly decorated men's longhouse. It's shaped like an axe head, its ceilings exceptionally high and painted with toucans and snakes, stars, the sun, all done with charcoal and white lime, and red from areca. I was apprenticed to the pigment maker and had the job of maintaining an offering of red flowers laid out on a red blanket."

"A blood symbol — the red?" Ruchevsky said.

"They think it's the color of souls. They're easily the fiercest and most feared of the Highlanders. The other tribes tell their kids scary stories about a clan whose warriors have tails and devour children."

Ruchevsky said, "How is it they came by this reputation?"

"They hunt humans."

We both came fully alert.

"For sport?" John said.

"For their blood. Sometimes their heads too. When the spirits demand a blood sacrifice, the Katu begin a ceremonial journey. They isolate themselves from the village for a day to get ready, then raid some distant community they've scouted. They kill the first male they come upon and smear themselves with his blood. Ritually dip their spears in it. When they return, they go into seclusion for a month to come down from the experience. The slayers see the soul of the victim as a brother. It stays in the village. Katu women — " He circled his face with his hand. "Their faces are tattooed. The women speak gently to the slain soul to comfort it."

"Jesus," Ruchevsky mumbled.

"Did you ever see the ritual?" I said.

Slavin looked straight at me.

"The Katu often declared their village taboo so my folks wouldn't interfere, but they took little notice of me. Kids were very free. I was nearly as dark as they from the sun, and young, nine or ten. One time I shadowed the hunters as they returned. I'd convinced myself they'd gone out after game. I didn't dare believe they'd actually stalk another human. I saw it though. The head. They had killed a chief. A very special victim. They'd decorated themselves with his blood, dipped their spears in it, cut off his head, and carried it home. That's where they think the soul is — in the head. With great ceremony, they put it in the men's house with the others."

"Good God," Ruchevsky whispered.

"That's not the worst of it, I'm afraid."

"I'm not sure I want to know," I said.

"Their preferred prey were foreigners. My father thought they were always fantasizing an honored place in their collection for his noggin, he said — or mine."

Ruchevsky said, "But you were just a kid."

"When their god or the spirits wanted blood from a living person, the raiders would bring back a captive, preferably male — and young."

"How young?" I asked.

"A year or two. Easier to carry in a basket, easier to direct."

"You saw this?" Ruchevsky said, quietly.

Slavin nodded. "There was a big ceremony and they brought the boy out. The raiders wanted him to grasp a sharp blade but he wouldn't, so they forced his hand onto it. They extracted some blood from the wound, then finished the rite . . . and added his head to the rest."

The two of us sat silent, speechless.

"When I told my parents, Mom couldn't stop trembling. We left the same afternoon."

Slavin stared at the dissipating crowd. Small boys in blue shorts dashed from an outbuilding at the corner of the property and bolted toward the river, raising a plume of yellow dust as they galloped.

"Reverend Slavin," Ruchevsky said, "we're aware you recently met with the Communists' province head."

He turned to us. "I see."

"Out in the jungle," I added.

Slavin didn't respond immediately. His face took on a sad aspect.

"Will this have to go into reports? Do you have to share this with Colonel Bennett?" He took out his pipe and fussed with it to cover his discomfort.

Ruchevsky sat forward, voice lowered. "Were you meeting with the commissar to demonstrate your neutrality, maybe? Showing deference to the revolutionary government in the province?"

He looked chagrined. "Not to put too fine a point on it, I went to collect payment."

"For?"

"Services rendered." Slavin sighed, at last realizing the reason for our interest in the Katu. "I had approached the Katu on the Front's behalf. Persuaded them to grow certain native medicines for the sick and wounded."

"You acted as a go-between for money?" I said.

"Not for me personally. The Montagnard villages I serve are desperate. They're barely subsisting on the provisions the province allows them. Kids' stomachs are potbellied from lack of a decent diet. The colonel's charitable efforts are commendable but they aren't nearly enough." He set the pipe aside. "I continually plead with the province chief, to no avail. We live alongside people ill with hunger. Nothing's been put right about their rice supplies."

"So the commissar offered his assistance if you persuaded the Katu to grow poppies?"

"No, Whalen Lund approached me. He said our military would never challenge the province chief about depriving the Yards of staples or selling off our donated rice. He said we only wanted Montagnards as mercenaries, that America's commitment was to the Saigon government, not the tribes. He said I was wasting my breath going to Chinh, that the South Vietnamese were perfectly happy to see the tribespeople culled by war and deprivation. Except for individual members of the American military — some AID agents like him and missionaries like me — he said nobody was going to intercede on their behalf. His solution was simple: the VC would get opiates for their military patients, and the Montagnards could count on a few thousand dollars at harvest time that could be the difference between surviving and not."

"And you bought this?" Ruchevsky said.

Slavin nodded. "Hard not to. Everything he said was the truth."

"Except," I said, "the part about what the narcotics are for."

"All I know is he approached me to propose it to the Katu. Poppies grow best at altitude, so the Katu were the obvious choice. Liberation Front people escorted me into the foothills to meet with them."

"VC accompanied you?" I said.

"I went the final stretch alone. They were afraid."

"Do Viet Cong oversee or protect the fields?"

"No. The Katu carry the raw opium down to them from the mountain to a nearby river."

"Where?"

"Three miles downriver from their village — that was the plan."

"They transport it by water?"

"I don't know. I never went back."

"But their village is near water?" Ruchevsky said.

"Yes, as always with the Katu. It's on the side of a sloping hill surrounded by peaks."

"A big village?"

"A hundred longhouses. Yes."

Ruchevsky had him mark it on our map and said, "Can we get a look at those opium fields of theirs?"

Slavin sat up. "The terrain is extremely steep. The Katu must have built a thousand bamboo steps into the mountainside so they could climb up. I downed two canteens on those stairs. At the top it levels off. It took another hour to reach the field."

Ruchevsky said, "You think we could observe the fields without their knowing?"

"There's no way you could climb that mountain except by their stairs. And they are closely guarded. A helicopter landing would give you away instantly. They're far too vigilant and untrusting. I'd advise against it." He looked from one to the other of us. "You aren't intending to hurt them, are you? The Katu, I mean."

"Reverend," Ruchevsky said, "you haven't been back to those fields, so you haven't seen the quantities of opium they're cultivating up there. Those poppies are putting hundreds of thousands of dollars in NVA coffers."

Slavin looked genuinely shocked. "I don't want the Katu to suffer for my stupidity."

"You think they deserve your concern?" Ruchevsky said.

"You may see their behavior as savage, but is it that different from what we're doing here? Except that we're far less concerned with the disposition of our victims. We stack up ours like cordwood and bulldoze them into pits. They practically worship theirs."

We thanked Slavin for his candor and left him standing on the porch.

Ruchevsky said, "What can you do to those fields?"

"Bombard them with mountain goats," I said. "It's not likely we're going to get any more air assets. Sounds like Mr. Lund has really been studying his crop science and not just pushing new strains of rice, the smug bastard. Talk about not knowing which war you're in or whose side you're on. You think Captain Nhu is only collecting tribute at Chinh's behest?"

Ruchevsky said, "I'll get my shop in Saigon to check out Nhu's family finances: work down the family tree, sniffing for money. Chinh's too. And Lund's. Wolf Man's agricultural adviser and air marshal needs to be shut down."

The last stragglers were leaving. The guards made ready to withdraw. I went over to Miser at the beer cooler.

"Get to the crypto rig and let Jessup know there's an American mixed up in all this."

"Who?"

"USAID man. Get the major to trace back Whalen Lund's time in country and see if he's done anything we can detain him for. I need to take him out of the equation here. He's collaborating with the hostiles, receiving kickbacks for expediting cultivation of certain agricultural products and maybe helping transport them. It would be a big help if Jessup could get him ejected from the country."

"Like a transfer?"

"Like arrested and deported. Hell, bust him for aiding the enemy and execute his ass. I don't care. Just run him the fuck out of Cheo Reo."

# 13

★ ★ ★

I DROVE COLONEL BENNETT to the stucco residence behind Roberta's clinic, as she'd requested.

"Captain, you seem . . . are you thinking I'm — "

"Sir, I don't get paid to think. I'm just wondering what I need to do if there's an alert."

"There's a field phone at the clinic connected back to our signal shack. Major Gidding knows to contact me."

"Yes, sir," I said, thinking his career was toast if we got attacked while he was unaccountably elsewhere. Or worse still, if someone passed along information to the VC concerning his whereabouts. What was the bounty on a shiny new American bird colonel?

"Thanks, Captain Rider."

"You're welcome, Colonel."

He looked guilty and a little forlorn. As well he might. The NVA were getting ready to launch some big operation, and we were that much more at risk without him in the compound. I put the jeep in reverse and backed out of the narrow alleyway into the bumpy street. Roberta was wrong. This wasn't some casual wartime romance for him either. He was closer than ever to his first general's star and risking everything for her. He had chosen her over us. I felt betrayed. Jealous too, since I would have made the same choice in an instant.

I had just finished my evening round of radio contacts down in the commo bunker when a VC came up on the frequency to say in decent

English that they'd be having their midday meal in our mess hall to-morrow. I took back the mike from the radio operator and said, "Yeah, hurry on over, fuckhead, and we'll hand you your lunch — personally. No problem."

Miser came halfway down the steps and beckoned me outside.

In the darkness, he whispered, "We got a situation."

"What?"

"Sergeant Rowdy. He's downtown, shacked up."

"He broke curfew?"

"Yeah. But that's not the problem."

"Sarge, it's been a long day. What's the problem?"

"There's VC in town tonight."

"How do you know?"

"We just got a call in the signal shack on the field phone from Dr. Roberta. She said to tell you right away. You'd know what to do."

"Right." I pushed at my cropped hair, wondering what the hell to do.

Miser said, "I should alert the duty officer and the guards on the wire."

"For sure, but don't say anything yet about Rowdy."

"Yes, sir."

"Where is he?"

"At the Brown Fairy."

"Opium den?"

"Seems like. Getting laid and blasted."

"Shit." A military scrip dollar would buy him a dozen pipes, and I doubted he'd ask for change. By now he'd be too far gone to stand, much less walk.

We set out over the gravel parking area toward the lone light of the night shift in the signal shack.

"Don't call a full alert," I said. "Call Ruchevsky at his place and warn him. Kill the perimeter lights. Have commo notify Pleiku we've got company in the area and we need gunships on standby, and Spooky on station here with its Gatling guns, immediately."

"And BUFFs?"

"Buffs?" I said.

"Big Ugly Flying Fuckers — B-Fifty-twos."

"Christ, *no!*"

Miser shrugged. "Okay, okay."

"Did Rowdy just stay in town all day or sneak out after curfew?"

"Crabbed out after the gate closed," Miser said. "His pals gave it up. They've got some secret back way."

"They'll have to show me. I'll go out that way too."

I went to gather my stuff. Miser jogged to the commo bunker to do his part. I burst into the signal shack, demanding to know Rowdy's trick. Geronimo escorted me to the wall of steel planks out back and showed me their "pet door," an eroded ditch where rainwater had dug its way underneath the barrier. The signalmen kept it covered with sandbags, which they pulled away to reveal a shallow depression. I took off my boots, shimmied through, and emerged into a dark world. I tied the laces together and draped the footgear over my shoulder.

Muzzle angled down, I crept away, trying to keep the dry ground from crunching underfoot. I followed the curve of the compound to the corner of the bare field where we had watched the young Vietnamese gather ground wood. I felt around with my toes for the diagonal path, hoping that no Vietnamese garrison guard would hear me. At the end of the path, I stepped on the road to town and let it lead me to the main street.

A single browned-out bulb was strung high on a bare pole, the town's lone streetlight. Reaching the edge of the deserted market, I sensed movement at the far end and heard men talking in Vietnamese. The rhythmic crunch suggested several of them, moving left to right, upright and confident. I didn't dare step out onto the wider expanse of the square. I hid in the blackness against the closed shop fronts and eased toward the alleyway that led to the clinic. More voices. Between the buildings it was so dark I couldn't see the sights on my rifle. I waded through the murk with my left hand outstretched, the pistol grip of the rifle in the other.

Gas lanterns burned painfully bright in the clinic, its screened sides open to the night air. Roberta leaned over a gurney. All around her stood armed VC. A few of the men held the patient down and one barked at her as she worked on their wounded comrade. He swallowed moans and grunted and tried to keep from crying out as she explored a wound on his shoulder. He lost consciousness for moments at a time. They hadn't permitted anesthetic: he'd need to travel fast, away from Cheo Reo, as soon as she was done.

Blood streaked her hands and arms to the elbow. She carefully withdrew a hemostat from the man's flesh as he winced and moaned. A shrapnel fragment clinked against the metal of a bowl. No sign of the colonel.

The men in the clinic had no night vision at all in that harsh light. When the wounded man's loud scream caused them all to turn toward him, I crossed to Roberta's house and slipped in. Bennett stood just inside the door, rifle aimed at my heart. He lowered the carbine. I held up my hand, fingers spread, signaling five hostiles. He nodded, face shiny with sweat.

The VC hadn't come for him or Rowdy — a relief. They'd come for Roberta's help. By the unwritten rules, since she was an unarmed female noncombatant, they'd normally leave her once she was done. But you never knew. Three missionaries had been seized years earlier and not seen again. There were no guarantees.

Bennett and I stood by the windows, helpless, rifles at our shoulders.

"The second from the left," he whispered, voice hoarse with fatigue and anxiety. "Wolf Man."

"I see him."

"Your eyes are younger than mine. If they make a move to harm her, drop him. I'll go at the rest."

We had Bennett's Viet Cong counterpart in sight, and though we were outgunned, we had all the advantage of surprise we needed to even the odds quickly. But Roberta was in the line of fire and there were undoubtedly more VC out there in the dark in blocking positions, securing the group's exit route. If a fight broke out, they could join in quickly.

"Is anyone with you?" Bennett said.

"No. I snuck over by myself."

*Me and my M-16*, I thought. I'd brought extra ammo for us but he was carrying a carbine. Wrong caliber.

The moans eased. The worst was over, or maybe the wounded man had fainted again. She worked steadily, sewing him up. The VC seemed less intent and anxious.

"I guess we'll know the score soon," he said. "I hope you won't be sorry for coming to the rescue."

Roberta worked on the wounded man for half an hour more, speaking easily to the circle in melodic Vietnamese. When she announced she was done, Bennett and I tensed and raised our sights. If there was going to be trouble it would be now. I estimated how many I could stitch firing on automatic. Wolf Man wouldn't be one of them. He was too close to her and too antsy, always moving.

Spooky's twin propellers droned overhead, its machine guns ready to pour down a thousand tracer rounds a second onto the unfortunate enemy in an unbroken red ray. The VC froze, looking up toward the sound. Wolf Man barked orders at his cadre to help the wounded man. Two stood him upright between them and half carried him away. Wolf Man didn't say another word. Just left. The rest sped after him.

Roberta slumped against the gurney for a few seconds, then stripped off her gloves, doused the lanterns, and crossed to the house. Once inside, she fell into Bennett's arms. She didn't even seem surprised to find me there. Her voice trembled as she talked herself down from the experience. Bennett asked about her patient.

"He's Montagnard," she said. "Three of them were. The rest Vietnamese, including their leader with the stubble beard. He's fluent in Rhade, though."

"That was a long procedure," Bennett said.

"The bullet's in pieces. The smaller chunks were hell to dig out. He's bleeding still. I sutured what I could. They really shouldn't move him."

Emotionally spent and exhausted, she sprawled across the thin mattress and the Western pillows that looked completely out of place. Three chairs, a table, and the plank bed were the only furnishings. She fell right asleep.

A chair creaked as Bennett sat down. "She called the compound when her nurses warned us Viet Cong were in the town. If they had come in here, I'd be dead. She kept them away."

"The doc takes charge."

"She does." He stood, arching his stiff back. "I'm in trouble. There's a train bearing down on me." All I could make out was his white forehead. "Were you ever that taken with anyone?"

"Once."

"How did it work out?"

"Train hit me and kept going."

He nearly laughed until he realized it wasn't funny. "You like her," he said.

"Yes, sir."

He started to say more but stopped himself. It occurred to me at that moment that I wasn't there by accident. Bennett intended to lure me into their circle — Roberta and his. Like the drive to Mai Linh, when I first met her, our being together wasn't serendipity. The colonel engineered it. I was the fallback. If he went home to his wife, if the Army discovered his adultery and cashiered him, if anything happened to him, I'd be there. To console and distract Roberta, to be infatuated. My anger rose.

I didn't want him to talk, so I said he should get some sleep too, that I'd stand guard. He didn't argue. He reversed his chair and sat backward on it, head resting on his arms, rifle across his lap. I leaned against the doorjamb and tried to see anything I could outside so as to distract myself and keep awake. There wasn't a lot. Toward dawn, I awoke abruptly, still standing, as vehicles screeched to a halt outside the house. With much shouting and gesturing, a large contingent of Colonel Chinh's regional militia pounded on the louvered door, demanding admission. Stripping off my fatigue shirt, I stood barechested in front of them, yawning. They all wore black pajamas and olive-drab hats strapped under their chins, and held their carbines at port arms. They were led by Captain Nhu, looking splendid in tailored fatigues and shiny insignia. He was clearly startled to see me, and slightly embarrassed.

The militiamen attempted to barge past to search the premises, but I barred the way and said the doctor was *fatiguée* and pantomimed her sleeping. Nhu ordered them back. He said something about a Viet Cong being treated in the hospital. I explained that an emergency patient had come and gone in the middle of the night but that we knew nothing about his affiliation. Nhu scowled, snapped at his men, and strode away. The militiamen piled back into the vehicles and drove off.

When the sun was fully up, I used the field phone at the clinic to call the compound and update Miser. After which I hiked down to Ruchevsky's house and borrowed a jeep to drive the colonel back to the compound. I picked him up and we drove to the Brown Fairy; I went in, and the colonel stayed in the jeep.

The place was basic: a two-story Chinese-style shop with a hinged wood-paneled front that would swing open later in the day. Crude shelving held the pipes and paraphernalia. There was a small Formica table with low stools for socializing, and two plank beds toward the back for patrons to recline on and drift into reverie.

The proprietress looked surprised to have a customer so early. How many pipes did I want? I brushed past her and roused Sergeant Rowdy from his narcotic slumber, his arms around a naked woman.

"Captain —"

"Morning, Sergeant."

"Sir, I . . ."

"You know," I said, warming up to some real bullshit, "you hold an extremely high security clearance. I'm not sure you're aware that I'm authorized to shoot your ass to prevent your capture. And I will, if you ever fuck up again. You're restricted to the compound until I say otherwise. Get your sorry self in the jeep."

The bare-chested girl stayed silent, only sniffed his cheek — a Vietnamese kiss. Rowdy dressed in record time and careened out the door. He froze, seeing the colonel, but recovered immediately and leapt in back. I tossed him my rifle.

"Look fierce," I said.

The perimeter seemed normal, the bunkers empty. Only one extra guard was on duty at the gate as the three of us rolled past like we'd been out reconnoitering. I don't think any of the men presumed anything. Actually, no one paid us much attention. They just seemed relieved to have made it through the long night without an attack.

# 14

★ ★ ★

MAJOR JESSUP'S RESPONSE to my inquiry came in the form of a radiotelephone call from an Army lawyer in Pleiku.

"There's precious little to be done about Mr. Lund," the JAG lawyer said, "since he's a civilian."

"Say if I'm wrong, sir," I said, puzzled. "I know the Uniform Code of Military Justice covers soldiers in combat and I thought also civilians in theater."

"It would apply to our civilians in the Republic of South Viet Nam if a state of war existed here. But . . . there's been no formal congressional declaration of the same."

"So the code doesn't apply to them?"

"That's correct."

"Could the Vietnamese do anything about him, if we caught him dead to rights?"

"As an American, Mr. Lund enjoys the same grant of immunity from the Vietnamese judicial system as you or I. We're all immune from their civil and criminal system."

"They can't touch him either."

"'Fraid not."

"Do you suppose he's aware of these little loopholes?"

"I wouldn't be at all surprised. Consider yourself lucky he's just a trafficker and not a murderer."

"Not for want of trying," I said.

An artillery battery across the street fired a salvo that screeched across the top of the compound.

"Funny, I could have sworn it was a war," I said.

The JAG major laughed pleasantly. "Conflict. The Viet Nam Conflict."

I offered Ruchevsky some attitude about JAGs, the code, and the Viet Nam Conflict. He laughed and ordered up an Air America helicopter. No door gunners or armament, just us and the pilots. It wasn't much but it was all he could think to do, short of taking Lund with us and tossing him out at a couple of thousand feet. The chopper flew us south to the coordinates where Judd Slavin had said the Katu transferred the opium to the transporters. We lay flat on the deck in back of the bulkhead behind the cockpit, doors open, and peered over the edge with binoculars. We couldn't spot anything until the copilot pointed out specks of red among the green. Poppies. They clung to a steep mountainside in an irregular patch. The Huey descended until we were within fifty feet. Two wooden boxes held Miser's Molotov cocktails, each glass jar with a primed grenade pickled in aviation gas, more volatile than kerosene. We dropped the glass jars onto the flowering buds. They broke on contact with the ground and detonated seconds later, igniting the av gas.

We hovered, watching the last explosions and flare-ups. My sense of satisfaction was short-lived. The fires weren't efficient. The green growth and dew smothered them in short order. At best, we'd done little more than announce that outsiders were aware of the opium. Maybe we'd put a scare in the Katu growers though I doubted they'd be frightened off that easily.

The helicopter swung south. We looked for the village but the Katu remained true to their reputation. A hundred longhouses, invisible. We followed their river, looking for the transfer point where the Katu delivered their crop. All we saw was a lot of wood debris floating downstream. Were they reinforcing their village stockade? Ruchevsky shot a roll of film and signaled the pilot to take us home.

· · ·

Colonel Bennett called me to an emergency meeting with Reverend Slavin and Joe Parks. We crowded into the tiny office. Audrey and Ted Baxter, the missionary couple who had come overland to the promotion party, had failed to confirm their safe return to their mission station.

"Both were recently hospitalized for malaria and dengue," Judd Slavin said. "They may be really ill."

"Or broken down on that excuse for a road," Joe Parks suggested, "or taken sick on the way home and laying over in a village."

"Might be just a busted transmitter," I added.

"Ordinarily I'd risk driving," Slavin said, "but it seems inadvisable at the moment with all the activity in the province."

Colonel Bennett rose. "Juddy, it's completely out of the question. Their place is far. They're practically in the next province."

Slavin said, "The Viet Cong have a liaison committee for missionaries. Maybe I should try to contact them."

I wondered anew just how chummy he was with local VC.

Bennett glanced at his watch. "We've got helicopter assets tomorrow. If they haven't called in by morning . . ." He looked at Sergeant Parks. "Should we, Joe?"

"Whatever you say, Colonel." Meaning *No, but you're going to do it anyway. It's on you.*

"Okay," Bennett said. "Captain Rider, organize the first aid and medications. We'll go in two ships and evacuate the Baxters if need be."

"May I come along?" said Slavin. "I'll stay out of the way and make myself useful."

The colonel came around from his desk. "I'd appreciate it if you would."

The meeting broke up. When we were out of earshot, Parks said, "I've got rumors coming out of two districts about enemy activity: Montagnard villagers pressed into work gangs to portage NVA supplies."

"You think the Baxters ran into trouble on the way home?"

Joe shrugged. "No telling. There's NVA regulars and VC all over the province. I'm running out of pins to mark the sightings."

The Baxters still weren't responding to radio calls the next day, but our assigned helicopters were diverted for an emergency. We wouldn't get a bird for another twenty-four hours. I was duty officer and went to catch a nap before going on. A runner got me up an hour later. I put on a sidearm and my web harness and slung my M-16.

Except for Mama-san Duc, our Vietnamese workers hadn't shown up for the second day running. Never a good sign. But the Yards who guarded us at night came in early, and I went out to the corner of the compound where they liked to build their small cooking fire and greeted them. I checked the perimeter and the gate, officially closing it at the 1800 curfew. Most of the rest of the evening I was down in the commo bunker. Rain inundated us around nine, and an hour later I draped myself in a poncho and went out again to check the perimeter. Coming back, I ran into Miser near the mess hall, his fatigues plastered to his body.

"Sent Jessup the weekly update," he said. "No screaming yet."

"Good."

I trudged toward my quarters and dashed across the small patch of grass to the walkway. I let myself in, hoping to lie down for another half an hour. The downpour roared against the roof of the overhang and the bungalow. My pant legs were sopping from the short run. I dried my hands on the towel at the end of my bunk and reached for the field phone to let the commo bunker know where I was. I went to crank it, to generate the necessary electrical charge for the ringer, when I glanced down at the terminals connecting the commo wire to the equipment. Each post had an additional wire.

I let go of the crank and brought the gooseneck lamp closer. The extra wires ran behind the rectangular green box and into the body of the phone. I uncased it and traced them back to a good-size wedge of explosive, molded like clay to fit the empty space inside. The wires attached to a pair of detonators sticking out of the plastique, just like the booby-trapped psy ops radios Grady had shown me at Mai Linh. The charge was large enough to eliminate me and the neighbors on both sides. The explosive probably came from our own modest ammo bunker.

I removed the detonators and yanked out the deadly wires. Hands trembling, I cranked the phone to call Ruchevsky at his villa in town. Big John answered promptly.

"Well," I said, voice tremulous, "at least you didn't blow up answering."

"You okay? You sound shook up."

"I am. I just neutered a bomb in our field phone. Watch yourself. Check anything electrical. Go over your vehicles too."

A runner burst in, summoning me to the commo bunker. I grabbed my poncho and weapon and we jogged together through the downpour and down the steps into the underground room. Radio static filled the smoky air. Mai Linh was reporting a casualty. Their intel sergeant was down, seriously wounded by an explosive planted in the speaker of his tape deck. Ignoring the danger, the Berets were driving him in on a stretcher. Medic Ed Sprague wanted Roberta's help.

I sent the runner to wake Lieutenant Lovell and had the radio operator call for a medevac on the sideband. Weather or no weather, we needed the bird. Lovell clambered down the stairs. I told him to warn the Special Forces teams at Phu Thien and Phu Tuc. They should immediately check possessions and equipment for booby traps, especially anything electrical.

I inspected the field phone in the bunker and cranked it to reach the clinic in town while the radio operator pleaded with Pleiku for a chopper. Roberta came wide awake as soon as she heard what was coming our way. Pleiku confirmed a medical-emergency flight was airborne.

"I'll meet you at the strip," she said.

I took a backpack radio, smoke markers, and flares, and tuned in the frequency of the approaching Berets and the commo bunker.

Westy was just going back to bed after checking his generators. I enlisted his help on the spot to commandeer the colonel's jeep. He jumped in behind the wheel and sped us up to the gate. Hump hurried to open it and passed Westy his pistol as we rolled by. The Berets were two kilometers out, approaching fast. Roberta's Rover passed us and we swung in behind her. She drove with only parking lights on. My taped headlights barely illuminated the road, but Westy knew the way blind.

He reached the airstrip and drove us past the empty ARVN sentry box, onto the perforated steel planks. Roberta pulled next to us and we all killed our lights. The rain had let up but the sky was overcast and starless: utterly dark. I couldn't so much as judge the distance to the Rover as I got out and groped my way across.

"Doc?"

"You got a flashlight?" she said.

I turned on my red-lensed light and held it over her medical kit as she hurriedly organized instruments, bandages, gels, and hypodermics and rattled off instructions about what to ask the Berets by radio about the wounded man's medical treatment so far. I left the Rover's door open so she could hear and went to the radio in the jeep to raise the Berets' medic. Sergeant Sprague acknowledged and I posed her questions to him. The answers were chilling. The man was comatose though breathing, pulse thready. The wound . . . A chunk the size of a coaster was missing from his skull.

Roberta stopped rummaging. "Ask Ed, can they see his brain?" she said.

"Can you see his brain? Over."

"Affirmative."

I rogered the call and signed off.

"How are you holding up?" I said.

"Sleep deprived. And hungry." I looked toward the sound of her voice. "I stopped being scared recently," she said. "Don't know why."

All we could do was wait. Westy announced headlights exiting the town. They passed our compound and made the turn for the airfield. A minute later their open jeep pulled up next to us, a stretcher with the wounded man laid out across the back. A second jeep, totally blacked out, stopped behind them. A soldier manned an M-60 machine gun mounted on a post in the back.

The medevac chopper came up on our frequency, reporting its approach. Roberta worked in the dark, aided by three red-lensed flashlights. The chopper pilot would need a light to guide in on. Westy strode into the blackness. I couldn't see him, just heard his boots clanking across the perforated steel planks. Faint *whomp*s drew closer. Westy struck the end of a flare, igniting the white magnesium tip, and held it aloft like a torch. Anyone could see it for miles — friend or foe.

"Just don't let him land on my ass," Westy shouted.

I alerted the pilot. He laughed and repeated the instruction: "Roger, no ass landing." The bird came straight in. When it was nearly on him, Westy tossed the flare aside and stooped. The helicopter settled thirty feet away. The Berets rushed their comrade aboard, and it lifted away, the drone of its jet turbine engine receding rapidly.

We all convoyed back into the compound, convened in the empty mess hall, and collapsed.

"What are his chances?" I asked Roberta.

"Zero to none," she said, "but he's breathing." She headed to our medic's room to crash. "He needs a miracle."

Sergeant Durando and Joe Parks went around with flashlights and checked all the field phones, doors, bunkers, generators, firing positions, and the ammo bunker. A slab of C-4 explosive had been freshly cut. They examined all the vehicle ignitions too and sent Westy to check backup generators.

The Berets at Phu Tuc reported the stock of C-4 explosive in their ammo bunker showed signs of pilfering. Ours looked nibbled at too. Possible VC suspects at the Special Forces camps were too many to count. But we didn't have a thousand Montagnard strikers and their families in our compound. I interviewed the sleepy gate guards and went over their logs, looking to see what outsiders had been in the compound the last twenty-four hours. With most of the Vietnamese workers hunkered down in Cheo Reo, the log was pretty bare. Other than Judd Slavin and some Special Forces people who'd come by for their mail, the list consisted of Mama-san Duc and the old Montagnards who came into the compound toward sunset to stand guard through the night. Hump confessed Americans weren't always noted in the log. Mostly just waved by. He couldn't remember who might have passed through without being recorded. The USAID reps from next door walked in and out all the time.

Only one ship was available in the morning to fly us to the Baxters. Gidding assumed command of the compound while Slavin and the colonel and I set off for the airstrip.

"Ted and Audrey are old Asia hands," the reverend said, sitting with me in back of the colonel's jeep. "High-school sweethearts from Missouri. They've got two teenage boys in boarding school in the Philippines."

The sentry box was empty so we parked on the apron to wait. Two security guards and Macquorcadale arrived a minute later. The speck on the horizon turned into a helicopter. I went up on their frequency and made contact with the copilot. They landed quickly, had the six of us sitting on the pebbled deck in seconds and on our way at a hundred knots, the jet turbine above our heads whining. Colonel Bennett donned a headset and asked the pilots to follow Road 7 southeast so we could look for the Baxters' vehicle in case it had broken down on the way.

We stayed on the deck and followed the unpaved dirt track, looking for their pickup. We saw nothing and no one. Every few kilometers the roadbed was interrupted: washed out, nearly grown over. When we reached the Baxters' district, the river led toward their village. There was no one on the banks bathing or washing or fetching water. Not even kids frolicking. Bennett and I exchanged looks. The door gunners leveled their weapons on the passing scrub and jungle.

Our pilot buzzed the Baxters' house on the edge of the settlement. Neither Ted nor Audrey came out. We snapped our safeties off as we set down by the village, a short distance from their house. The door gunner yelled in my ear and flashed all his fingers at me twice like a fight referee: "You got twenty minutes, Captain. Then we're out of here."

The prop slowed but kept churning. We exited rapidly and spread ourselves out, except Slavin, who stayed close to the colonel. An old woman approached from the village, complaining. She and her husband had been left behind, Slavin said, along with one young boy tending buffalo.

Had the ARVN come and relocated the villagers, Slavin asked, and left her? No. The others.

"Guerrillas?" Bennett said.

Reverend Slavin questioned her and turned to us. "*Chin guy.* Army regulars. NVA. But she says a sunburned Vietnamese man with a heavy beard and filed-down teeth addressed the villagers in Rhade. Said they must all go work for the soldiers and carry their rice."

"Your friend Wolf Man covers a lot of ground," I muttered.

"They took the boy of a government militiaman," Slavin translated, "to execute him as punishment for his father serving in the Saigon army. The boy's mother talked them into taking her instead. They walked her into the forest near the grapefruit tree." The old woman looked toward the tree. "She didn't come back."

"And where were the Baxters during all this?" Bennett asked.

Slavin conveyed the question. She responded slowly. He turned to look toward the house.

"What did she say?" Bennett asked.

"They hid in their bunker, behind the house."

"Were they taken too? Where are they now?"

Slavin translated the questions. She gazed around and spoke.

Judd Slavin looked puzzled. "She says they're in the bunker."

The old woman walked with us to the house and around the side, leading us to the circular mound that was the Baxters' shelter against bombardments. I opened the straps on my musette bag. The bunker's entrance was a few steps down. Something wooden lay across one side of the rounded earthen top, flanked by some pots and pans and a bottle of cooking oil. I attempted to go in the entryway, which was partly blocked with boards and drifts of dirt on the steps.

"Audrey?" Slavin called past me. "Ted?"

Bennett yanked out the boards over the entry and flinched. He pulled the collar of his green T-shirt over his nose and ducked inside, Slavin behind him, handkerchief over his mouth and nostrils. They were in there only seconds. They exited amid a putrid stench. Slavin was pale. It clung to his clothes and hands. He seemed undone: mute and choking. Bennett held a kerchief to his mouth, coughing.

Bennett looked stricken. "It's them."

The Baxters were decomposing rapidly in the tropical heat. The old woman gesticulated as she spoke. Slavin listened and translated.

"They took shelter in the bunker when the army men appeared. The red-star soldiers surrounded the bunker and summoned them. Reverend Ted came out. He scolded them in Vietnamese. The bearded man shot him twice, went up to the bunker with a grenade like a masher, and threw it inside. After the village emptied out and they all left, she went to the reverend. He was still alive. She helped him to the bunker, as he asked. His wife had lost an eye. She was mostly unaware, barely alive. They were finished, finished. They died in each other's arms."

I turned back toward the bunker. Scratched faintly into the sides of the mound were symbols I had seen in the Jarai cemetery.

"I closed it as best I could," the old woman said, through Slavin, "and took the cross they knocked down from our chapel to put on their burial house."

Bennett stood on the bottom step and replaced the boards, adding the ones I handed down. The three security guards kept watch as the colonel and Judd Slavin hurriedly finished the job of sealing the bunker's entrance, Slavin mumbling Bible verses, voice trembling, face running with sweat.

"'New gods were chosen, then war was in the gates . . .'"

His chest heaved as he labored, eyes tearing. They streaked the dirt on his cheeks.

"'Then I saw the beast . . .'"

He was babbling from the heat and despair that clutched at us all, and maybe the knowledge that he had taken money from the hands that had killed his friends. Audrey and Ted Baxter had devoted their lives to helping others and proclaiming their faith. Their reward was watching each other die.

Red dust and grit rose around us and stuck to our sweating bodies as we emptied sandbags into the entrance well. Slavin scratched their names into the wood of the cross and planted it firmly on the roof of their tomb.

"'. . . and the glory of the Lord shone round them,'" he said to no one in particular. He didn't look like a duplicitous spook masquerading as a cleric. He looked like a guy who had just buried dear friends without a moment's ceremony at an isolated outpost in the middle of a jungle.

The aged woman's husband appeared, hobbling toward us in a black shirt and a loincloth and speaking loudly. Slavin's eyes widened.

"He says VC are approaching."

Bennett ordered the guards to the chopper while we rushed to the modest two-room house to retrieve the Baxters' personal effects. The rotors whined louder.

Bennett took up a position at the door while Slavin and I raced around. I took a pillowcase and filled it with photographs of two blond kids, someone's elderly parents, the Bible on the nightstand, a hairbrush. I didn't know what to snatch up, what held meaning. Slavin added small sculptures, a figurine made by a child, a heart-shaped rock, an address book, two framed wedding photos. Bennett urged us to finish as I pushed objects into the sack and Slavin searched for a photo album — seconds to gather up a lifetime. I made for the bookcase.

"We've got to go," the colonel said, and waved Slavin out. I grabbed a handful of volumes at random and ran after him.

We had intended to look for the Jarai woman Wolf Man had executed by the grapefruit tree. No time. The old woman accepted Judd Slavin's rucksack of supplies and my two packs of cigarettes but wouldn't come with us. Slavin urged her husband to convince her, to no avail.

"She says she isn't getting into our iron insect. Says she must look after the village until everyone comes back."

The crew chief was frantically waving for us to hurry. My heart hammered my chest. We bade them goodbye and ran to the churning helicopter. The pilot lifted off the instant we jumped on board.

Armed men stepped into the open as we rose. They hadn't yet seen the old couple nearing the far side of the clearing; they were all looking up at us. With a final glance skyward, the ancient woman and her man slipped into the undergrowth and disappeared.

# 15

★  ★  ★

**T**HE HUEY STAYED on the deck as we flew back along Road 7 toward Cheo Reo, eventually climbing up to a thousand feet. Treetops sped by. Colonel Bennett cupped his headset to his ears, listening intently. He tugged me nearer the door and pointed down. In a short open strip of the road a flatbed truck lay half tipped over on the shoulder, its load of long hardwood logs spilling out. Four male figures lay prone around the vehicle: two civilians and two South Vietnamese soldiers in green fatigues stained dark with blood.

I jabbed earthward. Bennett nodded and spoke into his mike. The pilot signaled his assent. The helicopter dipped and slowly spiraled down. The warrant officers set the Huey down right on the road, raising a storm of dirt and small stones. Five of us jumped off. The pilot barely decreased the rotations and the downdraft pummeled us with grit. Bennett and I approached the disabled truck warily while Macquorcadale and the others secured the perimeter. The windshield and cab were riddled with bullets. A shot-up tire smoldered. The gaping entrance wounds and the large exit holes were undoubtedly made by the nasty, spiraling rounds from Kalashnikovs.

The roadbed had been hastily swept in two separate places to cover tracks. A few feet off the road, both spots showed a mass of boot prints. Several hundred NVA had crossed in two files and disappeared into the heavy growth along the stream.

"Maybe the driver refused to stop," I said.

"Or the ARVN escort panicked," said Bennett. "I would have thought a safe conduct came with the logging deal."

"Maybe the People's Army hadn't gotten the word or wasn't interested. Or just didn't want to leave any witnesses to who was marching through, or how many, or what direction they were going."

The pilot signaled us back aboard but I needed a closer look. I motioned toward the load. Bennett nodded and took up a position facing away, rifle stock braced. I jumped up on the truck bed and touched the thick raw timbers, three feet across, freshly sawed and aromatic. Mahogany. The bottom timbers were cut in half lengthwise, the flat halves face-down on the bed to make a steadier platform for the ones piled on top and chained to the rig. The two topmost logs had skidded off and lay half on the truck, half off. They'd been cut in two lengthwise and rejoined. One log lay open, its innards filled with coarsely wrapped packages: a hollowed-out container for contraband.

The loggers were smuggling raw opium, probably had been all along. The wooden debris I'd seen floating on the current in the Katu River was man-made: the transfer point for the opium was a sawmill. Madame Chinh's loggers. I ripped open a package and pulled out two wrapped bricks of raw opium, tossed one to Bennett, and shoved the other in a thigh pocket.

The only two roads in or out of the province, 7 and 2, crisscrossed each other at Cheo Reo. The opium was undoubtedly loaded onto the truck somewhere along the lower leg of 7 and driven southeast toward its junction with National Highway 1, which continued south to Saigon and the refineries in the Cholon District. The bank deposits to the Hong Kong accounts were never interrupted because the real traffic never faltered. If we had disrupted their marijuana harvest and singed a few poppies, we'd done nothing to the mainstay of their opium trade.

It wasn't safe to investigate further. Bennett ordered Macquorcadale to puncture the gas tank, opened a jerry can of gasoline and splashed the logs, then threw two cans of motor oil atop the pile. I took a jar from the cab, spilled its contents on the road, refilled it with sawdust and gasoline, stuck a sock over the mouth, and set fire to it. I hurled the jar at the rig. The bark and exposed flanks caught instantly. We ran to the chopper. The gas tank went up before we left the ground, sending a thick plume of smoke rising toward the layer of black cloud cover.

I typed an encrypted message to Jessup telling him to have our MPs stop all rigs hauling timber south on National Highway 1, toward Saigon. That door would shut in hours.

I went to find Big John and let him know that we'd discovered — and sealed off — the land route. He wasn't in our room, but I could hear him yelling. He was in the colonel's office, berating both Bennett and Major Gidding. I tiptoed into the outer bullpen and suggested to the civilian interpreter that he go for a smoke. Slight and sensitive, Mr. Cho looked grateful to escape Big John's disturbing volume. Checkman volunteered to go too.

"You don't smoke," I said.

"Neither does Mr. Cho."

"Go." I sat at Checkman's desk in the cramped bullpen, listening to Big John vent his wrath on Major Gidding.

"*Siphoning* our gasoline. *Selling* staples in volume at Chinh's wife's market. Sweet Jesus, the wife of a full colonel in the *South* Vietnamese Army is facilitating the resupply of the *North* Vietnamese Army under our noses. He's practically provisioning their rest-and-recuperation spas in the mountains, providing them with a rear staging area for whatever offensives they're planning . . . planning against us all."

"I seriously doubt the Chinhs are even sympathizers," Gidding said. "He's too much the capitalist, as is she."

"Oh, for — who *cares* about their motives or politics," Ruchevsky snapped. "What difference does that make? The result's the same, Major. NVA bellies are getting filled, NVA ammo replenished. And — surprise! — Chinh refuses to send out patrols against his best customers."

"That's pure supposition," Gidding spat. "He's only got four hundred soldiers. The NVA number in the thousands at the moment. He's simply being prudent and conserving his forces." He turned to the colonel. "If he goes, do we really think another province chief would behave any differently?"

"I hope to God," Ruchevsky fumed.

"Where does it stop?" Bennett said, genuinely torn. "Madame Chinh sells a license to log hardwoods, that's not our business. But I saw what was traveling inside those logs."

There was a thump. He had dropped the brick of raw opium on the desk to show John and Gidding.

"She's selling licenses to dope smugglers."

"Sir, we're not here to reform their system. We're expected to go along and get along — give them support in their fight and keep out of the way. We've got too much on our plate to become narcotics agents on top of it."

He shifted his attention to John.

"Look," Gidding said. "We're in Viet Nam by invitation. On their sufferance — Chinh's sufferance. We're here as advisers, not Chinh's superiors. As far as we're concerned, Chinh operates with impunity. I can't rein him in or order his men into the field. Neither can the colonel. We're not Saigon, we're not General Loc up in Two Corps. Their private undertakings are their business. They're none of yours."

I got up and stood quietly in the doorway.

Ruchevsky banged the desk. "My *business* is to protect your backs and ferret out Commies in the population, not local corruption. But Chinh's side ventures are lending significant aid and comfort to the enemy. And that is very much my goddamn concern, Major."

Gidding looked annoyed. "We all know Vietnamese military and civil servants aren't properly compensated. It's made exploitation of one's position part of the cultural norm."

"Cultural norm, my ass."

"We do not have operational control," Gidding said slowly, enunciating each word. He leaned across the desk toward Bennett to plead his case to his superior. "This isn't Schweinfurt, sir. Or Seoul. We don't have authority over their officers or officials. It's their military, their country. We can't very well impose our will or our values."

"Well, maybe we should start," Ruchevsky said sharply. "His customers are killing us, if you haven't noticed."

"I was *speaking* to the colonel."

"I'm *speaking* to you."

The colonel tried to calm them down but Ruchevsky wasn't listening.

"I'm risking my ass for nothing going out there," he said, "gathering intel for air strikes on a bunch of fucking Houdinis. I came here to tell you I just got the follow-up on the last sortie, and whaddya know — we destroyed another shitload of *trees* and jungle. *Our* actions against the enemy are being undermined because Cheo Reo's leaking and the enemy is anticipating our every move."

Gidding shook his head in disbelief. "So Pleiku's not leaking? Saigon's not? You have proof it's all only spilling out of Cheo Reo? Or is this more conjecture?"

"Oh, I'm *sure* Chinh draws the line at selling information," John said sarcastically. "Food, sure. Gasoline, why not? Beams for NVA bunkers? No problem. But intel, absolutely not. No doubt his code of honor forbids it." Ruchevsky glared. "You know what, Gidding? You're — "

"Gentlemen," Bennett said, rising to his feet.

" — full of seepage."

Gidding bristled. Ruchevsky barged through the bullpen, slamming the screen door as he exited. I ran out to catch up with him.

"That fucking Gidding," he fumed, walking across the quad.

"It's a nutty war," I said, trying to calm John down. "ARVN selling ordnance that gets shot back at them — and us."

"We're supplying all sides in this mess," John said. He fired up a wooden match to light his stogie. "The latest? ARVN keeps reordering and reordering this rubbery plastic from DuPont for military boot soles — more boot goo than they've got feet, it turns out. The VC scarf up the shipments and combine the goop with USAID fertilizer to make a high explosive. And guess who's been selling it to them?"

I felt a pang of pessimism. The corruption seemed overwhelming and impossible to stop. *Making a killing* was taking on a whole new meaning for me.

"Here," Ruchevsky said, and pulled a black-and-white glossy from a manila envelope: a peacock displaying its plumage in a huge fan.

"What's this?"

"The wages of sin — Chinh's hacienda. One of the exotic pets running around Colonel Chihuahua's garden in Saigon. He's got miniature deer too. And ponies for his kids."

A wide shot of the residence showed an ornate French-era mansion and outbuildings surrounded by a high brick fence topped with broken glass. Hand-printed at the bottom was an address in an exclusive district in the capital.

"Little John's best informant says the Chinhs are looking at land around Dalat for a mountain retreat near Madame Nhu's old place."

"Damn, I'm in the wrong army."

Mr. Cho's elegant gray head poked around the corner of the mess hall.

"Mr. Cho?"

He'd undoubtedly heard us. I sent him scurrying back to the office.

"So you heard how the opium's getting to Saigon?" I whispered.

John nodded. "Chinh's going to be more than a little annoyed when he finds out you've got MPs shutting down the route." Ruchevsky closed an eye against his cigar smoke. "And I'm looking forward to Lund finding out you're putting an end to his pension plan. You light up a couple of fields and suddenly there's a few extra wires in your field phone. I'm not liking your odds of survival once the MPs start confiscating those logs."

Checkman called me back into the bullpen. Lieutenant Lovell stood nervously in a corner of Bennett's little office. Sergeant Divivo had reported by radio that the ARVN company he advised was refusing to go out on a sweep in spite of all the mounting evidence of enemy strength increasing and drawing nearer. They wouldn't budge, citing the danger of nearby Communist forces. The rifle company was about to be dismissed.

"ARVN is completely intransigent," Bennett said. "Looks like we've got to put out patrols ourselves. Immediately. Captain Rider, take six men. Patrol a radius of three kilometers, looping northwest from Cheo Reo. Do a cloverleaf. Lieutenant Lovell, take a second patrol and loop a cloverleaf south. I'll go up with Major Hopp and we'll recon a twenty-klick circle around Cheo Reo."

I picked Sergeant Divivo, Rowdy for my radioman, and four off-duty perimeter guards, ordering them to stand ready in forty minutes, each man carrying a day's rations and four hundred rounds, every round of the first magazine a tracer. If we got into a fight I wanted an initial fusillade of screaming red. We'd fire blind and split. It wasn't brilliant but I'd seen it work: blast away like crazy and disengage. As in run like hell.

Cheo Reo's artillery battery would be of no use to us. We'd be on our own, except for whatever air assets might divert to help us. "Leftovers," Miser called them: warplanes coming off of missions with unused ordnance.

The Vietnamese sentries at the checkpoint on Road 7 watched us march past. One soldier squatted over a live duck, blade in hand; another lounged in a hammock. Others leaned on the sandbag walls piled chest-high around the roadblock, smoking as we trudged by.

We marched three kilometers and left the track to move west through scrub, counting off three hundred yards before turning back toward town. Avoiding trails, we patrolled cross-country, rifles up. My map indicated a Montagnard village less than a klick ahead. A hundred yards farther on we came upon a six-year-old youngster straddling a huge water buffalo wallowing in a mud hole. Just beyond him were the village longhouses. Young palm trees marked the community's borders. I led the patrol through, stopping to souvenir the chief an extra pack of cigarettes and try out the few words of Rhade I knew.

I asked if he had seen northern troops or Viet Cong. The chief said the VC had been there propagandizing. I didn't know how to ask him how long ago. I'd run out of vocabulary.

Near a stream fenced across with bamboo and clogged with fish traps, we came across a mass of footprints on a path. A large group wearing NVA boots. The impressions were less than a day old. Two klicks from Cheo Reo. NVA units were maneuvering that close, totally unchallenged, in mortar range.

I broke off our route and turned the patrol around to head out at an angle from the way we'd come. Three thousand strides farther, another village appeared on a rolling ridge above a river tributary. No children, no women — young or old. No men. Divivo pointed out branches laid across paths leading into the village, meaning they weren't receiving visitors. The village stood empty, weaving looms and threshing abandoned, cooking fires smoking in the longhouses. No one in the gardens or by the river. They'd hidden from us. All except the little boys herding buffalo in mud holes. They stood like birds, motionless on the large wallowing beasts. I wondered aloud why these kids had stayed at their posts.

"Lookouts," Divivo said.

"For the villagers?"

"Or the VC. You never know."

We passed by quickly, worried about being in the open, and forded a wide coil of river that came up to our waists. Crossing, I took the opportunity to pee in my clothes without stopping. What looked like a huge dead fish floated by.

"Body," Divivo said, as we pressed on, the younger men wincing at the sight.

We made two more loops, seeing signs of more booted traffic and the marks made by sampans beached on the bank. They'd bivouacked near the boats. No fires.

"You think it might be ARVN, sir?" a private asked quietly.

"I wish."

On the fourth loop our flanker stumbled on a shallow grave. We excavated enough of it to see three Montagnard men, hands still tied behind them, all recently slain by hard blows that had caved in the backs of their heads. Persuasion had given way to ultimatum.

"Poor bastards," Divivo said and crossed himself.

Rowdy offered me the handset. I waved him off. I didn't want to take the time to call in anything in the open or stop to encode a message. VC were undoubtedly monitoring our frequencies. The less aware they were of where we were and what we were finding, the better. If we didn't make it back, that would be message enough. I ordered Rowdy not to acknowledge calls with more than a click on his handset.

We covered the bodies again, dropped everything but our water and ammunition, and made straight for home base, praying all the way we wouldn't bump into the people's liberators maneuvering through the jungle and scrub around us.

Joe Parks was waiting at the front gate. He took the enlisted off to debrief while Lovell took me and Sergeant Divivo to the colonel. Major Gidding joined us. It didn't take long to give them the bad news. Gidding grew agitated. I asked about the latest alerts from II Corps.

"The NVA are on the move," he said, "maneuvering in large numbers. Two Corps is betting Pleiku City is one objective. NVA deployed to their south along Road Fourteen in blocking positions. They're expecting the road to their north will get cut next. Other enemy units are moving in the opposite direction, southeast — toward us. Road Seven is already blocked with trenches dug across; two small bridges were blown."

Bennett nodded. "I've got to light a fire under the ARVN battalion. Face Chinh down. Press him to take immediate action. Our Special Forces camps are at risk. So are we and Chinh's battalion."

"Not really," I said. "Our South Vietnamese neighbors seem to have an understanding with the enemy."

Major Gidding bridled. "That's an ill-considered comment, Captain. You and John Ruchevsky seem determined to undo every bit of what we've achieved here."

"Gentlemen," Bennett said, "we don't have time for this. I need to see Colonel Chinh, right now."

"You want us to come, sir?" the major asked.

"A show of unity and concern?" Bennett said. "It's a thought. God knows, private talks haven't done anything for us."

"The more the merrier at this point, no?" Gidding said.

Bennett gathered himself to his full height. "Maybe not just yet. We'll keep it respectful. Captain Rider and Private Checkman will accompany me. Major, secure the compound in the meantime. Radio me any further news of enemy movement."

The parade ground in front of the ARVN battalion office was empty. Checkman asked some officers where to find the province chief. Colonel Chinh, they said, was in his quarters.

We drove across the bare parade field, not a blade of grass on it, not so much as a weed, and pulled up next to the officers' billet, a refurbished French colonial residence circled by a wide veranda. A pair of bloody elephant tusks, freshly harvested, stuck out of an empty metal drum in front. We mounted three steps up to the porch and entered. Each officer had an individual room off a long, wide hallway, with a common mess at the end. On the far side of the dining hall we came upon Chinh's valet, who led us down a short corridor into the colonel's sitting room. Not much by way of décor: a faded couch, an armchair, a Ping-Pong table, a cloisonné vase on a teak stand. No wall decorations whatsoever, no pictures of the family or anyone else. The manservant led us through to the back veranda, where Chinh stood, espresso cup in hand, leaning close to his caged songbird, which fluttered and warbled as we approached.

Bennett didn't even apologize for the intrusion and wasted no time pressing Chinh about the lack of patrols and the cancellation of the day's sweep. Chinh remained in a benign mood as he contemplated the vista of the Cheo Reo basin and the mountains in the distance. He dismissed the valet and addressed us in a pleasant tone, Checkman translating.

"I am well aware of your many suggestions. We considered them just this morning and decided not to implement them . . . at this time."

"May I know why not, sir?" Bennett said.

"We require the troops in Cheo Reo. I cannot spare the rifle companies and disperse them as you suggest. They are needed here for defense. My superiors at Corps headquarters fear more violence from the Montagnards."

Bennett said, "Sir, with all due respect, Montagnards should hardly be your main concern at the moment, when we have — "

Chinh interrupted, his voice melodic with the tones of his language. Checkman listened for a minute, then translated.

"On the contrary. Your Special Forces lure young Montagnards to their camps, teach them to be saboteurs, to overthrow governments, violate international borders, assassinate Vietnamese. How many such camps now? Fifty? Sixty? When we are under threat, we are the most concerned with the army of aborigines at our backs."

Bennett colored. "The Montagnards harass and slow the invaders who march across the border into your province."

"Your A camps slow nothing." Chinh spoke rapidly; Checkman struggled to keep up: "Any Green Beret camp that interferes, the northern army overruns and brushes aside. They are too distant — too isolated — even from one another. There are no reinforcements, no artillery that can help."

In English he added, "You make same mistake as French, Colonel Bennett." He pressed a biscuit between the bars of the cage. "I always listen your advise. I advise you now." The bird pecked at the biscuit. "Camps too small. Job big. You cannot capture Ho's red fish with bird's nest."

"Exactly why you must not crouch here. Send out patrols, Colonel Chinh. Target your artillery, use our airpower." Bennett pointed at the vista. "A large enemy force marches this way. There have never been this many NVA soldiers in the province at the same time."

Chinh resumed his tranquil pose. His bird sang brightly.

"My job to protect from savage."

"Sir," Bennett said, "I beg to disagree."

Chinh returned to Vietnamese, his tone sarcastic and hectoring: "Your camps harbor murderous rebels," Checkman translated. "Green Berets sow discord between the savages and our citizens, and advocate separation of the Highland regions from Viet Nam. The French, you, the Cambodians, all plot and promote bloody rebellion."

"Savage loyal to you," Chinh said in English. "You loyal to savage."

Bennett fell silent, unable to deny the charge. "Colonel Chinh," he said, "we have lost enough men defending your country to prove our loyalty. Why would we encourage the Montagnards to secede?"

Checkman's freckles grew darker and his face whiter as he translated the province chief's reply: "I wonder myself. Saigon understands your government has conducted surveys, found important ore in the Highlands. Thinks you encourage the savages to establish an autonomous state, so it can be more easily relieved of its strategic riches."

"Strategic riches?" Bennett said, dismayed.

Chinh, looking smug—in possession of privileged information—drew out the moment. "Plutonium," he said, finally.

"Plutonium?" Bennett froze in disbelief.

"And ore of aluminum."

"I . . . I assure you—" Bennett stammered.

Chinh clasped his hands behind his back and spoke in English. "No need. Not embarrass. Maybe Washington not inform colonel, as Saigon inform me."

"Sir, why are we debating? You and I are both facing an immediate threat from large numbers of North Vietnamese," Bennett said. "The NVA has found a safe haven here in Phu Bon Province. They operate freely. We need to know how many. Where. And disrupt them."

Chinh grunted. He appeared affronted. "You want fight Communist. Okay, okay. American soldier stay year, sometime two. Me? Fifteen. Fight war fifteen year. Last five year, before I come to Cheo Reo, I have eight adviser. Soon you go. I wait. Get different adviser, different advise."

Chinh crossed his arms and looked out onto the volcanic plateau toward a small, dormant cone.

"Province have sixty thousand Montagnard. Several thousand NVA soldier. Me? With me — four hundred men, four hundred family."

"Sir, our circumstances are grave. I may have to contact General Loc at Two Corps."

Chinh lapsed into Vietnamese, pausing to let Checkman catch up.

"You like Montagnards more than us Vietnamese. In our marriages — " Checkman stopped, perplexed. "He must mean *alliances*. He says, In our alliances there are no vows of fidelity, no limit on other relationships. Our matches are not made for . . . love, not for desire. They are arranged for mutual benefit. Changing such alignments, after a decent interval, is acceptable. You need not feel guilty for shifting your affiliation. Taking other partners is acceptable . . . if such is your wish."

The barely veiled message was clear, and Bennett's discomfort evident on his face. Chinh would do nothing. And he knew about the colonel's affair. If Chinh notified his or Bennett's superiors, Bennett's career was over. Adultery was a court-martial offense in the U.S. Army. Chinh had flashed his trump card.

He grunted. "You have duty, Colonel. I same." He tapped his chest. "*Je suis responsable*. You have order. I same."

"Your orders are . . .?" Bennett said, barely containing himself.

"Keep soldier alive, keep command strong. Civilize Montagnard."

"Civilize how?" Bennett said, exasperated. "Push more Vietnamese refugees into their tribal territories? Force the Montagnards off their land into hopeless government hamlets and force them to assimilate?"

Chinh stared him down. "At home you have Indian. We have Indian. Same." He reverted to Vietnamese.

"Would you stand by and let your Indian reservations secede? How many states have you returned to your Sioux?"

Bennett pulled out a map of the province and asked Chinh to shell the three nearby trails being used by the NVA. Chinh said, "Okay, okay," and straightened. "Excuse."

Colonel Bennett saluted and Checkman and I snapped to. Chinh returned our salutes casually.

"Captain," he said, stopping me, and reached into the birdcage to pick up a colorful feather. "You and you friend interest in my birds." He handed me the yellow-gray feather. "Sorry not peacock."

# 16

★ ★ ★

I DROVE TO RUCHEVSKY'S house in town to give him a heads-up about Chinh's warning and found him sprawled in his wicker armchair, playing hearts with his guards. He waved his cigar at me and indicated the couch, draped with a long, handwoven Montagnard black cloth bordered in red and rows of small white stick-figure helicopters. I ran Chinh's crazy assertion past him.

"Plutonium. I love it." He got up, heading for the back. "Beer?"

"Got a Coke?"

"In a bright Commie-red can. Comin' up."

He was back in a second with our cold drinks, fresh cigar firmly clamped in his teeth. The guards took up their posts outside and I filled him in on the latest encounter with Chinh and all the activity our patrols had seen.

"Shit," he said and handed me the pop. "You up for another run through the forest?"

"Now? With all the NVA passing through the neighborhood?"

"Later. If there is a later."

"Just you and me again?"

"No. We'll need some manpower this time."

"What for?"

"A snatch. I'm clocking a courier coming down the trail with guards and a radio. He's being escorted by serious VC cadre on each leg. From what we know, he's carrying several kilos of paper from their higher command and he's due to pick up more from our fearless local VC leader, Mr. Wolf Man, as he passes by."

Last time, when John had taken me right into the middle of a VC mall, we had been lucky. But I wasn't eager to push my luck just now.

"Sounds tempting," I said, with bravado.

"Trust me. If he's carrying what I think he's carrying, this could nail Chinh's ass."

"In that case, I'm definitely in. What's the drill?"

"We take out the entourage, grab the courier and his stuff, and break the sound barrier exiting the area."

"Elegant. How many of us?"

"Maybe six. We have to smoke the guards to kidnap him."

"Sure," I said to the suggestion of another murderous close encounter. He must have sensed my hesitation.

"We go in, we come out," he said, checking me closely. "Simple."

"How many of them?"

His lips pursed. "Same as us. Half a dozen?"

"That a guess?"

"Almost. On some stretches they give him more escorts."

"When do we do it?"

"Don't know. Soon." He extended a fist. "Let's hope."

I tapped the top of his fist with my own and raised my Coke can. "To Operation Humpty Dumpty."

John pulled a classified sheet from under a folder resting on the chest.

"Here. A present. Reverend Slavin's bank records are clean. Captain Nhu's too. Poor boy's still going to have to work in mama's pharmacy after the war. Lund's Saigon account however . . . USAID man's regularly banking five-thousand-dollar deposits, transferred from a bogus company in Macao. Small change for a small fish."

"So Lund isn't the partner. And Province Chief Chinh isn't getting paid just to look away."

"Hardly. He's in it in a big way. Chinh banks his humble government salary in Saigon. His lovely wife parks her regular tribute monies in a Paris account. But nothing like multiple hundred-thousand-dollar deposits. Guess what, though: Madame Chinh's got a newly rich cousin."

"Where?"

"Taiwan."

"Doing what?" I said.

"Nothing. She's a spinster. Lives with her nephew's family. A sometime caretaker."

"Big bucks in child care, huh?"

Big John blew a smoke ring. "Her bank records should be in my courier pouch on the next Otter flight. Looks like the Chinhs have an awful lot invested in this drug trade you've been sent to fuck up. You may want to bunk with me for a while."

"I can't bail on the signal unit or my intel duties. Bennett's short-handed as it is."

"Rider, I got people watching me sleep, making sure I get to wake up. You've got a mosquito net and a screen door."

"And a deadbolt."

"Whoopee." Big John twirled his index finger.

"I sleep in an armed camp."

"My point exactly," he said. "There are weapons and explosives everywhere, common as heat rash. All you need is a mishap . . . a detonator and a couple of volts . . . You give 'em an opening . . ."

"I'll be watchful, John. Rest easy."

"Watch out you don't rest in peace. Mai Linh's a real armed camp and their intel guy lost half his skull just turning on Waylon Jennings. That country shit will kill ya." Ruchevsky grew somber. "We're on our own in this. Bennett can't help much and Gidding won't."

"Okay. I guess it's up to us to take him down."

"Yeah, before he cancels our ticket. Congratulations, by the way."

"For what?" I said.

"The bounty on you has doubled."

The Air Force intel from MACV reported a large enemy force moving piecemeal out of the mountains in the direction of Cheo Reo. Miser, Gidding, Parks, and I spent the late afternoon rounding up civilians—the three USAID guys, Little John, the two Korean doctors and their three nurses, and Dr. Roberta. It took a couple of hours to escort them all into the compound. Cots were erected for the men in an empty hootch, while the Korean women settled into two adjoining bungalow rooms. We hadn't gotten a replacement *bac-si* yet, so Roberta got the medic's cramped quarters and dispensary at the far end. Joe Parks returned late. In spite of their colleagues' fate, the Slavins refused to leave the Montagnards. As did senior missionary Reed at the leper village. The colonel sent Parks right back to tell the Slavins it wasn't a request. He wanted them brought to the compound immediately. Sergeant Parks and two security guards delivered the word and shepherded their pickup back to MACV. Reed was allowed to remain at the leprosarium. Given how wary all Vietnamese were of the disease, the NVA wouldn't go near the place.

In the waning light, Colonel Bennett read the formal escape-and-evasion plan to the civilians staying in the compound and the half of Team 31 that wasn't manning the perimeter. Afterward the mess hall looked like the first Thanksgiving: food and guns and pilgrims far from home, huddled together for protection. The missionaries led everyone in saying grace over the meal and held an impromptu prayer service right after supper. Our operations officer and a couple of enlisted men joined them. Just outside, you could hear Colonel Bennett reciting the escape plan again for the Team 31 members who had just come off guard duty.

Beyond the fence the world went silent. I climbed the water tower and stared straight along the main drag through town. Empty. The Vietnamese kitchen workers and hootch maids hadn't shown up for work again and the businesses in the vil had stayed shuttered all day. The Montagnard night sentries strode in right on time as if nothing were happening.

The town remained buttoned up and so did we. Bennett ordered the perimeter lights doused and the compound blacked out. Ruchevsky's cigar glowed in the twilight, his Schmeisser clamped under his arm like a loaf of bread. At sundown we all took up our defensive positions in the bunkers. The ARVN howitzers across the street started firing, their shells screaming and rattling over us.

"Huh," Miser said. "I didn't think they'd have the nerve to risk pissing off the NVA."

Around seven, a hot item came in on the secure teletype. ARVN units had occupied Da Nang to put down a full-blown revolt in I Corps against the regime and us. Premier Ky had deposed the popular Corps commander — one of the few Buddhist generals — and denounced the chief Buddhist monk as a Communist before arresting him. The Buddhists responded by burning down the USIS library in Hue and were hunger-striking and threatening secession. Soldiers in uniform joined the demonstrations. They wanted a civilian government — and our troops out of their country. Buddhists in Saigon were striking in sympathy. I ran it over to Colonel Bennett.

"Damn," he said. "The five Buddhist provinces want out, the Montagnards want autonomy for their twelve. How in hell is this country going to hold together? You got anything else I should know?"

"Three hours ago the NVA jumped a company of the First Cav forty-five miles northwest of us. They're fully engaged."

"See any connection to Cheo Reo?"

I bit my lip and pondered. "Not really, unless maybe they're trying to keep everyone focused elsewhere, away from here."

Bennett nodded, preoccupied, and dismissed me.

Nobody was going to get much sleep. I retired to the blacked-out signal shack. It was impossible to concentrate so Miser and I played cards with Little John, who turned out to be a real shark. After he'd taken us in half a dozen hands of poker, Miser urged me to show him the game I'd learned from a tailor in Saigon, an old Viet Minh company commander who had fought at Dien Bien Phu.

The tailor would lay out sixteen buttons in a pyramid: one button . . . three . . . five . . . seven. You took turns, removing as many or as few buttons as you wanted, but only from one row at a time. Whoever picked up the last button lost. I laid out the cards in the same formation. Miser urged Little John to try it but he wouldn't take the bait. Miser played instead. As usual, he lost over and over. My pot grew. He hated losing.

"What damn kinda game is this?" he groused.

"Don't know. Vietnamese. Maybe French. You go."

Miser picked up seven cards, wiping out the longest row. "How did you figure it out?"

"I kept asking the tailor but all he'd say was 'You play.' Later I'd play it by myself, backward, again and again, and cracked it a bit at a time. One day I beat him and he broke out his cognac. I'd figured it out."

"So what was the secret?"

"You lose in the middle before you even know it."

A couple of exchanges and he conceded again.

"Damn."

"Me play?" Little John said, tempted by the scrip piled up on my side. I finished off Little John in seven games and rose to go outside for some air.

*"Nuc?"* Little John asked, miming drinking.

"Water, hell," Miser said, "have a beer. May be your last chance in this life."

Out in the dark, I leaned on a wall of sandbags and gave Miser back the money he'd lost. "Stay away from that hustler," I said.

We stared in the direction of the river and let our eyes adjust.

Miser said, "Remember that wild VC in the wire at Dak To that Stolz and everybody shot at and couldn't hit because he was jumping around the minefield like a madman?"

"Yeah." I laughed. "Finally figured out it was an ape."

*Whump.* A mortar round launched into the quiet night.

Miser yelled, *"Mortar, mortar,"* as we dove back inside for cover. Two more shells thunked in quick succession, arcing toward us through the black sky.

The first whistled in and exploded by the water tower. The second blammed down between the gate and the back of the mess, peppering walls with hot fragments, spraying gravel and shrapnel onto roofs. A woman screamed. The third mortar round followed the second: the Charlies were trying for the main generator. A propane tank spewed gas and expired. Westy's generators kept churning.

After the three mortar rounds — silence. Helmet straps and rifle slings jingled as shadows trotted to bunkers. We took up our positions on the perimeter and waited. I had a thousand rounds in magazines stacked at my firing port. I seated the first round and checked the safety.

"This is gonna look like New Year's Eve," Miser said, ragged teeth white in the darkness. He was smiling, helmet set at a jaunty angle.

Damn if he wasn't enjoying himself. Rowdy, at his assigned spot, sounded like he was reciting Hail Marys. Macquorcadale unexpectedly swung his rifle around, smacking Miser in the shoulder.

"Jesus H. Christ!" Miser snarled. "Look alive, fucktard. I don't appreciate no fucking gun barrel crackin' me upside the head. And close that chin strap. This ain't no halftime. If you get blowed up and your brain bucket comes crashin' down on me, you'd best be in it, fuckwit."

Someone's rifle slid off the sandbag wall to the ground.

The sarge fumed. "Whichever peckerhead's weapon that is, he'd best pick it up — now!" Somebody gathered it in. "If it's out of your hands again," Miser growled to him, "I'm gonna use your asshole for a gun rack, you doofus motherfucker. And stay away from them jars before you blow us all to shit. I ain't runnin' your sorry ass through a strainer to send you home to your mama."

Even the possibility of VC surging into the perimeter was preferable to Miser's spewing, those ruined teeth an inch from the kid's face. A couple of them giggled nervously.

"What are you ladies gawking at?" Miser snarled. "Macquorcadale, you giant bimbo, ain't you noticed you're too fucking tall for your firing position. Dig a hole!" Miser barked.

The soldier stood dumbfounded, looking at Miser like he had lost his mind.

"You got sand in your pussy or something?" he shouted at the Canadian. "Dig a hole to stand in, before I use that entrenching tool to realign your brains. You" — he pointed to our two privates — "help 'im."

The three of them dug at the hard ground, using helmets and a shovel like pickaxes, their fear momentarily forgotten as they obeyed the absurd order. The rest of us trained our weapons on the perimeter wall.

"Last man standing," Miser announced with glee, "pop the thermite grenade in the crypto van."

A tense hour passed. Ten o'clock. Nothing.

I left Miser with the detachment and circled the defensive positions, where I ran into Colonel Bennett and Joe Parks. We went to ground at the southernmost corner, behind the sandbag bunker housing the .50, and stayed flush with its perforated steel walls.

"What do you think, Captain Rider?" Bennett said.

"Seems too early in the evening for a ground attack."

"Two in the morning would be more their style," said Joe Parks.

I said, "Do you get the feeling we're supposed to keep our heads down?"

Joe nodded. "Yes, sir. They're on the move and don't want us to see them."

"Passing that close?" Bennett said, concerned.

"Yes, sir," I said.

"Okay. We stay turtles."

I went back to patrolling the compound. At half past midnight, I noticed a lanky figure slipping along the bungalow walkway, heading to the medic's room. At 0300 Sergeant Rowdy sought me out.

"Captain," he whispered, "you should know. Either the ARVN stopped answering their field phone or the landline's cut. Gate guard wants you too."

I stayed in the shadows and announced my arrival with a hoarse "Hey, what's up?"

Something struck the roof behind us and tapped its way to the ground.

"Like that," Hump said. "Sticks and rocks have been coming over for the last quarter hour."

"Probers trying to draw your fire?"

"Or ARVN harassing us again from across the street."

"The signal shack called over there but they're not responding."

A stone struck the ground and skipped toward us. Another clanked against the steel of the encircling outer wall. Somewhere Deros was barking. If the enemy was coming, we'd know it when they scaled the perimeter or stormed the gate.

"Fire only if you've got a target or you're taking fire," I ordered. "Pass the word. I'm going for a look. Put up a flare."

I snuck up to the wall, hunched over, and peered over the top. No human sounds. A handheld flare punched into the air, whooshed up, and ignited, drifting slowly back to earth. Nothing moved except the odd quivering shadows cast by its magnesium light.

Not thirty feet away, five NVA wearing pith helmets perched like ravens on top of the steel wall. Hump cut loose with his M-16. AKs flashed rounds back. Hump fired again, and there were three. I blew the closest Charlie off the wall with a burst, hyperventilating as I did. The remaining pair smacked the sentry box with green tracers. Hump knocked another one backward. I accounted for the last one, discarded my empty magazine, and snapped in another.

The flare extinguished. I tossed a grenade over the steel wall and sprinted back toward Hump, yelling, "It's me, it's me!" The grenade crumped, throwing up dirt. My toe caught and sent me sprawling headfirst.

Hump spat curses, breathing rapidly, eyes white. I groped around for another flare. Hump beat me to it and launched one. Somewhere on the perimeter a short burst of a 16 clattered.

I crawled into Hump's position and shouldered my weapon, waiting for the artificial light. The flare popped and floated down. No one scaling the wall. No one in the barbed wire securing the gate. The field phone whirred. The colonel. I gave him the report: five North Vietnamese regulars probing the gate area, repelled.

We waited for the full attack. A short volley chattered from a bunker, red tracers arcing out. No other firing. The ARVN battery finally launched three illumination rounds, turning the world silver and black, straining our eyes with their intense, quivering light. Boots scurried toward us. Four more men joined our position.

Long minutes ticked by under the completely black sky, with only a little starlight. Hump fell asleep standing up, slumped against the sandbags, rifle butt at his shoulder. I was fully awake, high on adrenaline, my pupils like raisins. I took a deep breath and exhaled slowly through pursed lips.

It seemed like yesterday I'd processed stateside for the last time with a bunch of grunts like Hump. A short truck ride had brought us to an overnight shelter, a tent city for transients. All the flaps were raised. Each ten-man tent was encircled by a two-foot-high wall of sandbags, just slightly lower than the cots inside, hardly affording protection from small arms, and none from mortars. The transients bedded down and were asleep inside of two minutes. Nobody even removed a boot. The camp went black; no lights, no cigarettes. The unlucky few, myself included, drew guard duty.

Half the sentries were green newcomers; the other half, mangy GIs with just hours left in country. White rings of fungus spotted our sun-burned complexions. The newbies were coming, we were going. The veterans, bleary and thin, worked out their angles of fire and guard rotations. None of them gave a thought to a formal guard mount and I wasn't about to line them up for one. They were not to be fucked with their last night standing guard in Viet Nam.

The first watch filed out of the guard bunker. The rest passed out on bare cots. In seconds the short-timers were cutting Zs. They were skittish sleepers, coming sharply awake from time to time. See-ing where they were, they instantly fell back asleep again. In the dis-tance, big guns and small arms occasionally barked and burped. The new guys lay awake, thinking about those going home to the land of milk and green money, and wondering what lay ahead for the ones staying.

It was some ungodly hour when we landed in the States. In a rare gesture, the Army was laying on chow around the clock in a dolled-up mess hall, anything you wanted. Steak, chops, grits, ice cream, banana cream pie, rhubarb custard, whatever. You could indulge like a con-demned man. No one did. Just drank milk pretty much continuously, plain and chocolate, and waited. For new uniforms, for leave papers, or to muster out. Nobody said anything. Just played with light switches or examined their empty glasses, not having seen a glass glass in a year. Or real milk.

Now, waiting in the dark, I wondered where they all were. How they'd made out. Why I wasn't with them.

It was nearly four in the morning, too late for an attack. Bennett appeared, and he and I spent the rest of what darkness was left check-ing the American defenders and the Montagnard sentries. The sunrise was overcast and hazy, but to me it was spectacular.

My left sock was soggy. I'd been slowly bleeding into my boot. I limped to the dispensary, leaving bloody footprints on the concrete walk. Roberta finished wrapping a private's palm and what was left of his thumb. The first sergeant led him away. Dark circles rimmed Roberta's eyes. Curls stuck to her face.

"We have to stop meeting this way," she said, trying to sound brave.

Roberta cut the left leg off my fatigue pants, exposing a bloody gash across the back of my leg. I could see the sweat in her scalp. Her hands trembled slightly. A shard of something was stuck in the meat of the calf muscle. I hadn't felt much of anything when it happened. Now it screamed as she numbed it with Novocain and worked the jagged metal loose, sterilized the wound, and stitched it closed.

"Self-inflicted?" she said.

"Yeah, well. You can't blame a guy." The bravado sounded hollow. We were both exhausted. "You okay?"

She bit her lip. "Scared to death, but otherwise having a lovely evening, thank you." As she snapped off her rubber gloves, she kissed me on the forehead.

"I like your bedside manner."

She doused the wound with sulfa and dressed the sewn-up gash. "Get out of here," she said, and turned to a kid waiting by the door holding his arm, blood seeping between his fingers.

"Thanks, Doc," I said. She didn't reply, already focused on him. I limped to my room barefoot and put on fresh socks and boots.

An hour later, Sergeant Divivo snuck out the back with six men for a short first-light reconnaissance. No sign of the probers we had shot off the wall except for blood trails. Divivo radioed in that there was something odd at the designated escape-and-evasion pickup point we were supposed to sneak to in the dark if the compound fell.

Parks keyed the mike. "What?" he said. "What's odd? Over."

"Better come. You'll want to see this for yourselves."

Parks and I drove out to the pickup coordinates. A field. Olive-drab underwear hung head-high on wires strung like clotheslines between the few saplings, an American grenade lashed to each, the pins crimped flat, loops tied to the wire. The downdraft of incoming helicopter propellers would lift the T-shirts and shorts, yank the wires taut, pull the pins, arm the grenades.

"So much for superior technology," Joe said.

"I don't believe these dinks, Sarge. Now they're attacking us with our own underwear. I'm never wearing any again."

"Some sacrifice. You don't now."

How had the NVA gotten so close to the compound? How had they slipped past the ARVN perimeter to reach us? Were they so expert in the dark, or had the ARVN let them pass unchallenged? Our allies hadn't fired a shot, even after the shooting started.

The town remained shut, the Vietnamese battalion locked down. Checkman drove to the airstrip with an armed escort to meet the incoming courier flight. On the way back, he noticed four black splotches on the outside of the perimeter wall. The colonel and I went along with Joe Parks to investigate.

"There," Checkman said, pointing.

Sergeant Parks knelt next to a smudge. He clenched the pipe in his teeth and touched the stain, rubbed it between his fingers, and sniffed. "Motor oil."

Checkman was embarrassed. "That's all? Just motor oil?"

Joe Parks said, "I've seen this before. The VC splash motor oil on steel to make an adhesive for C-four charges. Makes the putty stick, even to wet metal."

"C-four is pliable," Checkman said. "Couldn't they just push it into the perforations in the planks?"

"NVA don't improvise," Bennett said. "They do it exactly as rehearsed."

"True, sir," Parks said. "They're rigidly disciplined. Crept up to here in the dark and prepped the steel with motor oil, as ordered." He scratched at his cheek with the pipe stem. "Maybe while we were distracted with the assault at the gate."

"Cut the commo wire to ARVN too," I said.

Joe nodded. "Planned on rain giving them cover when they stormed our perimeter. They were relying on the bad weather to deny us air support and keep from getting anviled from the air when they were done with us."

Joe stood up. "Except blessedly it didn't pour. So they canceled. They must have been sitting out there half the night, waiting for a downpour."

"They skipped us because it didn't rain," Checkman said, awe in his voice.

"Joe," I said, "you think they have some reserve force prepping to assault us the next time it pours?"

Parks shook his head. "Undoubtedly they left a reserve in the foothills. But the units that rehearsed the attack on the compound must be en route to their main objective by now. I think we're okay." He looked at the colonel. "The mobilized battalions are past us, sir. They're off our plateau and in the mountains . . . on their way to whoever's going to take the full brunt. We got a reprieve."

"No thanks to ARVN," I said, "who did absolutely nothing."

Bennett licked his dry lips, face bathed in sweat, his blond hair dark with it. "Damn. It's like someone walking on your grave."

When we returned to the gate, the civilians were just leaving. Lund and his colleagues were almost the last in line, driving out. Ruchevsky, in his Bronco, waved me over.

"Captain Cox and Sergeant Grady are waiting on us by the river," he said.

I got in and Ruchevsky sprayed gravel rushing through the gate. "What's up?" I said.

"The snatch. The courier is getting closer. We need a head session."

Ruchevsky drove us to the edge of town to where the Ea River joined the Ayun, and where off-duty advisers and civilians occasionally congregated at sunset, like Californians. A peaked thatched roof, like on a Montagnard longhouse, rose over an elevated earthen floor, supported by six wooden columns. The place was sunbaked and bare. Nearby, a gaunt Vietnamese watered a cadaverous herd of horned cattle. Captain Cox sat behind the wheel of the Special Forces jeep; Sergeant Grady leaned against it. The back bulged with essential supplies: ammo, Budweiser, a crate of Vienna sausages, a bag of mail. A bullet hole blistered the windshield on the passenger side.

Cox stepped out as we rolled to a stop. "Welcome, pilgrims."

"Captain." Ruchevsky greeted him and nodded to Grady. "Sarge."

"Vandals?" I said, indicating the punctured glass.

Grady said, "Some cracker tried to light us up on the way in."

I said, "I can't believe you drove in after what went on last night."

Grady snorted in derision. "Police action is all that was. Wouldn't hardly qualify as a fight."

Ruchevsky said to Cox, "You want to lay it out?"

Captain Cox slipped off his green beret and pushed it through an epaulet. "Big John thinks our target is accompanied by four or five escorts and hauling a radio and a couple kilos of paper."

"They don't trust radio communications," Ruchevsky said. "They commit a lot to paper."

"Is he transmitting as he goes?" I said, trying to get an inkling of how he was being tracked.

The pair looked to Ruchevsky. He hesitated a beat. "Yeah," he said.

"Morse or voice?"

"Not voice. He's using a key."

The guy wouldn't be transmitting that much while trekking. Had John substituted one of his agents for a VC guide along one of the legs of the trail? Easily done. The guides had little contact with one another or their Vietnamese handlers, and the infiltrators walking the trail were strangers.

Cox drew a crude map in the dirt film on the hood.

"We'll rendezvous with the chopper near the abandoned A camp at Buon Beng and load out from there. We dress and camouflage at the old camp, arm up with CAR-fifteens, silenced. The silencers are hand-made, but they work." He brought out two rifles from the jeep. "Sight them in ahead of time. Everything stays under wraps. We want as little attention as possible beforehand."

"Right," I concurred.

"Rider, you'll hump the radio and handle our communications. Sarge will haul the extra battery and a grenade launcher."

"How do we get put in?" Ruchevsky said.

"By Huey. I just spoke to the colonel. Bennett is laying on a flight of three ships the day after tomorrow to help cloak our mission."

"That soon?" I said, taken aback.

"Affirmative. The birds will make half a dozen touchdowns. Four will be false insertions. We'll get off at one of them. The colonel and his people will jump off at another."

"With any luck," Grady said, "we won't be detected. Then two hours of humping to reach the ambush site. It's not an area any Americans have been in, other than John. So we'll risk taking trails. Big John says there are plenty."

Ruchevsky nodded and Grady went on.

"We get to the ambush point, familiarize ourselves, and take up positions for the night."

"What's the pecking order?" Ruchevsky said.

Grady said, "Jarai Willie walks point. I follow, walking slack. Captain Rider, behind me, handles the radio. Followed by Captain Cox with the grenade launcher, followed by John. The other Yard, Rot, walks drag and covers up our tracks."

"And you're confident," I said, "that your Yards aren't VC?"

"Completely," Cox said. "Grady I'm less sure about."

"Where do we intercept the travelers?" I asked.

"They'll lay over in a rest station near a shallow branch that leads into the river proper." He drew an oxbow in the dust on the hood and an X for the rest hut. "The next morning they'll set out just before dawn and ford the little river a few minutes later. The water's not deep yet, about knee high. Their point man will cover their crossing." He drew a trail and tapped out dots along it. "We spring the ambush when they start up again on the other side. Okay?"

We nodded.

Cox pointed his chin toward Grady. "Sarge."

Sergeant Grady propped a foot up on the front fender and leaned on his knee. "The Yards will take care of the point guy and their rear guard. We'll each have a man to take down, except Big John. I'm hopin' the silencers do the job but, you know, out of half a dozen spooked gooks, somebody's going to yell out and like that. Still, it'll be remote, early morning, right on the edge of thick jungle. The next closest group traveling that stretch of trail should be ten klicks back. It oughta go okay."

He paused to see if we wanted to say anything.

"Right," he continued. "Big John's responsible for neutralizing the radioman and prepping him for travel. Smack 'im, gag him — whatever works, big man. Just as long as he's standing and mobile. We don't carry nobody. We do the snatch and cut out for the extraction point.

John, you got fifteen seconds to subdue him and get him up and running once we take 'em down. Fifteen seconds . . . and we're gone."

Grady said, "Our priority is the courier and whatever paper he's carrying. If we get into a jam, trash the Commie radio and abandon it — lighten the load. We won't have no backup team to drop in and save our sorry butt ends if we get in the shit. Comport yourselves accordingly."

"And if it goes wrong?" Ruchevsky asked, for the record. "Or the guy refuses to march . . . collapses from the heat?"

"We can't carry his sorry self," Cox said. "We'll go down with heat exhaustion ourselves. Encourage him. If he totally resists or is slowing us, don't think. It's *xin loi.*"

"Okay, we done?" Grady smiled broadly. "We're on."

Cox noted the time on his Rolex and slipped on his beret. "It's late, Sarge," he said to Grady. "Let's *di di.*"

Big John and Cox shook hands. Grady and I dapped.

"Don't forget the camo for your honky mugs," he said.

As the Berets drove away, Ruchevsky tossed me a padded envelope. "Merry Christmas."

Madame Chinh's cousin's bank records, as promised. Dates, deposits, amounts — the works. I sat up that night and went through the bank records of Mrs. Chinh's cousin in Taiwan and especially the itemized list of deposits, hundreds of thousands of American dollars. I compared them to the deposits made to the VC's Hong Kong account. Equivalent sums were deposited on the same days to both. Hong Kong's were withdrawn quickly, presumably to become goods and guns. The Taiwan bank account remained untouched and simply grew.

I exhaled and stretched. There was something important in the figures in front of me but I couldn't immediately pin the thought down. As plain as the hole on a gnat's ass, my dad would have said. In any case, there was no mistaking that Chinh — not Lund — was their main man.

# 17

★ ★ ★

THE PRIORITY CALL from Saigon came into the signal shack close to midnight, relayed along the American coastal bases up to Qui Nhon, directed inland through An Khe, across to Pleiku, and down to us. It was like calling long distance station to station to reach Cheo Reo. Any break along the way and you'd have to begin again. The caller must have spent hours getting through. Whoever it was, he was hot to get word to John Ruchevsky immediately.

Miser had summoned me to take the call. No one was answering the field phone at Big John's house.

"I'll bring Ruchevsky to the phone here," I told Miser. "Just keep talking to them. Don't lose the connection."

Curfew was long past but I had to go outside the wire. With headlights taped, I could barely navigate the short familiar route. I'm sure it wasn't any quieter than usual but it seemed eerily so as I pulled up to his house and greeted his night guards. When he heard why I'd come, John grabbed an Uzi and a sling bag of magazines from a guard and slid in beside me. We made it back in record time.

Miraculously, the spliced-together radiotelephone call had held. Saigon was still on the line. John took it in the shack, looking unhappier by the minute. By the time he signed off, I saw a new level of anger in him and not a little fear. Outside, he told Miser and me a warrant had been issued early that morning in Saigon for the arrest of Nay Lo.

"Who's Nay Lo?" I said.

"Little John."

"I thought working for you he'd be immune."

"He should've been," he said. "Nobody local would dare touch him. Sector headquarters here got Saigon to issue a federal warrant."

"Chinh."

"Who else?"

"They're actually going to arrest Little John?"

"Two white mice left Saigon yesterday, manifested for Cheo Reo. They could be here already."

"National Police," Miser said, "here?"

Of all the corrupt institutions in South Viet Nam, the Saigon police might have been the oldest and the worst. They were extortionists and plunderers. Everyone in the country loathed and avoided them.

"What's he charged with?" I said.

"I don't know." Ruchevsky tried to rub the sleep from his eyes. "No one's seen the writ."

It began to dawn on me. "Little John knows everything you know."

"And everybody. He's my go-between with all the agents and informants. If Chinh gets hold of Little John, he'll extract everything we know about him and who gave us the information." Ruchevsky smacked a sandbag. "We've gotta find him before the white mice do."

John wanted to go immediately. I barely talked him into waiting at least until it was light. I thought I had a way to distract him. Back in our room, I spread out the bank records of Madame Chinh's newly rich cousin in Taiwan. Alongside them I laid the front organization's account. Curious in spite of himself, Big John stopped pacing and took my seat to peer at the figures. I leaned over his shoulder.

"Remember the twenty kilos of heroin that landed on Grady's patrol?"

"Yeah." John nodded. "Just like the airdrops reported in Pleiku Province last year."

"You said word was the province chief there got five grand for every load parachuted into his domain."

"So?"

"What do you see?" I said, leaning over him.

"The deposit dates and amounts line up like twins."

"What does that tell you?"

He stared at the numbers some more. "That Chinh's not getting any measly five grand a pop. He's banking the same huge chunk as the VC. He's not just getting gratitude money for ignoring the drugs passing out of the province. It's his operation. He's their equal partner."

"That's damning enough, but there's more."

Ruchevsky looked at me, stared at the figures some more, and shook his head. "I don't see whatever it is you're seeing."

"The Taiwan deposits are *identical* to the Hong Kong deposits. Which means Chinh isn't kicking any part of the profits to his superior. He's sharing nothing."

"Shit. No tribute, no gifts to his patron."

"Exactly. Chinh's gotten greedy. He's keeping it all."

John rubbed the stubble on his cheek. "He's playing with fire."

"We can sink him with these financials."

John shook his head. "We can't show anyone these numbers or the window will slam shut on the account and the paper trail will start disappearing. The guy eyeballing the deposits will have his peepers plucked out." I started to protest but John held up his hand to stop me. "We need to think this through when we're not so distracted," he said, and resumed prepping his weapons. "Your gear almost ready?"

I taped together two magazines of M-16 ammo, one upside down, so there'd be no rummaging around for another, then loaded up two pouches with full magazines — enough for a siege. John got out his Schmeisser.

He ran down the contingency schemes he and Little John had, places he might hide — assuming the duo from Saigon didn't already have him. The possibility was torturing Ruchevsky. I tried sleeping for an hour but John's impatience made that impossible. He was itching to get going.

By three thirty there was no holding him. I commandeered the signal detachment's jeep and we set off through the gate, hours before the night's curfew expired. We drove to Little John's home village, where by protocol we woke the headman before searching. Little John wasn't in the men's longhouse or anywhere else, although the chief volunteered that Vietnamese had come looking for him toward dusk in an

ARVN vehicle. Both men were dressed in teal slacks, black shoes, and short-sleeved white shirts with epaulettes. No caps, no insignia — but white mice for sure. The taller one displayed a gold tooth, the other the gold-filled cap of a Parker fountain pen in his breast pocket. A status symbol — the suggestion of the pen — even if owning the whole instrument was beyond the man's immediate means.

"Great," Ruchevsky groused. "A bent cop too stupid to extort a whole pen."

Dark as it was, we drove down to the river and crossed on foot. The water was lukewarm and shin deep. In full monsoon season it would be chest high. Runoff streams that fed into the river during the wet season were still dry channels. We went along one of the sandy troughs and reached their emergency rendezvous point: a grove of bamboo on the bank of a tributary channel.

"Little John," Ruchevsky called quietly as we slipped inside the meeting spot, a patch of sand enclosed by a solid wall of bamboo trunks that soared fifty feet over us, each thick as a leg, making the grove impossibly dense. It buzzed with insects, the air inside hot and dead. The smell was almost as bad as the sight Ruchevsky's flashlight lit up: a head impaled on a bamboo stake.

A mass of tiny black beetles saved us from looking at his eyes. His features were rigid, teeth bared and jaw locked. I slapped away the insects with my hat. The ears were gone, lopped off. Coagulated drips of blood hung down onto the white sand, thick as paint. Ants scurried everywhere in a frenzy. Flayed, bloody soles protruded from the ground, the legs impossibly splayed. Fingerless hands, spiked to a bamboo trunk, held a halved chunk of bamboo with *Viet-gian* scratched into it: Traitor.

"I'd say he talked?" I muttered, my voice shaky, and swatted at the droning, blood-crazed flies.

"God, I hope he sang like a canary. Whatever got it over quicker."

Judging from the head's grimace, I figured the screams would have been unearthly. I thought of the live dogs Special Forces medics used in training, amputating legs and inflicting gunshot wounds they then practiced patching up. But first the medics disabled the dogs' larynxes.

I pointed at what had been his throat. "Doesn't seem like they were happy with what they heard. They cut his vocal cords after they got whatever they got and kept right on going."

Using a stick, Ruchevsky picked up a wedge of something that looked like a giant pig's knuckle. "Jesus."

It was a vertebra dangling loose. Ruchevsky dropped it and went to examine the hands.

"They bound his hands with wire — pierced it through his palms like he was a martyr."

My guts felt like strings being strummed. Big John didn't look so good either. He stepped back into the circle, eyes large, and held his hand over his nose and mouth against the slaughterhouse stench.

"Where's the rest?" Ruchevsky said, staring down at the carnage.

Turning slowly in the odd natural chamber, I saw what was draped in the bamboo all around us.

I had to wet my lips to speak. "We're standing in him."

Ruchevsky leaned closer to the staked head, swatting at the bugs.

"It's not him," he rasped.

"Are you sure?"

"Yeah, yeah. I think it's Tri, our best informant. Works as a cook for Chinh. Gave us the info on the NVA market." Ruchevsky looked like he wanted to throttle someone. "God, why'd they dice him like this?"

Agitated, he kept rubbing his upper arm. "Tri must have told them about this meeting place. But it wasn't enough. Little John wasn't here."

"Chinh must want him bad," I said.

We followed the dry streambed down to the riverbank, looking for signs of the inquisitioners and Little John. Finding none, we followed the sandy trough back to the bamboo cul-de-sac.

Ruchevsky and I decided not to try to reassemble the body, or what we'd found of it. We would need a story for Tri's family, but his wife and kids should be spared seeing him like this no matter what. Vietnamese needed to bury their dead intact, or at least diligently gather up all the parts. It meant everything to the family to have a whole body. A loved one missing his head was unthinkable. But this . . . The torturers hadn't just painstakingly slaughtered Tri and expelled him from this life. They'd doomed him in the next.

Vietnamese souls didn't immediately leave at death, and beheading or mutilation disrupted the process of dying, arrested the spirit's departure. The soul would know no peace. Unable to find its ancestors, the disfigured ghost would haunt the family.

We built a pyre of dry bamboo and added as many pieces of Tri to it as we could. We torched the whole grove. The dead trunks, held upright by the surrounding live bamboo, had no room to fall and added to the impenetrable wall. They burned hot enough to ignite everything and cremate the inventory of ruined flesh. The green bamboo popped like small-arms fire as we trudged away.

"Any chance at all this is VC revenge on Tri for telling you about the jungle market?" I said.

Ruchevsky shook his head. "When Viet Cong do awful shit — disembowel somebody's kid in front of them or bury somebody alive — they do it publicly, cold, a merciless object lesson. This is a private message, to scare the piss out of me and Little John and anyone else who acts against Chinh."

Ruchevsky rubbed at his neck.

I said, "Has it occurred to you that maybe they're not after just Little John? That maybe they put out the warrant to lure *you* out of the compound in the middle of the night?"

Ruchevsky shook his head. "Chinh knows what my people would do if I got iced."

"Don't kid yourself. The C-four in our phone wasn't intended for Little John. You could have been using it as likely as me. He's lined up on us both."

Ruchevsky said, "The only good news is it means we're really hurting him."

We crossed the river in silence. Ruchevsky took the wheel for the next leg, checking more hamlets within a few kilometers. No Little John. Ruchevsky drove us down a perfectly straight and deserted road, nothing but scrawny trees and brush on either side. And amazingly, paved.

"Where does this stretch go?" I said.

"Nowhere, really. The French probably laid it down. It rolls for a hundred yards and just stops."

Where the pavement ended, a dirt track took us to an abandoned one-story house with a tiled roof that stood alone in the scrub, its two wings fronted by a long patio. The walls were pitted and falling away. It could have been the residence of a small coffee estate, but there were no abandoned fields, no scents of coffee blossoms. Aside from two sad-looking ylang-ylang trees and a jasmine bush, no domesticated plants had survived the neglect.

John didn't bother to check inside the dark building. He slipped around the side to a concrete bunker, holding his flashlight away from his body, just in case. I switched mine off and followed him down a few steps. John's Uzi hung from his neck, the Schmeisser on his shoulder. He picked up a Montagnard bush ax.

"Watch your head," he instructed as he opened the heavy door and ducked to avoid a beam. "Stay behind me."

The bare bunker had the racks of an old wine cellar. Shadowy roots hung down from the gridded ceiling. Ruchevsky blocked me from entering. One of the distended tubers lunged toward us, hissing.

"Jesus!" I said, tripping backward. Ruchevsky swung with the ax but missed, then beat at it with the flat of the blade until the thing was still.

He shone his light on the snake. A krait: the deadliest. The ceiling was studded with them. They appeared dead, but Ruchevsky didn't take chances. Once they were lashed to the grid, nobody would have dared untie them. He hacked them all in half to make sure.

I said, "What the hell is this place?"

"The provincial interrogation center." He pointed at the hanging snake carcasses with the ax. "Inducements for guests of the state."

The space smelled dank and worse. One wall was smeared with something dark and unidentifiable. I peered into a large jar in one corner and shone my light inside. My eyes teared at the acrid odor. It clawed at the eyes.

"What's this for?"

John came over. "Water spiked with lime. They hose it through the nose into the stomach, jump on the midsection until it gushes back out the mouth. Even if you make it out of here, your gut forever reminds you of lessons learned. Chinh's interrogator's nickname is 'the Bartender.'"

"Sweet."

"Yeah," Ruchevsky said. "That restraint board there makes it easier to tip you back. But first they shove a stake in your nostril and break the bone so you can't breathe through your nose when they force the water down your throat." He looked around. "I only made the mistake of hanging around one time. Listening was actually worse than watching."

We turned to leave. Something shone in a crack in the floor. Ruchevsky picked it up.

"Shit."

"What?"

"It's a little gold Buddha on a chain. Like Tri's."

"Lots of Vietnamese wear them, John."

He nodded. "The Cambodians pop them in their mouths going into battle."

I said, "How do you know about this place?"

"We underwrite the local security enforcers."

"You fund the people who do this?"

"We finance the interrogation centers in every province. That's just a fact of life."

John drove toward Cheo Reo with no headlights. Though we were filthy and shaken, our night's work was unfinished, and we drove to several other spots to check for Little John. The sun haloed the horizon. Reaching town, we drove the dirt streets slowly, hoping he would see us and come out. After the first circuit, we noticed an ARVN jeep driven by two National Police running parallel to ours. They turned toward us onto a side street.

Ruchevsky spun the wheel and drove straight at them. The passage was too narrow to play chicken. The cop swung left, smashing into the butcher's stand to avoid a collision, bringing down a rack of impaled creatures. The carcasses kept coming loose and falling on the cops. The driver and the butcher raged at each other, not quite daring to direct their anger at us. John backed our jeep out and we continued on, unmolested.

Big John stopped in front of the barbershop and hopped out. I beat him in. The proprietor sat in his barber's chair, waiting for customers.

No, no one had seen Little John, and everyone seemed glad of it. The barber was openly nervous, avoiding eye contact and swinging a silver piaster coin on a silver chain, like a hep cat, until it wound around a finger. Then he spun it the other way, unwinding it.

We returned to the jeep. John Ruchevsky rested a foot on the fender, his forearm on his knee, and surveyed the town.

"He would've shown himself by now if he was here."

I said, "I assume our little run-in with the mice means they haven't got him either."

"That or they're done with him and looking to do something to us."

"Maybe we should put a watch on the airstrip," I said, "in case they've got him and try to fly him out."

Ruchevsky took the wheel. "You're right. Let's go. We're not doing any good here."

We made for the compound.

I said, "What were your instructions to Little John in case of trouble like this?"

"Aside from the bamboo grove, you mean?"

"Yes."

"I told him to hide where he was the most certain they wouldn't look for him."

"Did he ever say where that might be?"

"No," Ruchevsky said, "unfortunately." He braked sharply. We skidded to a halt in a cloud of grit.

"What the hell?" I blinked against the road dust rising around us.

"I think I know where," he said.

We drove back through town and hung a right onto a track. Ignoring caution, we went some kilometers and pulled up outside a Montagnard village near a river: half a dozen longhouses and a Western building with a corrugated metal roof. I pointed to two spears suspended above the gate.

"What are those about?" I said.

"A Jarai warning—contamination."

John drove in. A slight figure stood in front of the largest longhouse, seemingly waiting. Before I could even make him out, I recognized the glove. At Little John's feet rested a small valise made out of sheet metal repeatedly printed with a beer logo. He must have been relieved that Big John had found him but was too shaken to show it. Instead, he seemed rigid.

"Someone say Saigon police look to me," he said. "I hide. Two police drive into village at sundown. I run into bush."

That they had come all the way from Saigon and knew to look for him at the village had made him worry they might also know the emergency meeting place. Instead of going to the rendezvous point, he had snuck cross-country to the leprosarium, a place deeply feared by Vietnamese.

"Mother here," he said, "father here. He indicated the couple standing nearby. The woman looked normal except for malformations of her feet. The old man stood holding a cigarette, blowing smoke out of an opening in his face roughly where a nose might once have been. One foot was an ulcerated stump.

Little John and his parents quietly embraced. Their son was a liability for all sides. He would never be safe in Cheo Reo and they all sensed it. He clutched them both, loath to let go and eager to leave. Finally he was ready and we drove away. Little John sat motionless behind us, the valise on his lap. I looked back at the receding figures. He never did.

Ruchevsky stashed Little John in our room and got on the radio to his superiors in Pleiku while I guarded our guest. When John returned, we reloaded our magazines and waited.

Ruchevsky said, "I've gotta get Little John out of the province — to protect him and what's in his head. But once he goes . . . Little John's the go-between with everybody working for me. How am I going to operate without him?"

"Chinh didn't have to risk doing anything to you," I said.

"You got it. The bastard neuters me without harming a hair on my head."

"So far."

Ruchevsky sighed. "They're about to get another chance. We still have to get Little John past the two gentlemen from Saigon."

"And Chinh's soldiers at the airfield."

Checkman appeared with instructions: "Go to the airstrip immediately."

"Right," I said and gathered up Little John's valise and my rifle.

We loaded Little John back into our jeep and I drove us out, our weapons across our laps. A good seventy yards from the tiny sentry box that secured the otherwise deserted airstrip, we stopped and sat. Two ARVNs slouched by the guard post.

A minute later a field phone rang in the sentry's booth. A moment passed. The barrier pole came down. Four South Vietnamese soldiers emerged from hammocks slung in a grove of scrawny trees. They milled around nervously until ordered to assume positions on either side of the barrier, rifles at the ready.

A shiny speck approached from the east and came straight in. A twin-engine Beechcraft, brilliant silver against the roiling black sky. It landed and taxied onto the round apron just beyond the sentry box and stopped, shut down its engines. Onto the wing stepped a civilian in mirror sunglasses and Hawaiian shirt, hefting the most fantastic-looking assault weapon, like something out of an old British sci-fi movie, with a normal barrel sitting above a fat barrel. Evidently it fired two calibers, atomic and apocalyptic. He stood on the wing in open defiance. The South Vietnamese soldiers circled one another, confused.

"Okay," John said. "*Tien.* Advance."

I stepped on the gas and we rolled forward at a steady five miles per hour.

"John," I said, "promise me you aren't going to put Little John aboard and jump on yourself."

"Damn, I hadn't thought of that. Great idea." He squinted at the ARVNs. "Take your safety off."

"It's not on."

"Whatever you do, don't speed up or stop. Just drive."

My foot never went near the brake. We just rolled toward the lowered barrier, the longest fifty yards I'd ever driven. It was clear we weren't going to stop. At the last possible second the barrier came up. We passed onto the apron and right to the waiting plane. Clutching his beer-can valise, Little John mounted its two steps in a flash and disappeared. The man on the wing dropped to the ground and slipped inside, drawing the hatch closed after him. The engines turned over and revved. The plane spun back onto the metal-plate runway and rolled right into its takeoff.

"Small victories," Ruchevsky said, watching it climb. I never saw Little John again.

# 18

★ ★ ★

FROM OUR SHARED desk, Ruchevsky gathered up a miniature bottle of cognac made out of paper, a tiny paper television, an equally small paper motorbike, and a refrigerator, playing cards, an air conditioner, and stacks of black-and-white paper money. The miniatures were an Asian thing—for burning—luxury items the deceased could enjoy in the next life. Since the next world was spiritual, converting the paper miniatures into smoke to pass them over was as effective as burning the real things, and considerably more affordable.

The miniatures were for Tri's memorial ceremony. His widow and their four children wore traditional mourning garb: coarse white garments with large patches. Neighbors stood along the wall next to a table laid with food and drink, the few relatives wearing white headbands. Custom forbade mention of Tri's name. A color print of the Sacred Heart of Jesus hung behind the altar, partially obscured by flowers. The widow and kids were reciting the rosary.

Ruchevsky hadn't told her how her husband died or that we'd cremated him. Fire was an especially bad end and left *con hoe,* very unhappy ghosts, to plague the relatives. To explain why the body hadn't been recovered, he told her Tri had drowned and was swept away, which was only a marginally better death than being murderously butchered and cremated. To help his disquieted ghost, the widow had hired a local sorcerer to call forth her man's spirit from the river and capture it in a jar, which now sat on the ancestral altar next to offerings of rice and wine and the burned-paper replicas of major appliances.

Candles flanked the charred-paper remnants and joss sticks burning in a vase of sand. Ruchevsky placed an envelope with the solacium payment on the altar: the sum allocated by the United States to compensate for an unintended civilian death. Thirty-five American dollars. In a separate envelope, John slipped the widow four hundred more in piasters, liberated from the strongbox under his bed.

The snatch was on. Two ships would lift Colonel Bennett and a small force of a dozen officers and men, nominally going out to reconnoiter trailheads. Talk about fingers in dikes. A third chopper would follow, carrying the six of us in full camo to our insertion point.

We didn't want the ARVN or anyone else seeing what we were up to, so we didn't use the airstrip. At dawn we set out in a truck and jeep for the abandoned Special Forces A camp at Buon Beng. I hid one trembling hand in my pocket and clutched my weapon hard with the other.

Over his shoulder, Colonel Bennett casually said, "You're somber this morning, Captain."

"Yes, sir. I'm not looking forward to engaging the enemy at close quarters."

"You're in good company," Bennett said, "historically speaking. The Union forces collected twenty-four thousand muzzleloaders from the fallen after the Battle of Gettysburg. The rifles were stuffed with minié balls they'd only pretended to fire. It happens war after war."

You could see him relax as he spoke. It was easy to imagine him lecturing at West Point, far from this war.

We rolled up to the empty gate. The structures were overgrown and crumbling. Sergeant Grady and Captain Cox were waiting along with their Montagnards, Rot and Willie. Both wore sleeveless black tunics, carbines slung over shoulders and crossbows in hand — the Montagnard version of silenced weaponry. The shafts were each a foot and a half long, the arrowheads wound with threads soaked in poisons that would "fry your wiring in seconds," Grady said. "They left 'em stuck into an antjar tree all night, absorbing the poison sap."

Cox confirmed it with a nod. "Believe it. Plus, they can put a shaft in your eye at forty yards. You can't see the arrows fly, they go so quick."

"Just don't give them any grenades," Grady said. "Yards can't throw for shit. Vietnamese either."

Colonel Bennett ordered a few saplings cut down that might interfere with the helicopters' landing while Ruchevsky and I changed into camouflage fatigues in a roofless bunker and set about turning ourselves into walking bushes. Grady mixed camouflage grease with insect repellent.

"I've got the natural advantage here," he said, smiling, as he dabbed on a few strokes of the bug-dope-and-camouflage-grease paste and passed the rest. "Don't forget the backs of your big white ears."

Our silenced CAR-15s were already expertly camouflaged. Even the black pistol grips were taped to break up their solid color.

"We're gonna look like crazy minstrels," Sergeant Grady grumbled, "wearin' overgrown hydrangeas."

Jarai Willie grinned.

"What's he so jolly about?" I said to Grady.

"Oh, he had hot-shit dreams last night. He seen deer. Good omens. Me?" Grady muttered, "We seen crows this morning. Don't tell young Willie, though. It's bad Yard juju. Last time one landed on a bunker we were building, they made us tear it down."

I said, "Maybe we should tell the colonel and call it off."

Grady scowled. Turning to the Jarai, he announced loudly, "Remember, fellas, we're goin' after Vietnamese. Man, this is your chance to knock their dicks off."

The colonel shot him a look.

"Well, hell, sir," he said sheepishly.

Ruchevsky approached, weapon in hand. I cleared my throat.

"What're you gawking at, Rider?"

"You look like a topiary on acid."

Grady frowned. "What the flamin' hell is topiary?"

"A fancy overgroomed plant," I said. "Only this one happens to have a gun barrel sticking out of its ass. You could use some additional pruning." I pulled off some extraneous branches. "What do you think, sir?" I said to the colonel.

Bennett pursed his lips. "You're still a little overfoliated, John." Ruchevsky yanked away a few more.

Barefoot in their loincloths and black shirts, the two Jarai took in our strange costumes with some curiosity. They could blend into the woods in a second just as they were. We worked hard and still couldn't match the effect.

"Can we get a Geiger counter too?" Grady chirped. "I wanna try findin' some of that plu-to-ni-um. I think I can get good coin for that shit in Cholon."

"Hey," I said. "I'm hearing rumors the Japanese are buying up beachfronts in Viet Nam, looking to the future. And that we've secretly found oil offshore. Hell, why not plutonium? It gives me hope there's really a good reason for all of us being here."

"That's more than I've got," said Cox, all business.

Helicopters were approaching. Cox called us together.

"Stick to the center of the trail. The VC don't mine the middles, only the sides, where growth hides the devices. Don't step on piles of leaves or brush. Don't dive off the trail if we run into NVA. If you see knotted rattan or a knotted fern, that's a VC warning of booby traps ahead. A stick laid straight down the trail — same thing."

The three choppers landed on the smoke canister Grady had tossed out onto the unused helipad. We boarded the last ship as Bennett got everyone else on the first two and lifted off. We lay on the floor and slid the doors shut. The soldiers in the other two made a show of their presence on board, riding with doors open, feet out. All three choppers headed northwest, twenty feet over the river.

A few minutes into the flight, we left the river and rose over the unbroken canopy of heavy jungle. The air was chill at altitude. Morning fog flowed down from the higher mountain valleys and billowed out of the passes onto the lower elevations. The first false insertion was in a long narrow opening in the jungle, eleven minutes into the flight. Our chopper circled like a gunship. The other two touched down for four seconds and lifted off again. The second spot was at a river's edge. An unlikely place to insert.

"Okay, dudes," Grady yelled over the slipstream. "Be heroes, not zeros."

We piled out and were gone in an instant.

The flight would make three more decoy stops to try to confuse anyone observing its progress. The colonel and his patrol would bail out at the sixth and last.

Twenty yards into the green, we deployed in a circle, feet touching, weapons at the ready. We were far beyond any U.S. artillery fan or the seven-mile range of Chinh's howitzers, not that we could have relied on the ARVN gunners. If we got spotted, we'd have to call for Army gunships and the Air Force to save our butts. We lay motionless in the underbrush beneath single-canopy trees that towered over us. No movement anywhere, no signal shots announcing our presence.

Twenty minutes ticked away. We hadn't been detected yet. The adrenaline backed off. A foot touched mine, passing Grady's signal to move. From here on, rank meant nothing: we were playing by Special Forces rules. Grady, with the most experience, was the leader and would call the shots.

We set out, Jarai Willie leading, Grady following, me third with the radio, Ruchevsky and Cox, Rot walking drag. We zigged and zagged for nearly an hour, looped an eight to backtrack on our trail, and set an ambush for anyone following us.

Nobody. Twenty more minutes passed and we moved off again through vines and tangles. As we trekked over a ridge, I managed radio contact and reported in, whispering "Crazy Fox" into the mouthpiece. Cheo Reo acknowledged. I depressed the mike button once, signing off.

The Jarai led us under heavy canopy that arched ten stories over our heads. The deeper we went, the thicker and higher the green ceiling soared over us and the easier our movement, because the lower growth was thin in the diminished light.

The canopy turned a deep emerald. Nothing snapped or rustled on the jungle floor: the mossy deadfall underfoot muffled our passage. It was as still and dark as a cathedral. The jungle grew larger and we shrank. The trees dwarfed us. We were insects. The air sweated, saturated with moisture. Every surface dripped and glistened in the murk. The humidity was total, a jungle sauna. We were soaked.

Soon we couldn't see much beyond thirty feet. Whole sections were impassable, blocked by tangles of tree trunks uprooted and toppled by the raging growth. We diverted around them, under them, human specimens in some giant's terrarium.

The huge roots of triple-canopy trees formed steppes of ferns and moss. Parasites and fungi gnawed at everything living, us included. I brushed away termites, worms, ants, centipedes, straw-thin land leeches, and scratchy-sticky vegetation. Our skin, our hair, our clothing were smeared with decay and growth.

Forty minutes farther in, the canopy thinned. Willie led us along a broad animal track, so wide that I hoped we wouldn't meet whatever had made it. Probably wild boar, judging from the path's width and height where it tunneled through growth. The track took us to a shallow brook hemmed in by water palms. We bunched up behind him, preparing to cross. Willie found a breach in the palms and stepped into the water and stopped. He raised a fist — danger — and summoned Grady forward. Willie pointed at the water. I saw nothing and shrugged at Cox, who was kneeling alongside me. He leaned against my ear and whispered, "Clay mud flowing down. Somebody's upstream."

We crossed carefully, one at a time. It always surprised me. Like all flowing water in Viet Nam, it looked cool but the stream was warmer than my body and not the least bit refreshing. The flora thinned further as the canopy cover increased. Birds chirped, lots of them. Willie led us toward the sound until we could see feathers flashing, vivid orange and yellow against the green. Parrots, myna birds, canaries, skylarks scattered and took flight. Willie pointed to the reason for the gathering — a cache of rice bags piled on a low platform with a tarp roof. Each bag was imprinted with the logo of the American international aid program: one dark hand, the other white, clasped beneath a Stars and Stripes shield. A bag at the bottom had split open, drawing the beautiful, wild crowd.

A path led toward the stash of rice from the other side. Willie followed it. Forty yards on, stumps of young trees and saplings dotted a light area where strong, straight timber had been cut down for construction. Tracks went every which way. Willie took one, seemingly at random. We passed garden plots next to a flooded bomb crater. Something broke the surface. Reflex swung our rifles toward the splash.

Fish. The crater was stocked with live fish.

We had stumbled upon a base camp for a hundred men. An NVA company. The occupants couldn't be far. Wet shirts hung on branches. Thirty feet away, the unmistakable odor of human waste announced their latrine. A-shaped bunkers bulged out of the ground, covered with earth, some interconnected by trenches. Outside a large one, built from heavy timbers and soil, were impressions in the hard ground, unmistakably a mortar's, probably an 81-millimeter. Like the camp, the bunkers were empty. Nobody home.

Three Bren-like Czech ZB-26 rifles and cans of their Mauser ammo lay tarnished and damaged alongside rusted grappling hooks trailing ropes — devices the enemy used to drag their dead from the battlefield to their improvised graves. A volleyball net of woven vines stretched across a dirt patch. Huge trees arched high overhead, their canopies thick and dripping. Around the court stood bamboo platforms: classrooms with easels, mess platforms with chopsticks protruding from empty number-10 cans, storage platforms with nylon sheets protecting mounds of salt, sleeping platforms with mats — one of them occupied.

We trained our CARs on him. Cong in the flesh. Barefoot, in dark green shorts and armless gray undershirt. The scourge of our Free World Forces. He slept with mouth open, dead to the world, the crook of his arm across his eyes, ribs protruding. He was tiny, maybe ninety pounds, frail, half naked, hair spiky, unkempt, consumed with fever from the look of him.

Grady eased up to the youth, making sure he was unarmed. He pointed away. We didn't linger. Cox signed to Willie, who led us silently on a southeast heading. The signs of habitation fell away. We were back under triple canopy and moving well, praying we were walking away from and not toward wherever the People's Army was having its jamboree.

We covered a thousand meters and reached the fording point where we would lie in wait for the VC courier and his minders. They were due to pass by in the wee hours of the morning, urgency making them risk daylight travel, albeit under jungle canopy.

The modest river, no more than the width of a road, lay at the bottom of a trough cut by past monsoons. The water was only knee high. We descended the bank and crossed quickly, one at a time.

Grady selected a slight knoll in a grove of saplings we could exit from in any direction, and we hid out. Cox set the two Yards to provide security, and the four of us stuck our heads together under a poncho liner.

Grady whispered, "This place is crawling with major VC."

"Yeah," Cox whispered back, snapping on his red-lensed flashlight to study the map. "It's sure not uninhabited jungle anymore."

"What do we do about the ambush?" Grady asked, directing the question to all of us. "If we don't do this real quiet, they'll know we're here. The odds of a chance meeting are sky-high. Even if we dust his babysitters without being detected and nab this commo guy, I don't know what we'll run into around the next bend between here and the extraction point. The VC keep their larger units spread out as a precaution. But we could be in an interval between smaller elements."

"Or between battalions," Cox whispered.

"You saying we should scrap it?" said Ruchevsky.

"I'm saying it's a total gamble. They could be anyplace. How many more campsites like that one are out here? We don't know what shit we're in the middle of."

Cox shifted the light toward the sergeant. "You're the man, Grady. It's your call."

"Hell," he said. "It's too hinky now for me to call it by my lonesome."

He put it to each of us in turn. No one was going to be the one to veto the thing, even as everyone prayed someone would. It was unanimous: proceed as planned, testosterone and glory. Fuck.

"Jeez," Grady said, grinning. "You're crazier than fire ants. Okay, most likely our man will be somewhere in the middle of the line. Wherever he is, don't kill 'im. I'll wait until the radio gook is past me in the ambush before I spring it. Remember — if I fire, it's on. If I don't shoot, we pass it up and sneak the fuck home. If it's gonna happen, I set it off. No one fires unless I do."

He looked us over. "Once it's sprung and we take 'em down, we beat feet right away and go for the landing zone. So don't miss. Check your silencers. You don't want the NVA hearin' this. We need kill shots, right between the antlers. Knock 'em down fast. We gotta be away from here quick. Fifteen seconds."

He pointed to where we were on the map and to the landing zone.

"It's thirty minutes to the LZ, John says. There's a narrow trail. As soon as we're on the way, Captain Rider radios for the pickup. Anybody got anything to add?"

Ruchevsky said, "None of our long-range recon units have snuck in here. It's virgin territory. So Charlie should be feeling safe — and let's hope a little lax."

"Amen," Cox said.

"Okay," Grady said. "Everybody stay cool. Everybody stay lucky."

We used the remaining daylight to set up two mines on our flanks and prepare our positions. At sunset we bedded down together on a slight slope. I radioed in for two seconds and we set the guard schedule for the night. We were exhausted but too wired to sleep. When I finally did, it was like falling into a black hole.

We were nudged awake. Before I could rub my eyes, three VC passed our position in the dark, heading north toward the base camp. Judging from how chatty they were, they had no suspicion of our presence. Since they weren't laden down with packs and a radio, none of them was our quarry. Cox gave up on sleep and took a dex candy. Just as I radioed in at midnight, a heavily loaded raft floated by on the river, pushed along in the shallow water like a scooter. Four more bamboo rafts floated by. For an isolated region, there was an awful lot of traffic.

Two hours before dawn, we rose from the night perimeter and shifted into our places in the one foolproof and perfect military configuration: the firing squad. Rot crossed the river in the direction they would come from to lie in wait for their rear guard, in case their last man didn't cross with the rest of the party, which was likely. Willie hid up ahead to deal with their point man once he moved away from the party on our side.

I couldn't make out my colleagues among the fronds, and I knew where they were. Ruchevsky, the closest, unpacked his second weapon, an M-79 grenade launcher that looked like a stubby shotgun. He loaded a single fat shell, a beanbag round to knock down his target if needed but not kill him.

I was groggy from interrupted sleep and immobility, and grew steadily unhappier with whatever bugs were sharing my fatigues. Chiggers, ants, spiders — all God's creatures taking communion on my flesh. I looped "California Dreamin'" nervously in my head to distract myself as they dined.

The light was still vague when we heard them approaching. The song in my head switched off. Big John's intel was impressive. The silencer would slow velocity but this close that wouldn't matter. If they bunched up, I was putting all eighteen rounds in my targets in one burst.

The Charlies' point man arrived at the river's edge and waited on one knee. The rest caught up and paused with him. The first man crossed and stopped to take in the jungle. He listened to the insects, a good sign, and signaled.

Five more forded one at a time, a few seconds apart, not terribly alert. Three in NVA helmets and khaki, two in *cao ao* pajamas. After the fifth man, I raised the muzzle a quarter inch, waiting for them to advance along the trail into our kill zone. Mercifully, it was just growing light and they presented as little more than silhouettes, faceless shadows I wouldn't be disinclined to pull the trigger on.

At that moment, on the far side, a sixth helmeted soldier stepped out of the jungle and proceeded to cross. A seventh waited on deck and then waded over. No others followed.

Seven on our riverbank. Possibly an eighth bringing up the rear, Rot there to dispatch him with his crossbow. More than we expected. The kidnap victim for John to deal with — was he identifiable? Number four's squarish pack bulged: the radio. The stub of an antenna stuck out of it. My pulse leapt.

Would Grady spring the ambush or give them a pass?

Their point man didn't start out from the riverbank ahead of them as he should have. That meant six VC for three of us to take down, leaving John to wrestle the seventh. I'd have to knock out the three in front; Cox and Grady, the trio in back; John, the radioman in the middle. Three head shots seemed risky. I'd spray the torsos. Body mass. They just needed to stay close.

They started forward, bunched. Grady fired . . . then Cox and me. A muzzle flashed back.

One burp had emptied my clip.

With all the firing, I'd missed it, but now the unmistakable *clack* of a Kalashnikov echoed back to us along the valley. A shot one of them had gotten off. Fuck. We'd been announced.

I slapped in a new magazine one-handed and advanced, eyes on the three in front. All of them were down.

*"Dung le ban,"* the radioman squealed. Don't shoot.

Ruchevsky, lying on top of him, whispered for him to shut up. I covered as Cox helped strip the radio off. Big John cuffed and gagged the radio guy and bound him at the elbows. They were on their feet, the captive's eyes like silver dollars.

I stepped toward my downed targets. The light seeping through the jungle turned faintly white. The third man I'd hit was in a black top and shorts. There was no mistaking him. His teeth were filed down like a Montagnard's. Pronounced five o'clock shadow darkened his cheeks. Wolf Man.

I motioned Cox over to confirm his identity and tore away his rucksack. Ammunition, salt pork, a Russian Zenith camera. The canvas satchel on his shoulder . . . paper! I turned him to get it. The exit wound in his back was a bright red bowl. Ribs and a lung gone. I tossed out everything but camera, maps, and papers, and slung on the bag and his weapon.

The next body wore a field uniform. NVA didn't wear insignia, and he wore no distinctive Commie belt buckle, like some officers. But he was armed with a pistol, an American .45, which meant he might be one. I unstrapped his ruck. Besides a Hungarian transistor radio, it was full of medicines and morphine in a nylon bag. A medic, maybe a doctor. I liberated the medicine bag and tossed the pistol and rucksack into the jungle.

Rot was crossing the river in a hurry, exuberant with his success. Willie appeared from up the trail, looking disappointed he'd missed out. Cox, standing over one of his targets, popped a coup de grâce shot.

I moved to the point man, sights fixed on his chest. Shit, he was breathing, still alive. A barefoot Montagnard VC in shorts, carrying nothing but ammunition and a sleeve of cooked rice. My heart sank. It was the father of the child we'd delivered, Roberta and I. He choked, grunting from pain, blood trickling from his chest. His eyes blinking, disbelieving.

Cox came up to me, signaling to hurry, then saw his face. He recognized the dad too. In one motion he covered the man's face with his boonie hat and filled it with a muffled burst from his CAR. Gratitude and revulsion swept through me.

Willie touched Cox on the arm. He was looking off the trail, toward Grady. We pushed through the foliage to where Sarge lay against a tree trunk, pressing a field dressing hard against his groin. The gauze and his fatigue pants were sodden.

"How bad?" Cox said.

"It must've hit bone and zigged everywhere. I'm cut up all over inside. Feels like a piece is comin' out my lower back. I think I'm bleeding out my ass. I'm sittin' in blood."

Cox said, "Cut away his pants," as he sawed a strap off a rucksack and hurriedly tightened it around Grady's thigh. I exposed the wound. Cox rifled the medic's musette bag. Grady took him by the arm.

"Don't."

The heavy caliber had devastated the leg, split it open all the way down the back, ass to ankle. White bone shone through the filleted flesh. The tourniquet slowed the bleeding but not enough. The leg seeped steadily, a rich heavy red. An explosion that took off a leg might cauterize the wound and stop its bleeding, but nothing sealed the arteries severed by a caroming bullet. If he was medevaced to a hospital, the surgeons could use Teflon and Dacron tubes to replace them, but here we could do nothing but slow the blood loss.

"You won't get to the bleeding," Grady said, voice hoarse. "The leg is hamburger in back. I'm leaking like a stuck pig. Just lousy luck. Wolf Man had a round in the spout and the safety off. Must've jerked the trigger when he got hit."

Cox looked scared. "We can't get a helicopter in here. We'll have to carry you."

Grady grimaced, teeth clamped. "In this heat, through this shit? You can't."

"Sarge — "

"All that jostling, I'll just bleed out faster."

"Grady — "

"Don't give me that nobody-left-behind crap. I don't want to be tits-up in Arlington with them ring knockers and honky fucks. I'm gonna kiss the bitch right here."

The Montagnards had finished dragging the bodies off the trail and took up defensive positions facing the far bank of the river and up the trail.

Cox tore the filter off a Salem, pushed it between Grady's lips, and lit it. He took short drags, sucking smoke in small increments. A shot sounded. A signal we'd been spotted.

Grady arched his back a little from pain. "Visiting hours're over, old son."

Cox licked his lips. He hesitated for a second, then stripped off Grady's web belt and harness, taking the grenades and ammo, and slung the sergeant's rifle across his own back.

"I'll leave two morphines."

"Leave me a grenade. And some tear-gas powder."

I put a pack of dry CS in his lap, and Cox handed over a grenade. Grady held it up.

"Pull the pin for me."

Cox did. "If it gets too bad, use the morphine," he said.

"No. Take it. My watch too. I don't want them to get it."

Cox slipped off the Rolex and pocketed it.

Grady said, "Either I nod off and the grenade does the job . . . or they'll find me. I'll wait till they're close. The gas should help slow them up too. Go."

Cox signaled Ruchevsky, and John shoved the VC prisoner past us. The captain touched Grady on the shoulder and rose.

Grady looked gray. "See you on the other side."

"Don't think so, Sarge," Cox said, squatting again. "I'm going to that better place, unlike some."

Grady took small sips of air. "Sure you are. Fuck you . . . sir. Get outta here."

Cox went. I fell in behind him. Willie passed me, going forward to take the lead. Rot took up the rear as we pressed toward the rendezvous, a half an hour away, risking everything by taking an established trail, leaving Grady farther behind with each step.

Counting strides was one of my jobs. At a hundred and four we heard the grenade.

# 19

★ ★ ★

**W**E HAD GONE a mile, nineteen hundred paces, dogged by two of their scouts who fired signal shots intermittently to summon the pack. We were traveling fast but their signal shots never receded: they were keeping up. Cox gestured to halt and waved us off the trail about fifteen feet. The Yards disappeared to act as our security. While we thrashed through the jungle, big and overburdened, they slipped through it like fish in water. We collapsed in a circle, facing out; Ruchevsky and I lay on either side of Cox as he consulted the map. Our objective might be obvious to the pursuers by now if they knew the area and the few open spaces. Their comrades might be on faster trails, trying to beat us to the pickup. In which case, we were done.

Cox whispered, "We've gotta nail at least one watcher. They can't know when we turn off. Rider, take the lead. You're maybe twenty minutes from the pickup point." He showed us on the map. "You should find a stream a quarter of a mile ahead. Leave the trail there and hang a left into the stream. It will slope up toward a rise. The foliage will thin out."

"What are you gonna do?" Ruchevsky said.

"Hang back and try to pop a scout, then run the trail. Gotta keep them from following us long enough to make the turn at the stream without them seeing."

"Let me hang back," I said. "I don't know if your Yards will take direction from us."

"Negative," Cox said, and signaled us in motion.

Just then the first scout appeared, moving warily but fast along the trail. An NVA. Cox took aim. The man staggered and clutched his throat, the shaft of an arrow protruding out the back of his neck; wound tightly around its head was the thread impregnated with poison.

We stepped out of the bush and covered Cox as he checked the man writhing in agony. Cox raised the CAR to his shoulder to finish him but Willie trotted up, crossbow in hand.

"What's he doing?" I whispered.

"He wants him to suffer."

Willie said something. I looked to Cox.

"Says it'll be over in a second."

It was. Willie cut off his ears and threw them away. The deformity would disorient the VC's spirit so he wouldn't reincarnate easily to avenge himself. Captain Cox booby-trapped the body. As soon as they were done, we resumed our rush. A little farther along, he propped the empty outer casing of a claymore mine on its tripod at the side of the road.

"Something for them to mull over."

He tossed the ends of its wires into the undergrowth.

"Devious," Ruchevsky said, chest heaving.

Willie took the lead and we were off again, Cox right behind him, I was relieved to see. We loped after them, practically jogging. We crossed the stream and kept going until the first patch of hard ground. Cox whistled to Willie and signaled for us to step off the trail to the left. We all stepped off simultaneously, avoiding leaving any sign, and turned around. Rot, now in front, led us back through the undergrowth in reverse order to the stream. He headed into the current, flanked by reeds. We rushed after him, Ruchevsky in front of me with his prisoner, Cox and Willie trailing.

The stream flowed straight and we made good progress. The reeds and foliage thinned as we ascended. After fifteen minutes it grew distinctly lighter. We'd reached a savanna of high grass towering over our heads, tall as corn and topped with silky plumes. Cox planted a second claymore — this one no dud — and unspooled the wires as he pressed straight into the dense grass. The trail we left was obvious. Thirty yards in, we made a hard right for fifteen yards. Cox wired up the clicker that would detonate the claymore.

"Okay," he whispered, "knock down the grass," and hurled himself at the stalks, using his body to press them flat. Ruchevsky pushed the prisoner to the ground and we imitated him, opening a circle. Chaff and insects rose all around us as we crushed the blades.

"Rider," Cox said, "go back to the elbow turn. Stay out of sight best you can. Watch for our hunters. If it's a single scout, he'll sit and wait for the rest. If it's a whole bunch, empty a magazine at them. Keep their heads down. When the bird's coming in, hightail it back before it gets too close. The downdraft will flatten all this around us. I'll blow the claymore as soon as we're on board."

"It may get lively long before that," I said.

"Yeah. Go."

I got to the turn and lay down flat to stick half my face out. The heavy camouflage made me hard to spot but I still felt exposed. AKs would scythe right through the grass.

Rotors thudded. The bird was coming. Distant shouts in the jungle: they had heard too.

The chopper was close, dropping straight in. I listened for firing, hoping they didn't have the bird in their sights. As the tops of the grass stalks began to dance, shots clacked up at it. A door gunner's 60 answered back. The stalks bent halfway. I fired a full magazine down the alley and dashed for the circle. The grass went flat from the full blast of the downdraft, completely exposing us and the Huey. Ruchevsky threw the prisoner on board and ordered the Yards to follow. Cox knelt by the door, firing. Ruchevsky launched grenade rounds at them with his M-79.

I emptied another magazine at the woods as I went. Cox too. He jumped butt-first onto the chopper and detonated the claymore, sending up a geyser of dirt and fronds at the corner of the field.

I ran up to the bay door and dove in. The bird rose the instant I was on. A shot clanged off the chopper's armor under the pilot. Another screeched through the aluminum overhead. We were away.

I sat up, panting, my fatigues soaked with sweat, and vowed never to smoke again as I checked myself for wounds. I accepted a lit cigarette from Ruchevsky and inhaled it deeply. It tasted bitter. Cox, legs dangling out the door, kept his face turned away from us all. Willie shifted over next to him and held his hand.

I took the contraband medical supplies to Roberta at her clinic. She looked relieved to see me.

"You're okay?"

I didn't reply.

She turned pale. "Is the colonel . . .?"

"He's on his way back, he's fine. But he's got a full plate waiting for him."

"Of course," she said. She resumed washing her hands in a basin; failing to find a towel, she dried them on her white lab coat.

"Just wanted to bring you this medical stuff."

"Everybody made it okay?"

"No. We lost a Special Forces noncom. Sergeant Grady."

"The black sergeant at Mai Linh?" she said. "Poor man."

"What's that?" I pointed at the jars on her bench.

"This?" she said, touching one. "*Kabang* tree resin. The Montagnards use it as a poison. This one — *ipoh* tree sap — is poison too. It's possible these substances could have medical applications."

Her face tipped toward me.

"Something on your mind, Rider?" She looked at me quizzically.

I needed to tell her about the father of the child we'd delivered, but I couldn't. Didn't.

"No," I said. "I'm ripped up about losing Grady the way we did, is all. Wanted to drop these supplies off," I said, holding out the haversack, my hand unsteady.

"Oh, Erik."

"I think it's mostly morphine in there."

"Thanks. You're an angel of mercy. We're always so short on everything."

She took the sack from me and laid out dextran blood thickener, vials of morphine, and two bottles of liquid sulfa. Out came a dozen lengths of commo wire, coiled. Except the wire was stripped out, leaving just the insulation.

I was baffled. "What the hell is that for?"

"Tubing," she said, stretching out a section. "God, it's an IV. They've improvised an intravenous line." She locked me in her gaze. "You captured this."

"Yeah. Didn't want to see it go to waste."

"How will you ever beat these people?" she asked, returning her attention to the contents of the sack.

"I don't know."

"They're beyond determined." She turned toward me. "You sure you're all right?"

She called a nurse to take away the supplies and made tea. We took it out on the bare concrete slab at the back of the house and stood with our cups, looking at the trash-strewn lane. The sky was threatening again. Clouds rolling in a solid gray avalanche. It was going to pour later. The full monsoon was drawing closer.

"Everything's going to turn to goo soon," she said.

"Yep. The ARVN will stand down and snooze away the rainy season. The VC will maneuver through the mud and launch their monsoon offensive. And we'll curse the bad flying weather and our jeeps and trucks and armor."

"Some things don't change."

A Montagnard family marched toward us in a line, grandfather at the front, followed by his son-in-law, his daughter, and their children. The old man carried the youngest boy in his arms. They stopped in front of her and spoke in their language. Roberta pinched the boy's skin. It remained bunched when she let go.

"Dysentery. He's totally dehydrated. Nearly gone. Rider, I've gotta go."

She led them into the dispensary, calling out instructions to her nurses.

Miser laid it open on a bit of plastic sheeting in the grass in the quadrangle between the bungalows and the mess hall.

The NVA radio nested in a .50-caliber ammo can, one of ours. The whole rig was hand-built. The knob of its Morse code key was a mahjong tile. The set was housed in aluminum, precisely wired, well machined, the tube sockets drilled out, capacitors aligned, resistors grounded to the chassis.

Miser sniffed at it with professional coolness. "Hand-wound coils."

"Impressed?" I said.

"Built from scratch."

"Let me see." Ruchevsky leaned closer.

The courier was already in the air on the way to Pleiku. Cox was accompanying him to II Corps headquarters for MACV. No way were we exposing him to Colonel Chinh's intelligence officers and field police across the street, even though the official demand to see the prisoner had arrived soon after we returned. Bennett wasn't yet back from his mission, so he couldn't be held accountable for any alleged slight or violation of directives. I was all too happy to play the offending party and shoo the ARVN lieutenant away from the gate. I lied and said the captured documents had gone with the prisoner. Joe Parks offered some sage advice as we walked back toward the bungalows.

"A word of caution. Translate the enemy documents before you pass 'em back to the head shop in Pleiku."

"They won't do it?" I said.

"They will, but you'll never know what was in them, even if they're plans for another attack on Cheo Reo. The higher highers will tell you that you haven't got the clearance to see it. It's too sensitive, and like that. Intel's a one-way street. Tap off what you need before passing it on."

"What a way to run a war," I said.

Checkman hunched at his desk, slaving over the papers. We had risked our lives to gather the raw intelligence, and we wanted to learn what we could about what was really happening in our backyard before sending the stuff down the rabbit hole to headquarters.

Colonel Bennett, still in battle dress, returned and summoned Ruchevsky and me to his office, along with Gidding and Parks.

"Incredible," he said. "You got Wolf Man. A special courier comes at first light tomorrow to fetch all this. It's getting its own chase ship." Bennett motioned at the materials spread over Checkman's desk. "Do we know any more about what's happening locally?"

I held up a classified teletype message. "Intel from Two Corps. Confirms the NVA are still on the move setting fire to mountainsides along the way to block overflight sensors."

Bennett said, "What's your take on what's happening, Joe?"

Parks clamped down on his pipe. "They'll march three nights running, twenty to twenty-five miles a night, their companies spaced an hour or so apart."

"That's what passed by the night we were probed?" said the colonel.

"Yes, sir. Probably four or five companies maneuvering past us, single file, their soldiers two meters apart. With maybe two other similar columns following different tracks farther out."

"They needed to get out of this basin and into the mountains," Ruchevsky said.

Sergeant Parks sat down, facing the colonel's desk. "Right. Once the NVA near their targets, they'll lay low again until everyone's assembled. They'll distribute extra ammo, put casualty-recovery squads in place, set up aid stations along their withdrawal routes, dig graves . . . and it'll be on. Some base or airfield will take a major hit; at least two battalions.

"The assault," Parks continued, "it'll be precisely timed. May take sixty minutes or several hours. Whether or not they take their objective, at the appointed time the NVA will stop their attack and disperse into the jungle, taking their wounded with them, while mortuary squads drag away the dead. They'll drop off the live casualties at triage points, and by morning the battalions will be miles away, scattering through the jungle, breaking down into ever smaller units . . . separated again. They'll disappear."

Checkman's typewriter ratcheted as he tore out a page. Red-faced with excitement, he spoke rapidly. "The confiscated documents and precisely drawn map were the Northwestern Zone Order of Battle," he announced.

They confirmed what we'd guessed: the first mission of the newly formed battalions was to march sixty miles in three nights, heading southeast along three land routes. Mass up as two reinforced battalions and launch a major attack.

"Their objective's Tuy Hoa," Checkman stated. "The air base and Army installation on the coast."

"From which a lot of our air assets originate," Bennett added. "The river running past us leads straight there."

"The Hundred and First Airborne is in Tuy Hoa," Gidding said.

"The NVA are moving southeast," I said, pointing at the map. "Downriver. They'll go past our Special Forces camp at Phu Tuc and on to Tuy Hoa."

"They skipped our small piece of it," Gidding said.

"They can afford to," Joe chimed in. "We're inconsequential."

Checkman stood and resumed his summary. The captured maps, he explained, marked out the routes of approach and the routes of withdrawal, ammunition-distribution points, first-aid stations serving the battlefield, field hospitals farther from the fighting, the sites being prepared in advance for quick burials. He sat down and started typing again.

Bennett exhaled. "Joe, what's your estimate of their total rice supply?"

Parks paused to do a quick calculation on a scrap of paper.

"Their daily requirement is eighteen ounces per man. Figure fourteen hundred men, that means . . . fifteen hundred pounds of rice a day, sir."

"Three quarters of a ton," Ruchevsky said. "No wonder they're emptying the villages along the way and replenishing their rice stash at their camps in the mountains." He absently worked the lid of the mahogany box back and forth. "All those mouths to feed. Mrs. Chinh must be getting ready to order her next season's Paris couture."

Major Gidding glared at Ruchevsky.

"Not if we can help it," Bennett said, ignoring his XO's look of disapproval.

Checkman stopped typing just long enough to give us the showstopper. He held up classified sheets by way of demonstration.

"Our SOIs with next week's radio codes. A list of all our frequencies and Pleiku's. Operational area assignments. A schedule of air assets and target clearances in process. MACV intelligence estimates on the NVA presence in the Highlands. Harassment and Interdiction fire coordinates for the Vietnamese artillery to target."

"Good God," Joe said. "So much for their harassment shelling."

Ruchevsky whistled. "Or bothering to clear air strikes through them. A total waste."

Joe Parks leafed through the documents.

"All this is eyes-only. And found on a VC corpse — their top political officer for the province. Son of a bitch."

Ruchevsky could hardly contain himself. "Which means Wolf Man was rushing classified information to the enemy command to encrypt and pass back to their headquarters. The highest-ranking VC in the province carrying information that could only have come from one of two sources."

Bennett looked sallow. "Me and my Vietnamese counterpart, and our immediate staffs."

"Colonel Chinh," Parks said. "Well, unless you've gone over, sir, Colonel Chinh's responsible for supplying the enemy with highly classified information."

Ruchevsky raised his hands and said, "Hallelujah." He was elated, arms thrust in the air. "The wicked witch is dead!" He stopped when he saw Bennett's expression. "What's the matter, Colonel?"

"Think about it, John. Finding this on Wolf Man isn't ironclad evidence it came from Chinh. Think about what Saigon and MACV will say if we — if I — accuse a province chief of something like this." Bennett draped his web belt across his chair and leaned on his desk. "His benefactors won't appreciate our threatening him with exposure, since they're beneficiaries of his corrupt practices."

And he didn't even know about Chinh's major source of extracurricular income, the revenue he didn't share with his betters.

"If they have to investigate him," Bennett said, "they'll investigate me. In the interim, the new province chief will send me packing just to even things out and save face."

I hadn't thought about the backlash against Bennett, the effect on him of a clash with the supreme civil and military authority in the province. It seemed unfair that he should suffer, maybe lose his post, be separated from Roberta. Roberta — the other reason Bennett might be hesitating. Chinh would be vengeful. Revelation of Bennett's adultery would end him as an officer and a gentleman. He looked deflated.

"Whatever else he is," Bennett said, "Chinh's one of them. They'll protect him and their injured national pride."

Ruchevsky toyed nervously with the mahogany presentation box on the side of the desk and lifted out Chinh's gift pistol. "You mean, protect their collective asses since they all partake of the spoils, pack away their gold for the moment when . . ."

"We need to tread carefully," Parks said. "Exposing Chinh will make them nervous, which doesn't bring out their best qualities."

Ruchevsky gave an exasperated groan. "Come on, people. We're not talking graft anymore. This is way beyond black-market profiteering. It's not even merely collaborating. This is total fucking treason."

"What's the punishment?" I said.

Ruchevsky glanced up. "For treason in wartime? The firing squad if they like him. The guillotine if they don't. Take your pick."

"Get real, John," Gidding exclaimed. "It's happened on his watch, is all."

"True." Joe Parks agreed with Gidding. "More likely Colonel Chinh will just find himself transferred, pending an investigation that will never get off the ground."

"You being cynical or serious?" I said.

"Both. A couple of months ago we could've turned him in to their anti-corruption committee in Saigon, but it was just disbanded for corruption. If I had a nickel for every sticky-fingered province chief transferred out of harm's way to a better job elsewhere . . . Chinh could easily walk away free and richer."

I said, "Isn't there any way to bring him down and not catch the recoil?"

"Yeah," Ruchevsky snarled, "kill the son of a bitch in his sleep. His rat wife too." He dropped the Chinese pistol back in its box.

Bennett wiped his face and addressed Ruchevsky. "Chinh may not be able to touch you, John. But by the same token, he's protected too. You can't just put his name on a list."

"A damn shame too," Ruchevsky said.

Parks said, "If we give him time, he'll find a way to weasel out of this, blame someone on his staff, blame us, leaks by VC agents at higher headquarters, his astrologer — whatever. Leaning on him immediately with the suggestion that we have absolute proof—that might just work."

Bennett opened his canteen. "You really think Colonel Chinh would give up his sinecure, just write it off and go quietly?"

Joe Parks sucked on his pipe. "If we acted fast enough, he wouldn't know what we've got on him. He could only imagine the worst. We won't know if it's enough to lever him out of here if we don't put it to him, sir."

Bennett recapped his canteen. "Tell him we want to spare him embarrassment—or worse. Say we're giving him the chance to resign and save face."

"And neck," I said.

Bennett looked to Ruchevsky and Gidding. "Are we agreed?"

Gidding looked undecided. Ruchevsky started to giggle. We all looked at him, puzzled.

"Colonel," he said, "Chinh may assume he's already won your goodwill and cooperation."

"What are you talking about, John?"

Ruchevsky turned the box around to display the big circular colonel's insignia replicated on the inside of the lid.

"Your solid silver eagle? It's platinum."

We found Colonel Chinh taking late-morning coffee with his officers at the one decent café off the market square. The colonel was treating his men, looking content and prosperous, a gold Dunhill lighter resting next to his Marlboros on the low table. He rose as Bennett approached, and his officers stood up with him.

"May I speak with you?" Bennett said and stepped back into the street before the man could reply. Colonel Chinh scooped up his cigarettes and lighter, waved Captain Nhu and the others back into their seats. Bennett led him away, but not before I heard him say, "We need to speak privately . . . without an interpreter. Do you think we can cope without having someone translate?"

Chinh said, "Yes," and lit a cigarette. Bennett began to speak very softly, calmly laying out our case against him. Chinh's features grew stony as he listened, snapping the lighter open and shut. The ash grew. Finally Chinh spoke, smoke punctuating his words. I couldn't make out what was said, but he was stern and displeased.

"Colonel," Checkman called from the jeep, holding up the handset of the radio. "It's urgent."

Bennett excused himself and hurried toward the vehicle.

"He's not budging," Bennett said to me as he passed. Taking the handset from Checkman, he gave his call sign and listened. He had trouble hearing and covered his other ear to hear better.

I looked back at Chinh, arm across his waist, holding his elbow, and made a quick decision. Chinh might not fear accusations of treason from us, but he'd be mad not to fear his superiors if they found out he was denying them their financial due. The corruption was a system, elaborate and unforgiving, with no real means of contrition and mercy. Anyone who flouted its customary practices would be made an example.

He turned back toward the café. "Colonel Chinh," I called. He stopped and waited for me to catch up. "I have intelligence you should consider before choosing your next steps."

"I speak your colonel already," he said. "I tell I punish when I find."

"This is a separate matter, sir." I stepped closer. "In my position as intelligence officer, I've learned that General Loc may soon be made aware of your wife's cousin's overseas account."

Chinh grinned. An Asian reflex when stressed — or panicked.

"Of course," I went on, "the information might not reach General Loc . . . if you were to resign your position as province chief. Which unavoidably leads to a delicate matter." I paused to stoke his anxiety. "Your wife's part in all this. She may have to face charges as well."

"Captain Rider," Bennett called out. "We have to get back."

I turned on my heel and hurried to rejoin Bennett and Checkman. We drove hastily back to MACV.

Bennett said, "Three columns of NVA are nearing the Special Forces camp at Phu Tuc."

As soon as we pulled in, Bennett vaulted out of his seat and jogged to the commo bunker. After conferring by radio with the Green Beret commander at the A camp, he returned to his office. Joe Parks dismissed Mr. Cho for the day, and Bennett gave us all the lowdown on his exchange with Chinh.

"I gave him our ultimatum. He tried not to show it, but he was definitely shaken."

"And?" Ruchevsky said.

"No sale. He seemed confident he could shift it all onto someone else, is how I read it. You know, sacrifice a subordinate to pay for the dishonor and blame the compromised intelligence on him."

Only Major Gidding seemed relieved by the idea that the status quo would be maintained. The rest of us were disheartened. I hoped my threat had carried more weight than Bennett's, but I saw no reason to raise anyone's hopes.

Checkman knocked. "Call for you on the landline, sir. It's Colonel Chinh."

We stepped out to let Bennett take it. He mostly listened for a minute, rang off, and joined us in the bullpen.

"Chinh's had a change of heart," Bennett announced, surprised and smiling. "As soon as the current threat abates, he says he'll submit his resignation."

Joe Parks let out a low whistle. Checkman hooted and high-fived him. Big John beamed and offered everyone a celebratory cigar like a new dad.

"In the meantime" — Bennett raised a hand for attention — "his headquarters in Pleiku is alarmed by reports that the VC are seizing rice caches. They want villagers to surrender it to the provincial governments and deny the enemy food stores."

Sounding amused, Ruchevsky under his breath said, "No more rice sales to the People's Army. Downright tragic. Watch, Chinh will squeeze every last dime out of this damn province on the way out the door, the bastard."

Bennett massaged his neck. "Orders from Two Corps are to seize all the rice stores he can locate. He's issued instructions to his district administrators and troops to compel all villages — Montagnard and Vietnamese — to dig up their emergency storage jars of rice and surrender them to his troops. Three of his ARVN companies will truck into the field and meet up with Vietnamese militia from Phu Thien to sweep the villages and escort the rice back to Cheo Reo. He wants four birds to fly his officers and their American advisers around to supervise, make sure none is held back or diverted to the NVA. We have air assets assigned to us at dawn."

Parks shook his head. "I'm sure VC cadre are already telling villagers the Americans and their Saigon puppets are indifferent to their hunger and seizing the last of their rice supply — that they won't see a grain of it again."

"Probably true too," Bennett said. "It's a propaganda windfall for the Viet Cong. But we can't help that at the moment. At least if we're there, we can try to help the villagers keep enough back that they don't starve."

Bennett moved his helmet to a hook on the wall. "Major Gidding, Lieutenant Lovell, and Sergeant Divivo will each take a flight tomorrow. Captain Rider, you'll accompany me. We pick up our Vietnamese counterparts down at the airstrip at oh-seven-forty."

"ARVN actually leaving their billets," Ruchevsky said, looking victorious. "Hell must be getting chilly."

# 20

★ ★ ★

RUCHEVSKY AND I managed only a few hours' sleep before heading out to put our pouches aboard the courier flight.

"I have a suspicion about you, John."

"Oh, yeah? What?"

"I think you knew Wolf Man was accompanying that courier, and that we had a shot at taking him down and grabbing the documents that would incriminate Chinh."

"No kidding."

"You set 'im up."

Ruchevsky smiled. "Wolf Man had personally delivered Chinh's intel before. There was a good chance. We got lucky. He was there, the classified stuff was on him."

I pointed to the four dots in the lead-gray sky — choppers coming in from the southeast.

"The rice roundup," I said.

Three jeeps appeared, passed the raised barrier, and drove onto the apron to surround us. Ruchevsky waved to the colonel and pulled away in his Bronco, heading back to the compound.

"Morning, Captain," said Bennett. "Sergeant Divivo's presence has been requested for a patrol with his ARVN company."

"Wonder of wonders," I said.

"You'll take Divivo's mission," Bennett said. "I'll take Captain Nhu with me. Here's the list of all the villages we're going to overfly. Chinh wants each of us to land at at least one to make sure all is actually proceeding as planned. I've got the hamlet of Hiong Cham. You take the second one I've circled. Lieutenant Lovell the third, Major Gidding the fourth. Chinh has ARVN and regional militia clearing and securing the vils we're landing at. Don't go into the villages before you're sure the army or the militia's there."

"Yes, sir." A hundred yards back on the regular road, Chinh, in his open staff car, was leading a convoy loaded with troops standing in the truck beds. Bennett saw me staring and turned to look himself.

"Colonel Chinh in the field," he said.

"Yeah, a historic moment. Now that the main-force NVA have departed, he's rolling into action."

The four Hueys came closer, their long blades whopping the hot air. A solid layer of dark clouds blanketed the north.

"Monsoon later," Bennett said.

We leaned against a jeep and watched the four helicopters land close to the fuel truck to replenish their tanks, engines running, props turning through the process. Bennett gazed at the retreating plume of dust raised by Chinh's command car and ARVN trucks.

"Can you spare a cigarette, Captain?"

"Didn't know you smoked, sir." I offered him my pack, shaking out a butt.

"Haven't in years. Saw forty coming and quit."

I held up my lighter and he sucked in the flame. Bennett was oddly subdued for somebody who had just won a very personal fight by a knockout. The last helicopter finished topping off and signaled for us to load.

"Here we go," Bennett said and took a long drag. He tossed the cigarette and got in his jeep. Nhu and I jumped in back and Checkman sped off, heading for the first bird. The other two jeeps fell in behind as we lumbered down the steel plates.

Checkman dropped me at the second bird and drove on toward the lead chopper to deliver the colonel and Nhu. We loaded in seconds and were airborne. The Hueys half circled the field and sped off in different directions: the colonel, west; my ship, northwest. We sailed out over the endless green. The cold light beneath the solid layer of black clouds turned the rivers silver.

We arrived at the first village and orbited slowly, observing ARVN on the ground confiscating rice, then proceeded to the next location, where farmers were resisting the insistent troops. After much gesticulating and shoving by the soldiers, the villagers finally surrendered their stores. And so the morning droned on. As we neared the sixth hamlet the ship suddenly broke off its approach. The crew chief handed me a miked headset.

The pilot came on. "Captain, we just got a mayday from the lead ship."

"The colonel's bird? What's their situation?"

"Don't know. Can't raise them. They're on the ground . . . We're heading over."

The jet turbine howled, churning full out. The sky grew even darker, the jungle shrouded and shadowed beneath us. The seconds tortured. I leaned into the air streaming past us, squinting to see. We banked and descended. Out the open door, I could see a small village abutted by rice paddies. Men trotted toward the thick jungle and disappeared into the fronds. Next to some huts the colonel's Huey sat smoldering.

Our bird shot over the area, the door gunners fixed on the ground. The gun on the left side opened up, sweeping the foliage. Red tracers floated up in response, momentarily confusing the gunners. Both quickly resumed firing. Red pulses crisscrossed.

I lay on the floor and fired into the tree line where black figures in conical hats hid in the broad leaves. One of our sister ships arrived and joined in, firing continuously. There was no more return fire. Our pilot dropped in for a quick landing. I leapt out and raced for the colonel's helicopter, ran to its right side and pushed open the spring-loaded panel at the base of the rotor shaft to reach the fire-extinguishing system, then slid open the copter door. The colonel lay slumped on his back, clothes smoking, his glasses melted to what was left of his face. Lips and eyebrows gone, head burned bald.

The pilots were in their seats, the door gunners at their posts, the colonel and Nhu prostrate on the deck in the compartment behind the two fliers. All six of them shot to pieces. The crewmen and pilots had on their white helmets, their bodies black and blistered from soot and fire, much of their uniforms and skin burned away. They were slippery with blood and exposed layers of yellow fat.

For all the pomp surrounding the profession of arms, in that instant it seemed barbaric and crude, about as noble as an abattoir. I felt nothing but the indignity of his dying like this: roasted, ruined, the silver eagles mocking his charred remains.

The downed chopper pilots' unit rushed three helicopters to the site, and a sister outfit laid on four gunships to fly cover. They offered as many slicks or shooters as we wanted: they'd divert everything. Gunships circled like angry hornets as more Hueys landed.

John Ruchevsky, Major Gidding, Checkman, and Sergeant Parks arrived to help with the recovery. The corpses leered as we struggled to get them into green mortuary bags. Each had been shot multiple times, the copilot nearly cut in half. He and the pilot were difficult to extricate from the well of the cockpit. The men from their unit bent to the task, faces grim, fatigues smeared with offal.

The colonel lay on the metal floor close to the door, his clothes burned into the singed flesh. Gunshot wounds riddled his torso and one leg. Captain Nhu lay across the aluminum bench, punctured and destroyed, the canvas seat burned away and collapsed under him. Parks inspected what was left of the chopper as I collected their weapons. Ruchevsky was talking to some villagers.

I said, "The ship's radio and both door gunners' machine guns are missing."

"Yeah, they stripped them out. Left their personal weapons."

I laid out the small arms and proceeded to clear them. Major Gidding watched me remove magazines and eject rounds from the pilots' .45s and the colonel's and Vietnamese captain's carbines.

"They didn't get off a shot," I said, clearing the last rifle.

Major Gidding stepped closer. "Damn. You sure?"

"Yes, sir. Not from these weapons." I turned to Joe Parks aboard the helicopter. "You find any casings from the door guns?"

"No," he said.

Gidding squatted in the wrecked passenger section. "I don't suppose it matters," he said, "but I wish they'd had the chance to go down fighting." He seemed almost offended.

Ruchevsky came over and we gathered around him. "Checkman's questioned a couple of farmers. And I debriefed the other chopper pilots about what they heard on their radio net as the colonel's ship came in."

Gidding turned abruptly. "What are they saying?"

"Provincial militia came into the village two hours before the colonel's helicopter arrived and told the villagers to keep working. The farmers say the helicopter approached and hovered. The pilots say no radio contact with the vil was overheard on the net. A red smoke marker popped on the ground."

"The operation's signal color," Gidding interjected.

"The copter landed. The militiamen waved a greeting. Someone aboard the bird waved back. The pilot shut down the engine. The tall American officer and the South Vietnamese got out."

"They cut the engine?" Parks said, incredulous.

"Yeah, according to the farmers. Bennett and Captain Nhu climbed down and walked toward the militia. They were gunned down over there." He pointed to a spot forty yards off, near a young palm tree, the broad leaves punctured with round holes. "Simultaneously, the militiamen closest to the chopper drew down on the crew, riddled the American pilots and door gunners."

Parks stepped down from the gutted chopper. "That was clever, what they did with the red smoke, enticing them to land. Seems like the ambushers knew exactly what to do."

"What arms did the VC carry?" I asked.

Ruchevsky said, "U.S. carbines."

"Like the militias," Gidding said. "They were supposed to be Ruff Puffs — Vietnamese Popular Forces militia — but they must have been Communist irregulars. VC."

Parks circled as he spoke: "I'm not so sure of that. This was really planned out. For sure not just a piece of bad luck."

He led the four of us to the spot where Nhu and the colonel had been slain. He indicated the ocher dirt stained dark with blood, the young palm tree stippled with bullet holes. Spent carbine casings lay scattered everywhere.

Parks policed up some of the cartridges and removed his cotton hat to mop his forehead and cheeks with a handkerchief. "The pilots never would have shut down their engine unless Colonel Bennett or Nhu identified the armed men on the ground as friendlies. That's standard procedure. They'd never deviate."

"Poppycock," Gidding disagreed. "We're all capable of mistakes."

Joe Parks turned to him. "I promise you, unless he was dead certain who they were, Colonel Bennett wouldn't reassure the pilot, much less get out of a chopper and walk toward a bunch of armed irregulars. He must have recognized some of the militiamen."

"Recognized individual VC?" I said.

Gidding slapped his hat against his leg. "You're not making sense," he half shouted over the engine of a Huey lifting away.

"The other odd thing," Parks said, "the ambushers put the bodies back on board the helicopter." Parks pinched his lower lip. "Taking the armament and destroying the ship, I get that. But why move the two bodies?" Parks brushed a hand across his tan scalp. "They didn't lay them out like trophies or anything, to get in our heads. Why squander time to put them back on board and risk being caught out in the open instead of concentrating on getting away as fast as possible?"

"Why do *you* think they moved them?" Gidding said, growing visibly annoyed with Parks's insistence that something was amiss.

I stepped in to deflect some of his building anger and said, "They wanted us to think what you're thinking, Major. That the colonel and Nhu never got off the ship, that the chopper landed, and the crew, the ARVN captain, and Colonel Bennett all died in a hail of VC bullets. It was meant to look like they had mistaken Viet Cong for friendly militia and landed in the middle of an enemy force."

"Yes, sir," Parks said. "They didn't want us to know that they'd deceived the Americans."

"Fuck me," Ruchevsky muttered. "Why would they bother?"

I touched Parks on the arm. "Joe, you said Bennett may have recognized them."

Ruchevsky rubbed his face with a cloth. "The province paramilitaries are thoroughly infiltrated. Some are certainly VC."

"Like the militiamen who were here," Parks said.

I faced Ruchevsky. "John, you think the Communists would do this just to protect their man and keep him where they need him?"

"Wouldn't you," Ruchevsky said, "in their shoes?"

"What man?" Gidding said, blinking and sounding worried. "You're suggesting—"

Ruchevsky's eyes stayed on me as he answered. "That's right—their spy and protector. Chinh's worth a lot to them. They'd do whatever to keep him in place. Then again, Chinh could have laid this trap himself."

Brow furrowed, Parks said, "Chinh commands the Vietnamese militias personally. He could order up any platoon of territorials he wanted."

Gidding colored. "Good God. You're saying this is murder."

I looked at Joe. "South Vietnamese militiamen known to Bennett? A unit he was familiar with?"

"Phu Thien District headquarters," Parks said. "He knew the militias there pretty well." He rested his weapon across his shoulder like a yoke, one arm over the barrel.

Ruchevsky stared off toward the mountains. "Chinh sees to it the province serves as a safe staging area for the NVA, provisions them, sneaks them our classified information. Bennett threatens his operation, Chinh orders Bennett killed by his militia." Big John turned back toward us. "We're scrambling to figure out how the shooters did such a good job deceiving the colonel. But that was the easy part."

Gidding held his forehead. "You've got to be kidding."

"Get serious, Major," Ruchevsky snapped. "You still think Chinh is intending to resign? He only told Bennett he would to buy himself time to set this up. This"—he pointed back at the mayhem—"this is all about saving his ruthless ass and his cash flow. He's outmaneuvered us all and you're refusing to see it."

"Sweet Jesus," Gidding exclaimed. "If what you're suggesting is even possible, how could you ever prove it?"

Abruptly he set off toward the downed chopper. Big John and

I walked the area and obsessed, growing more convinced the more we turned over the facts. Little John was eliminated—gone from the province—rendering Big John completely ineffective. With Bennett's death, any accusation of treason by the ranking American officer vanished. If the suggestion ever surfaced, Nhu was also conveniently dead, so it would be easy for Chinh to discover his trusted aide had been a traitor all along, meeting with VC commanders in the jungle, accepting their money in exchange for our intelligence and classified procedures. As John talked, it dawned on me that if I'd been on the chopper as planned, my threat to expose Chinh's greed to his superiors would have ended too. Like in the Saigon tailor's game, we were left staring at the last pieces on the board, not realizing we'd lost before we had even known what was happening.

The gunships made a low pass. We put the burned corpses aboard two slicks for transport: the helicopter crew to Tuy Hoa, Captain Nhu and the colonel to the military morgue at Pleiku. The rest of us flew back to Cheo Reo. On the way Miser reached me on the radio. He was cryptic but I got the gist: Army intelligence reported the NVA assault on Tuy Hoa had been called off because the order of battle had been so badly compromised. A lot of guys owed Sergeant Grady and Colonel Bennett their lives and limbs. That same afternoon, fifteen Vietnamese militia at Phu Thien deserted.

The light was white, the sky gray. A monsoon rain burst as I drove to her clinic. She wasn't there. The Bahnar head nurse looked stricken. She said I might find her at the sun hut by the river, and I drove on alone through the warm rain.

Roberta wasn't under the eaves. I spotted her below, sitting at the river's edge. Mist rose from the large drops pummeling the ground and the water. The river boiled from the blows.

I slid down the steep embankment and walked out to her through the tepid downpour. Rivulets snaked past her into the monsoon current. She might have been weeping. I sat down alongside and drew her against me. We sat like that for a long time.

# 21

★ ★ ★

RUCHEVSKY STOOD UNDER the overhang of the concrete walkway outside our room, pondering.

"You know," he said, "it wouldn't have occurred to us to suspect anything if they'd just left them for dead."

"You're probably right," I agreed. "Casualties on the battlefield. Who would have questioned anything?" I stared at his ankle boots. "I should have gone with him, should have had his back."

"Yeah," Ruchevsky said, "if you had I wouldn't have to listen to this bullshit. Had his back . . . Get real. They were done for when they shut down their engine."

"They were done the minute I tried to strong-arm Chinh with those bank figures of his wife's cousin."

"Information I supplied you, if you're looking for someone to pin it on." Ruchevsky got to his feet. "We almost had him."

"John. I'm sorry."

He just nodded.

As John had predicted, with the loss of Little John and the death of Tri, his web of informants was compromised beyond repair. He rolled up his operation and made ready to leave. Miser expected us to be recalled to Saigon at any moment. The daily routine went on, but the compound remained subdued after Bennett's death. Cohesion was done — over. Everyone withdrew into his own countdown of days left in country.

Major Gidding escorted the colonel's body home. He stayed for the funeral at the request of COMUSMACV, meaning Westmoreland himself. In Washington, D.C., an immaculate Class A uniform was prepared, insignia perfectly placed, two different unit patches sewn on the shoulders, combat stripes on the sleeve, every badge and citation and medal ribbon assembled and exactly pinned, including his posthumous Silver Star. But the body was too badly burned to wear it. Instead the uniform was placed in the casket atop the bagged remains that bore an admonition against viewing. Gidding accompanied the widow to the cemetery at West Point. An honor guard fired three volleys at the graveside and folded the flag in the prescribed triangle. The commandant presented it to the widow with the thanks of a grateful nation.

Miser was tired of doing all the gump work and started agitating for us to leave. Our work was done, he argued. The local VC commissar was dead and doing no business of any sort; at least part of the Viet Cong money supply had been pinched off for a while. And he was right. Whatever damage we could do to the drug business had been done. Chinh wasn't going to let us disrupt the works any further. John had called it: the VC account in Hong Kong disappeared. That window on their operation shut. Mrs. Chinh's cousin's account mysteriously closed too, no doubt converted to bullion — or emeralds. She'd left Taiwan and shown up in Vancouver, British Columbia, with a brand-new Canadian passport. Even if Chinh couldn't clean up that trail entirely, he'd come close. Whalen Lund went on an overnight trip to Nhatrang and never came back.

We were in disarray. Outmaneuvered, out of commission, outta luck. Expertly picked off. At the bar one night Joe Parks and I tried to work out how to bring some justice down on Chinh's ass.

"MACV headquarters in Pleiku seems a possible back door," Parks said.

"Yeah, but we're not Colonel Bennett. We can't go right to the top. And that's what it would take."

"No, we haven't the time to work our way up the chain of command. But we can present the situation in Cheo Reo like a security breach, go to the head of the intelligence section in Pleiku and tell him our story."

I was beginning to get it. "And he'll sound the alarm that'll let us jump the queue."

"Uh-huh. Just don't ever own up to it."

We got a ride on the courier flight. Checkman saw us off and wished us luck. Visibility seemed unlimited in the unearthly light beneath a black front rolling in. At Pleiku we were met by an old pal of mine from the 5008 OSI detachment who loaned us a jeep. We presented ourselves at the MACV intel shop and were shown in to the major in charge. The major listened attentively, soon losing his relaxed demeanor.

"Jesus H. Christ," he exclaimed when we'd finished, and he hurriedly called higher headquarters to get us in to see the MACV commander. He synopsized our story to an aide and we got penciled in. At ten of ten we sat in the anteroom, waiting for the general to come free. Out of his office strode a rotund Vietnamese general officer, starched and polished and looking imperial.

"Chinh's boss," Joe whispered, "Major General Vinh Loc."

The general swaggered past, trailing an entourage that grew as he crossed the room. He swept up aides like iron filings and exited with more than half a dozen in tow.

"Coincidence, you think?" Joe said, sarcastically.

A sergeant escorted us into the raw, unfinished office of the general's adjutant, a Lieutenant Colonel Blackwell. We reported and were waved into seats facing a teak slab laid across a pair of sawhorses: the man's desk. Overhead, beams and joists were exposed, as were the studs and two-by-fours in the walls. A nail driven into the wood in back of the colonel held his pistol belt, holstered sidearm, and canteen. A major wearing the JAG insignia of an Army lawyer straddled a chair backward.

By now, Joe and I had the story of Chinh's treason down and we recounted it in record time.

"Why amn't I hearing this from your acting CO?" Colonel Blackwell said.

I said, "Major Gidding accompanied Colonel Bennett home and stayed for the funeral at General Westmoreland's behest. He's in transit now, sir, on the way back."

"I see." Blackwell shook his head, looking displeased. "And the chief evidence supporting this . . . murder allegation against Colonel Chinh is classified material found among captured enemy documents that point to treasonous actions on his part."

"Yes, sir," I said.

"They'd have to be produced," the JAG lawyer put in, "if you're going to try to convince anyone of the veracity of this story."

"How's that going to happen?" Blackwell said. "They're classified. Their intelligence value trumps any other consideration."

"Colonel —" the lawyer started.

"There's no way the captured documents will be shared with our esteemed allies."

Blackwell watched the statement slap us and waited for an outburst. Joe and I sat silent.

The lawyer looked at us sympathetically. "You do realize everything you've put forth is conjecture and suspicion or circumstantial in nature."

Blackwell sighed audibly. "Accusing friendlies of complicity in the death of a high-ranking American officer would undermine the U.S. effort in South Viet Nam, sow discord among allies, and embarrass our government and the government of South Viet Nam — not to mention pissing off General Loc."

"The man's a prince," the JAG major said in a sardonic tone.

Blackwell glanced over at the attorney. "He means that literally. He's cousin to the last emperor to rule Viet Nam, who's presently enduring the rigors of exile on the French Riviera with his many wives and concubines."

Blackwell propped a foot on a wooden box and leaned back to stare at us, antsy and dissatisfied. We hadn't made his day.

"General Loc's the commander, for Christ sake," Blackwell said. "We can't just accuse one of his top people of murdering an American officer and betraying his country. Though you've made me wish the son of a bitch dead."

I said, "Are you ordering us to desist, sir?"

"Captain, last week I had a report in here that two sergeants advising an ARVN company were killed in the field. No one else got so much as a scratch. ARVN called in a helicopter to come collect our bodies and strolled home. The wounds on the Americans were . . . suspicious. Single shots, close range. The ARVN didn't look like they'd even been in a fight. I like this situation even less."

Blackwell's spit-shined combat boot came off the box as he sat up, hands flat on the slab. "No accusation of murder will be leveled against Colonel Chinh. Treason either. God help us, you will not discuss your suspicions or communicate them to your families or the press. You're officially gagged. Is that understood?"

"Yes, sir," I said. Blackwell turned to Joe.

"Sergeant?"

"Understood, sir."

"Incidentally," Blackwell said, and slid a single sheet of paper across to us. "The Vietnamese interpreter who worked for Colonel Bennett — name of Cho? — was tried for espionage at the sector headquarters in Cheo Reo and summarily executed this morning."

Chinh had played us and won. Sunk us like pool balls, one after another. We'd pursued him like he was a corrupt official instead of a lethal foe, and he had had his way with us. Run the table. The NVA trails and base areas remained open for business, and so did he. We had done some temporary damage but surely the Chinhs would adapt, rebound. Already the housecleaning was well under way.

Joe and I started at the Air Force compound bar because it opened early for the night shift coming off duty. We worked our way back toward the MACV bar, staggering in there in the middle of the afternoon. My OSI pal decided we needed food. He drove us all into Pleiku for a French-Vietnamese meal at a typical rundown establishment built on the Chinese design: restaurant fronting the dirt street, panels folded open, patrons propped on tiny stools, kitchen in the rear, alley beyond that, family quarters on the floor above. We sat right by the door and were treated to a sumptuous meal, complete with a magnificent French wine. All for eight bucks each. As sundown neared, we hit the road for the base: Joe curled up in back, my pal at the wheel, me next to him. Doing thirty miles an hour along the oil-treated roadway in an open jeep felt like racing. A solid front rolled toward us across the volcanic plain that looked like Nevada: the earth orange, the dark sky enormous. The odd light made everything ominous and eerily clear.

"What's that noise?" Joe said. "I think your jeep's crapping out."

"What noise?" my friend said, but Joe didn't respond. He mentioned it again as we drove up the side of the dormant volcano toward the MACV compound. We hit a pothole and I heard the clunk too.

"Stop!" Joe yelled. We skidded to a halt — "Out! Out!" — and all three of us bailed.

As we dove for the ditch, the spare gasoline can strapped to the back went up and took the gas tank with it. The gasoline in the jerry can had eaten through the adhesive of the tape holding down the arming spoon on the grenade, its disintegration expertly timed to get us before we reached the base. We had escaped its killing range, but the wire that was wound around the charge pitted Joe's back with razor-sharp fragments, leaving countless tiny black punctures that wept blood.

The jeep was done for but the gate guards rolled out to help and we had Joe in the 71st Evacuation Hospital in minutes. Joe sat on a gurney clutching the one field dressing from his web-belt pouch, too dazed to decide which of the many punctures he needed to cover. It took hours to extract the bits of metal, and the docs couldn't even get them all. They'd join other such souvenirs floating around in his well-traveled hide and work their way out over time.

"Joe," I said, still tipsy, "you're a living metaphor."

By morning he was stabilized, by afternoon he was halfway to Tokyo, and I stood alone on a square metal landing pad on the barren slope well outside the perimeter wire, waiting for a chopper ride to Cheo Reo. I couldn't imagine a lonelier spot on the planet.

Miser met me when I landed. Major Gidding was back and wasn't happy with what Joe and I had done in his absence, correctly concluding that we'd gone over his head, since we had correctly concluded he wasn't going to do anything except try to make his temporary command permanent. A shiny new lieutenant arrived the next day and took over my intel duties. I was relegated to the signal detachment.

The following morning there was a funeral for Dr. Roberta. I attended the ceremony with her. We didn't speak much. She had announced she was going home, and the Montagnards threw the funeral for her to commemorate the bond they felt — and the loss. They built her a burial hut, interred a wooden egret in an elaborate ritual, and presented her with its twin. Best as I could make out, when she passed away sometime in the future, that second egret would carry her spirit back to her grave and she would remain among them forever.

Toward the end she bent her head and trembled. "'We have erred and strayed from Thy ways like lost sheep,'" she recited. "'We have followed too much the devices and desires of our own hearts.'" Then, barely audible, she mumbled, "Fuck."

"*Chia buon,*" the chief said to us. I share your sorrow. She left for Da Nang and the States a day later.

Captain Cox sold Sergeant Grady's watch for four grand while on R and R and added the greenbacks to the Montagnards' cash box, their hedge against future catastrophes. The snake eaters hosted a Special Forces party out at Mai Linh in Grady's honor, an appropriately rowdy wake. One of the team celebrated his late comrade by sailing through the sky, fifty feet up, towed in a sling beneath a chopper, arms outstretched like Peter Pan, something Grady always liked to do on his birthday. Major Hopp did a flyby in his Cessna, trailing red and blue smoke canisters. Afterward the Berets kept their distance from MACV. They'd pick up their mail and supplies at the Cheo Reo airstrip but rarely came into the compound. The rains soon made the road pretty much impassable and we hardly saw them at all.

Big John Ruchevsky announced that he was manifested on an Air America flight out in a week's time. I asked him to get me and Miser on the bird too. Neither John nor I was hungry that night so we retired to the bar. When we were good and drunk, and toasting the colonel and Little John and Tri, he confessed his rage at Chinh. The only satisfaction he'd been allowed was a quiet message to the National Police, one service to another.

"Remember the white mice who came to town looking to arrest Little John?"

"Sure. The guy with the gold Parker pen top and his little pal with the gold tooth."

"They never made it back to Saigon."

The day before John Ruchevsky and I were to leave, the two of us and Captain Cox met at the sun hut by the river one last time. We drew cards. I'm not sure if I won or lost, but I had the high card and set about my task. I'd already prepared . . . in case. Back at the compound, I gathered up my stuff, and Miser and I donned ponchos and slipped out during the afternoon's downpour. He dropped me outside town and drove away.

Draped and hooded, I made my way to a bare knoll, armed with a snub CAR-15 and carrying, in pieces, all twelve blessed pounds of the heavy rifle I had first fired in the Army. It was considered obsolete, inferior to the M-16 invented for us to employ in the jungle. Ridiculously touchy and easily jammed, the 16 fired a small-caliber bullet at an enormous velocity that carried it on a flat trajectory, straight, with no arc. The barrel was designed to give it a particular rotation that caused the round to tumble when it struck its target. Penetrating flesh, it somersaulted, building up tremendous pressure. When it exited it took a great deal of the person with it, leaving a devastating wound. The intent wasn't so much to kill as to injure, horribly, perhaps to circumvent international prohibitions against dumdum bullets, perhaps to make its American inventor a millionaire with his own private plane. It had managed both.

Unlike the enemy's ammo, the M-16's bullet was light and easily deflected by so much as a stalk of tall grass in the jungle terrain. The round also lost velocity after two hundred yards. I needed it to carry farther, and I wasn't looking to wing or maim.

So I had procured a rusted American M-14 no one would miss. I took it apart and cleaned and oiled and tested it. The M-14 fired a hefty .30-caliber cartridge, roughly the same as an AK and the Belgian FAL .50 that Ruchevsky had offered me. But the old American rifle delivered the round far more accurately than the Kalashnikov, which got iffy after fifty yards, and the sights were better than the Belgian field piece — simple and easily zeroed in. The M-14 had an old-fashioned wooden stock and kicked like a mule, but it could put a bullet through an engine block.

The rain stopped. I spent the late afternoon concealed at the base

of the knoll, assembling the weapon, wiping and oiling the new ammunition. Though I'd only get one shot and wouldn't need a magazine,
I loaded one anyway to make the rifle feel more familiar. I could smell
the sheen on the cartridges and firing mechanism when I raised the
stock to my cheek, testing.

I had once mounted the guard at a serious military prison. The Sergeant of the Guard threatened that if a prisoner escaped, we would
serve out the prisoner's time until he was recaptured. We were to shoot
anyone who attempted flight. No warning shots. If we wounded or
killed the man, our court-martial and a finding of guilty were automatic. As was the penalty: eleven cents. The cost of the bullet. Legally,
no further charges could be filed.

I felt serene, my hands steady. The waiting didn't make me impatient or anxious. It reminded me of the happy hours I'd spent sitting
with my dad in that rickety blind in the back pasture, watching him
reassemble a target rifle a piece at a time. I thought about my distant
life in the States, from which I now felt as divorced as I did from my
wife, and about the profession of arms that also seemed to be slipping
away. I wondered why on my last leave I'd been afraid to cross bridges,
and what I would do with myself if I ever made it home.

I took a bit of a chance not using a scope, but I didn't really want
to see his face. My one regret was that he'd never hear the shot, never
know it was coming.

It rained again. Afterward the sky grew opaque with indeterminate
cloud cover the color of rusting iron: a light yellowish orange tinged
with red. The odd light exaggerated everything. Colonel Chinh normally took his evening coffee on his private porch at the back of the
wooden French-era building he occupied with his officers. He came
out at his habitual time, dressed in his usual khaki, and hung up his
caged songbird. Chinh stood enjoying a demitasse after his dinner,
taking in the dramatic sky and the bird's song. No wind, no impedi-
ments of terrain, three hundred meters distant. His posture unmistakable.

It was simple. I'd dismantle the rifle, scatter the pieces in the swollen river, and walk away. No South Vietnamese was going to come out

after me in the dusk. John would pick me up on the road and I'd spend our last night in Cheo Reo at his place.

The sights fit him exactly, head to toe. I eased the tip of the sighting post down to the middle of the body mass and slowly exhaled as if blowing away dandelion seeds. Then brought the front blade up to align with his head.

# EPILOGUE

⋆ ⋆ ⋆

**T**HE WINTRY SKY grew lighter. Celeste Bennett sat without speaking, her forehead in her hands. She took a deep breath and sat up straight.

"Were you ever suspected?" she said.

"Officially? No. Though my boss in Saigon, Major Jessup, had some choice remarks for me off the record, and the brass were clearly uneasy with the whole situation. I ran into Colonel Blackwell at a supper club in Saigon some months later and he flat-out asked if I'd done it."

"What did you tell him?"

"I said entertaining the possible complicity of friendlies in the death of a high-ranking Vietnamese officer and civil official could only undermine our efforts in South Viet Nam, sow discord among allies, and embarrass our governments."

"What did Blackwell say to that?"

"Nothing. Just stood me drinks. After the second round he said your dad deserved better. I said as how I agreed."

Celeste pushed back her hair. "What happened to them all? Miser? Checkman? The others?"

"Checkman got sent to the Army's language-immersion course at Monterey and went back to Viet Nam as an interpreter. Had two kids with a Vietnamese woman and made the mistake of marrying her five years into their relationship."

"Mistake?"

"Sure. Because the instant he did, the Army notified him that she and the kids were henceforth American dependents and couldn't remain in the country. Never mind that they were Vietnamese. The Checkmans left with their kids."

"Miser?"

"Miser, last I heard, was running a bar in Bangkok and sponsoring an annual film festival."

"And your friend Ruchevsky?"

"Big John was transferred elsewhere in country and distinguished himself. Sometime later he finally got to Eastern Europe, which is what he'd trained for. Once a year I'd get a postcard, never from the same place twice. His work remained covert and unsung but he seemed happy enough doing it. He lives in Boston now, spends part of each year in the old country, visiting his Ukrainian cousins. Took his father's ashes back a few years ago."

"And Captain Cox?"

"Cox I ran into in Las Vegas. He was there for a Special Forces reunion. We caught up while his former colleagues rappelled down the side of the hotel, scaring the hell out of unsuspecting guests, then went to one of those swank shooting galleries just off the Strip and fired Soviet assault weapons all night. We were still talking when they got back."

"Did he stay in the Army?"

"Cox went home after his Mai Linh tour and was assigned to Special Forces at Fort Bragg as an instructor. After Martin Luther King was killed, they were called out for riot-control duty in Baltimore. An Army colonel ordered them to rip off their shoulder patches and remove their berets, like they were something shameful. The Pentagon didn't want it known that elite troops were being deployed against American citizens. Occupying a U.S. city upset Cox enough. Hiding his beret and Special Forces insignia was the last straw. He resigned his commission. Green Beret alumni help sponsor a community in North Carolina for the few Montagnards who made it out, and he did that for a while. Occasionally they corral some congressman or senator and repatriate a few more from refugee camps in Laos, where Yards sometimes show up."

I said, "Do you remember Sergeant Sprague, the Special Forces medic at Mai Linh who couldn't leave the A camp to deliver the breech birth?"

"Vaguely."

"He left the Army but went back to Viet Nam with USAID, back to Cheo Reo. South Viet Nam started to unravel in March of seventy-five. The NVA went after the Highlands again, built a secret road to Ban Me Thuot — as they'd done at Dien Bien Phu — and seized the town. The South Vietnamese Army fled Pleiku in hundreds of trucks but couldn't continue south on Fourteen because it was blocked at Ban Me Thuot. So they all turned off onto Road Seven. It ran like Broadway, cutting diagonally through the province, through Cheo Reo. The town just exploded as the huge lawless mob hit. The retreat was a rout, civilians and soldiers mixed together, shelled by armor and gunned down by NVA. Sprague sent the Montagnards on a march to the coast and got himself to Saigon, where he said he extracted a promise from the U.S. embassy to send a ship to pick up the tribespeople."

"So a lot of them got out."

I shook my head. "They waited and waited. No boat ever came."

"Not our finest hour."

"No."

"What happened to the Montagnards who were left behind?"

"Nothing good. The North Vietnamese had guaranteed them autonomy after the war."

"But they never got it."

"No. Hanoi reneged completely. Vietnamese settlers flooded the Highlands. They're converting the plateaus to rice paddies and fields, cutting down jungle and pushing the Yards aside. The leadership negotiated a ruinous deal with China to let them mine for ore in the Highlands."

"Not plutonium, I hope."

"Aluminum. Billions of dollars' worth. Open pit. It will make a few comrades very rich, destroy a lot of lives. The Highlanders are protesting. The Communist government keeps the Yard villages under surveillance, quashes anyone who resists."

A ray of morning light cut the room and haloed her hair.

"The Montagnards fought the Communists for another dozen years after Saigon fell. I always pictured them carrying on with Grady's stash and all the equipment they appropriated when ARVN collapsed."

"And you?" she said.

"Me? I stayed in for a while. But things went steadily downhill. The war got stupider. Morale plunged. The enlisted men just quit obeying orders, stopped believing. A lot of fed-up career soldiers left the military to avoid getting sent back. Soon it was just hard-core lifers and teenagers going over, officers looking to get their promotion tickets punched and pick up some gongs. Our government got desperate for troops."

I looked past her at the black silhouette of the mountains.

"When the secretary of defense ran out of kids to conscript, the Pentagon developed a brilliant hard sell for getting GIs to extend their service commitments. They'd helicopter reenlistment teams to especially bad battlefields right after the action ended, with the ground still smoking, a moment when a lot of guys would've sold their souls to get away from the body bags and the blood — do just anything not to be there. Any soldier who signed on for another three-year hitch was promised specialized training that would put him in the rear. They'd escort the guy straight to their chopper without so much as a goodbye to his friends. They were evil scenes to witness. Men slinking away, humiliated, shaking. I stuck around for a while but my heart wasn't in it. I came home and saw it was a merciless war for some of us and another evening-news story for the rest. They didn't even waste rhetoric on us, much less look to our wounds."

"You left the Army."

"I was in Los Angeles on a furlough and went for a walk on Rodeo. Stopped at a store window to look at a female mannequin. It had on a sun helmet with a small red star on the brim, and an olive-colored NVA uniform — shirt buttoned to the throat — belted with a bandoleer of linked seven-point-six-two rounds, polished like gold. I quit the next day."

"Listen," she said. "I want to thank you for telling me."

"He was a fine man, Celeste. I hope I haven't tarnished his memory for you."

"Just the opposite. For the first time I feel like I know him."

"I'm wondering if you feel you need to share all this with your mother."

"She died eight years ago."

"I'm sorry to hear that."

"Yeah. Me too. She was difficult, but it's a lot bigger, lonelier world without her."

"Breakfast?"

The picture window looked out over the road up from the valley. The winter sky was backlighting the mountains in the distance. The peaks were hazy and you couldn't see terribly far. But even half hidden, they were beautiful.

"It's morning," she said, squinting at the window.

"Yeah."

"Let me do something." She rose, arms wrapped around herself for warmth.

"Make some more coffee," I said, "and I'll handle the rest. How do you like your eggs?"

I was efficient in the kitchen after all these years of involuntary bachelorhood and had rye toast, eggs, and bacon laid out on the dining table in no time. The cooking warmed the room.

"Tuck in," I urged. She didn't really need the encouragement. As we ate, a red band rimmed the highest ridges, and soon the first rays projected long shadows at us from out of the pine woods below the house.

Celeste said, "I'm a little surprised she gave up her clinic and left."

"Dr. Roberta? Yeah. She got the team's new medic to take over the clinic and she worked to raise money for it, but she never went back. Things caught up to her — other responsibilities. She resumed her career, had a child."

"She found someone. I'm glad."

"Not exactly. I don't think she ever got over your dad. She never married."

"You stayed in contact."

"After a fashion. She's director of public health at a teaching hospital. In San Francisco."

I went to the trove of framed pictures, took down an old photo, and brought it back to the table.

"Her daughter, Denise. At six."

I took a tiny notepad from my shirt pocket, and the small Swiss ballpoint I habitually kept with it. When I finished writing, I tore the page out for her.

"What's this?"

"Denise's address. She lives not far from her mom, in Novato. Just north of Frisco."

Celeste looked puzzled. "Why are you giving me — ?"

"I thought you might look her up, since you're heading south anyway."

"Why?"

"You've never met your sister. Maybe it's time."

I hadn't ever made anyone cry so fast.

"Sister?" Her voice wavered.

"Yeah. She has a child herself now. I guess that makes you an aunt."

She clutched the paper, staring at the address, the name, the fact of it sinking in.

"That's why Roberta left," she said. "She was pregnant."

Celeste sat crying quietly. When she'd recovered herself, she said, "Thank you, Erik Rider."

I drove her back down to her car. The day was starting out pasty, but I knew the weather in the mountains. It would be crisp and sparkling by noon. I gave her a badly folded map of northern California and reminded her to go slow on twisty 36. Once she reached the ocean, the Pacific Coast Highway would take her the rest of the way. She hugged me with that thin body and drove off.

It was a long haul to Novato. The road along the coast was only two lanes and full of dips and curves. But I had a feeling she'd drive straight through.

# AUTHOR'S NOTE

★ ★ ★

That there is so little fiction in *Red Flags* is owed to the generosity of many. I am indebted to the veterans who helped me remember and who offered their own memories of what they experienced and witnessed during their time in country. Most especially Harry Pewterbaugh, George Ruckman (who loved Vietnam and stayed seven years), Jeff Barber (who left his leg there), supermarksman Rick Stolz, Jerry Rowland (who just missed boarding the fateful chopper), and Ellsworth "Little Smitty" Smith. Our local missionary Robert Reed, who devoted thirteen years of his life to the Montagnards, also graciously shared his memories of difficult days and corrected some key details.

It is Harry's theory that we all started looking for one another once we hit sixty, and I think he's right. The vets' online forums surge with floods of searchers. Three of us met up in California. Soon afterward, we located two more of our brethren and visited by phone. Rick I visited in Oconomowoc, Wisconsin, one Fourth of July as his son deployed to the new counterinsurgency wars in the Middle East. The Internet made the reunions possible and also allowed me to connect with Vietnam veterans who served before and after we did. My thanks to them all.

Augmenting these memories is a cache of more than a thousand volumes of nonfiction and fiction, many declassified documents, maps, downloads from a wide array of archives and websites, learned monographs, and a host of memoirs. Most memorable among them: Hilary Smith's self-published *Lighting Candles* and Lady Borton's wonderful translation of Dr. Le Cao Dai's *The Central Highlands: A North Vietnamese Journal*, issued by the Gioi Publishers, Hanoi (2004).

Thanks too to editor Thomas Bouman of Houghton Mifflin Harcourt for his sensitivity to the subject of the Vietnam Conflict; to Beth Burleigh Fuller for coordinating so ably the many steps required to actually produce the book; to Tracy Roe for saving me endless embarrassment with her brilliant copyediting; to publicists Christina Mamangakis and Hannah Harlow for their thoughtful promotional efforts on its behalf; and to Laurie Brown for so capably leading her sales and marketing troops to victory.

For those still suffering guilt incurred during the Vietnam era, I offer this salve: Donate online to the Vinh Son Montagnard Orphanage in Kontum at friendsofvso.org. Or send a check to Friends of Vinh Son, P.O. Box 9322, Auburn, California 95604.

Lastly, the civilian called John Ruchevsky in these pages seems to have come in from the cold and resettled in the States. I hope to thank him personally when I drop by with a copy of this story, which he in great part inspired. I would call ahead, but of course his number is unlisted.